THE RED AND

Iris Murdoch was born in Dublin in 1919 of Anglo-Irish parents. She went to Badminton School, Bristol, and read classics at Somerville College, Oxford. During the war she was an Assistant Principal at the Treasury, and then worked with UNRRA in London, Belgium and Austria. She held a studentship in Philosophy at Newnham College, Cambridge, and then in 1948 she returned to Oxford where she became a Fellow of St Anne's College. Until her death in February 1999, she lived with her husband, the teacher and critic John Bayley, in Oxford. Awarded the CBE in 1976, Iris Murdoch was made a DBE in the 1987 New Year's Honours List. In the 1997 PEN Awards she received the Gold Pen for Distinguished Service to Literature.

Since her writing debut in 1954 with *Under the Net*, Iris Murdoch has written twenty-six novels, including the Booker Prize-winning *The Sea, the Sea* (1978) and most recently *The Green Knight* (1993) and *Jackson's Dilemma* (1995). Other literary awards include the James Tait Black Memorial Prize for *The Black Prince* (1973) and the Whitbread Prize for *The Sacred and Profane Love Machine* (1974). Her works of philosophy include *Sartre: Romantic Rationalist*, *Metaphysics as a Guide to Morals* (1992) and *Existentialists and Mystics* (1997). She has written several plays including *The Italian Girl* (with James Saunders) and *The Black Prince*, adapted from her novel of the same name. Her volume of poetry, *A Year of Birds*, which appeared in 1978, has been set to music by Malcolm Williamson.

ALSO BY IRIS MURDOCH

Fiction

Under the Net
The Flight from the Enchanter
The Sandcastle
The Bell
A Severed Head
An Unofficial Rose
The Unicorn
The Italian Girl
The Time of the Angels
The Nice and the Good
Bruno's Dream
A Fairly Honourable Defeat
An Accidental Man
The Black Prince
The Sacred and Profane Love Machine
A Word Child
Henry and Cato
The Sea, The Sea
Nuns and Soldiers
The Philosopher's Pupil
The Good Apprentice
The Book and the Brotherhood
The Message to the Planet
The Green Knight
Jackson's Dilemma
Something Special

Non-Fiction

Acastos: Two Platonic Dialogues
Metaphysics as a Guide to Morals
Existentialists and Mystics
Sartre: Romantic Rationalist

Iris Murdoch

THE RED AND
THE GREEN

WITH AN INTRODUCTION BY
Declan Kiberd

VINTAGE

Published by Vintage 2002

16 18 20 19 17 15

Copyright © Iris Murdoch 1965
Introduction © Declan Kiberd 2001

First published in Great Britain in 1965 by
Chatto & Windus

Vintage
Random House, 20 Vauxhall Bridge Road,
London SW1V 2SA

www.vintage-classics.info

Addresses for companies within
The Random House Group Limited can be found at:
www.randomhouse.co.uk/offices.htm

The Random House Group Limited Reg. No. 954009

A CIP catalogue record for this book
is available from the British Library

ISBN 9780099429135

Penguin Random House is committed to a sustainable future for
our business, our readers and our planet. This book is made from
Forest Stewardship Council® certified paper.

Printed and bound in Great Britain by Clays Ltd, St Ives plc

TO
PHILIPPA FOOT

CONTENTS

Introduction   1

Chapter One   9
Chapter Two   33
Chapter Three   49
Chapter Four   62
Chapter Five   72
Chapter Six   86
Chapter Seven   102
Chapter Eight   124
Chapter Nine   134
Chapter Ten   144
Chapter Eleven   160
Chapter Twelve   170
Chapter Thirteen   182
Chapter Fourteen   194
Chapter Fifteen   201
Chapter Sixteen   211
Chapter Seventeen   225
Chapter Eighteen   232
Chapter Nineteen   238
Chapter Twenty   246
Chapter Twenty-one   256
Chapter Twenty-two   269
Chapter Twenty-three   279
Chapter Twenty-four   294
Chapter Twenty-five   304

Epilogue   310

INTRODUCTION

IRIS MURDOCH was born in Dublin of Anglo-Irish parents in 1919, a year of revolution across Europe. She was educated in Bristol and Oxford and, like many Anglo-Irish before and after her, came to know the strange condition of declaring herself Irish in England while feeling herself to be English in Ireland.

It is a conflict recreated in Lieutenant Andrew Chase-White, who finds Ireland at once familiar and alien, and, as a consequence, 'not real'. The Ireland of the prelude to the Easter Rising is a provincial place in which 'nothing happens', as the Great War rumbles on in other parts of Europe. The characters of this novel feel the fatal pull towards some sort of redeeming 'action', yet find it almost impossible to achieve such authenticity. Using the Irish rebellion of 1916 as backdrop, Murdoch is enabled to explore many of the themes of European existentialism, about which she wrote as a leading academic philosopher through the 1960s. Her own background allows her to hint at the mingled, unclear nature of identity – her most colourful character here, Lady Millie Kinnard, is hard put to to know where one person ends and another begins. The treatment of the Rising in terms of the existential dilemmas which it poses in the personal lives of a range of characters helps Murdoch to bring out the inherent modernity of that historical event. There is a real whiff of the 1960s from every page of a book set half a century earlier in time.

The Red and the Green was published in 1965, just a year before the fiftieth anniversary of the Rising. The Ireland of the 1960s commemorated the Easter rebels fulsomely, but not the tens of thousands of Irish dead in the Great War; yet to Murdoch, viewing those distant events in a long retrospect, the soldiers in both armies seemed hauntingly similar. Both Andrew Chase-White and his rebel cousin Pat Dumay evince a fear of sex and a fixation on long-suffering mothers, a complex of attitudes which was by the 1960s being recognised as a pathology. To Andrew the sexual act was 'a secret murder', and to Pat it was 'the part of himself which disgusted him'. In a book which is a study of the relation between an image and an action, this assumes some importance: and it is very likely that Murdoch's treatment of the theme had a palpable influence upon William Irwin Thompson's *The Imagination of an Insurrection: Dublin 1916*, a psychological study published in 1967 which treated the rebel leaders as sexually-inhibited masochists who made a cult of self-denial and who sought an outlet for their frustrations in the zones of revolutionary action. Or, it may be that the texts of 1916 read Murdoch and Thompson as closely as these writers read those texts. There is a whiff of Wilhelm Reich from Thompson's analyses too.

As an Anglo-Irishwoman Murdoch was an astute interpreter of those trace-elements of Englishness in the Irish nationalist tradition. She knew that many Irish Republican Army training manuals were based on texts stolen from the British army, and that the chivalric codes of honour practised by the rebel leader Patrick Pearse had strong roots in nineteenth-century English society. The young Andrew Chase-White knows that by 1916 the very notion of a cavalry-charge is an outmoded hangover from heroic literature, yet he persists in joining a mounted regiment – only to see unarmed lancers mown down in the streets of Dublin as an opening gambit in the Rising. Yet Pearse would to the very end comport himself like a knight in a gentlemanly epic, even to the extent of surrendering a symbolic sword at the moment of submission to the British commander at the end of Easter week.

Beneath the surface traditionalism of such symbols in *The Red and the Green*, the modern world struggles to be born. Andrew's assumed fiancée, Frances Bellman, is amazed at the fact that there isn't a general revolt against the prevailing order, not just by soldiers but by women and by the poor. 'Being a woman is like being Irish', she suggests, finding as a woman that people often tell her that she is important but then act as if she doesn't count. As if in revolt against the system, Millie Kinnard wears trousers, smokes cigars, takes lovers (like Flaubert's Madame Bovary) and feels that 'she might have been somebody if she'd been born a man'. Murdoch's portrait of this slightly dotty aristocrat who plays with revolvers and outrages the bourgoisie seems based (to some extent) on the rebel countess Constance Markievicz.

This in turn reminds us that over seventy women fought as soldiers in the Rising, whose republic addressed its opening proclamation to 'Irishmen and Irishwomen' at a time when most women in Europe still had no vote. The Proclamation was radical in assuming that women were part of the body politic. Although Pearse might clothe the event in the rhetoric of ancient Gaelic tradition, its underlying ideals were often social-democratic and even revolutionary. It is to that futuristic element that Iris Murdoch most richly responds. By 1965, of course, social-democratic governments had been elected to power in many parts of Europe, but she was fully aware that the Easter rebels (whose Proclamation guaranteed that they would 'cherish all the children of the nation equally') would, had they been victorious, have instituted the first welfare state in Europe. They would have appointed Hanna Sheehy Skeffington to be the first female government minister anywhere in the world (a year before the Soviets named Alexandra Kollontai in 1917).

The tragic backdrop to these struggles is the nineteenth century, in the course of which the English tried to extend their identity over Ireland, following the Act of Union in 1800. It was a paranoid fear of modern French republican ideas which not only led to that forced Union but also destroyed Irish civilization – or so Christopher Bellman contends in a memorable passage of the book. If the Patriot Parliament of 1782 had survived, he suggests, Dublin would not have become a cultural back-water (whose decrepit Georgian mansions with broken door-knobs and peeling paint are well evoked by Murdoch). But the Union is shown here to have been doomed by the forces of Nature itself, for in Ireland even the rain is different from its English counterpart, 'seeming to materialize in the air rather than to fall through it'. The Rising, however, sought to undo that coercive Union and to make Ireland once again metropolitan to itself.

Andrew Chase-White, although nominally a member of the British army, tries (however dimly) to understand the underlying forces at work. Being Anglo-Irish, he may feel himself superior to both the Irish and the English, but he is also enabled to stand back from and study the latent realities. He intuits that the British may be subconsciously willing the natives to revolt. His rebel cousin Pat certainly thinks so, viewing the English as 'less than ruthless': and Andrew himself laughingly reports that his own reserve squadron in Longford has just one hundred rifles, about half of which are functional. When he goads his Irish cousin with his taunt that 'At least I've joined the army', it is as if he is inviting them to come forth with a countervailing gesture.

At much the same time, the young men's aunt, Millie Kinnard, is pointing her revolver at the oil paintings of her Anglo-Irish ancestors.

Andrew has many reasons for his constant passivity in the face of the challenge represented by his republican cousin Pat. And there is a definite sense in which the authorial voice of Iris Murdoch seems to endorse that passivity, despite the disapproval of Andrew's pro-British acquaintances, as a kind of high intelligence: 'the realization that there are people we shall never conquer comes to us as part of the process of growing up'. Whenever Andrew ceases vying with Pat in his own mind, he feels free for the first time in his life, free to construct his own self. Murdoch's reading of the meaning and destiny of the Anglo-Irish relationship is impeccably Sartrian.

INTRODUCTION

Pat Dumay is a strikingly pragmatic (rather than mystical) rebel. He opposes the wearing of uniforms by the Irish Volunteers for much the same reasons which led Sean O'Casey to criticise their adoption by the Citizen Army – they would only highlight their wearers as targets for enemy guns. The deeper point is also existential: that a real revolution would be no costume drama but an event in which a freed people felt able at last to wear their own clothes. Pat is appalled at the folly of rebel leaders whose taste for melodrama causes them to seize the General Post Office. The building was hopelessly exposed on three sides to enemy attack but marvellous in its symbolism as the largest official site in the main thoroughfare of the national capital, thereby permitting the rebels to cut across all aspects of Dublin life.

Pat is said to be critical of Pearse's 'archaistic visions of virtuous manly society whose manners were somehow to be restored'. but responsive to the tenderness and sweetness of the leader's temperament. In fact Pearse was as much of an empiricist and of a modernist as his fellow-leader, James Connolly. Both men shrewdly gift-wrapped the modernity of their ideas in the images of a Gaelic past, the better to secure converts amang a people who liked to think of themselves as traditional. Preaching socialism, Connolly said that it would be no more or less than a form of Gaelic revival, a return to ancient codes according to which the chieftain held the land in the name of all the people, with the exception that now it would be the government rather than the chieftain who did the holding. Likewise, Pearse suggested that his liberal ideal of a child-centred education would simply be a revival of ancient Gaelic methods. Posing as conservators of Gaeldom, both men were in fact radicals – something which is intuited by Cathal Dumay who cites the old socialist aphorism that 'a child may stick a pin in a giant's heart'. As a sixteen-year-old who yearns for a revolutionary role beyond his tender years, Cathal becomes an embodiment of Lenin's theory that the real misfortune of the Irish was to have risen too soon, before the revolt of the European proletariat had matured. If they had waited for a further year, the rebellion might have led disillusioned Irish soldiers to mutiny against their leaders in the British army, with copycat effects among the allies and even among the German ranks, precipitating a wider uprising against Europe's ruling class. Then the pin in the hand of the child really would have destroyed the heart of the imperial giant.

All of Murdoch's characters feel that life during the long decades of peace before the war had become unreal and inauthentic. It was a widespread delusion among a people who did not know at first hand the terrible effects of a technologically-conducted war. Even a liberal humanist like Sigmund Freud succumbed to the general mood: unless life is placed in constant jeopardy, he wrote, it may become 'as shallow as an American flirtation'. It was only with the prospect of ten thousand deaths a day, he contended rather amazingly, that it could 'recover its full content and become interesting again'. The poet W. B. Yeats wrote on Christmas Day 1915 of a feeling of anticlimax, reviewing his entire life as a preparation for something which had never happened.

Millie Kinnard seems almost to be quoting Yeats when she speaks of her longing for 'some golden thing which never came', and of a desire for 'some great glittering event that would change everything, some great act'. As a thinker, Murdoch is fascinated by the relationship between an idea and an action. She is haunted, as the existentialists were, by the fear that all too often what is intended as a profound action becomes merely an act, so that the meaning which should have accompanied the action is taken away from it even as it is performed. The Easter Rising was a particularly appropriate backdrop to such a philosophical investigation, since it had to be imagined many times before it came to pass (as, indeed, it is often prefigured in *The Red and the Green*).

In order to deepen her exploration of this theme, Murdoch plays fast and loose with some of the facts, for it is very unlikely that relatively junior figures like Pat and Cathal Dumay would have known of the Rising days before the event. But, by endowing them with a kind of foreknowledge, she not only adds a tragic resonance, but also raises a crucial question of ethics. That question recurs in different forms throughout the story – as when Barney Drumm or his wife Kathleen or Christopher Bellman are each tempted to tell someone else a truth of which each feels that the person should be informed – yet each of them hesitates lest that telling hurt the receiver of the information and lest it turns out to be motivated more by the self-interest of the teller than by the objective welfare of the receiver. Ultimately, in a rich twist to the plot-line, this becomes a question for Andrew Chase-White himself in the climactic scenes of the book.

Murdoch skilfully weaves various domestic and personal sub-plots around the major political theme: yet the underlying philosophical issues are always pressing. One of the young men is refused by his beloved in terms which, once again, revolve around the effects of an action: 'but the cold touch of action awakens the spirit to a world where what is dreadful has slowly and minutely to be lived'. While this humiliation is being endured, another of the young men is suddenly and surprisingly embraced by Millie in a richly contrapuntal scene. 'You want to test yourself', explains Millie, 'to the point where you can will the death of all that you are'. Millie feels her life to be useless and empty: and Barney Drumm knows that feeling too. He can only ever impersonate the sort of holy-man he wishes to be, and even in prayer at mass he knows 'it was only play-acting'. Both of these characters, the desiccated aristocrat and the spoiled priest, are attracted by the idea of a real action, in hope that some authenticity of feeling will redeem a shabby life.

As a novelist, Murdoch unflinchingly includes herself and her art in this search and this indictment. Barney's memoir – which is really a record of his masochistic resentment against an equally masochistic wife – confronts the problem of its own self-interested distortions by having the words 'All this is not quite true' written across it. The parallel with *The Red and the Green* is surely intended. It may refer not just to possible errors of fact (for example, Thomas MacDonagh was not in the Post Office during the fighting) but to those many scenes which so strain the reader's credulity that Millie herself feels the need to describe them as 'like a comic opera'. Men come to her in incredible coincidences 'to fill up the void'. Others seek to flee that void by an escape into religious ritual. In either case, the reading is existential. The Easter eucharist impresses Barney with 'the notion of an event, a change'. Some hours later Andrew, caught up on the edge of the Rising, realizes that he is 'in action for the first time'.

Iris Murdoch once wrote a book about Jean-Paul Sartre, describing him as a romantic rationalist. So are many of the characters here. So is the central event which defines them all. Easter 1916 was a strange blend of visionary and the pragmatic. To hold a Rising at Easter-time was to appeal to ancient poetic notions of sacrifice, redemption and renewal. It was also to invoke the power of spring, with the idea of new life coming from a dead land. But it was also to act at a moment when the British administration was on holiday and its soldiery off guard. The use of ancient Gaelic symbols to promote some futuristic ideas is an example of that same moment of Irish modernism which, even as the Rising was being enacted, led JamesJoyce to cast the most experimental prose narrative of the modern period, *Ulysses*, in the framework of one of Europe's oldest tales, the *Odyssey* of Homer. Few of those who have written about the Easter Rising in the years since it took place have captured that mixture of the archaic and the avant-garde as faithfully as Iris Murdoch does in the following pages.

Declan Kiberd
2001

Chapter One

TEN MORE glorious days without horses! So thought Second-Lieutenant Andrew Chase-White, recently commissioned in the distinguished regiment of King Edward's Horse, as he pottered contentedly in a garden on the outskirts of Dublin on a sunny Sunday afternoon in April nineteen sixteen. The garden in question, secluded behind substantial walls of rough golden stone, was large, and contained two ailing but gallant palm trees. The house, a dignified villa called 'Finglas', with big square windows and a shallow slate roof, was washed a light slightly streaky blue. It was both neat and spacious, built in a style of confident 'seaside Georgian' which in Ireland had felicitously continued until the beginning of the present century and after. The house and garden, the walls and palm trees, the property of the father of Andrew's fiancée, were situated in Sandycove Avenue, Sandycove, one of the bright little roads of multicoloured villas which run down to the sea from the main road which leads from Dublin out to Killiney and Bray. The road on which Finglas stood, or from which, conscious of a certain superiority over the other houses, it withdrew, was clean and very quiet, seeming always full of a grey luminous light from the sea, which could be seen and indeed heard at the foot of the hill where the road ended casually in the water and the pavement turned into yellow rocks, folded and wrinkled and shining with crystalline facets. The road partook indeed of the hardness and cleanness of the rocks and the coldness and clearness of the water. Visible to the left, if one went right down to the end, and visible too from the upper windows of Finglas, was the bulky headland with the Martello tower upon it, the Acropolis of the village. The headland concealed the view of Kingstown, but from the sea's edge could be seen the folded back arm of Kingstown pier, its terminal lighthouse

9

rising in the middle, seeming to end with the gaunt obelisk, happy commemoration of the departure from Ireland of George the Fourth. Straight ahead, across the very light dirty grey-green waters of Dublin Bay, lay the blue couchant silhouette of Howth Head, and to its right the open sea horizon, a line of cold mauve above the grey: whereon even now Andrew, pausing in his task, saw the smudge on the skyline which was the approaching mail boat. In spite of increasing activity from German sub-marines, the mail boats reached Kingstown with scarcely diminished regularity, though an erratic course, adopted in the interests of safety, brought the smudge of smoke into view at various and unpredictable points of the horizon.

The scene was, for Andrew, intensely familiar and yet dis-turbingly alien. It was like a place revisited continually in dreams, both portentous and fleeting, vivid to the point of necessity, but not entirely real. Here too it was as if his senses worked at a half pace, and smells of houses, rough feels of garden walls, echoes of voices in conservatories, were spread out and enlarged into something weird, too big and too close for comfort. Andrew's family were Anglo-Irish, but he had never lived in Ireland, although he had spent most of his child-hood holidays there. He had in fact, by what he regarded as a somewhat tiresome accident, been born in Canada, where his father, who had been in the insurance business, had once spent two years. Andrew had grown up in England and more especi-ally in London, and felt himself unreflectively to be English, although equally unreflectively he normally announced himself as Irish. Calling himself Irish was more of an act than a descrip-tion, an assumption of a crest or picturesque cockade. Ireland remained for him a mystery, an unsolved problem: and a prob-lem which was in some obscure way disagreeable. There was of course the religious question. A far from devout and, in England, an uncontentious, uninterested, almost entirely non-practising Anglican, he felt, on arrival in Ireland, his Protestant hackles rise. There was an aggressive tingling, and something deeper which was unnervingly like fear. Today was Palm Sunday and Andrew, together with his mother and his fiancée, Frances Bellman, had attended matins at the Mariners' Church in Kingstown. On emerging from the church they had found the streets filled with those others who, streaming in far greater numbers out of their chapels, were now parading about, more slowly, more confidently, carrying palms in their hands. For them it seemed, and for their sins Christ was even now entering Jerusalem, and their demeanour exhibited already a satisfaction, even a possessiveness, which made the congregation of the Mariners' Church, trotting more soberly homeward with averted eyes, feel unreal and perfunctory, unconnected with the great events to honour which these arrogant strollers were almost casually decked. Andrew's personal apprehension of this difference, this contrast with something gaudier, more vital and more primitive, was heightened by the fact that a number of his Irish relations had, to the extreme almost incredulous horror of his mother, become Roman Catholic converts.

Andrew's father, who had died just over two years ago, had been himself a scholar *manqué*, a gentle bookish man who had passed thoughtfully and ineffectually through life, always a little diffident and puzzled. He had wanted Andrew to be a scholar, and had been overjoyed when his son effortlessly collected a history scholarship at Cambridge in the year before the war. This achievement, however, seemed to have exhausted Andrew's academic capacities and ambitions, and he had spent an idle though not particularly riotous year at the university when the war came. He left Cambridge with the intention of enlisting, taking with him a passion for Malory and a vague ambition to become a great poet, and very little else in the way of higher education. His desire to serve his country was checked, however, at the outset by a prolonged bout of asthma, an ailment from which he had suffered intermittently since childhood. Pronounced fit at last, he had joined up in the autumn of 1915 and had been rapidly commissioned.

Andrew detested and feared horses. It was therefore, to those who knew him well, a matter of some puzzlement that he had chosen to serve in a cavalry regiment. The key to this phenomenon lay in Andrew's Irish cousins. He was himself an only child, and as such had pondered long and with fascination upon the mysterious and frightening sibling-relationship of which he was deprived. His various cousins, all of whom lived in Ireland, had served him in those long hated and yet loved holidays of childhood as sibling-substitutes, temporary trial brothers and sisters, for whom his uncertain affection took the form of an irritated rivalry. He felt himself indubitably superior to this heterogeneous and, it seemed to him, rather unculti- vated and provincial gang of young persons, always noisier, gayer and more athletic than himself. But his superiority was rarely recognized. More often he found himself forced to play the dull one, left out of the game, not understanding the joke. This had especially been so in the matter of horses. All his cousins were natural, casual riders. They were a race of young horsemen, passing him by with the insolence of the mounted. Indeed, his earliest memories of Frances, who was herself a remote relation and had belonged to the 'gang', were of a swift mounted girl, a graceful side-saddle Amazon, outdistancing him, disappearing.

So it was that Andrew's now so distressingly close associa- tion with horses had come about through a simple desire to impress his cousins. There was in it too, though Andrew recognized this less clearly, an element of masochism. It was like his irresistible desire always to dive off the highest board in the swimming baths, although he was terrified of heights. He had, for very fear, to press close to him the object of terror. He had established his relationship with King Edward's Horse long before, in peacetime, with no other idea than that of getting some inexpensive equestrian experience. Since he could count himself for these purposes as a Canadian, he had found it easy and convenient to attach himself to this eminent and predominantly Colonial regiment. The arrival of the war converted his game into a dreadful seriousness and hoisted him with his own petard. Pride forbade any contemplation of a change of unit. And now in his dreams he found himself pursued and cornered by enormous horses wearing German uniforms.

Andrew had had a brief but entirely uneventful glimpse of France. He had completed a strenuous training at the cavalry depot at Bishop's Stortford, where at that time hard-riding Australians were arriving weekly, and in February, shortly after receiving his commission, had been sent to join C Squadron of the regiment which was then stationed in exceptional luxury at the Château of Vaudricourt. When he arrived the squadron, besides enthusiastically enjoying the amenities of the Château, were mainly engaged in felling trees and building stables, and the communal aims seemed distinctly domestic rather than military. It was only later that Andrew learnt that the desire to make one's surroundings convenient and comfortable is one of the more important motives in the economy of war. After a week or so of this, the divisional mounted troops were all moved to Marthes to spend some days in the First Army training area. Here they encountered not the Germans but a devastating snowstorm, and for some time Andrew's only concern was finding dry unfrozen places for horses. The horses survived the experience with equanimity, but Andrew himself went down with severe pneumonia and had to be shipped back to England. Pleurisy followed the pneumonia, and he crawled out of hospital at the end of March, an exhausted convalescent, told to report to the Reserve Squadron of his regiment in a month's time. More than half of that month had now elapsed.

Andrew was a confused soldier. The role of 'soldier' was perhaps the first role in life into which he had made a positive attempt to fit. He had played the part of an 'undergraduate' casually and, somewhat to his own surprise, not very wholeheartedly. He did not entirely like the *mores* of those who set the tone at Cambridge and, what was perhaps a more serious matter, he lacked the money to compete with them. So he had set himself up a little defiantly and yet not very confidently as a recluse. His work had benefited little. The idea of himself as a soldier, an idea which would have been entirely repugnant to him in peacetime, was now of course backed up by the enthusiasm of an entire community. Yet Andrew had still not been able to draw on to him the skin of soldiery or to swagger into the part with the ease which he envied in many of his contemporaries. His persona as a soldier was still disparate, composed partly of childish romanticism, partly of schoolboy conscientiousness, and partly of some yet veiled adult attitude of fear and resignation. Of these perhaps the first was at present the most active, though Andrew would have blushed to admit how much his zeal depended on early impressions of the more patriotic passages of Shakespeare and a boyish devotion to Sir Lancelot.

From the details of warfare his imagination still shuddered away. A knowledge of the facts of the war in the trenches had not destroyed his attempt to make sense of it all by means of romanticism, but it had increased the quite separate and veiled area of his fear. In the snowstorm at Marthes, as on training exercises at home, it was his plodding conscientiousness that he relied upon, and he hoped that in a situation of danger it might at least serve him in lieu of courage. Whether he possessed courage was an agonizing mystery. He despised himself for being glad that the routine concern for the welfare of the horses tended to keep the mounted troops behind the front line. He could not help being relieved rather than otherwise that the concept of the cavalry charge appeared to be outmoded. But he viewed these sentiments with alarm as deep symptoms of funk. He was intensely disappointed that he had not, during his short time in France, broken his duck in this respect.

It was an additional sorrow to him that, since he had to do a soldiering trade, he had not managed to get himself into some more modern and highly mechanized unit. He was a keen amateur of wireless telegraphy and of motor cars, and at Cambridge had been much in demand as a mechanic among his wealthier car-owning companions. He had even at one time privately decided, though he never told his father this, that he would go in for motor car design when he was through with his tripos. He would have been prepared now, though with his imagination strictly switched off, to interest himself in machine guns, and he had learnt what he could at Bishop's Stortford about the Vickers and Hotchkiss guns which were there in inadequate and intermittent supply. But during his training he had spent much more time with his rifle and even with his sword, an object which had given him initial pleasure and which he now detested. At Vaudricourt he gathered that little wireless work was to be hoped for and that C Squadron had not yet been issued with machine guns. The most directly war-like regimental occupation, now popular in B Squadron, was something known as 'bombing from horseback', which involved galloping in single file past Boche gun-emplacements and hurling in Mills bombs. Andrew, who did not like the sound of this, noticed that his senior officers approved of the Mills bomb and suspected the Hotchkiss because with the former a mounted detachment could still emulate the traditional behaviour of cavalry. There was a nostalgia, among the regulars especially, for a vanished superiority, a once useful expertize; and when one evening in the mess young Andrew had loudly remarked, 'After all, a horse is only a means of conveyance', there had been a shocked and scandalized silence.

The Reserve Squadron of the regiment had moved to Ireland the previous year, and after being stationed at the Curragh had just now moved out to Longford. It was there that Andrew was to report at the end of his leave. Meanwhile he was trying, with a certain amount of success, to ignore the future and to live as fully as possible within the little world of feminine claims and pamperings represented by Frances and his mother. He found himself almost loving the complex pre-occupied triviality of the lives of these two near and dear beings, and he stayed close to them as if to claim the protection of some small, forlorn yet powerful innocence. It was not only that he grasped their little world as a contrast to 'out there'; it was also that it somehow represented a necessary defence against all the other things that Ireland meant, the men of Ireland, his male cousins. Andrew put it to himself: I really cannot be bothered with Ireland just at the moment. And he had in fact put off, now disgracefully long his mother told him, going to visit other members of his family.

Andrew's mother had lately and precipitately decided, very much to Andrew's dismay, to sell her London flat and move to Ireland. The efficient cause of this decision was the Zeppelin raids on London, which Mrs Chase-White represented to her eager and credulous Dublin friends in vivid, even lurid terms. Her nerves, she claimed, could not stand it, with those Zepps always coming over. Andrew felt extreme irritation, not only at what he regarded as a shameful lack of stamina on the part of his parent, but also at what he suspected to be the formal cause of her decision, an atavistic urge to return to the soil of Ireland. Hilda Chase-White, *née* Drumm, was, like her husband, Anglo-Irish; but whereas Andrew's father had spent most of his childhood in Ireland, Hilda and her younger brother Barnabas had been brought up in London. Andrew was vaguely aware that his mother and his uncle had in some way not got on with their parents, but he had never troubled to diagnose what was wrong, nor indeed been in a position to, since his grandparents both died when he was a small child. His maternal grandfather had been a civil servant of small means, but well known in his circle as a gay social man and a party-giver. He was also by way of being a famous practical joker. It may have been that these antics offended Hilda's sense of dignity, or it may more simply have been that she compared the London ménage unfavourably with the bigger, grander and altogether more ceremonious houses of her Irish relations. Andrew recalled from childhood the tone of slightly querulous envy with which she spoke of these establishments: a sentiment not shared by his father, who, although he retained a strong nervous interest in his family there, and especially in his half-sister Millie, seemed always thankful to have escaped from Ireland.

The purchase therefore, just completed, of a house in Ireland no doubt represented for Hilda the fruition of a very long-term intention; and, especially since her head was turned by the extreme cheapness of Irish properties, it was with difficulty that Andrew had persuaded her not to acquire one of several available castles, each one damper and mouldier than the last though undeniably inexpensive, and had coaxed her at last into buying a pretty and reasonably sized house in Dalkey. His uncle Barnabas, for some long time now settled in Ireland, had been of little assistance. But as Hilda often said, not much could now be expected of Barney. Barnabas, who had figured as notable in Andrew's childhood because he was a crack shot rather than because he was a promising mediaeval scholar, had latterly, it was generally agreed, gone to the dogs. Barnabas too had felt the urge, as Hilda herself put it, 'to escape from the parents', though Andrew could not understand what in this case was felt as menacing. His uncle was the reverse of snobbish. But he too had evidently felt some imperative need to return to Ireland, had married into another branch of the family there, and, to Hilda's and indeed to Andrew's intense horror, had become a Roman Catholic. He was even, so Hilda would sometimes report in a whisper, said to be writing a history of the Irish saints, an activity which his sister found for some reason highly improper. It was in addition said of him that he had at one time wanted to become a priest, but Hilda would never publicly countenance this rumour. The fact that Uncle

Barnabas had also apparently taken to drink was almost welcomed as a more normal manifestation of black sheepishness.

That some of the family were converts was something which Hilda felt as a continual affront to herself. It caused her real pain, and she spoke about it as little as possible, even to the point of keeping it dark. She had been deeply wounded by her brother's defection, for although her conception of family ties in general struck Andrew as rather worldly, she was, or had been, extremely fond of Uncle Barnabas. 'The family' was a great subject with Hilda, and Andrew had become a little reluctantly interested in the matter himself, especially as he somehow found it necessary always to explain that Frances was a distant relation. The situation was complicated. 'We Anglo-Irish families are so complex,' Hilda used often to exclaim with a kind of pride, as if complexity in families were a rare privilege. 'We're practically incestuous,' his Aunt Millicent had once added. 'What does that mean?' the child Andrew had asked, but no one had enlightened him. He sometimes felt now that 'the family' had indeed something of the fascination of the snake that eats its own tail. He was both interested and repelled, and the sense that the family occupied or pervaded Ireland, managing to inhabit most of its corners, largely composed for him the sinister power of that island.

In fact, Andrew had in recent years seen happily little of his remoter relations who owned farms in Clare and Donegal. Frances and her father, Christopher Bellman, who had at one time lived in Galway, had now moved to Sandycove, and Andrew felt no urge, though his mother sometimes suggested it, to go on a familial tour. Dublin and its neighbourhood contained quite enough of the cousinry, and those indeed with whom Andrew had always had most to do. The exploration even of this branch of the family, which was needed in order to make clear his relationship with Frances, was in fact complicated enough. His paternal grandmother, Janet Selborne-Doyle, 'a great beauty' as his mother always said when she was referred to, had married twice. Her first husband was John Richard Dumay, from whom she had had issue two children, Brian and Millicent. Of these, Brian, it was always said whether truly or not as a result of a nervous breakdown, had become a convert to Catholicism when still a student at Trinity. The 'great beauty's' second marriage, after the death of her first husband, had been to Arnold Chase-White, and the one off-spring of this union had been Henry Chase-White, Andrew's father. Henry married Hilda Drumm, and Brian Dumay had married one Kathleen Kinnard who was in fact a connection of Hilda's mother's family, and who had caused pain and scandal by forthwith adopting the religious faith of her husband. Millicent Dumay then married Kathleen's brother, Sir Arthur Kinnard, and the third sister, Heather Kinnard, married Christopher Bellman, Frances' father. Both Mrs Bellman and Sir Arthur Kinnard had died fairly young, and Andrew could not recall having met them. His Uncle Brian had produced two sons, Pat Dumay, who was a year older than Andrew, and Cathal Dumay, who must now, Andrew reflected, be about thirteen or fourteen. Uncle Brian had died when Andrew was about fifteen, and his Aunt Kathleen had caused some surprise and a good deal of adverse comment by subsequently marrying her co-religionist in the family, his Uncle Barnabas, who it appeared had been one of her early admirers. That marriage had been childless.

Andrew's mother had been impressed and continually pre-occupied by the goings on of her Irish relations, particularly the Kinnard family, possessors of an enviable mansion and an even more enviable title, who, especially in the days of Arthur's father, had set a standard both of grandeur and of social freedom which must have made Hilda discontented with her restricted London life and with the 'mad' yet cosy society of her parents. There was no doubt that she coveted not only the traditional ease of the Kinnard household but also its Irish remoteness from the pettier aspects of the 'bourgeois' world.

Hilda had never been quite sure that her father and mother were blessed with good taste.

Although Hilda had talked about these things to Andrew all his life, he had only very recently begun, in relation to her, to understand them. He had much earlier, and with a kind of nervous distress, apprehended his father's quite different and strangely deep anxieties about Ireland. Some family demon haunted Henry Chase-White. He was fond of his relations, and especially fond of Aunt Millicent. But the source of the trouble, Andrew soon came to conjecture, was his half-brother Brian. Brian Dumay was older than Henry by several years and was a very different kind of man from Andrew's father. Uncle Brian had occupied some post in the Bank of Ireland which never seemed to provide matter for discussion, but in so far as he entered into the life of his nephew he did so in the guise of the perfect all-round out-of-doors uncle. Andrew recalled the scenes, always the same, on hills or beaches, with Uncle Brian leading the way, leaping from rock to rock, followed by the shouting children, while Andrew's father picked his way cautiously behind. And Andrew must have been about ten when he realized, with a tender protective pang which seemed to make him on the instant much older, that his father was a little jealous in case Andrew should compare him unfavourably with Uncle Brian. It was an occasion when they had all been swimming, except for Andrew's father who had found the sea too cold and was sitting in the sandhills with a book. Andrew had run to him and been told almost roughly, 'You don't want to be here with me. Go back to your uncle.' Since then Andrew had liked Uncle Brian less. But it was not until his uncle died that he realized how extremely attached his father really was to his half-brother who must have represented something robust, attractive and puzzling, which produced in him a characteristic tremor of awkwardness. Andrew met with the same awkwardness, the same shy disguised puzzled fondness in his father's attitude to himself; this barrier was never removed and

ONE

Andrew felt a special pain when his father died to think that perhaps he had never known how much his son loved him.

Andrew had felt as a child an acute and uncomfortable interest in all his relations, but the magnetic centre of that field of forces had usually seemed to be his cousin Pat Dumay. It occurred to Andrew later that his own peculiar anxiety about Pat somewhat resembled his father's anxiety about Uncle Brian, only Andrew had never exactly felt any liking for his cousin. His interest in him was something more obscure and disturbing. He had spent a good deal of energy in earlier years in trying to impress Pat, and indeed it could scarcely be denied that the folly with the horses which had had such far-reaching results was an attempt to get even not so much with Frances as with Pat.

Pat, who was known in their childhood as 'the iron man', and who effortlessly excelled in all their sports and games together, had never paid much attention to Andrew. Andrew, a slow-growing child, had often, with rage, been relegated to play with 'the little boys', and he still felt that Pat casually took him to be younger than he was. There had never been any sort of confidence or friendship between them, although on a few occasions when they were older Andrew had made advances. Pat, who was not much given to talking, would then withdraw into a taciturn dignity, while at the same time seeming not to notice Andrew at all. He moved quietly, his eyes elsewhere, like someone avoiding a small obstacle in his path. In moments of revolt Andrew referred to his cousin as 'pompous' and affected surprise that he was not more frequently ragged. Yet somehow Pat's formidable dignity seemed to impose itself on others less concerned than Andrew. Other children were usually a bit afraid of Pat, who was capable at times of a good deal of violence. Andrew was reluctant to admit that he had ever feared him. But he had, when younger, felt a sort of awe which had perhaps partaken of a childish horror at Pat's religion. With years of reason and tolerance the horror had diminished,

21

but in the quality of his persisting interest in his cousin there was still a sort of shudder as at something primitive and dark.

The younger brother Cathal, though commonly said to be cleverer than Pat, was of course of less moment to Andrew. He had spent a good deal of time in the past avoiding Cathal, who, being so much younger, had usually figured in one way or another as an impediment. The relations between the two brothers seemed not of the happiest, and Andrew conjectured the existence of some ferocious jealousy. Pat had always, ever since Andrew could remember them together, enjoyed knocking his little brother about, sometimes with a brutality which was alarming to witness. Andrew most poignantly recalled a scene when he himself was about thirteen when he had intervened to save Cathal, then a small child, from a particularly vicious attack. Pat, who had retaliated by giving Andrew a black eye, was subsequently beaten, presumably for this misdemeanour, by Uncle Brian. This occurrence had somehow, for Andrew, defined and confirmed his unhappy sense of connection with his cousin; though he doubted very much whether the incident had had any significance for Pat.

Since he had become more or less grown up, and more especially since he had become a soldier, Andrew felt with some relief that his childhood obsessions about Ireland were beginning to fall away. The tradition of the annual holiday was discontinued, and the dark wet island seemed less of the menace that it used to be. He had not been over there for some while, nor seen any of his relations apart from Frances and Christopher, who were frequent visitors to England. During this period Pat Dumay had been studying law at the National University, and was now apparently working in a solicitor's office. Andrew, rather vaguely hearing news of him from time to time, was gratified to learn that he had not specially distinguished himself in his studies: and the notion that he was after all more talented than his cousin came as a salve to his, in any case diminishing, consciousness of that old rivalry. He was rather surprised that Pat had shown no sign of enlisting, a matter commented on adversely by Andrew's mother, who, vaguely conscious of him as a competitor with her own boy, rather disliked Pat. But this unexpected blemish in the heroic figure of his boyhood was in fact far from displeasing to Andrew, and although he publicly disowned his mother's scornful opinion he secretly shared it.

Andrew's satisfaction at being liberated from Ireland was a little checked by the excessive nervous disturbance which he now felt on visiting the place again, and especially on hearing that his mother proposed to settle there. He had reckoned on seeing very little of Ireland in the future. He had decided, though without announcing this to anyone, to remove Frances from it completely as soon as this could be arranged. The removal of Frances indeed represented for him a sort of final triumph over the past. He felt irritated, and in a curious way a little frightened, to find that the severance could not be quite so complete. He told himself rationally that he must really begin to behave about the whole thing in a more grown-up way. Yet when he thought of the visit which he was to pay the Dumay household on the following day, he was not only childishly pleased at the idea of showing off his uniform and his newly grown moustache: his heart beat faster, he did not know why.

This visit, and a subsequent visit to his Aunt Millicent, had been urged upon him as a duty by his mother, although as he well knew she felt no particular affection for any of the people concerned. Hilda regarded 'the family' as having an import- ance which, while she might not have used this language, transcended affection. She would not have professed actually to *like* any of her relations, with the exception of Christopher Bellman, Frances and her own brother; and even in these two latter cases there were cross-currents of a hostility very obvious in origin. Millicent Kinnard and Kathleen, as she now was, Drumm, aroused in Hilda, whenever they were mentioned, a particular sort of almost physical jerky nervousness. These two very different persons were, Andrew knew, in different ways a disappointment and a scandal to his mother. Stationed at important points within the family machine they simply failed to turn the right handles.

Andrew's father had been extremely though rather nervously fond of his half-sister, and this may not have endeared Millie to Hilda. He had also been devoted to Kathleen, though not in any way which could have caused rational annoyance to his wife, his gentle and complete devotion to whom had been a show-piece of the family. It was for Andrew felicitously axiomatic that his parents had been a happy united pair, and he was even now curiously conscious of his father's presence as a support to his mother and himself. Hilda's irritations with Aunt Millicent and Aunt Kathleen were more largely social in origin. Andrew was tolerantly aware that his mother was a fearful snob and that 'keeping up with Millie', which was presented as a tiresome duty, was made considerably less disagreeable by the fact that Millie had a title. There was also the wealth, the splendour and what was left of the ceremony. But it was just here that Aunt Millicent failed.

Andrew could remember when he was quite small hearing a side-whiskered gentleman at a garden party saying to another, 'I say, Millie Kinnard is rather fast, isn't she?' The idea seemed to please the gentleman, but Andrew's mother, who was standing near by, had indignantly hustled Andrew away in the course of the reply. There had never been, as far as he knew, any positive scandal connected with his aunt, but he was given to understand that she was a person who habitually 'went too far', although whither it was she proceeded with unwonted celerity, overstepping what barriers, he never altogether discovered. Millie was of course known to hold rather progressive views on 'the woman question', had taken a nurse's training, contrary to the family's wishes, during the South African war, and had managed to get herself briefly to the scene of action.

She had, it was said, not mourned too long after her husband's death. She was rumoured to wear trousers and smoke cigars. She possessed and could fire a revolver. She had a great many gentlemen friends.

'Millie has style' was the sort of remark which people tended to make and which Hilda hated to hear. For her, Millie's style was bad style and Millie's undeniable form was bad form. Andrew's mother was anxiously conventional and indeed regarded convention, which she preferred to think of as ceremony, as a fortress against all that she most feared. Perhaps in the end it was a fortress against her father's practical jokes. Aunt Millicent represented, just where one might have expected an access of strength, a dangerous breach in the defences. Andrew had chanced not to see his aunt for some years, since she had been away on his last visit, and his memories of her went right back to a scene in some summer garden where what seemed a pretty girl in a white dress, under the dappled shade of a parasol, had laughed at him, but not unpleasantly, making him laugh too. He felt a certain interest in seeing her again.

Aunt Kathleen was quite another matter. While Aunt Millicent failed through frivolity, Aunt Kathleen, *née* after all Kinnard, failed through dullness. Millie's form might be regrettable, but Kathleen was formless; and it was this, even more than the monstrous fact of being a Roman Catholic, which Andrew's mother held against her. The Dumay house in Blessington Street was shabby, disorderly, even dirty; and in this Hilda deplored a sheer lack of inherited discipline. 'When you think of Kathleen's opportunities,' she would say as prologue to a denunciation. Nor could she forgive Kathleen for marrying Barnabas, and thereby confirming her benighted brother in a state of insanity from which he might otherwise have recovered. Hilda also resented, though for fear of giving it further publicity she never mentioned, the fact that Kathleen supported her husband financially. Barnabas, who had latterly been employed in the public service, gave up this work soon after his marriage to devote himself entirely to research. Hilda blamed his wife for what she regarded as his progressive demoralization, and when the drinking bouts began she would say, 'It's all of a piece!': meaning Catholicism, Kathleen, alcohol, and the Irish saints.

As Andrew meditated rather vaguely in the cool April sunshine of that Sunday afternoon concerning his forthcoming visit to the Dumays, he was engaged in the task of fixing Frances' red swing. The swing, its wooden seat painted with a sort of peasant design of white hearts upon a scarlet background, had been ever since long ago a feature of the Bellman's much larger and wilder garden in Galway. That morning when he had been looking at a photograph album with Frances they had come upon a picture of her, a little girl with a big straw sunbonnet, sitting upon the swing, while Andrew in a sailor suit stood rather ungraciously by. As Andrew began reminiscing about the swing Frances had said that in fact they had brought it with them, it was somewhere around, and Andrew had said that of course he would fix it up forthwith. Then they had both fallen silent.

Andrew thought of and indeed referred to Frances Bellman as his fiancée, although nothing had yet been quite formally fixed between them. It was rather that an understanding, dating from somewhere very remote in their childhood, had gradually grown up, like a tall genie taking shape between them and joining their hands. They had been, on the many occasions when they had been able to be together, 'inseparable' as children; and as soon as Andrew was ready to fall in love he fell in love with Frances, as if this were an inevitable and natural aspect of growing up. The frenzy of love had been calmed almost at once by the sense that he could not possibly lose her. There was already the security of a long attachment. He had felt no interest in any other woman although he had had his share of opportunities and indeed of flattering attentions.

He was sometimes surprised at the ease with which he had been immediately conducted into this congenial haven, and attributed it somehow to the same kindly gods who had made him the only child of happily married parents. Frances too was an only child, and this made her seem quite especially of the same race as himself. Andrew adhered to no general theories of a romantic nature concerning the importance of a stormy initiation into love, and particularly now, with the prospect of a return to the war opening before him like a black hole, he was prepared to settle gladly for a security in his personal life which seemed likely to exist nowhere else. France, not Frances, would lay his soul naked.

Andrew had never formally proposed, though he assumed that some absolutely explicit suggestion, such as the naming of a day, would be necessary before the ceremony could be performed. In a way he would have preferred simply to wake up one morning and find that Frances was his wife; and he felt sure that she felt exactly as he did. She accepted and completed his half-voiced assumptions about the future, and their conversations were like a song sung in snatches by persons who know their parts so well that they need only by a note or two suggest them. He knew that Frances understood him perfectly. That was why they had both fallen silent suddenly together when they were speaking of the swing, since a swing suggested a child.

Andrew was still a virgin. Where Frances was concerned, two ideas were curiously enlaced in his mind, the idea of his first introduction to sexual intercourse and the idea of his death. The hours of both these events he pictured as flying towards him through the darkness like great scarlet darts; and although he did not doubt that the former would arrive before the latter, he sometimes, and especially in sleepless nights, thought that the latter might not come far behind. This returned his thoughts to what had made him and Frances suddenly silent.

The connection between the two ideas in fact went, for Andrew, deeper than anything suggested by the casualty lists.

He profoundly feared the notion of the sexual act, and whenever he imagined himself doing *that* to Frances he felt appalled incredulity. This act, an act of terrible violence involving the destruction of both the aggressor and the victim, seemed something quite separate from his old deep love for Frances, and separate even from the uneasy excitement which he had felt during the last week at living in the same house with her and accompanying her as far as her bedroom door. It was as if the act in question would have to be committed in a clandestine manner, like a secret murder. He could not imagine it as a part of ordinary life, and as the scarlet dart flew nearer and nearer he had times of feeling most dreadfully afraid.

Another consideration which joined the two fearful ideas together and made him confused and frightened about what was to come was a vague sense that people surrounding him, his family, perhaps society, expected him to make Frances pregnant before he was sent to the Front. An old aunt had practically blurted out something like this in his presence; and he divined some such thought in the mind of his mother, who was in some ways ambivalent about his relationship to Frances. This sort of dubious 'survival', offered as a kind of duty, made Andrew upset in a rather self-pitying way which he usually avoided. He wanted to live and be happy with Frances himself and to be under no obligations of that sort to the human race or even to her. He felt too, in these moods, hustled, and more inclined to procrastinate about the whole business. However, the moods soon passed, swept away by his sheer tenderness for the girl and his increasing sense that this was the moment to settle his destiny, or rather to confirm a settlement which seemed to have been so felicitously made long ago.

Andrew's mother was very fond of Frances, but had sudden little sharp bursts of hostility towards her, as he imagined she would towards any girl that Andrew proposed to marry. Frances let them pass, shaking her head like a pony, which she in many ways resembled, and Hilda would at the next moment be especially affectionate. Andrew was exceedingly fond of his mother, sometimes he felt alarmingly fond of her, although she exasperated him extremely almost all the time. He disagreed with her views on everything and her ambitions made him shudder. He particularly disliked the social half-truths which she constantly told as a matter of instinct. She would imply that she had attended gatherings of which she had only heard, and when in Ireland would portray the glittering nature of her London social life in a way which amounted to serious misrepresentation. He flattered himself that he could observe with a sharp eye the world which so dazzled his mother; yet while he blushed for her vanity he could not see her as corrupted.

He had, in the past, felt a good deal of nervousness on the subject of whether his mother would think that Frances, an untitled, unfashionable girl, who had never even properly 'come out', was good enough for him. He had gradually with relief become aware that Hilda regarded Frances as a rather special young person. He only subsequently realized that there was a particular reason for this. Christopher Bellman was extremely rich. Children are usually oblivious of any except the most evident differences in wealth, and Andrew had only lately acquired an adult awareness of how much, in that sense, particular men had 'behind' them. He felt this awareness to be an onset of worldliness, especially when he noticed that such knowledge did in some way alter his view of people. But of course he had loved Frances and even wanted firmly to marry her long before he had apprehended her as an heiress. He was only thankful that this fact about her seemed to pacify his mother completely, who otherwise would certainly have been on the warpath in London in ways which would have greatly displeased him. He excused this covetousness in her, as he excused in himself a certain quiet satisfaction at the idea of marrying, quite accidentally, a rich girl: his parents had always been very poorly off and Andrew was just at an age to appreciate how inconvenient this was.

His prospective father-in-law, Christopher Bellman, was still a rather obscure and alarming figure to Andrew. He was constantly surprised to see how easily his mother managed to get on with Christopher. It was as if she simply failed to notice that he was a dangerous animal. It was indeed the spectacle of Hilda and Christopher gambolling together that most especially brought home to Andrew what seemed to him an adult insight: that someone can seem, and in fact be, quite different with one person from what he is with another. It was as if Hilda's mechanism was simply not designed to pick up a whole range of rays given off by Christopher, to which Andrew was sensitive and which led him to find Christopher 'dangerous'. Andrew thought that it was also very adult of him not instantly to dub his mother, for that reason, deficient. But neither did he, as he would when younger have done, regard her as daring. He searched rather for irrational features in his own attitude.

Christopher was in fact English, though Irish by adoption through his wife Heather, and an Irish 'enthusiast' in a way which sufficiently marked him as an alien. When younger he had worked in the Civil Service, first in London and then in Dublin, but had retired in middle life to devote himself to scholarship, wherein, Andrew noticed, he concealed his systematic seriousness under an air of dilettante trifling. He was an expert on the antiquities of Ireland and possessed a large library on the subject, destined in his will for Trinity College, Dublin. He was familiar with Gaelic, although he had never joined the Gaelic League and was hostile to the wholesale cultivation of the Irish language which had come to be, for many of his acquaintances, such an important political end. He knew a good many of what he called 'the Irish Ireland mob', but kept aloof from all politics and controversy. Andrew judged him, though not always confidently, to be a cold man. Yet his pursuits were harmless, he was obviously very attached to Frances, and had always encouraged Andrew.

Sometimes Andrew, forever making little of his fright, de-

cided that it was simply Christopher's appearance that unnerved him. His future father-in-law was very tall and looked
anything but English. He might have been southern French or
even Basque. He had extremely black hair and large dark eyes
and a long thin very red mouth. He had always been clean-
shaven, with a dulled sallow complexion. His longish hair was
looped back behind his markedly pointed ears and his bushy
triangular eyebrows met and grew for a considerable way
down the bridge of his narrow and slightly hooked nose. The
brow was prominent, yellower than the rest of the face, and
much scrawled over with fine wrinkles, so that it sometimes
seemed that he was wearing a cap pulled down to eye level.
This gave him a secretive air. Yet he managed to look handsome and even young, and his eyes, always rather cautious and
watchful, were very often humorous. Perhaps it was simply
that Andrew suspected that Christopher was frequently laughing at him. He felt, however, an immense respect for Christopher, for his learning and for his rather mysterious detachment.
Exhorted for some time to call him by his Christian name
instead of 'Sir', he had found this difficult.

Andrew had by now almost finished dealing with the swing.
It had not been a complicated operation, but he had dreamily
prolonged it, simply glad to find himself mechanically occupied. The ropes were securely knotted on to a projecting
bough of the big chestnut tree which stood beside the lawn,
and as they chafed to and fro they dislodged a light dusting of
bark which descended on to Andrew's blond head in a peppery
rain, making him sneeze. The ropes slipped neatly through the
slots in the seat and were knotted together below. Andrew had
mended an incipient crack with a slat of wood and filled up a
hole with putty. The red-and-white painted surface was as
bright as he remembered it, the central spot of scarlet in those
green childhood scenes, polished by many childish posteriors
into a warm soft glow. He was rubbing it over with his sleeve,
almost as if for some magical evocation of the past, when he

caught sight of Frances coming from the house to call him in to tea.

A number of blackbirds, who had been threatening each other upon the lawn, flew up at her approach. The garden was in that disturbing expectant condition of the spring when everything is exuberantly leafy but nothing is in flower. All was green, that particularly pale vivid, damp-looking green which emanates from the Irish soil or is perhaps elicited by the dark brightness of the Irish light, a green washed over with silver. The slender spears of montbretia which fringed the house, the pallid waxy stripes of hemerocallis, the fuzzy shifting masses of fuchsia gave to the scene something of the air of a lush reedy water meadow. Against this dense vegetable harmony Frances advanced, wearing a full-skirted dress of white spotted voile and Irish lace with a wide sash of mauve satin. Andrew, who had been drooping lazily, sprang to attention, his glance darting involuntarily to her ankles which the new fashion left clearly visible

Frances was a small girl, inclined to plumpness, with something distinctly bouncy or frisky in her gait. Andrew had once punched another boy who called her 'dumpy'. There was in fact a brightness and vitality in her which forbade such a description. She had more the plump grace of a pretty pony. She had Christopher's dark hair which, travelling to a complex bun behind, was looped over her ears just like his. She had, too, his long mouth and the large prominent brow about which she could never decide whether to hide it or to reveal it. But the slightly exotic look which in Christopher suggested the south, gave to Frances an almost gipsy appearance, or perhaps rather she just looked Irish, of the Irish of Ireland, wide-faced, a little tousled, with a long powerful smile.

Without speaking to Andrew she hopped at once on to the swing and began to urge herself to and fro. The ropes groaned upon the bough and the chestnut bark descended like black confetti on to her white dress. It began very mistily to rain.

Chapter Two

'WHAT'S on at the Abbey?'
'Some stuff by W. B. Yeats.'
'The Countess Cathleen man? I don't think we feel strong
enough for that, do we. What about the Gaiety?'
'D'Oyley Carte. I believe it's *The Yeoman of the Guard.*'
'Well, we might go there. Only don't forget my furniture is
arriving at Claresville on Thursday.'

It was about half an hour later and tea was nearly over. They
were sitting round the low wickerwork table in the conservatory, while outside the garden was being caressed or playfully
beaten by the light rain which drifted a little in the breeze from
the sea. Rain in Ireland always seemed a different substance
from English rain, its drops smaller and more numerous. It
seemed now to materialize in the air rather than to fall through
it, and, transformed into quick-silver, ran shimmering upon
the surface of the trees and plants, to fall with a heavier plop
from the dejected palms and the chestnut. This rain, this scene,
the pattering on the glass, the smell of the porous concrete
floor, never entirely dry, the restless sensation of slightly damp
cushions, these things set up for Andrew a long arcade of
memories. He shifted uneasily in his basket chair, wondering
how long it took to develop rheumatism.

Christopher had lighted his pipe, Frances was sewing,
Hilda, without occupation, was sitting very upright as if the
organization of the party had suddenly fallen upon her. Her
hair, a pale blonde striped with grey, rather scanty and silky,
pulled well away from the face and banded by a black velvet
ribbon, looked like a neat cap, and she appeared older than her
age. Her face, lightly wrinkled or rather perhaps crumpled,
was a uniform colour of soft parchmenty gold, and often gave
the impression of being weather-beaten or sunburnt, although

Hilda in fact shunned the open air. The large straight nose and rather stern dark-blue eyes completed the picture of a person of authority, although an inherent vagueness in Hilda's principles made her in practice a less commanding person than she seemed.

'I'm longing to see your house finished,' said Frances.

'Thank God you didn't buy that crumbling pile at Dundrum,' said Christopher. 'I'd have had to help you keep it upright, and it would have been a full-time job.'

What about me? thought Andrew, with a sudden pang, but then decided that he was being morbid.

'Kathleen said she'd find me a maid. I gather one has to pay ten shillings a week now.'

'And most of them would steal the cross off an ass's back and can't be trusted to cook anything but rashers and eggs!'

'Oh, I'm good at training servants. I had a perfect little jewel in London. And of course I shall have the telephone installed.'

'The telephone is fine here if you only want to talk to the exchange! Have I convinced you on the motor car question?'

'Yes, Christopher. I think after all it would be foolish to buy a motor car just now. There are too many difficulties. I hear Millie has just bought a Panhard. She is so extravagant.'

Andrew knew quite well that his mother was aware that she could not possibly afford a motor car.

'We might think in terms of a pony and trap, though. After all, one must get about. And when the war is over I shall certainly purchase a touring car. Andrew shall learn how to operate it.'

A Vauxhall Prince Henry, thought Andrew dreamily to himself. When the war was over he would have money to spend. It was nice to think that he had a rendezvous in the future with a Vauxhall Prince Henry.

'I think I shall always stick to my bike,' said Christopher. 'The bicycle is the most civilized conveyance known to man.

Other forms of transport grow daily more nightmareish. Only the bicycle remains pure in heart.'

'I was very relieved Andrew didn't want to go into the Flying Corps,' said Hilda, speaking as if her son were not present.

'What's on tomorrow, Aunt Hilda?' asked Frances, revealing a long straight row of white teeth as she bit a length of thread off from the spool. Andrew's mother had always been content with this formal mode of address, which increased Andrew nomenclatorial difficulties with Christopher, since to address him familiarly in Hilda's presence would seem a kind of disloyalty.

'*Tomorrow*, my dear,' said Hilda, with the confiding eagerness she always evinced over any social plan, however trivial, 'tomorrow Andrew goes to tea at Blessington Street. I can't manage it, I've *got* to be at Claresville then to see the builder. You'll go with him, won't you?'

'I don't mind,' said Frances. 'I like to watch Cathal growing up. He looks entirely different now every time I see him.'

'He's such a big boy. It's hard to believe he's only fourteen. Children grow up so much more quickly nowadays. You'll go along too, Christopher?'

'Please not. That house depresses me. And Kathleen always makes me feel guilty!'

'I don't see why she should. But the house *is* gloomy, and there's always that curious smell on the stairs. Don't you think Kathleen has become awfully sour and self-absorbed just lately? And so dreadfully pious! Someone told me she goes to chapel every day.'

'She does it to spite Barney,' said Christopher, puffing his pipe, his gaze upon the quietly dripping palm trees.

Hilda, as usual, did not follow up a remark which made reference to her brother's religion. She went on, 'And on *Tuesday*, I know it's a terrible bore, but we *must* go and see Millie, I did promise. She's back from Rathblane now, it's her time for being in town. How do you think Millie is these days, Christopher? Going downhill?'

'Not specially,' said Christopher. 'She's been hunting like a maniac all the winter.'

'She certainly has plenty of energy,' Hilda conceded. 'I sometimes think she really might have been somebody if she'd been born a man.'

'Can't one be somebody if one's born a woman?' asked Frances.

'Well, hardly in that way, dear. Though in plenty of other ways which are just as important,' said Hilda vaguely.

'I think being a woman is like being Irish,' said Frances, putting aside her work and sitting up. At such moments she had an unconscious gesture of pushing back her hair to reveal her large brow. 'Everyone says you're important and nice, but you take second place all the same.'

'Come, come, women have always had Home Rule!' Christopher always jestingly set aside his daughter's sometimes rather ferocious attempts to turn conversation into serious channels.

'The emancipation question is certainly a grave one,' said Hilda. 'I am not at all hostile to the idea myself. But there are so many values— And I'm afraid that your Aunt Millicent's idea of emancipation is wearing trousers and firing a revolver in her own house.'

Christopher laughed. 'That's about it. But one must start somewhere! Will you be coming to Millie's, Frances?'

'No, thanks.'

Andrew had long been aware that Frances did not like Aunt Millicent, but he had never been able to make out why. Among the generalizations about women which passed freely around his regimental mess was one to the effect that women never like each other, since every woman regards every other woman as her rival. Andrew, while attending with interest to all such distillations of worldly wisdom on a subject which was still very mysterious to him, suspected that this one was over-simple. It was true that women, leading more isolated and emptier lives, were naturally, when opportunity offered, more frantically anxious to attract attention and more ruthless in their pursuit of the opposite sex than were men who had, after all, other interests, as well as more chances to know each other in an atmosphere of free fraternal co-operation. Or so it seemed to Andrew, who saw men as inherently dignified animals and women as inherently undignified animals. However, in his own experience, when he had noted a marked dislike of one woman for another there had usually been some reason for this other than the postulated general rivalry.

In the matter of dislike of Aunt Millicent, his mother for instance disliked her out of envy for her title and her money, and because she failed to further Hilda's social ambitions. While Aunt Kathleen disliked her because of Uncle Arthur. Kathleen had it seems been very attached to her brother Arthur and had, rightly or wrongly, felt him to be in some way slighted or belittled by Millie, who was in fact fairly universally said to have married Arthur for rather worldly reasons. Uncle Arthur's early death was also somehow vaguely felt to be Millie's fault. 'Poor Arthur,' Hilda used to say. 'Millie simply ate him. Kathleen never forgave her.' Frances' dislike, which could hardly be put down to loyalty to either Kathleen or Hilda, persons from whom to say the least she felt detached, could perhaps after all be more simply explained as the nervous envy felt by a young girl who, however much she might officially despise such values, recognized in an older person a kind of elegance and glitter which she could never hope to emulate. Or more simply still it might be that Frances had weighed Millie in some spiritual balance and found her wanting. Andrew noted, sometimes a little uneasily, that his fiancée was capable of making quite uncompromising moral judgments.

'I hear there is to be mixed bathing at the Kingstown baths,' said Hilda, pursuing some train of thought concerned with the enormities of the modern world. 'I cannot approve. Not with the bathing costumes people wear nowadays. Frances and I saw a girl at the Ladies Bathing Place at Sandycove who was showing nearly the whole of her legs. Do you remember, Frances?'

Frances smiled. 'She had very pretty legs.'

'I'm sure you have very pretty legs, my dear, but they're nobody's business but your own.'

Andrew, feeling an entirely private amused resentment at this judgment, suddenly found himself catching Christopher's eye. Christopher gave him a faint secretive smile. Distressed, Andrew dropped his gaze and pulled at his moustache. There was something curiously improper about catching Christopher's eye just then. It was almost like an exchange of winks. He felt suddenly mocked and threatened. He could never make Christopher out.

Christopher, perhaps to cover what he had apprehended of Andrew's embarrassment, went on at once, 'In fact nothing may come of the mixed bathing idea. Father Ryan has already protested about it. You and the Holy Romans see eye to eye on this, Hilda.'

'They're certainly very full of themselves these days,' said Hilda, 'protesting against this and demanding that. I expect it's the prospect of Home Rule. "Home Rule will be Rome Rule" may prove but too true. We must prepare ourselves.'

'Indeed,' said Christopher. 'And yet they've opposed it all along the line. It's the Church not the Castle that has really kept this country down. All the great Irish patriots have been Protestants, except for O'Connell. The Church was against the Fenians, against Parnell.'

'Oh well, *Parnell*—' said Hilda. The judgment was vast, vague, crushing.

Andrew here caught the eye of Frances, who was a devotee of the great man thus dismissed. He saw her draw breath to protest, decide not to, and half smile at him as if asking for approval, all in two seconds. He was pleased by the quick little exchange.

His mother was going on, 'I can't understand why recruiting is going so slowly in Ireland. I saw an article about it this morning.'

'I don't think it's going slowly. Irishmen are streaming into the British Army.'

'Well, yes, but so many remain behind. And the *attitude* of people. Last week I heard a man singing a song in German in the public street. And in Clery's yesterday I heard a woman say to another that Germany might win the war. She said it casually as if it were quite an ordinary thing to say!'

Christopher laughed. 'Of course, the English never ever for a second conceive that they can lose a war. It's one of their great strengths.'

'Why do you say "they", Christopher, and not "we"? You're English after all.'

'True, true. But having lived over here for so long I can't help seeing the dear old place a little bit from the outside.'

'Well, I think it's very disloyal to talk in that way about the Germans, as if they could possibly win. After all, England and Ireland are really one country.

'So the English soldiers evidently think when they sing "It's a long way to Tipperary". But it's always easy for the top dog to extend his sense of identity over his inferiors. It's a different matter for the inferiors to accept the identification.'

'I can't understand this talk about inferiority. No one regards the Irish as inferior. They are loved and welcomed all over the world! And I can't stand this jumped-up Irish patriotism, it's so artificial. English patriotism is another thing. We have Shakespeare and the Magna Carta and the Armada and so on. But Ireland hasn't really had any history to speak of.'

'Your brother would hardly agree with this judgment.'

'I am not impressed by a few moth-eaten saints', said Hilda with dignity.

'Ireland was a civilized country when England was still barbarous,' said Frances, tossing her hair back.

'My dear Frances, you are parroting your Uncle Barnabas,' said Hilda. 'You know very little about it.'

This, Andrew thought, was probably just. Frances was no scholar, and her views on politics, though often vehement, were extremely confused and discontinuous. Frances had always been very attached to Hilda's brother, and had never associated herself with the scandalized or mocking attitudes of the family towards the convert. Uncle Barnabas and her father between them had been her school and her university, and once for a short while she had helped her uncle with some aspect of his study of the early Irish Church. It was something, she used vaguely to say, about the date of Easter, and more Andrew could not gather. Long aware of a friendship between Frances and 'Barney', Andrew felt an undiminishing jealousy which he recognized to be both unworthy and irrational. He had never for a second been able to take his Uncle Barnabas seriously. While Christopher seemed to him, and rather formidably, a real scholar, he could not imagine Uncle Barnabas's toils as other than childish vanities, and Frances' muddled account of them seemed to confirm the view. 'Barney' shambled on the outskirts of the family caravan, an irredeemable figure of fun.

'And all this nonsense about reviving the Irish language,' Hilda was going on. 'With all due respect to you, Christopher ...'

'Oh, but I entirely agree with you. Gaelic should be left to us scholars. One should be content to be born to the language of Shakespeare. And in fact the Irish have always written the best English.'

'The Anglo-Irish have.'

'True for you! Those aristocrats who think themselves superior both to the English and to the Irish!'

'And when you think of all the money we've poured into this country.... The Irish farmers have never been better off.'

'Not everyone would agree with that,' said Christopher. 'I read an article in the *Irish Review* only yesterday saying that Alsace-Lorraine was far better off under German rule than Ireland under English rule.'

'That couldn't possibly be true. It's just Irish spite. I wonder why people think the Irish have such sunny characters? Don't they realize there's a war on? Now they've been promised Home Rule and everything they want they ought to be grateful.'

'Perhaps they don't feel they've got much to be grateful for,' said Frances. 'A million people died in the potato famine.'

'My dear Frances, that was regrettable but has nothing whatever to do with the present situation. You argue like a street-corner orator. There may have been some unfortunate things in the past, but they're all long ago now, and I'm sure England never purposely hurt Ireland, it was just economics.'

'There's something in what Hilda says,' said Christopher. 'Ireland had several bits of sheer historical bad luck, and one of them was that the potato famine coincided with the hey-day of Manchester free trade. In the eighteenth century England would have relieved the famine.'

'What were the other bits of bad luck, sir?' asked Andrew.

'Eighteen hundred and one and nineteen fourteen. It was very unfortunate that this war started just before Home Rule went through. Remember Churchill saying that if Belfast wouldn't submit to Home Rule the British fleet would teach them to? The Liberals were really exasperated with the North. A year or two of enforced religious toleration and everything would have settled down. Whereas now we shall have endless trouble. But the Act of Union was the big Irish disaster. English government in the eighteenth century was the most civilized government in history. Fear of the French put an end to eighteenth-century civilization. Perhaps it put an end to civilization. It certainly put an end to the Irish parliament. Ireland was really becoming an independent country, the great land-owners thought of themselves as Irish. And of course that began to scare the English stiff. Hence the Act of Union and all our tears.'

'You think Ireland might have had a quite different history if it hadn't been for that?' said Andrew.

'I do. There was a real Irish culture at that time, a culture with its own brilliance and with international ties. Do you remember that monument I once showed you, Hilda, in St Patrick's Cathedral, which talks about "that exalted refinement which in the best period of our history characterized the Irish gentleman"? The date of that is twelve years after the Act of Union. Oh, they knew what had happened all right. If the Irish parliament had survived, Ireland wouldn't be the provincial backwater it is today.'

'Home Rule will make it even more provincial,' said Hilda.

'I fear it may,' said Christopher. 'And idiots like Pearse don't help when they invent a romantic Irish tradition which just ignores the English ascendancy. Ireland's real past *is* the ascendancy. Ireland should turn back to the eighteenth century, not to the Middle Ages. Goldsmith and Sterne would turn in their graves to hear the nonsense about Holy Ireland that's talked nowadays.'

'All that can't be quite right,' said Frances. 'I mean, you seem to be talking as if Ireland were just the grand people. You remember what Grattan said about *we* are not the people of Ireland. It's everyone having always been so poor that's awful. Compare the Irish countryside with the English countryside. There are no real towns and villages in Ireland. There are the same little featureless houses or hovels everywhere, and then nothing else till you come to the country mansions and the cathedrals of Christ the King.'

'Catholicism is the curse of this country,' said Hilda. 'If only Ireland had followed England at the Reformation.'

Christopher laughed. 'You mean the Irish, having rejected the most civilized religion in the world, Anglicanism, deserved their fate? That's arguable! But they were just that much farther away, and the Fitzgeralds and the O'Neills went on being Catholics and being warlords in a quiet way. As for Ireland being the grand people, it's unfortunately true that until lately history has been made by the grand people. Frances is really right, though. What this country lacks is a yeomanry. The Irish peasant remained primitive and remained poor.'

'Why?' asked Andrew.

'It's largely the same answer. No parliament. Think how important parliament was in England from the very start. Ireland remained a country of overlords. The big estates were political prizes. Ireland was always a property being handed about. An insecure ruling class without a parliament is soon demoralized. And ever since the Irish princes sold out to Henry the Second there's been collusion between Irish gentry and English power. "Her faithless sons betrayed her", as the song says. Ireland's only hope of pulling herself out of feudalism was to develop a steady ruling class with its own culture and its own civilized organs of power, and that began to be possible in the eighteenth century, only the Act of Union wrecked it all just as it was becoming a reality. And by eighteen-fifteen standards in English political life had declined so much, England was so gross with triumph, there was no help for Ireland there.'

'So it looks as if the French are the villains of Europe,' said Andrew. 'A view I've long held!'

'Why do people in Ireland always talk about *history*?' said Hilda. 'My head's always swimming with dates when I'm over here. English people don't talk about English history all the time.'

'They don't have to ask the question, What went wrong?' said Christopher. 'For them nothing went wrong.'

'Well, I'm afraid Ireland is a thoroughly self-centred country.'

'All countries are, my dear Hilda. Only selfishness shows more in the unfortunate.'

'And now there's all this Trade Union nonsense and stopping the trams. It's so demoralizing. And all this playing at soldiers and marching about in green uniforms and so on. Even Barney got tied up with it at one time. Something ought to be done about it. People ought not to play at war when there's a real war on.'

Christopher blew out a curl of blue smoke and watched it rise to where the rain was running steadily and now almost silently along the glass roof of the conservatory. A soft salty mist was filling the garden, penetrating the curtain of the rain. There was a raw smell of the sea. Christopher spoke now with a more deliberate slowness, like one who feels he has been too vehement or is afraid of becoming so. 'After the Ulster Volunteers came into existence, and especially after they were armed, it was inevitable that there would be a similar movement down here. After all, it's the right of free men to prepare themselves to defend their freedom.'

'The British Navy will defend their freedom. It always has done!'

Andrew, who sensed that both Christopher and Frances were getting a bit tired of hearing from his mother, interposed in his most objective and manly manner, 'Wasn't it rather a mistake, sir, for the British Army not to recognize the Volunteers in the South? I gather General Mahon recommended it to Kitchener. Especially after the Ulster Volunteers were formed into a division.'

'Yes,' said Christopher. 'You'll find the Red Hand of Ulster in the British Army, but there's no sign of the Harp.'

'Kitchener is afraid to arm the Irish,' said Frances.

'I'm sure he's no such thing,' said Hilda. 'He told Mr Redmond and Lord Carson that he'd like to knock their heads together.'

'Do you agree,' said Andrew, adopting Christopher's slow tempo, 'with the people who say that Redmond ought to have demanded immediate Home Rule in exchange for Ireland's participation in the war?'

Christopher laughed. 'Good heavens no. I'm not an extremist. Home Rule is a certainty after the war. Or else a hundred thousand men back from the army will know the reason why!'

'Is it conceivable that the Castle would be so insane as to try to disarm the Volunteers?'

'No, no. The English will behave correctly. After all, people are watching them.'

'So you agree with Casement that the Irish question is an international question now, and not a local British matter any more?'

'Oh no! The notion of "joining Europe" is just another illusion. Poor old Ireland will always be a backwater. Imagine the most god-forsaken hole in the world and go on several hundred miles into the unknown and there you'll find Ireland!'

'I can't hear calmly about that man Casement, 'said Hilda. 'To go over to the Germans and try to stab England in the back like that just when she's up against it. . . .'

'It's the old story. "England's difficulty is Ireland's opportunity." Casement belongs to a classical tradition. And in a way I can't help admiring the fellow. It must be a lonely bitter business out there in Germany. He's a brave man and a patriot. He does it purely for love of Ireland. To love Ireland so much, to love anything so much, even if he's wrong-headed, is somehow noble.'

'He does it for love of gold, you may be sure,' said Hilda. 'It's the traitor mentality.'

Christopher thought for a moment. 'I think that word "traitor" ought to be removed from the language. It's just a muddled term of abuse. Casement's crime, or mistake, if it is one, is much more complex than anything that blunted word could name.'

'So you don't think there'll be any trouble in Ireland?' asked Andrew quickly before his mother could expostulate further.

'Trouble with the Sinn Feiners? No, I don't. And what

could they make it with, hurley sticks? I was talking to Eoin MacNeill's brother about it all the other day. Eoin has quite returned to his Gaelic studies. He was never a firebrand leader in any case. The Volunteers are really just like Boy Scouts and James Connolly's lot, the Irish Citizen Army, are ten men and a dog. If the Germans actually invaded Ireland, a few hotheads might help them, but with the blockade that's an impossibility. And anyway, as I say, what trouble could the Irish make, even if they wanted to? They've got no arms and they're not insane. I saw a squad of Volunteers drilling the other day with ten-foot pikes. It was pathetic!'

Andrew laughed. 'Don't tell the Sinn Feiners, but our reserve squadron at Longford only has about a hundred rifles, and half of them are D.P., drill purposes only. They'd probably explode if you tried to fire them!'

'Your lot at Longford had better look out then,' said Christopher. 'That place is a hot-bed of disaffection.'

'You shouldn't say things like that, Andrew,' said his mother. 'You never know who's listening.'

Andrew felt justly rebuked, and recalled suddenly to mind a rather unpleasant incident which had marked his arrival in Ireland. The one really constructive thing which he had managed to do when in France had been to get hold of a magnificent Italian rifle with telescopic sights. This extremely precious object had somehow or other disappeared at some point between the mail boat and Finglas. Christopher's gardener had sworn that the rifle had simply not been with the luggage when it arrived from the boat. Andrew now of course realized that it had been insane of him to take his eyes off it for a second in this gun-hungry country. Some time later he overheard Christopher saying casually that his gardener was connected with the Citizen Army. Andrew thought he would probably never know the truth of the matter: but he felt the disappearance of the rifle as a hostile act, upsetting and menacing.

'No, no,' Christopher was going on. 'I don't exactly see

Ireland as explosive material. I agree with Bulmer Hobson. Ireland is a damp bog which will yet extinguish many a flaming torch and gunpowder barrel! The fact is the Irish are far more sentimental and emotional even than one imagines. It all ends in talk. This morning, for instance, when I was down in town I witnessed a curious little scene. I meant to tell you of it earlier. I was passing near Liberty Hall, you know, the Transport and General Workers Union place, and I saw that some sort of ceremony was going on. There was a big crowd, and a girl in the Citizen Army uniform was climbing on the roof and un-furling a flag. It was a green flag with the Irish harp on it. And the I.C.A. men were all drawn up in ranks presenting arms and the bugles were blowing and the pipe bands were playing and then everyone started cheering, and do you know, quite a lot of people in the crowd had tears in their eyes.'

Andrew was disturbed by this account; and he felt that Christopher had perhaps been more interested than he pretended to be. Frances had put down her sewing.

'But what did it mean?' said Andrew.

'Nothing. That's my point. The Irish are so used to personi-fying Ireland as a tragic female, any patriotic stimulus produces an overflow of sentiment at once.'

' "Did you see an old woman going down the path?" "I did not, but I saw a young girl, and she had the walk of a queen." '

'Precisely, Frances. St Teresa's Hall nearly fell down when Yeats first came out with that stuff. Though in fact if you recited the Dublin telephone directory in this town with enough feeling you'd have people shedding tears!'

'Well, I think it ought to be stopped,' said Hilda. 'I can't imagine how they can do it, with the town full of wounded soldiers, you'd think they'd be ashamed. And I'm very sur-prised indeed that Pat Dumay hasn't enlisted. I really must have a word about it with his mother. An able-bodied young fellow like that ought to be longing to get out to the Front. I have the impression that he's becoming a rather disagreeable young man.'

'I shouldn't say anything to Kathleen if I were you,' said Christopher. 'And I'd advise you not to show your opinion in any way to Pat himself.' As he said this, Christopher looked quickly at Andrew.

Andrew felt an immediate pang of annoyance and the familiar sense of a threat. As if he would be such a fool as to bait his cousin for not having enlisted.

'Well, you may be right,' said Hilda, getting up. The sea mist now shrouded the garden and enveloped the house, curling damply in through the interstices of the conservatory. The rain had stopped, but water now hung on the interior of the glass in rows of glittering beads which would suddenly start rolling, coalesce, and fall with a small splash on to the stiff linen table-cloth. Frances was packing up the tea things. As they began to drift in toward the drawing-room, Andrew heard his mother saying to Christopher, 'I've been meaning to ask you for such a long time. What *exactly* did Wolfe Tone do?'

Chapter Three

'HAVE you heard this one?

> *As a beauty I'm not a star.*
> *There are others more handsome by far.*
> *But my face I don't mind it,*
> *For I am behind it.*
> *It's the people in front get the jar.*'

'That's not very funny.'

'It's not meant to be funny. It's philosophical. Well, and it is so, funny. And have you heard this one, "There was an old man of Rathmines"—'

'Oh, shut up, Cathal.'

'Don't be always telling your brother to shut up,' said Kathleen, who was laying the table for tea. Her sons did not reply, but waited with an air of abstracted politeness for her to leave the room, which she did a moment later.

'It's today the lilly-white boy is coming.'

'That's a fine way to be after talking about your cousin.'

'I mean it complimentary,' said Cathal.

'You do not.'

'All right, I don't. And you don't like him either. Isn't he a sort of a bloody English chancer.'

'I don't mind him. I like him all right.'

'Will he be in his uniform?'

'I expect so.'

'Will he be wearing spurs?'

'How do I know? Yes, I suppose so.'

'I shall laugh at his spurs. You'll hear me laughing and it'll be at his spurs.'

'You'll behave yourself decently or I'll belt you.'

'You will not.'

'I will so.'

'Yah! Yah! Patsie's not me da!' sang Cathal, waltzing the length of the drawing-room.

The Dumay's house stood at the upper end of Blessington Street, a wide, sad, dirty street due north of the Pillar, which crawled up the hill and ended at the railings of a melancholy little park. It had, under the pale bright sky, its own quiet air of dereliction, a street leading nowhere, always full of idling dogs and open doorways. Yet in form it closely resembled the other great Georgian arteries of Dublin, with its noble continuous façade of sombre blackened red brick which seemed to absorb, rather than to be revealed by, the perpetual rainy light. Looked at closely, the bricks of these houses showed in fact a variety of colours, some purplish red, some yellowish grey, all glued together by a jelly of filth to form a uniform organic surface rather like the scales of a fish, the basic material of Dublin, a city conjured from the earth all in one piece by some tousled Dido. Iron railings guarded deep cave-like areas where dandelions and young saplings flourished, and a few steps led up to each front door, above which was a graceful semicircular fanlight. The ornate pillars which flanked the doors, battered and flattened by time, had the air of Grecian antiquities. The windows alone were, the length of the street, handsome and elegant as upon their first day.

The doors varied. They were serious affairs, solid and many-panelled, and if well painted and provided with handsome knockers and a brass plate or two could sufficiently announce, even here, the residences of substantial citizens, well-bred reticent professional men. But by now many of the doors in the street were broken-down, their paint peeling off, chequered with mysterious holes, and lacking their knockers so that visitors had to shout through the letter-box. Various strange activities had meanwhile developed in the basements, such as a bicycle shop in one, a carpenter's workshop in another, and in one area a man sat all day mending cane chairs. While through grimy glass the fanlights displayed, besides the usual gaudy little figure of Christ the King, the cards of hairdressers and of chimney sweeps. At the end of the street there was even a house which had a sweet shop on the ground floor.

Yet the street had a spirit above these matters and in the evening when the lamp-lighter was just going his rounds, or on certain soft days when the sun shone through cloud, making everything vivid and exact as in a print, the street looked beautiful, with that particular sad, resigned, orderly beauty of Dublin. Those squared, cliff-like, blackened Dublin streets, stretching on and on, still had some inkling of perfection, even though the terraces sometimes looked more like warehouses, even had become warehouses, or in the poorer streets had gaping holes for windows and doors. Even then they seemed to know that they represented, they still in their darkened condition were, the most beautiful dwellings which the human race had ever invented.

The Dumays' house was not the finest in the street, nor was it the shabbiest. The door had been painted dark green some six years ago. It had a large brass knocker in the form of a wreath which the servant Jinny, a single girl of advancing years, who was paid eight shillings a week and lived in some nearby tenements affectionately called 'the little hell', occasionally polished when the matter came into her mind. On entering the house the first impression was of an ecclesiastical darkness and of the smell referred to by Mrs Chase-White. The ecclesiastical air was contributed by a stained-glass window on the half-landing which was in fact inside a lavatory, the door of which, when untenanted, stood always open. This place may also have accounted for the smell. The upper landing, which was long and lit by a skylight, was divided into two, for no very clear reason, by a faintly jangling bead curtain; while along the walls stood a series of shrines or side-chapels containing stuffed birds, cairns of wax fruit, and cascades of disintegrating butterflies under glass domes.

The drawing-room in which Cathal was now prancing was a long brown room, dimmed by brownish-white lace curtains, and very full of bulbous mahogany furniture. There were a number of coloured pictures of flower gardens, a large pinkish print called *The Love Letter*, and a prominent crucifix. Both Kathleen and Pat were indifferent to their surroundings and accepted the miscellany of brass bowls, ginger jars, embroidered clothlets and photos in upholstered frames as a natural part of the daily scene, as little remarkable as the rocks upon the seashore. Only Cathal displayed any concern with interior decoration and his interests so far were limited to the collecting of model animals, which now jostled the other inhabitants of the tall and extremely complicated overmantel, causing Jinny, when the day for dusting them came round, to utter under her breath words which would have startled Father Ryan. In the midst of the overmantel, whose unsymmetrical undulations suggested a natural growth rather than the workings of the human mind, was a slim extremely tall elliptical mirror, which showed in reflection an even more melancholy room filled with an atmosphere the colour of strong tea.

Kathleen had returned now and was placing upon the blue-and-white cross-stitch tablecloth the large silver milk-jug and sugar-bowl reserved for special occasions. Her sons fell silent. They never addressed each other now in her presence. They watched her with a faint detached curiosity as one might watch an animal which had wandered into view close by. She for her part was irritably aware of them. She was wearing an old-fashioned skirt of brown serge which reached almost to the ground and a high-necked white blouse over which she had drawn for the occasion a long knitted jacket of purple and orange stripes. Her hair was still fairish, though dulling now towards a peppery grey, and strained straight back into a large round bun. She had a small straight nose and large light-brown eyes. Her forehead was not so much wrinkled as pitted and crumpled with anxiety. She had been handsome and still looked strong, but in rather a haunted way.

The two boys had returned to their books. Pat was reading a novel by George Moore, and Cathal was studying O'Growney's *Simple Lessons in Irish*. Pat was fond of his mother, but there had always been much awkwardness between them. Pat had been nearly sixteen when his father died, and Kathleen, out of an anxious fear that the boys might now get completely out of hand, had attempted to impose a strict regime upon him. Pat had accepted his father as a force of nature to be endured, evaded, and in later years challenged, but never resented. His mother appeared as an arbitrary human will, and his struggle with her produced in him excitements and emotions which he found in some way loathesome. He punished her subsequently by his silence and had now got into the habit of speaking to her very little. He had found her second marriage entirely incomprehensible; and although he liked rather than disliked his stepfather he felt contemptuous of him and had never regarded him as a person with any sort of authority.

'They're here now,' said Jinny, ushering Frances Bellman and Andrew Chase-White into the room. Kathleen kissed Frances and complimented her on her dress. There was a mumble of greetings and a rumble of heavy chairs as everybody settled down about the small low tea-table, knocking it a good deal with their knees.

Pat stared at Andrew Chase-White without troubling to conceal the fact that he was inspecting him. Andrew had grown up a good deal since their last meeting. He had, almost, the face of a man, and an imposing blond moustache which he plucked at affectedly. He looked well in uniform, seeming taller and broader, and Pat felt no inclination to laugh at the glittering spurs and highly polished boots. Even Cathal seemed rather impressed and silenced. There entered the room with this smartly turned-out young officer the strong atmosphere of a larger public world. He seemed almost too good-looking, too typical, as if he had been chosen as a special envoy, a role which he seemed almost consciously to be playing, as he twitched his moustache and talked gallantly in a loud voice to Mrs Drumm, casting sidelong glances at Pat. He also spent a good deal of time examining the room as if to make sure that there had been no unauthorized alterations in his absence. His gaze returned uneasily to the crucifix.

Pat was surprised to find how much he was affected by seeing Andrew in uniform. He had no particular interest in his cousin, though as he had said to Cathal he 'didn't mind him'. As a boy he had only been concerned with children older than himself and Andrew had always been among the small fry. What struck him now was simply that whiff of the public world, that incarnate image of the soldier, official, stamped and approved. Actually to have this large topical object planted, as if by a practical joke, in his own drawing-room affected him not so much with annoyance as with surprise. There was also a certain envy, though not of Andrew personally. The young officer was an emblem of power. But Pat had his own reasons for not joining up.

Pat, who was vaguely aware that he had been, at various childhood times, rather 'hard on' Andrew, was conscious now of his cousin's almost frantic desire to impress him. There was an atmosphere of revenge in the air. Pat noticed it absently, casually, since he felt himself entirely invulnerable through being completely superior. He was prepared, even with a sort of amusement, to let his opponent enjoy what he took to be an advantage, easily inhibiting an assertion of personality which would have put young Andrew definitively in his place. As far as Pat was concerned, Andrew was still the little shouting boy who had followed him about, making a nuisance of himself on beaches all round the coast of Ireland. The present phenomenon was interesting not as an individual but as a type.

Kathleen was now talking to Frances, laying down certain principles for dealing with the servant problem which were to be passed on to Hilda. The conversation among the other three was staccato: Andrew condescendingly over-friendly, Pat distantly polite, Cathal, now recovering from his first discomfiture, definitely truculent. Andrew addressed his remarks to Pat, who offered minimal replies, while they both ignored provocative interjections from Cathal.

'I see you have an Irish grammar there. How interesting. Who's studying it?'

'Cathal is.'

'Is Irish a difficult language?'

'I understand that it's not an easy language.'

'It must be grand to know it.'

'Why don't you learn it then?'

'Do you think it important that the Irish people should learn it?'

'Sure, aren't you Irish yourself?'

'It has a certain symbolic value.'

' "A country without language is a country without a soul." '

'Yes, I appreciate that it has a symbolic value. On the other hand, if one is born to the language of Shakespeare—'

'You mean the language of Cromwell.'

'Don't keep interrupting, Cathal.'

'Well, I know when I'm not wanted!'

Cathal turned his chair right round to face Frances and his mother. Pat felt, like a small electric shock, a change in the emotional temperature which he realized to be Andrew's apprehension of their being left as it were tête-à-tête. Pat began to feel extreme irritation. He hoped that the conversation would not start to come round to the question of the war. He thought he could feel, and that with even more annoyance, Andrew deliberately avoiding the subject. At the thought that the 'lilly-white boy' might see himself as tactfully sparing his interlocutor an embarrassment a jeering scowl invaded Pat's face. He composed his features with difficulty.

'You must come round and see my mother's new house.'

'Oh yes.'

'She's always asking after you.'

'I trust Aunt Hilda is well?'

'She's fine now. She was awfully upset by the Zepps, you know.'

'Was she?'

'And how is my Uncle Barnabas these days?'

'Very well, I believe.'

'I'm so glad. You see, I haven't had time to come and see him since I came over, actually.'

'Really.'

Calmly determined to let the conversation run if necessary to a stand-still Pat fixed his eyes upon the crucifix above Andrew's head. He realized that this object somehow upset his cousin. Andrew squirmed in his seat. Pat thought he would try to force Andrew to look at the crucifix. But at that moment there was a little uproar from the other group.

'Our Lord said, "I bring not peace but a sword".' Cathal, who was incapable of tolerating a conventional conversation, had somehow steered the talk on to more general topics and was raising his voice.

'He meant the sword of the spirit,' said Kathleen in a subdued way. Having spent so much of her life as a widow with two high-spirited boys, she had cultivated a particularly soft rather dispiriting voice guaranteed to lower the temperature of any discussion.

'No He didn't, and I tell you why, because He was a Socialist.'

Frances laughed.

Pat, unable to resist contradicting his brother, turned round and said, 'Even if that were true, which it isn't, it wouldn't be very relevant.'

'How do you know if it's relevant since you don't know what we're talking about?'

Frances said, 'We're discussing pacifism.' She emulated Kathleen's slow soft voice.

'I told you it wasn't relevant.'

'It is so relevant. War is right when it's a fight for social justice.'

'But you don't have to kill people fighting for social justice,' said Kathleen. 'I agree with Daniel O'Connell, "No political reform is worth shedding one drop of blood".'

'Are you a pacifist, Aunt Kathleen?' asked Andrew. His air of friendly condescension made Pat want to kick him.

'No, not really. I just feel about this awful trench warfare—it can't be right. War has changed its nature.'

'It's all a matter of ends and means,' said Cathal.

'But some means are so terrible they can't really *be* means any more because the end gets lost. And some means are wicked in themselves, like torturing people or murder.'

'We call killing murder when we think it's a means to a bad end,' said Cathal. 'Of course this war is senseless, but that's because it's an imperialist war, and not because—'

'You don't even know what "imperialist" means,' said Pat.

'You want to say,' said Frances slowly and softly to Kathleen, 'that it could be all right with bows and arrows, but *this* sort of thing couldn't possibly be all right. I think I agree with you. When you really look at what's happening the world seems to have gone mad.'

'So you think Cousin Andrew's acting wrongly?' said Cathal, in a loud voice.

'Oh no, no!' said Kathleen. 'I was only speaking for myself.'

'Something can't be right or wrong just for yourself, if it's right or wrong it must be right or wrong for everybody.'

'Not at all,' said Pat, 'it depends what you mean—'

'Of course in a way I agree with you, Aunt Kathleen,' said

57

Andrew. 'It's all very well for people in places of safety to exhort us all to fight. But once one's been at close quarters with the business it's another matter.'

There was a short silence. 'How close quarters have you been at?' asked Pat, who very well knew the answer to his question.

Andrew flushed and frowned. 'Well, I can't say I've seen any action yet. I wasn't long in France.'

'It was smart of you to join the cavalry,' said Cathal. 'We all know the cavalry are kept miles behind the front line.'

'That's not true as it happens. And at least I've joined the army, I'm not just sitting at home or playing at soldiers in the back garden like some people.'

Cathal stood up, almost overthrowing the table. Frances and Kathleen started to speak in raised voices.

At that moment an extraordinary sound was heard just outside the room. It consisted of a series of loud resounding bumps accompanied by a tinkle of breaking glass and a human voice protesting in a traditional manner. Silence followed. Pat, interpreting the phenomenon, which was familiar to him in analogous forms, concluded that his stepfather, carrying some bottles of whiskey, must have fallen down the second flight of stairs, which, after creeping past the drawing-room door, he had been cautiously mounting. 'Oh dear, oh dear, oh dear,' said Kathleen. There was a general rush to the door.

Barnabas Drumm, wearing his hat, was sitting on the floor with his back against the newel post. A wide area of broken glass surrounded him, and from an extensive dark stain on the carpet there rose an overwhelming odour of whiskey. Barnabas looked sideways at the group in the doorway. Although he must have been perfectly aware that his predicament could amuse nobody and indeed must be causing a variety of different chagrins to all present, he could not help clowning it a little. He sat there with legs outstretched and began to whistle through his teeth.

Kathleen passed him by, stepping over him, and half ran along the landing. She returned in a moment with a dustpan and brush and, ignoring her husband, began to pick up the larger pieces of glass and put them into the pan. She worked slowly, in a resigned manner resembling the low voice she used to her sons, putting a quiet bitterness into the droop of her head.

Frances said, 'Are you all right? Have you hurt yourself?'

Cathal retired back into the drawing-room and shut the door sharply behind him. He was always wounded and affronted by his stepfather's total lack of dignity.

Andrew put his hand on Frances' arm, as if to protect her from a rowdy scene.

Annoyed by all these reactions and infuriated by the author of the incident, Pat said, 'For God's sake get up!' He pulled off his stepfather's hat and jammed it on to the post with a force which nearly split the crown.

With a good deal of dumb show, rubbing his bottom and his elbows, Barnabas began slowly to rise. He said, 'Isn't it just the like of me to do a thing like that.'

Barnabas Drumm was a short round man with a mild flabby face and a large golden moustache a little grizzled at the ends or soiled with Guinness. His brown hair fuzzed tonsure-fashion round a neat bald spot. The puzzled light blue of his eyes, invaded now by streaky reds and yellows, retained a childish quality. He still had a mouthful of good teeth and showed them often in a smile which though invariably gentle was also a reminder that he had once been better armed for the battle of life than he now seemed in general to be. Women, speculating about why level-headed Kathleen Dumay should have taken up with this muddle of a man, were divided between those who said that she had been pushed around by her first husband and now wanted someone she could push around, and those who voted Barney to be 'really rather sweet'.

'Hello, Andrew,' said Barnabas. 'We meet at last, though

not in the happiest circumstances. Think of all that excellent whiskey gone bang. Oughtn't we all to go down on our knees and lick the carpet.'

'Barney, will you please see me to the tram?' said Frances suddenly. Her voice sounded strained, as if she were about to burst into tears.

'Why, my dear, of course—'

Andrew said, 'But, Frances—'

'No, don't you come, Andrew. You stay here. I've got something special I want to say to Barney. Thank you so much, Aunt Kathleen. I've so much enjoyed myself.'

Frances had already seized her umbrella and her boa and was leading Barnabas away along the landing. Kathleen murmured something with her head still well down among the glass. Laboriously she was picking up tiny glittering splinters between her fingers.

Pat went back into the drawing-room and joined Cathal, who was standing stern-eyed at the window. Together, like a grim tribunal, they looked disapprovingly down upon their stepfather as he disappeared down the street arm-in-arm with Frances, sheltering under her umbrella in the light rain. He contrived to look jaunty. Pat detested jauntiness.

Andrew Chase-White, looking distracted, came running back into the room. The brothers ignored him. He seemed to run about for a little while like a dog. Then he returned to Kathleen and tried to help her with the glass, but the task appeared to be completed. He came back again and started to look for his raincoat. Pat wandered from the window and took up the George Moore novel. Andrew got as far as the door and then suddenly came back and stood before his cousin.

'Pat—'

'Yes?'

'Oh—sorry—nothing—'

'Goodbye, then.'

Looking wretched, Andrew left the room, colliding with

Kathleen, who was returning with the tea tray. Murmuring thanks, he made for the stairs.

Kathleen, watched by her sons, began slowly to stack up the tea things. Pat noticed that she was crying. Big tears welled from her eyes and fell from her cheeks on to the tray. She always stooped double over any task she performed. Pat could not fathom his mother's frequent and unconcealed tears, but he felt them as an aggression upon himself and averted his eyes. These exhibitions displeased him without troubling him deeply. He found women obscure and mysterious but not interesting. Kathleen left the room.

'Ah well,' said Cathal. '"Up the long ladder and down the short rope, to hell with King Billy and long live the Pope." What did he want, I wonder?'

'He wanted to apologize. He would have done so if you hadn't been here.'

'Well, let him go. We don't mind him. He's nothing. Are you going to belt me?'

'I'll let you off this time.'

'Pat—'

'Yes?'

Cathal came up behind his brother and gently put his arms round his waist. 'When is it to be?'

'I don't know what you're talking about.'

'You do so.'

'I do not.'

Chapter Four

Over and over, like a mighty sea,
Comes the love of JESUS, rolling over me!

Several hundred youthful voices pealed it forth enthusiastically as Andrew and his mother went with quickened step and stiffened gait past the big marquee. A large red banner above it read *Children's Special Service Mission*, and *Saved by the Blood of the Lamb*. Neither Andrew nor his mother referred to the phenomenon. They were on their way to visit Aunt Millicent.

'You really must fix things up properly with Frances, after all it's up to you,' said Hilda, as they began to pass out of range.

Once I was blind, now I can see,
Once I was bound, but now I am free,
And that's how I KNOW there's a Saviour for me—
OH such a Saviour!

Andrew reflected, as the horrible sounds died away, that in Ireland religion was a matter of choosing between one appalling vulgarity and another. Wondering which he would vote for if he had to choose, he concluded sadly that of course he would have to be with the young people in the marquee and their boisterous mentors. 'Yes,' he said absently.

At the moment Andrew could think of nothing else but Pat Dumay. He regretted everything about yesterday's scene. He felt he had cut a rotten figure. He had failed to protect Frances from a sort of grossness in the atmosphere. He had construed her rushing off with Uncle Barnabas as a reproach to himself. He had helplessly witnessed his uncle playing the buffoon. And worst of all he had allowed himself to be provoked into taunting Pat. He had scarcely troubled to formulate any intention or resolution about this beforehand, so impossible had it

FOUR

seemed that he should affront his cousin. It had been for
Andrew an axiom that Pat was a little larger than life and far
too dignified and authoritative to be in any way goaded or
jeered at. Such behaviour would only belittle the jeerer; as he
now felt himself belittled. More than this, he felt an acute
regret, almost a sentimental pain, to think that he had probably
ruined his chances of becoming Pat's friend. He now realized,
inordinately, surprisingly upset by the incident, that so far
from being 'liberated' from his uncomfortable interest in his
cousin, he had returned to Ireland with the ardent hope of
being treated as his equal, of winning his respect and even his
affection. Yesterday's encounter had been very important to
him and now that it had misfired he was left with an emotional
problem. He had hardly been able to bring himself to leave the
house, he could not remember whether he had said goodbye to
Aunt Kathleen, and he would certainly have attempted some
reconciliation scene then and there, had not the maddening
Cathal been standing by.

'After all, Frances wants a formal proposal, any girl does,'
Hilda was going on. 'It's a great moment in one's life. She'll
want to be able to remember it later on. It is really time there
was an announcement. And you must do something about a
ring. It isn't fair to other young men, and now that Frances is
going more into society you don't want to land her in difficulties.'

With an effort Andrew switched his attention to Frances.
Yes, he really must get Frances fixed up. And of course, yes, a
great moment. My dearest Frances, I have something of very
great importance to ask you. I wonder if you can at all guess
what it is? Indeed, dear Andrew, I cannot conjecture. You will
have to tell me. I wish you to do me the honour of becoming
my wife. 'You are quite right, Mama,' he said.

'I do hope Christopher will be on time. I saw him this
morning at Bewley's in Grafton Street and he swore he'd come.
It's such a job to get him round to Millie's. I do find your aunt

63

rather a strain and I know he does too. Thank heavens it's stopped raining, so perhaps he'll wait for us outside. You say everything looked just the same at Blessington Street? I really must get round there and see the boys, Kathleen keeps pestering me. I am surprised she does not re-do her drawing-room. She could easily afford it, and it must look so shabby and old-fashioned now.'

'It looked exactly as I always remember it.'

It was a room that receded into his earliest childhood like a long dirty corridor, always twilit, stuffy, melancholy, vaguely menacing. And yet perhaps it was not quite the same, or rather he himself had changed. He recalled seeing yesterday, as he checked the massy drifts of furniture and the myriad objects still rooted in their old places, an oriental table with innumerable pieces of glass set into its gilded legs. He remembered this, which had once seemed to him an object of exotic beauty; it now looked as his mother would see it, tawdry, vulgar. Some glory had gone from the room, something which at least it had had which resembled beauty. The presence of the big crucifix, which had formerly seemed both thrilling and alarming, now just seemed a piece of rotten bad form, characteristic of the particular undiscriminating muddle in which his aunt and uncle lived. Well, well, he would take Frances to England, away from all this. Yes, Andrew, she whispered gratefully, yes, yes. Her little hand sought his, and as he drew her to his breast he could feel the violent beating of her heart.

'Ah, there's Christopher waiting outside, bless him, wearing that comical mackintosh hat. Hello, Christopher, we were hoping you would be punctual. Oh, before I forget, Kathleen was at Claresville just after luncheon and said she'd looked for you at Finglas and there was something special she wanted to see you about.'

Christopher seemed a little depressed by this news. 'What have I done now? Did she say what it was? Was she upset?'

'No, she didn't say. She wasn't upset. You know Kathleen's

never exactly bright and gay. I shouldn't think it's important, so don't worry.'

'Ah well. Once more into the breach, dear friends.'

Aunt Millicent's town house was what Hilda called 'one of the better class houses' of Dublin. It was a 'double-fronted' house in Upper Mount Street, several times wider than the house in Blessington Street, but otherwise not unlike it in structure. In the watery sunlight the brick façades of Upper Mount Street glowed a rusty pink and yellow, only Millie's house, together with one or two others, had been washed over with a powdery red preparation, currently fashionable, and the interstices between the bricks outlined in black. The sagging steps up to the door were immaculately reddened to match. Beneath its magisterial fanlight the door was a radiant newly painted rose pink, its brass knocker, shaped like a fish, polished as softly bright and smooth as Saint Peter's toe; while at each gleaming window a heavy froth of lace curtain was symmetrically looped back. Just beyond, at the end of the street, the elegant green dome of Saint Stephen's, Church of Ireland, rose into the lucid blue sky. Long green coppery streaks trailed down the light grey stone of the tower and fingered the clock which was just now striking four. Its particular high cracked tone struck with a melancholy authority upon the heart of Andrew, recalling to him the church's rational empty interior where he had sometimes worshipped as a child, if participation in those calm, prosaic rites could be called worship.

A maid with long white streamers depending from her cap informed them that her ladyship was out in the garden. As they passed through the dark belly of the house Andrew tried to revive his memories of it. But it was many years since he had been there, and the rooms seemed unfamiliar. He glimpsed great mahogany surfaces gleaming like black mirrors in twilit interiors. There was a vernal smell of furniture polish.

The garden was more fresh in memory. He recognized, though he could not have pictured it beforehand, the wide terrace of slightly reddish paving stones, with its intermittent clumps of iris and rosemary and rue, and its square fish-pool, the brown beech hedge beyond, still clothed in its crisp twirled winter leafage, and the little lawn with the propped-up mulberry tree. The scene was wet and glistening, the paving stones reflecting hints of light and form, the mulberry tree dripping. Then suddenly the sun became brighter and a light seemed switched on in the garden. The great hump of the mulberry tree glowed into a golden green. Aunt Millicent came through the gap in the hedge.

Andrew felt a perceptible pleasurable very rapid shock as if a needle had passed right through his body without hurting him. It was many years since he had seen his aunt, and although he retained intact, like old snapshots, some attractive memories of her, these had been gradually overlaid by his mother's continual though vague remarks about Millie being so 'tiresome', or being about to 'go to pieces', a fate which was for some reason persistently foreseen by her sister-in-law. These prognostications, together with the reports of hunting, cigar-smoking, pistol shots and trousers, had made him, without reflection, expect something slightly, by this time, gaunt and sourly tweedy, something a little weatherbeaten, smelling of tobacco and even of whiskey, although drink had not in fact figured so far in his mother's denunciations. What confronted him now was a plump youngish woman with a radiantly smiling face, elegantly dressed in a tight-skirted slightly old-fashioned mode, and positively, oh very positively, pretty.

'Oh, hello my dears', shouted Millie across the terrace, You've come! Oh, goody!' She swept up to Hilda and began kissing her. 'Hello Christopher. Glad to see you, you old stranger. I absolutely adore your hat. And this is the golden-haired soldier boy! My, doesn't he look fine! I can remember him when he wasn't interested in anything but farthing lucky-bags. Can you remember those farthing lucky-bags, Andrew?

Many a penny you begged off me for them, to get them at Nolan's shop. But I mustn't remind you of that now, must I? Why, I think he's blushing, the pet!'

Andrew, smiling rather stiffly, felt he had gained a little insight after all into what his mother meant by 'tiresomeness'.

'It's very nice to see you, Millie', said Hilda. 'You seem to be keeping well. We had such a pleasant walk here. Merrion Square is looking lovely, with the lilac and the laburnum all ready to flower. And I'm glad to say the rain seems to have given up at last.'

'Oh yes, and I thought we'd have tea in the garden,' said Millie. 'Wouldn't that be fun? I haven't done it yet this year.'

'Won't it be a bit wet and cold for tea in the garden?' said Hilda, not concealing her displeasure.

'I'll lend you all woolly shawls from Connemara. I've just got some new ones and they're such pretty colours. And as for a little wet, sure I don't mind it, and you won't either when you've been over here a bit longer. One's getting oneself wet all the time in Ireland, isn't that so, Christopher? Sure I don't mind it at all.'

This appeared to be true, as Andrew observed that his aunt's high-necked dress of dove-grey silk, which with the enthusiastic gesturing that accompanied her words constantly swirled against the low bushes, was darkened with water and even muddied all round the lower hem. He also noticed as she swayed the rather old-fashioned flounced bustle effect at the back, unless it was indeed perhaps Aunt Millicent's shape. He looked elsewhere.

'Well, I think we shall be cold,' said Hilda firmly. She seemed to have decided it was a matter of principle to show the flag to her sister-in-law straight away.

'The sun's shining and it'll be dry directly,' Millie went on inconsequently, 'Wouldn't you like to walk down the garden? The little brick path is a dry way.'

'How's the camellia?' said Christopher.

'Oh, but it's in *flower*, it's a *sight*. You take Hilda down to the greenhouse to see the camellia and young Andrew shall stay here and help me with the tea things.'

Christopher led Hilda away. The murmur of her protests could be heard receding beyond the hedge.

'Aren't they a well-matched couple?' said Millie, looking after them. Then she laughed. 'Well now, young Andrew, come and sit down and let me look at you.'

She drew him to a wooden seat and they sat down. The long twisting branches of rosemary swept the pavement at their feet. The seat was extremely wet, as Andrew instantly realized. The dove-grey silk took the matter in its stride.

Millie sat for a moment staring at him, and he, half annoyed, half amused, returned her stare. She was not perhaps as handsome as she had seemed at first sight. Her complexion was rather coarse and her mouth too large. She had big dark brown eyes which she continually narrowed, perhaps because she was short-sighted. Her reddish brown hair, to which a fine and scarcely perceptible scattering of grey gave a metallic patina, was much plaited and entwined. Two small ears held their own against it, adorned with bright blue lapis lazuli earrings. After having been a very laughing face, it was now a very serious face. It compelled Andrew, and only after he had been looking into her eyes in silence for half a minute did he realize how unusual this proceeding was.

'Yes,' she said. 'You *are* like him. I could never really see it before.'

'Like—?'

'Like your father. You are really very like him now.'

'I'm glad—,' said Andrew lamely. The scrutiny now embarrassed him, and he averted his eyes.

'I wonder if you remember a picnic at Howth—well, why should you, you were very young. Tell me about yourself. So you were in France, but not for long, you got pneumonia, and you're still on sick leave?'

Andrew was a bit surprised and flattered at this knowledge of his lot. 'Yes. I'm afraid I haven't seen much action yet.'

'Don't worry,' said Millie. 'This old war is going to last quite a while. You'll have plenty of time to behave with reckless courage on some battlefield.'

'I hope so.'

'Well, you're a fool to hope so. I really think one should be a pacifist. I'm sure they could all make peace now if they tried. But what with the wicked old men and the silly young ones—it's about time women had the vote. Are you political?'

Andrew was not sure how serious she was. He answered lightly. 'I don't understand much about politics. I'm leaving that for later.'

'I think we should all be political nowadays. I say, my bottom says it's wet, what does yours say? Let's walk about a bit, take a turn, as your mother would say.'

She jumped up, and as she did so swept her hand along one of the rosemary branches collecting the small narrow leaves in her palm. A delicious musty fragrance arose which almost made Andrew sneeze.

'I love things with grey leaves, don't you? Well, rosemary hasn't actually got grey leaves, or rather they're only grey underneath, but that was the idea of this garden, and the rue has, and that stuff called trimalchio or whatever it is. There—' As she took his arm she strewed the leaves of the rosemary over his khaki sleeve.

'That's for remembrance. And rue—what is rue for, I forget?'

'For sorrow, I suppose,' said Andrew.

'Such a pretty plant. Well, sorrow we shall all have, especially you as you are so young. I keep thinking I have grown out of sorrow, but it keeps coming back. Don't worry about the tea, Maudie will lay it inside whatever I say, and I declare I think it's going to rain again after all. Come and see my fish.'

She released him, and moved to the other side of the little

fish-pool, regarding him across it. The brown surface of the pool quivered a little at their feet, perhaps with some preliminary drops of rain. The sky behind Millie was now a bright hazy yellow.

Andrew stared at his aunt across the pool. The blue earrings glowed in the dark convoluted hair.

She murmured, 'Yes, you are confoundedly like your da. What are you thinking at this moment?'

Andrew framed in his mind the sentence, How beautiful your earrings are, Aunt Millicent. He said, 'How beautiful you are, Aunt Millicent.'

There was a second's silence before Millie's loud laugh. 'Why, you naughty boy, are you flirting? And you engaged to the dearest girl in the world! Well, you must bring her to see me. You must come to tea next Thursday at Rathblane, the pair of you. And next Thursday, but not before, you shall call me Millie.'

She knelt down on the pavement beside the pool. Andrew knelt too, embarrassed at what he had so unaccountably said, but also, unaccountably, feeling rather pleased with himself. He pretended to be investigating the fish.

As he looked down into the dense brown vegetable depths of the pool something suddenly flashed past him. There was a glint of blue and a splash and a receding sinking glimmer. 'Dear me,' said Millie. 'One of my earrings has gone west.'

With an exclamation of distress Andrew peered down into the pool where the earring had completely disappeared from view, and his first instinctive idea was that it was lost forever. He looked up at Millie and found her regarding him coolly, her eyebrows slightly raised. She seemed unmoved by the incident and only interested in what he would do.

'Of course,' said Andrew, as if laboriously working it out, 'the pool's not very deep, is it? I'll get it for you'. His hand broke the surface of the warm water. He hesitated. Rather awkwardly he removed his watch and put it in his pocket and then began to take off his jacket. Millie stared at him. He folded the jacket and then could not think what to do with it, being unwilling to lay it on the wet pavement, until Millie reached out and took it from him in silence. He rolled up one sleeve of his shirt to the shoulder and loosened his tie and undid the shirt at the neck where it was a little tight. These preparations seemed to take a ludicrously long time. He plunged his arm into the pool up to the elbow, deeper, without touching bottom. A pale oval, the reflection of Millie's face, danced disjointedly on the disturbed surface. Andrew lay down full length upon the pavement. As the water lapped at his shoulder his hand explored the soft sludgy bottom. He touched something hard, and the next moment had fished up the earring. He handed it quickly to his aunt and they both rose.

Andrew felt distressed and discomfited by the incident, chiefly, as he now confusedly felt, because he had paused to take his jacket off; and yet it would have been idiotic to plunge his arm in without doing so. He quickly resumed his jacket. He coughed and began to brush down his breeches to which a greenish slime from the pavement adhered in streaks. He was beginning to feel annoyed and put in the wrong.

'Andrew,' said Aunt Millicent.

He straightened up to look at her. At once with a quick gesture she dropped the earring down inside the front of his shirt. A second later Hilda and Christopher appeared through the gap in the hedge. The terrace rang with Millie's unexplained laughter. It began to pour with rain.

Chapter Five

'I THOUGHT they'd never go,' said Christopher.

'How did you give them the slip?'

'I said I was going into town.'

'You don't think Aunt Hilda suspects?'

'Darling Hilda knows nothing.'

'Did she say anything special?'

'Only that it was just like you to want to have tea in the garden. I must say I agree!'

'But that was on purpose,' said Millie. 'I thought if we were all shivering out on the terrace they'd go all the sooner!'

'So you're not as feckless as I thought. A shrewd calculating person lives inside you.'

'Well, not really. I only invented the reason afterwards.'

'Whatever did you do to young Andrew, by the way? You must have bewitched him. He said practically nothing all through tea and just fumbled with the neck of his shirt.'

Millie laughed. 'Oh, I did something to embarrass him. Never mind what. He is so touchingly like his father, one can't help teasing him. Do you fancy him as a son-in-law?'

'He's all right. He's not as intelligent as Frances, but he's got sense and a very sweet nature. And they know each other very well and love each other.'

'Love—ah well—'

'Ah well, indeed.'

This conversation was taking place in a long upper room, originally a billiard room, which Millie used as a combination of personal boudoir and shooting gallery. The combination of these two atmospheres unnerved, and doubtless was intended to unnerve, Millie's friends. The room was thickly carpeted and at the near end, by the door, looking obscurely ecclesiastical, stood a low white dressing-table with a tall mirror surmounted by a large lace canopy not unlike those which are held above the Host in religious processions. A plump pink stool, gathered in to a waist-line of silken roses, was placed before the mirror which was flanked by a pair of gilded candlesticks containing candles, unlit at the moment. All round about was a cluster of extremely comfortable satin-covered armchairs, all facing the mirror, placed as if for some ceremony at which Millie would adorn herself or possibly undress before an admiring audience. This ceremony, as far as Christopher knew, never took place, nor did he suppose, though he had never investigated, that the jars of Waterford glass on the dressing-table actually contained cosmetics. They were more likely to contain liqueurs. As far as he knew: for sometimes for a fleeting moment he had the suspicion that Millie led some secret life where, with other recondite suitors, she proceeded to lengths of which he never dreamed. But in fact that was impossible; he knew all about Millie: and even if he lacked, certainly no one else enjoyed, the ultimate privileges.

The wall at the far end of the room, faced with wood and pitted with revolver fire, was bare except for the row of targets at which, standing among the satiny chairs, Millie took aim with her small nickel-plated revolver. The side walls, lined with a furry green vegetational wallpaper, were thickly covered with tolerably good oil paintings of members of the Kinnard family. At these, with suitably pugnacious exclamations, Millie often pointed her weapon, but had only once loosed off a bullet in their direction, which happily lodged in a frame. Christopher disliked these sports. He hated the noise and the horrible sensation of the impact. Millie, armed, cut a pretty figure. But he took the menace of it painfully to himself.

Although it was still light outside, Millie had pulled the curtains and lit the gas, and the fierce bright mantles purred along the room under their red tasselled shades. During the time in which Christopher had been engaged in 'giving the slip' to Andrew and Hilda, she had changed out of the tight grey dress into a looser shorter dress of purple crêpe-de-chine, rather oriental in appearance. She kept nudging the skirt of it against her leg as she stood, as if unused to the length, while she played absently with the revolver, spinning the barrel fast and then stopping it abruptly with her finger. Christopher, outstretched in one of the armchairs, watched her with exasperation, fascination, adoration and fear.

'You know, Christopher, when you play Russian roulette it isn't really dangerous because the weight of the bullet always pulls the loaded chamber down to the bottom.'

'I have no intention of playing Russian roulette. You are quite breath-taking enough as a pastime. Don't change the subject, my darling.'

The process of falling in love with Millie had, for Christopher, taken place over quite a long period. Yet there had never been any moment when he had both understood clearly what he was doing and been still able to control it. At moments of control he had not understood, and at moments of understanding he had been helpless. He sometimes told himself that if he could have prevented this thing from happening he would have done so. He knew, now, what Millie did, but he did not know what Millie thought, and he feared, coming upon them suddenly, certain blank moments of ruthlessness in her. Yet even the process of coveting Millie, at first as it had seemed so vainly, had renewed the world for him, and in her light he had seen every flower, every leaf, every bird designed with a wiry clarity and plumped out with a celestial untainted colour.

When Christopher had first met Millie, at a time when he himself was courting Heather Kinnard, she was already married to Arthur. He had disliked her, chiefly, as it seemed in retrospect, because she had tended to put Heather in the shade. Yet Heather had adored her dominating sister-in-law and defended her heartily against Christopher's criticisms. He had thought Millie loud, vulgar and thoroughly selfish. He still thought her loud, vulgar and thoroughly selfish, only now these things were meat and drink to him; or rather, he saw her faults with a difference, touched by romance into gaiety and by charity into innocence. Kathleen, whose conceptual armoury did not include the idea of vulgarity, disliked and indeed feared in Millie a merciless rapacity upon which she blamed Arthur's early death. Kathleen once said of Millie, 'She respects no one. She does not see where another person begins.' But Heather enjoyed Millie's flamboyance, her noise. This paler, frailer quieter soul took from her boisterous sister-in-law the reflection of a more abundant life. Perhaps, Christopher had often felt, Arthur's attitude to Millie was of this kind too. He had enjoyed being digested by this larger organism. And it also occurred to Christopher to wonder: had he himself similarly engulfed Heather? Was he able to 'see where another person begins'? No one had seemed to blame him for the way in which Heather had faded from life. Yet perhaps something in himself, less noisy, less overtly colourful, but just as ruthlessly and largely egotistic, had thrust aside that gentler, weaker spirit. But of course these were strictly irrational speculations. Heather had died from a disease of the liver and Arthur from cancer of the stomach. Science proclaimed their deaths normal, unavoidable.

Perhaps, in the long run, it was some deep sense of identification with his sister-in-law, some feeling of the similarity of their temperaments, of a profound likeness underneath a superficial unlikeness, which had made Christopher so interested. Arthur's demise had preceded Heather's by some eighteen months, and at the time of these deaths Christopher's dislike of Millie had been at a maximum: possibly because he felt himself associated with her in some kind of guilty pact. All the same, she had by now become an object of speculation, irritation, fascination. Perhaps too he had in a way learnt from Heather to regard Millie as one of the world's more significant objects. When her name came up in conversation he would jump and listen nervously, and when she was present he was always unusually argumentative. Then one day she asked him to lend her some money.

That was now about eight years ago. It had been a significant moment and Christopher had felt it to be such at the time. It had been, for him, the first indication that all was not well with Millie's finances. She lived extremely lavishly and it had been and still was confidently assumed by the world at large that Millie Kinnard was 'pretty well heeled'. Christopher was surprised, interested, and in a prophetic way curiously pleased to find that this was not so. He lent her the money at once, without comment, happy to be, and happy to be tacitly expected to be, supremely discreet. She was grateful, he was politely, reticently dignified; and at once their relationship was altered. Christopher's money had come to him from his father, who had been a teacher of mathematics at Trinity, an amateur economist and an expert gambler on the Stock Exchange; which expertize had augmented an already comfortable family fortune. Christopher himself was neither rapacious nor mean and had not inherited his father's taste for playing with money. Yet money was important to him, its presence was a deep source of security, and it was somehow a stuff through which he was vitally connected with the world. A part of his life-blood ran through it. And when he became financially connected with Millie some warmth passed from him to her with the connection. It was this primitive touching, more even perhaps than the more obvious sense of a power over her, which made him begin to fall in love.

But of course these explanations, upon which he himself later meditated, were in a way otiose. Millie was a gorgeous desirable object. He wondered why all men were not in love with her, and soon began to suspect that they were. She was an overflowing vessel, a plump, gay, generous woman. There was some coldness, some shivering, shrewd thinness in Christopher which needed her desperately, which clung to her as to a source of warmth and life. He only half concealed his need, watching her with a large affectation of detachment, and enraptured by the cool amused gaze which, in the formality of their new relationship, she with equal affectation adopted. He remembered how, in the old quarrelling days, Millie would sometimes shout out, 'But I adore Christopher!' Now, as their poker-faced relation gradually broke down into tenderness and laughter, he realized that Millie was not only grateful, she was prepared in effect to adore him. This made Christopher very happy indeed.

Time passed, and Millie's affairs became more involved and difficult. Christopher lent her more money. He gave her advice too, but he was a prudent rather than an original capitalist and an ineffective helper. Millie took advice in other quarters, without revealing the seriousness of the situation, and merely increased the muddle she was in. She was incapable of economies. Christopher watched these developments with mixed feelings, and gradually an idea which seemed to him both sinister and delightful formulated itself in his mind. Millie's difficulty would be Christopher's opportunity.

That he might ever ask Millie to marry him was a notion which, after he had fallen in love with her, he had early dismissed. He wanted to be happy, to enjoy the deliciousness of her company, not to ask too much; and it seemed clear that she could not possibly want to marry him. She was a spoilt girl, he was not by any means her only admirer, and she ostentatiously enjoyed her freedom. She 'adored' him, but she was not in the least in love with him. 'Adoration' was something different. Millie skipped about, bounded like a dog, shouted more than usual when Christopher arrived. But she let him depart without repining. She liked the intermittent character of their converse. He would have wished to be with her day and night. He coveted her body with a passion which his shrewd hedonism constantly quieted and checked. He did not care, at his age, to suffer the sleepless nights of unsatisfied desire, and he did

77

not in fact suffer them. But he wanted Millie; and he knew that she did not, in that way, want him.

Discretion about money had somehow cast a veil of secrecy over their whole relationship. It was not generally known that they were fond of each other or that they met so often; and Christopher kept up for the benefit of some of his relations the fiction that he found Millie 'trying'. He did this partly out of an innate taste for the clandestine, partly because of the money question, and partly because Millie wanted it that way. Christopher was realistic and resigned about Millie's desire for secrecy. A popular woman who enjoys her admirers and is also kind-hearted will naturally want to keep her friendships strictly sealed off from each other. To each man Millie seemed available with an undivided attention and a full heart. Christopher was consoled by being more in her confidence than most. He at least knew about the others; and he was fairly certain that, at present at any rate, these 'relationships' which Millie cultivated remained at a level of innocuous flirtation, although hearts other than hers were sometimes cracked in the process.

There was, however, yet another and graver reason for Christopher's secrecy, and that was the attitude of Frances. Frances disliked Millie, perhaps because, although Christopher had always, and quite automatically, concealed it from her, she sensed her father's interest and was jealous, or perhaps out of a strong temperamental disparity. 'I don't like being bounced at,' Frances had once said coldly after some demonstration of Millie's. And Millie indeed, who was always made nervous by the presence of Frances, whom she felt as a critic, had made various effusive but vain attempts to win the girl round. Christopher loved Frances dearly, though he had always treated her, even as a child, in the cool ironical manner which he used to the world at large. In this respect, he and his daughter, early left to each other's company by the vanishing of Heather, perfectly understood one another, and made no display of a strong affection which passed freely between them under a guise of such calmness that not everyone realized that they loved each other at all.

Before Christopher had formulated the idea of asking Millie to marry him he had not too much troubled about the hostility of Frances. It had merely provided another motive for a total discretion. But when the notion of such a marriage had appeared in the background the view which Frances might take of it became an appalling source of anxiety. That Frances disliked Millie was of course in itself a serious impediment; and there was also the possibility that a projected match between her father and 'that woman' might produce in Frances some unprecedented reaction of violence. Christopher was aware that in some respects which were relevant to this problem he did not know his daughter very well. Their relations had been, in a sense, too perfectly organized. Being so much in each other's company they had early developed an adult language of understatement, and their feelings, just because they were so harmonious, had been tacit. But Christopher divined in his daughter the presence of an as yet unpractised stubbornness, the presence of ferocious will.

The marriage question, for some time hovering in the background, had now suddenly and automatically been brought into the foreground by the almost complete collapse of Millie's fortunes. This collapse was not yet known to the world. At Upper Mount Street the maids with the white streamers still tripped confidently about the house and under the windows of Rathblane the hunters still strolled and nibbled the green grass. The chauffeur still polished the brass fitments of the Panhard. But all this must shortly vanish like a dream, dissolve like Aladdin's palace, unless . . .

Christopher, faced with the supreme temptation, did not attempt to resist it, did not even formulate the idea of it as a temptation, so confident did he now suddenly feel in his gods. He would save Millie, he would save her by marrying her. The idea that he was in effect proposing to buy Millie was perfectly clear in his mind, but seemed in the context entirely innocuous. The one who is in love has the significant destiny and Christopher felt that, beyond his hopes, a path had been made, a door had been opened, especially for him. His significance would felicitously espouse Millie's misfortune. There was indeed an inevitability about it, the other side of which was that it was somehow clearly 'impossible' for Christopher to save Millie without marrying her.

Although the idea that there was only one solution had been taking shape over a period of months, as Millie's financial affairs went into the final phases of collapse, it was only in the last four weeks or so that Christopher had used explicitly the words which named his intention. This had happened during scenes in which Millie would say desperately, 'I'll sell this house and Rathblane and go into lodgings,' and Christopher would say, 'Don't be foolish. You know you can't face it. You'll marry me and everything will be all right.' Then Millie would laugh loudly, say, 'It looks as if I'll have to!' and change the subject. It was true that Millie could not face it, that she would in the end do anything rather than face it; and meanwhile she played a little for time.

This period of their relationship had had, for Christopher, a special rather sad charm. Millie had been of late, even in the last year, more subdued, less boisterous. It was not that she seemed older or positively melancholy, but her beauty wore a sort of gauzy veil which perhaps only he could see. She was less rowdy and her gaiety sometimes seemed 'switched on', an effort, and she was often thoughtful. Christopher had her cornered, and she knew it. She used now her resources of irony and humour to cover the loss of her dignity as a free being. She seemed without resentment. There was something beautiful and sad in this loss of power which made him feel very tenderly towards her. It was like a stage in taming a wild beast when it becomes suddenly gentle and puss-like. It plunges far off, but feels the rope that draws and draws it. Now it trots

FIVE

more soberly near by. Soon it will come to the hand. It will
have to.

This was how Christopher saw it most of the time; but there
were moments of uneasiness when he felt that the closer he
came to her the more likely it was that Millie might suddenly
bolt. He would have been prepared to let her decide very
slowly indeed. He rather enjoyed his state of undeclared
sovereignty. But financial pressures set the pace and Millie
herself seemed increasingly anxious to settle her fate although
she still avoided any clear commitment; while Christopher,
who had intended not to press her, could not now prevent
himself from advancing upon her as the situation itself relentlessly advanced. No, he did not really think that she could
escape him. Yet with a woman like Millie one never knew. She
was used to doing things on the hunting field which seemed
equivalent to suicide; and although she was probably incapable
of facing poverty, she was not incapable of pulling the house
down, of provoking some total catastrophe on the assumption
that the world was going to end immediately.

'Have some of your special cider and sherry mixture,' said
Millie. 'I've got some here in a jug.'

'Thanks.' Christopher was partial to a mixture of two parts
of Tio Pepe to one part of dry cider.

She released the glass into his fingers, but kept her hand
lightly resting against his, looking down at him. The purple
silk brushed his knee.

'You look Chinese today, Millie. It must be the dress.'

'Good. I shall need all my inscrutability for dealing with
you.'

She suddenly laughed and moved away. 'Do you know,
poor dear Hilda, I was watching her at tea. I think she thinks
she's got you hooked.'

Christopher laughed too. 'Not hooked, no. She pictures us
as two ancient craft driven by the storms of fortune into the
selfsame anchorage!'

81

'When is Frances getting married?'

Christopher drew a quiet breath. Millie's jumpy nervy mood both frightened and exhilarated him. How endlessly she must have thought about Frances. Yet the name was rarely mentioned between them. 'Soon.'

'How soon?'

'I don't know. That foolish boy still hasn't fixed it. But he will directly. I'll make him.'

It was a sad thing to Christopher, and perhaps the only thing about which he really felt guilt, that he was now actually impatient for Frances to be married. Indeed she must be married before anything else could happen. He feared that will of hers, roaming unoccupied and uncaged.

'Christopher—'

'Yes, dear?'

'Do you think I'm getting old and ugly?'

'You know perfectly well what I think.'

'I must be getting old. I need to hear somebody saying that I am gorgeously attractive. Once I didn't need to be told, except by my looking-glass.'

'You are gorgeously attractive, Millie.'

She paused by the tall mirror and with a large gesture lit the candles on either side of it. Like a new ghost in the flickering light her reflection gazed at Christopher, and the reflection had suddenly the remote distinction of a work of art, and something too of the eternal sadness of art.

'Well, it's not true, but bless you for saying it. This soft light suits me, don't you think? It makes me hazy. One mustn't look too close. I am getting old. I'm nearly ready to retire. Perhaps I'll retire with you and we'll go and live in the hotel at Greystones and become a well-known old couple taking a turn on the front.'

'I wish you would! You know how much I wish—'

'Sssh, Christopher.'

'Yes?'

'I like you because you are so clever.'

'Oh, Millie, do stop tormenting me.' He had not meant to strike this note, but suddenly it was unbearable, the enclosed scene and her proximity. The straight silk dress moved upon her body as if she were naked beneath. She was very close and it was an agony not to touch her.

'I'm sorry,' she said in a suddenly desolate tone, and moved out of the soft aura of the candles.

After a pause she said, 'I don't want to sell Rathblane.'

'I know you don't.'

'I like being Lady Kinnard of Rathblane.'

Christopher gripped his glass. Millie was now going to say something which he had long guessed to be in her mind although she had never explicitly uttered it. 'Yes?'

'Yes. Christopher—would we have to change things altogether? You know you could have anything that you wanted. I am that sort of girl. Or rather I could be for you.'

'But I am not that sort of man. Besides—'

'Besides?'

'I should require—shall we say moderate faithfulness.'

Millie laughed but became tense again the next moment. 'You are modest! I would be faithful to you—moderately.'

'That is what you will be with marriage, my dear. Without marriage you would be nothing.'

Millie sat down on the stool, smoothing the purple silk over her thighs and gathering it tightly with one hand behind her knees. 'Yes, you are clever. I could say that I might find someone else more accommodating. But unfortunately you know quite well that I could only tolerate an arrangement of this sort with a very old friend and a highly intelligent one at that.'

They were silent for a moment.

Christopher said with emotion, 'Millie, I want you to be Mrs Bellman. I want Mrs Bellman to be you.'

'It doesn't sound so good,' she said with a sigh. 'Well, you are my last temptation, the devil come to buy my soul.'

'Hardly your last temptation, darling Millie. But sell, please sell!'

'I'll think about it!' said Millie, jumping up. 'Or perhaps I shall shoot myself instead. Do you think I have the temperament for suicide?'

'No. You love yourself far too dearly. We are not suicidal types, my darling.'

'I'm afraid you're right. And now I'm going to turn you out because I've got another visitor coming.'

'Who?' said Christopher. He got up, trembling with irritation and jealousy.

'Barney. He's coming for his evening bowl of milk. And he's to help me sort some papers. He's so devoted and useful.'

Christopher could not understand how Millie could encourage the futile crawling homage of someone like Barnabas Drumm. For many years now Barney had had, unknown, Christopher suspected, to Kathleen, a sort of position as a lackey, or serviceable buffoon in Millie's household. How this curious relationship had started, or why it continued, Christopher did not know. He supposed that Millie was simply incapable of refusing a devotion however absurd. He was hurt by this lack of dignity in her, and he was a little affronted too on behalf of Kathleen whom he respected. This little game of Millie's, he felt, would have to stop. It had of course never occurred to him to be jealous of Barney.

Millie had gone to the door. 'Barney'll take a knock,' she said thoughtfully.

'How do you mean?'

'If I say yes.'

'If you say yes. Dearest Millie—'

'All right, all right. Come to me on Wednesday. Come before luncheon, about midday. Or no, I'll come to you. Isn't that the day when Hilda and Frances go to town? I'd like to come to Sandycove. It would feel so dangerous! I'll give you your answer then. Now please go, I'm so tired.'

FIVE

They moved out on to the dark landing. There was a stirring down below and Millie looked over. 'Why, I think that's Barney coming up. Come, boy, come, boy!' She whistled shrilly as if for a dog. 'Good boy, good boy, come, come!'

Chapter Six

WHEN Cathal had asked his question, 'When is it to be?' Pat Dumay had not known the answer. He knew the answer now. The armed rising was to begin on Easter Sunday at six o'clock in the evening.

Pat had known for some long time that it would happen, that it would come. He had long felt it as inevitable, had taken it as it were into his own body. It was as if he were fixed to a steel chain the other end of which was hidden in that imagined mystery of violence, and he could feel it almost as a physical pain, a physical pleasure, drawing him towards it. But it was one thing to know, however certainly, that it would come; it was quite another to be given a date and a definite diminishing final interim of five days. What had been imagined had entered time and now the pattern of the hours lay under its authority. The news, which Pat had received this very morning, Tuesday the eighteenth of April, had been itself like a moment of violence, a blow which spread out through his flesh like a red rosette of anguish and delight. He was afraid. But such fear was a glorious decoration. He was afraid, but he knew himself too to be a brave man. He had not enjoyed the spectacle of others suffering in a war which he could not join, and he had not liked it either when they distinguished themselves. There had been moments when his own war had seemed an unreal sham. But there had been for him no alternative to that war.

It seemed to Pat that he had been born to a vision of fighting for Ireland. His parents had had little Irish patriotism and this lack was for him a part of their utter commonplaceness. His own recognition of himself as far from commonplace came with his early sense of his Irish destiny, his sense of belonging not to himself but to some design of history. He knew himself, even as a boy, as one chosen and already under orders. His first vivid memories were of the South African war, Dublin decked out in Transvaal flags, Boer songs sung in the streets, and the crowd at the *Irish Times* office to cheer a victory over the English. He had seen the Union Jack burnt and plumed troopers charging a crowd. The shock, the experience of subjection, the knowledge of belonging to a subject race, came into him with his first consciousness, together with a cold fierce will to freedom. And when, at George the Fifth's coronation visit, the town had been decked with hostile streamers declaring 'Thou art not conquered, yet, dear land', Pat had felt himself come of age for Ireland. The enormity of the insult laid upon his people, matched with his own unshaken sense of his worth, produced in him such a charge of power and resentment that at times he felt himself almost capable of acting and succeeding alone.

His patriotism was not of the diffuse and talkative kind, and though it was certainly romantic it was with some distilled essence of romanticism, something bitter and dark and pure. He had small use for 'Cathleen ni Houlihan', nor was he interested in Patrick Pearse's archaistic visions of a virtuous manly society whose manners were somehow to be restored. He had never joined the Gaelic League, and though he had attempted to learn Irish he did not think the language important. He was himself a matter-of-fact practising Catholic, but the pattern of his religion, though it remained secure, did not enter into the chief passion of his life. He was not one of those who made their Catholicism into nationalism. He was unmoved by the Holy Ireland affected by his stepfather, nor was he, like his younger brother, an ardent theorist. His Ireland was nameless, a pure Ireland of the mind, to be relentlessly served by a naked sense of justice and a naked self-assertion. There were in his drama only these two characters, Ireland and himself.

When the Irish Volunteers were founded in nineteen thirteen Pat joined them at once. He was in fact at the time on the point of attaching himself to James Connolly's Irish Citizen Army.

He had been much affected by the Labour troubles and much impressed by the great strike earlier that year. The courage and discipline of the unions stirred him deeply. Here again he had seen uniformed men attacking a crowd and had digested a violence of anger which nearly choked him. He had taken young Cathal to hear Jim Larkin speak, and had received certain new complexities into his concept of justice. So there were two kinds of masters to be reckoned with; and he listened, and his young brother listened even more avidly, to the words of those who said that the fight for freedom was a single fight and that the capitalist tyrant and the English tyrant must be driven out in the self-same battle.

However, when it came to it he joined the Volunteers. Without calling himself a Socialist, for he would never have called himself anything, he had no doubt at all that the capitalist system was irrational, tyrannical and wicked. The sense of being a subject, a serf, which his sensitive awareness of his nationality had brought home to his pride at such an early age made him ready to identify himself with the Dublin workers. But whereas he envisaged the liberation of Ireland as something singularly simple and pure, he could not picture the liberation of the working class without becoming entangled in ambiguous speculations and theories. He was not convinced that the two fights could be fought at once and he was sure that the affair of Ireland came first.

He joined the Volunteers also out of a sense that here was his place. He despised the genteel snobbery of many of the Volunteer supporters and their 'employer's Ireland'; but he felt that the hour of bloodshed would sufficiently separate the sheep from the goats. The men who were prepared to shoot and kill would be men of the right kind, and when the day came they and the Citizen Army would form one brotherhood. Meanwhile there was of course much less nonsense about the Citizen Army, whose discipline and fanaticism Pat observed with respect; and when he learnt that Connolly had lately interviewed each Citizen Army man individually and asked him if he would be willing to fight if the Army had to act without the Volunteers, and that each man had said yes, Pat felt something very like envy. But for just this reason, that the Volunteers represented something less compact and clear-headed, Pat had decided that his task lay with them. He conceived that the Volunteers needed backbone: he proposed himself as a stiffening agent; and he was influenced too by the idea that, in the Volunteer organization where there were fewer enthusiasts, he would receive a more rapid promotion.

Soon after joining the Volunteers, however, he discovered two things, first that the desired backbone was already present in the guise of an extensive secret group of the Irish Republican Brotherhood, and secondly, that he was not destined to shoot rapidly to the top of the military hierarchy. He was, he was never quite sure why, a little looked askance at. He overheard himself referred to as 'Hotspur' and 'that mad boy'. He felt the unfairness of this, as he knew that in matters of action he was cold, all cold with a chilly clarity which even surprised him. But he hid his disappointment as he hid everything else. After the beginning of the war, when the Volunteers had divided in two and the traitors had shuffled away into the British Army, Pat rose to the rank of captain. He still felt himself misjudged by those above and he did not seek their friendship. Equally he did not encourage the personal loyalty of his men, though when it sometimes seemed to him that they idolized him he was not displeased. He lived privately, going to his work each day at the solicitor's office, but conceiving of himself entirely as a soldier.

There was another reason why Pat had not joined the Citizen Army. He could not have served under James Connolly. He admired and respect Connolly, and there had been a time when, holding Cathal by the hand, he had followed often in the procession while the great man marched dourly, followed by a supporter with an orange box, to some chosen street corner. Connolly would mount his box and the two boys would listen spellbound, though Pat was always the first one to want to go. But Connolly was both too human and too theoretical to command the devotion which Pat wanted to offer; and given the structure and temper of the Citizen Army it would have been impossible to be in it without feeling an intense emotional loyalty to its leader. Pat was a man of savage independence and yet it often seemed to him that he would have brooked a limitless discipline from a perfect master. He felt himself as a person surrounded on the whole by second-rate men and dangerous to his surroundings. He would gladly have given up his dangerous will to one who should have been worthy to use him as an instrument. For someone truly great and ruthless he would have embraced both slavery and suffering. But there was no such person. It had once seemed to him that he might so have served Roger Casement. But he had only met Casement twice and Casement was now in Berlin. There were men in Dublin, such as Thomas MacDonagh and Joseph Plunkett, whom he could respect. But the only one who really moved him was Patrick Pearse.

Pearse troubled Pat, attracted, annoyed and disturbed him. He had first met Pearse in connection with the Wolfe Tone Memorial Committee, and he had heard him speak at the funeral of O'Donovan Rossa. He recognized there the power of a pure spirit, the sheer selfless strength which was in the end the only thing that Pat bowed to. Hundreds of things about Pearse irritated him. The man was given to all kinds of infantile nonsense. He romanticized Ireland's heroic past, which he peopled not only with Red Branch Knights, but also with ghosts and fairies and leprechauns in which he himself seemed half to believe. He was a blatant admirer of Napoleon, an alleged lock of whose hair he fatuously displayed to his friends. He also romanticized war in a way which Pat found alien and undignified, babbling about 'the red wine of the battlefields warming the heart of the earth' and other rubbish of this sort.

But nevertheless he was something like a great man and Pat was emotionally troubled by him in a way he could not entirely understand and would often have been glad to be rid of.

Admirable too was Pearse's chastity, his abstemiousness and his solitariness. He never smoked or drank or went to parties; and Pat approved of the absence from his life of women and all that they represented. In a way it made a barrier between them that Pat apprehended in Pearse a man in some ways rather like himself. He sensed in him, too, a sort of generalized tenderness, a sort of sweetness, something which Pat had long ago recognized in his own bosom as an enemy and attempted to destroy. Pearse was not the iron man who could have made of Pat a slavish tool. But Pat was prepared to accept him as his remote leader, and although Pearse was not officially the head of the Volunteers Pat regarded him as his chief. More near at hand he could perhaps not have brooked him. Pat detested his work in the solicitor's office and it had once been suggested by some friends that he might apply for a post as a teacher at St Enda's, the school of which Pearse was headmaster. Pat liked boys and he admired what he knew of St Enda's, but he could not have had, at such close quarters, Pearse in authority over him. Pat was glad too that circumstances had not taken his brother Cathal to St Enda's. He would not have wished Pearse to be Cathal's teacher.

Pat had little use for women. He connected them with the part of himself which disgusted him. He found them somehow muddled and unclean, representative of the frailty and incompleteness of human life. He despised the stupidity and frivolity which characterized their talk, and he was positively nervous of being touched by one. He did not, in fact, like being touched by anybody. The human touch reminded him of a fact which he preferred to forget, that he was incarnate. The desires, the disturbances, consequent upon being a sexual being he either suffered with a bitter consciousness or else disposed of by his own means, despising himself for this servitude.

In a spirit of pure enquiry, or perhaps to kill within himself a troublesome demon of curiosity, he had made his explorations in the world, both lurid and pathetic, of the Dublin prostitutes. He had discovered there exactly what he sought and took the filth of the sport into which he was initiated as a symbol of what he had in his more respectable surroundings already divined. He avoided married people.

His experience with the prostitutes had been in some ways his most momentous experience so far. It was something to which he had had to bring himself with violence. What seemed the greater part of him had felt such extreme nausea at the mere proximity of these grotesque animals: to force himself to seek their company and actually to embrace their atrocious bodies had been both a supreme degradation and a triumph of pure will. These two conceptions remained for Pat very close together. There was a satisfaction and a certainty in forcing himself to go down to the very bottom, to feel as it were the absolute floor of the world and know there was nothing under it.

Of the regions above him he did not very well know how to think. The pure perfection which he somehow knew about and from which he derived his steel-hard absolutes, his sense of justice, his love of Ireland, remained itself veiled and beyond experience. He did not call it God, nor did he connect it with the simplicities of his Catholic practice. He did not, as it were, even trouble to doubt his religion, but took from it quietly only those disciplines which suited his temperament. What served Pat, perhaps exclusively, as spiritual experience was the ripping apart of his will from the rest of his being. When he had been a boy he had pictured himself as a monk in one of the more ferociously austere religious orders, envisaging this as a supreme triumph of the will: the will riding alone, naked, over the trembling mediocre human desires. Pat had long ceased to dream of the cloister and he did not any more visit the dark doorways off the Dublin quays, but he found in a systematic thwarting of the flesh a partial remedy for the self-loathing which came over him so often. On manœuvres with the Volunteers in the mountains he would set himself almost impossible physical endurance tests. He avoided all regularity in his eating and sleeping, and would, in the midst of his most ordinary working days, harden himself with hunger and fatigue. He would have welcomed a military discipline more ruthless than anything he had yet encountered: he would gladly have accepted, and also inflicted, corporal punishment. It would have pleased him to have his flesh beside him, like a beaten subject animal, entirely cowed by his will.

Yet physical suffering was merely the symbol of what he wanted. If he could have believed himself a poet, a creator of any kind, capable of lifting out of the muck and mess of life some self-contained perfect object, this would have seemed to him a goal worthy of his powers. But he knew, bitterly, that this salvation was not given to him. He could put no name to what he wanted: it was certainly not love. There was in his life only one piece or fragment or strand of ordinary human love, one place where he needed and was needed, and he regarded this, and his inability to erase it, with the utmost dismay. His aim was something very much more like freedom. He despised the ordinary imperfect mechanics of the human personality, wherein the command of the pure Mentor was never obeyed until the impure mass of tissue, the gross living Self, was ready to obey it with ease. The Mentor's command would be only half listened to, half heard, and the gross Self might then slowly, lazily, begin to adjust. This could be suffering, but mild, confused, scarcely conscious, dim. There would be no direct relation between the Mentor and the Self until the moment of easy obedience was reached, and the two could be related emotionally, indulgently, in the making intelligible of an act of coercion now almost completed. This method of operation enabled the gross Self to remain fat and healthy however often it might be forced to change direction. Whereas, so it seemed to Pat, in perfect life the command would be obeyed immediately, and the Mentor would not be a consoling though reproachful friend, but would be more like an executioner, bringing about a real loss of tissue in the Self and causing extreme pain.

This was the freedom Pat desired for himself in the purest inner recesses of his intent. But in his more ordinary being this desire was almost entirely fused with his resolve to free Ireland and his sense of having been born as a liberator. The Ireland which he loved was not personified or described, it was the refined purified counterpart of his own Irishness, the necessary magnetic pole of his own resentment of the bondage which he saw about him and most of all within him. For this he would fight, and the fight could only be a bloody one. He agreed with those who said that, after all that had passed, Ireland's freedom must be bought with blood. So it was that for Pat the idea of the rising in arms, now suddenly imminent, had come to be the target of his whole existence.

*　　*　　*　　*

At this moment, on Tuesday, April the eighteenth, Pat was down in the cellar of Millie Kinnard's house in Upper Mount Street. The cellar, which was lit now by two candles, was big, low ceilinged, and vaulted like a crypt. Thick blankets of cobwebs, stirred by the warm air rising from the two flames, undulated rhythmically overhead like vegetation in a stream, and cobwebby streaks shivered a little upon the dull white walls. There was a cool, rather pleasant, musty earthy smell, as of a comfortable well-cared for tomb. In a row of domed side chapels at the far end the round bottoms of bottles glinted greenly under long draperies of dust. In the centre, ranged neatly in piles and covering almost the whole floor, was a large collection of miscellaneous weapons.

Pat had been very uneasy, and was still uneasy, about trusting Millie with this secret. He did not greatly like Millie, and although he knew that she was brave, he thought her incurably frivolous. He saw her as merely playing at politics, enjoying the excitement and the secrecy and the spice of danger. She had observed an impeccable discretion about the contents of her cellar and had also been conveniently discreet about her patriotism, so that hardly anyone knew her for a sympathizer. But Pat did not like having this frail link in the chain, and there had been much speculation and misgivings about Millie's loyalty. However, it had been necessary, on an initial occasion two years ago, very rapidly to find a hiding place for a quantity of arms, and Pat had made the quick decision, for which he still felt entirely responsible, to trust her.

The occasion of his originally trusting Millie had also been the occasion of his first bit of active service with the Volunteers, when Erskine Childers had landed a load of rifles at Howth. That was a summer Sunday of two years before when, in a contingent of eight hundred unarmed and unsuspecting Volunteers, Pat had marched down to Howth harbour. As they came on to the quay and saw the yacht waiting there was a sudden thrilling suspicion, and then they were told to advance at the double. They unloaded the yacht in ten minutes, taking possession of more than nine hundred German Mausers. As they passed the guns from hand to hand, so happy was each man to hold a real weapon at last that he kept the first gun he touched and passed on the second. Marching back with his rifle on his shoulder, Pat could have wept with emotion, and several of his comrades actually did. Now they were armed men. Nor did they have to wait long before confronting their enemy. A company of the King's Own Scottish Borderers awaited them at Clontarf. Happily perhaps, the newly acquired Mausers were not loaded. Cunning prevailed over force, and while the leaders on both sides were parleying, the Volunteers melted away into the gardens at the side of the road. The British soldiers marched back to Dublin and later that day fired upon a hostile crowd. Three people were killed, and Pat's next public appearance with his rifle was when he carried it reversed in the slow march at the funeral.

But these seemed old childish days now. Then they had been clumsy recruits. Now they were hard well-trained troops, real soldiers as good as their enemy and better. They had felt their power. This year on St Patrick's day they had taken the city over. They had marched straight from mass, two thousand strong, to College Green to be inspected by MacNeill. Traffic came to a standstill, police were swept aside, as they marched, disciplined and armed, to the sound of their pipe bands. Dublin stood and watched them like a breathless enchanted girl. Pat felt they could have taken Dublin that day.

Not that he had any illusions about either the difficulty or the sheer ugliness of the kind of struggle he was engaged in. He felt a detached envy of the simple open public war which he could not join. Although in a curious way he was not really a man of action, he knew himself to be brave, and if he had any identity now he had the identity of a soldier. He would have liked a cleaner, straighter fight, 'a steed, a rushing steed, on the Curragh of Kildare, a hundred yards and English guards . . . .' The sort of song that Cathal sang. As it was, his choice and his justification would be lonely and secret, and the killing he would do would look like murder. But that was how it had to be.

He had no illusions about the difficulties. Bernard Shaw had justly likened their struggle to an encounter between a pram and a Pickford's van. Nor was Pat at all reassured by the military strategy of his superior officers. There had been a long controversy about uniforms. Pat had been opposed to a uniformed force. He envisaged nebulous mobile irregular columns which could strike and disappear. He had studied the methods of the Boers who, with a much larger army, had preferred guerrilla tactics. In the face of heavy artillery, mobility seemed an obvious essential. But the military mind in the Volunteers, and even in the I.C..A, seemed old-fashioned in cast. There was much talk of *ésprit de corps*, and other even wilder talk of status under International Law. It was imagined that the green puttees, the slouch hats and the Sam Brownes would bestow on their wearers the status of belligerents, and entitle them to the privileges of the International Code in battle and as prisoners. Whereas Pat knew perfectly well that if they failed they would be treated as murderers and traitors.

Although the troops were tough and the discipline good, the training was not always very rational. There had been some excellent courses in street fighting, but there were still too many textbook exercises out of old British Army drill manuals. The chief difficulty always, of course, was arms. Here again many illusions were cherished. There were those who spoke of the imminent arrival of fifty thousand German troops with Roger Casement at their head. Pat neither believed in these men nor wanted them on Irish soil. He disliked the Germans as much as he disliked the English, and echoed Casement's own bitter cry: the Germans want cheap Irish blood. German arms, German technicians even, that was another thing. Give the Irish the weapons and they could do the job themselves. But though there were frequent rumours of German arms ships that were to slip through the blockade, nothing came of it and Pat dismissed this too as a myth.

On the other hand, he did not hold with Connolly that they should 'start first and get the rifles afterwards'. It was a matter of scraping together a minimum armament. Every week brought in, from various sources, fresh rifles. But what was chiefly needed was machine guns, machine guns, machine guns. James Connolly had hopefully set his engineers to devise a simplified Lewis gun, which was then to be mass-produced in the basements of Liberty Hall, but the men had been simply unable to do it. There had also been some experiments with bombs, but these instruments turned out to be far more dangerous to their inventors than to the British. Pat cursed them all for incompetent oafs. He felt that if he had been an engineer he could have solved the problems involved by sheer will-power.

In the flickering light of the two candles Pat surveyed his arsenal. It was extremely miscellaneous. Besides the Howth Mausers, there were old big-game guns, German sporting rifles, old Italian weapons, British rifles stolen from soldiers on leave, or bought from their drunken owners outside pubs for the price of a drink. There were a good many bayonets, mainly slim Italian ones, but these would not always fit the guns for which they were intended. There were also a number of old Fenian pikes, a weapon much favoured by Eamon de Valera, a young man of whom Pat was emulous. Ammunition was plentiful, not all of it very straightforward. This was a subject which caused Pat a good deal of doubt and anxiety. There were a lot of sporting cartridges with heavy slugs and leaden blunt-nosed big-game bullets. These would make terrible wounds, and Pat felt almost persuaded that it would be improper to use them. Yet bayonets and shells could make terrible wounds too, and no one thought that they were unsporting. He recalled his mother's view that warfare was all right when it was bows and arrows. Then he bitterly concluded that bows and arrows were just about what they had.

But the shortage of weapons and even the fallibility of the men were not the last difficulties. Pat knew of another and yet more demoralizing problem which concerned the leadership. The apparent structure of the Volunteers was not its real structure. The actual power in the movement, together with the plans for the rising and for co-operation with the Irish Citizen Army, lay with a group of militants, mainly men of the Republican Brotherhood, who had kept these plans secret from the more moderate nominal leaders such as Eoin MacNeill and Bulmer Hobson. The soldiers would obey their militants, at least they would in Dublin. But the divided leadership was a possible source of confusion; and Pat had been dismayed to hear of a speech made by Hobson at the weekend in which he had said that the duty of the Volunteers was 'to influence the Peace Conference' and that no one should 'take the responsibility for shedding blood'. This suggested both that Hobson had heard a certain rumour, and that he might be prepared to act vigorously upon his own beliefs. There was no doubt that the situation was tricky. If Pat had had his way he would have ordered Hobson, MacNeill and several other persons to be taken into immediate custody. It was not safe, at this stage, to let their voices be heard at all.

Pat had now completed his survey and checked his list. He let the strange blue daylight in through the heavy cellar door and then returned to blow out the candles. He locked the door behind him. He hoped that he would not meet Millie on the way out. She was often hanging about to accost him after his visits to the cellar, hiding in doorways or leaning over bannisters. As a precaution Pat had acquired copies of the keys of the Upper Mount Street house and of Rathblane, where various other items were in store. He had not mentioned this fact to Millie. He did not like women playing at soldiers, and Millie must be regarded as dispensable. He mistrusted her curiosity and abhorred her almost sexual excitement about the possibility of bloodshed. He saw her as depraved and frivolous, a mixture of prostitute and adolescent boy.

As Pat reached the dark hallway there was the tap of a shoe and a pale flurry as Millie appeared from the direction of the garden where she had evidently been waiting. He saw her plump eager face thrust forward in the half light, her big rather damp eyes glistening and bulging with interest.

'Oh, Pat—any news?'

'News? No. I've just been looking things over as usual.'

Millie swept round him and the stiffish satin of her skirt ran rat-like over his foot. She leaned her back against the hall door, her hands spread out, breathing hard, barring his way. 'There *must* be some news.'

'I don't know what you mean. There's nothing particular.'

' "Thou wilt not utter what thou dost not know, and thus far will I trust thee, gentle Millie." Is that it?'

'I must be getting along.'

'I have a very *special* reason for wanting to know. Things can't go on like this, can they? Something is going to happen, isn't it? Something is going to happen soon?'

'Nothing whatever is going to happen.'

Millie gave a long sigh and her arms dropped to her sides. 'Well, it makes an easy war.'

Pat ignored this. Lowering his voice he said, 'You shouldn't talk so. Now please let me out.'

There was a sudden sound from behind the half-open door of one of the front rooms. The room was in semi-darkness as the huge red velvet curtains had been released from the cords and covered half the window. In the centre a little yellow light entered through the thickly worked lace. It was raining outside.

Millie gave a startled hiss, and then darted to the door of the room, throwing it wide open. Pat followed her. In the soupy twilight he saw a rotund figure stretching and uncurling in a big leather armchair. It was his stepfather Barnabas Drumm.

Millie was transfigured. She bounded furiously forward and cracked the flat of her hand down upon the table. 'What are you doing in here, you beast? Why are you spying on us? What do you mean by it? Get up!'

Barnabas got to his feet, gaping miserably at Millie and over her shoulder at Pat. He was hunched up, shrinking into himself like a disturbed spider. 'Sure I just fell asleep. I wasn't spying, Millie, word of honour. I meant no harm. I don't know why, I just fell asleep.'

'I know you creep about and listen. I know your mean ways. Well, take your drunken sleep somewhere else. Go on, get away with you!' Her long skirt swirled as she aimed a kick at him.

Barney edged round the chair and then bolted past them as

if fearing another kick. He fled, not out of the house but toward the back quarters as if to take refuge dog-like in the kitchen.

The incident disgusted Pat. He knew, but preferred not to reflect on, the fact that Barnabas trailed about after Millie and she contemptuously tolerated him. But what angered him now was that Millie simply did not seem to have realized that the person she was thus humiliating was Pat's stepfather.

Millie herself seemed to become aware of this a second later. She put her hands to her face and said, 'I'm sorry—'

'Well, goodbye.' Pat quickly opened the front door and let himself out into the rain. He turned up his coat collar. She is trash, he thought as he strode away, she is trash, she is trash.

Chapter Seven

'AT this period of my life I imperceptibly became aware that I was becoming steadily estranged from my sister Hilda. Perhaps such slow partings, who knows, are our inevitable rehearsals for the final severance. Hilda and I had been united, at an obscure but effectively deep level during childhood by our joint opposition to our parents. But, as time and circumstance shook our characters into position, it became clear that we abhorred the parental way of life for different reasons: Hilda, because it was brittle, noisy, shrewdly inexpensive, and not socially grand; I, because it was utterly unspiritual.

'There was also, and I felt this increasingly whenever Hilda visited Ireland, the fact that she did not understand either of the women in my life or appreciate the subtle threads of my relationship with them. She was simply not "in the picture"! The dumb devotion of Kathleen, the tender possessive raillery of Millie: Hilda could make little of all this. Indeed, self-absorbed as always, she *saw* very little; but what her intuition silently told her was that there were women, and women whom she variously deemed unworthy, who were rivals for the monopoly of her adored brother.'

Barnabas Drumm had penned these words that very afternoon as he sat at his 'work' in the National Library, and they now ran through and through his head, all pure and glittering like a clear brook. Or perhaps the words were the stones in the brook, speckled and smooth, which through a trembling translucent medium he saw steadfastly arrayed before him. His words, it seemed to him, rang out with a quiet authority; and when he had uttered a convincing passage it remained with him and eased his spirit for the rest of the day. For several years now Barney had been secretly working on his Memoir.

SEVEN

The tattered notebooks about the Irish saints had been touched more intermittently and lately not touched at all. Barney had become completely absorbed in the more interesting task of self-analysis.

Barney had commenced this task when, after a Lenten retreat, he had decided that he must make a serious effort to find out 'what had gone wrong'. He must, in the most relentless way, examine himself. He had for too long assumed that he could lay it all at *her* door, could count himself a man ruined by a single catastrophe, a catastrophe which passed in a matter of weeks. But a man's life is not so easily destroyed; and as he realized this later he wished that he had known it *then*. He could have picked himself up. So if he was now the wreck that he was it could not simply be *her* fault. There must have been ancient reasons why he had made of himself the young man that he had, so lately it seemed to him, been, and other reasons, or perhaps the same ones, why he had gone on, with all the appearance of a ruthless intention, driving himself into a wilderness of the spirit. He was very unhappy and he felt that he deserved not to be. He did not especially hope that finding out what had gone wrong would help to put it right. He started his project in a mood of pure self-castigation. Sometimes he felt very old and told himself that the least he could do before he died was to face, clear-eyed and squarely, the wreck of his life. Later he found that the task he had undertaken was curiously consoling.

He had been a talented boy for whom much was hoped. He gained a top classical scholarship at Cambridge and mastered Hebrew while still at the University. He was a crack shot and a noted rowing man. He had loving parents, an adoring sister, and plenty of friends. He had loving parents, and yet somehow, from the earliest times he could remember, Barney had resented his parents. He could not think what, in a small child, that resentment could have been. Later on it took form as a thorough impatience with the noisy frolicsome frivolity of the parental world. His fashionable-on-a-shoestring mother laughed, or rather screamed, too much, and his father's ingenious set-piece parties and elaborate much screamed-over practical jokes seemed to him unbearably vulgar. He was hurt by their whole mode of being, although when he reflected upon their misdemeanours they did not really seem very grave. He decided to go to Ireland.

Barney's mother, Grace Drumm, née Richardson, was Anglo-Irish, a connection of the Kinnard family, and Barney and his sister had had their share of Irish holidays, during which Hilda had had her eyes dazzled by the splendours of Rathblane. Other things impressed Barney. Ireland was for him a dark place, slow, dignified and mystical: everything that was unlike the gay little, bright little flat in South Kensington. He lost his heart; and it was not long before, the focus shifting a little, he perceived that the mystic beauty of Ireland resided in the Catholic Church.

This perception developed into a great spiritual crisis during which it became clear to him that he had an extreme destiny. He must forswear the world and aim at perfect sanctity: anything less would be, for him, a meaningless, perhaps a disastrous, goal. He took himself away alone to the saint-haunted solitude of Clonmacnoise and stood beside the round tower in the holiest place in Ireland. Here he felt himself, in what later seemed to be a mystical experience, confronted, captured, claimed. What claimed him then was something very old and pure, a Christianity still simple and innocent of blood, whose humble and unpretentious saints lived in little low-roofed cells. The sacred river Shannon, flooding yellow-reeded between the small barrow-like hills, turned under his gaze from pewter-grey to blue and Barney decided that he must become a priest.

To the despair of the family he entered Maynooth and soon donned the soutane. He lived in a perpetual exaltation, giving himself up to austerities and enthusiasms which earned him many a shrewd rebuke from his spiritual advisers. He developed a passionate relationship to the Eucharist. He constantly pictured himself, as it was soon to be, holding the very Body of Christ in his hand and feeding a starving kneeling flock which stretched away to the confines of the earth. At nights he dreamed of the Chalice from which the blood of his Master streamed to take away the sins of the world. He held the cup in his hands, turning with an unspeakable happiness to say, *Ite, missa est.* But he was never ordained. He quite suddenly fell in love with Millie.

Millie in fact, as it seemed later, simply coerced him into love. She was recently widowed and in a condition of intoxication with her new freedom. She had been but vaguely aware of him, had largely ignored him, at their few meetings since her marriage, and Barney had been equally unobservant of her. But when Millie saw him in his soutane she suddenly, recklessly, coveted him. She never deceived him, at least not verbally. She simply wanted this black-robed priestling as her slave, a pet to fondle and caress. She wanted to arouse a blasphemous passion in this pale long-skirted half man. She told him constantly that she was not in love with him. She just needed him to be in love with her. Barney found this absolutely pure-hearted wickedness quite irresistible.

He had had some vague emotional involvements with girls at Cambridge and had counted these as his wild oats. The experience with Millie was entirely different. He was shattered, scattered; and he could not help in fact believing that she loved him. She certainly behaved as if she did. His body, which had seemed a pure vessel, a spiritual temple, scoured, empty and awaiting the final installation of a ghostly visitor, now hotly and needfully enclosed him, a tugging animal of unquiet flesh. It was as if his veins had been emptied and given new blood. He became horribly incarnate; and when the desperately beautiful, desperately desirable Millie looked meltingly into his eyes and inclined her warm lips slowly upon his he felt that God was become man indeed. Of course, Millie restricted her

favours to the most superficial caresses, thereby reducing him
to a state near to madness. The end came with a party at
Maynooth where Barney was discovered with Millie sitting on
his knee. He left the College shortly afterwards.

In what order things happened then was never very clear to
Barney in his memory: whether he repented and gave up
Millie, or whether Millie dropped him and he repented. He
often felt able to give himself the benefit of the doubt, since
the shock of his dismissal brought back to him an appalling
sense of what he had lost. While falling in love he had not
explicitly told himself that this meant the end of his vocation.
He suffered continual sharp pangs of guilt about what he was
doing, but he still felt that he was acting somehow within the
framework of his former intention. When that whole numinous world vanished from him and he found himself outside,
with nothing to help him except the daily bread of the Church
and the penny plain machinery of repentance, he felt himself
so broken that he could hardly envisage himself any more as a
man. Here Millie, even if she had not at once removed herself,
could have been no use to him. In fact, when Millie saw Barney
outside Maynooth, stripped of his soutane, a miserable confused young man running round Dublin looking for a job, her
interest in him ceased abruptly; and after a meeting at which
she treated the whole matter as a joke and then practically
accused him of having invented it all, she ceased seeing him
altogether. Perhaps she felt ashamed. If so, the only sign of it
was that she kept this interlude a close secret and never spoke
of it to anyone. Barney's superiors at Maynooth were discreet,
and Barney himself had no motives for being talkative, so the
part which Millie had played in his life remained almost
entirely unknown. It was thought that 'some woman' had been
involved in his decision not to be ordained, but beyond this
even rumour did not go.

Kathleen, however, knew. By a curious accident, which
Barney later felt to have been decisive in his life, Kathleen,

admitted unexpectedly to the house in Upper Mount Street, found Millie and Barney in an embrace. Barney was never sure whether, if that had not happened, he would have chosen to confide in Kathleen; very possibly not. In any case the shock, the sudden appearance of Kathleen as a spectator, and her continued existence as one of the few people 'in the know' gave her, for him, a privileged position. Through her surprised censorious eyes he saw himself, a robed ordinand passionately embracing a pretty widow of dubious reputation. He resented her knowledge, but it also brought her near to him. In his dereliction, with both Millie and the priesthood lost to him, he had to turn to someone and he turned to Kathleen.

But why did he despair so quickly? he often asked himself. Why did he not accept the full force of the blow, regard himself as someone who, for years perhaps, must remain a broken, humbled man? He ought to have left Dublin and joined himself in a menial capacity to some remote religious house. There were places for such as he. For the disaster had not broken his faith. It had not broken it, but it must, he later felt, have temporarily cracked it, or he would not so quickly have attempted to rearrange the whole pattern of his wishes. He ought to have kept his attention fixed upon the priesthood, regarding that great treasure, which had been so nearly within his grasp, as having simply receded far away, perhaps impossibly far away, but still presenting itself as the only good. He ought to have repented relentlessly, ferociously, and been prepared to lie upon the ground. He ought, strip by strip, to have divested himself of his former mind, of everything that had made him frail and false. Instead of which, without hope, turning his back entirely upon all that had happened, he sought an immediate consolation.

Kathleen, herself lately left a widow, was several years his senior, and he turned to her at first as to a mother or an elder sister. He told her everything, everything not only about Millie but about his whole life, his childhood, his parents, everything. He came to her again and again; and Kathleen listened to him with a plain gentleness and wisdom which made her seem to him a supremely good woman, the first good woman that he had ever met. She uttered no reproaches, but she made no allowances and he was grateful for her willingness to judge him. Then there began to be a kind of meaning in his escape from the bad woman to the good woman. With an easeful sweetness which was quite unlike his recent frenzy he started to love her. And it seemed that she loved him too, loved him for his history and for his need of her. She represented suddenly and as it were all complete the possibility of the good life which he had previously sought in a mistaken quarter. He now saw himself as a Catholic husband, a Catholic father, the upholder of a pure, robust, cheerful Catholic home, his house renowned as a refuge for the guilty and the unfortunate. He saw a way here which led straight back to innocence. He proposed to Kathleen and she accepted him.

What went wrong? It seemed to him that he was settling down. He found himself a small job in the Civil Service and started work upon his history of the early Irish Church. He published an article, which was lengthily though adversely criticized in *The Sword of the Spirit*, entitled 'Some Druidic Origins of the Christian Mysteries'. He became interested in the struggle between the Irish and the Roman Church which preceded the Council of Whitby. He began to perceive important affinities between the Irish Church and the Eastern Church. Ireland and the East, he proposed to demonstrate, had spoken the pure tongue of the Gospels, preserving a mystical freedom and a spirit of love which were increasingly lost to the over-organized and over-theorized Roman machine. He published a tract called *From Athos to Athlone* and began to correspond with some very sophisticated French Jesuits who chaffed him about the dangers of heresy. He made a detailed study of the origins of monasticism in Ireland and formed a strong attachment to Saint Brigid, generous, gentle, miraculous saint, and went on devout pilgrimages upon her tracks. He projected a book entitled *The Significance of Brigid* as the first volume of his *œuvre*. It seemed like the good life. Yet during all this time he had not consummated his marriage with Kathleen.

Perhaps it was that after all there was really no short way back to innocence. As soon as he had tied himself to Kathleen, Barney began to feel subdued resentment which had to do both with the priesthood and with Millie. At a conscious reflective level he made out the irrevocable and tedious nature of the marriage bond which linked him to a material, cheated him of a spiritual, destiny; while in the deeper thoughts of his flesh he hopelessly missed Millie and knew it would be sacrilege without zeal to accept a second best. He had missed two absolutes and was left with a compromise. Symbol of two losses, he retained his virginity.

Of course, Kathleen never reproached him, never indeed mentioned his remarkable failure. But of course, too, after a while she began to withdraw. It seemed to him that she had withdrawn slowly, step by step, her eyes fixed upon him, waiting for a sign or gesture which he simply could not make. If he could only, as in the old days, have sought her forgiveness. But he could not. He needed now to defend himself against her, to make fortifications. He began to feel a little afraid of her. He kept formulating and then of course rejecting the theory that she had married him to spite Millie. He formulated more confidently the theory that what she had loved in him was not the whole muddled human person but simply his fallen state. As he put it much later in his Memoir, 'Millie loved me because I was a blasphemer, Kathleen loved me because I was a penitent'.

He regretted what he had lost, he wished that he had waited. With a curious pain, which was like remorse in reverse, he judged that he had been far too hard on himself at the time of the original fault with Millie. He had exaggerated his guilt. He had been guilty of nothing but inopportunely falling in love. It now began to seem to him that he had done something far worse in marrying Kathleen. He became moody, gave up his job in the excise department, and tried to concentrate on his work on the Irish Church. He spent a great deal of time away from home, ostensibly at the Library, but in fact more and more frequently sitting in bars by himself or with chance acquaintances. Then one day by accident he met Millie in Sackville Street.

She immediately began to laugh. She laughed and laughed while Barney scowled at her sickly. Then she took his arm and said he must come to her house forthwith for a glass of sherry. He came there and immediately fell at her feet. Extreme love is like certain kinds of conditioning in animals. It exists at a level where there is no such thing as time. Barney was simply back where he was. A few kind words, a touch, from Millie re-established and confirmed his servitude. He did not accuse her of the past but told her in a trembling voice that *now*, *now* she must never send him away again. Moved herself, she promised that she would never send him away, that he could always come to her. Carried away, she even expressed a sort of love for him. Perhaps, being older, she was now more appreciative of an absolute devotion. And when Barney began, slightly sobered, to explain that of course he didn't exactly mean that he was going to leave Kathleen, she began to laugh again, and laughed and shook him until he laughed too. Barney was very happy on that day.

Later times were less happy. He took to frequenting the house at Upper Mount Street. He said nothing to Kathleen about having met Millie and nothing about these visits. He noticed too that Millie, following the instincts of a much-courted woman, quite automatically made a secret of his status with her. When others were present he was merely 'a relation'; and indeed most of Millie's grander friends were in any case incapable of focusing their attention upon so drab a figure. Barney, for his part, watched Millie closely, more closely than she realized, coming with relief to the conclusion that she had no lover. He began to feel a little security in his new life. Christopher Bellman, who knew vaguely of his existence as Millie's friend, was a man of the world and no gossip. Barney had been shaken, surprised, and rather especially pained at twice meeting Pat Dumay at the house. But he knew of Pat's morbid reticence. Nothing would reach Kathleen from that quarter.

Kathleen did not know; but Barney's secret life with Millie took nourishment, took blood, from his existence at home, and Kathleen certainly felt this extra deprivation, this increased rate of emaciation of their common world. And Kathleen, as it seemed to Barney, took perhaps unconsciously her own steps to punish him. Since his re-instatement with Millie, Barney had been less than constant in his attendance at mass. He had taken no stand with himself, formulated no policy; he just found that, giving this or that explanation to his wife, he just went to church less often. He shunned confession or else went through it in a kind of dream. During this time Kathleen became noticeably more devout. She began to go to mass daily and, almost ostentatiously, to collect 'lame ducks' of all kinds. She spent a lot of time in the poorer parts of Dublin doing strenuous kinds of social work, and became an organizer of a league for helping ex-prisoners. She had never been particularly house-proud, but her attention to the house was now minimal. She was too busy helping people in distress. Her appearance also she neglected, and began to look noticeably shabby, untidy, old. She was often up half the night with her charges and invariably seemed tired. It was as if she had taken over the pastoral function which had once seemed reserved for her husband. She was the priest now.

Barney felt these excesses to be directed against himself. What charm, what beauty, she had had she was now deliberately destroying; and when he saw her trudging along Blessington Street, her shoulders hunched with tiredness and preoccupation, her old unfashionable serge dress bobbing on the pavement, her bulging shopping-bag knocking on the railings, he felt both exasperation and pity, but the pity was the more fleeting of the two. This was her way of being merciless to him. His reaction was a further withdrawal, more drink and more Millie. More of the Mountjoy bar and considerably less of St Joseph's Church. At the same time he still felt capable of judging himself; things had not yet gone too far. He still had a fairly clear head and could measure where he was. But effectively his repentances took the form of isolated orgies of regret: if only he had not married he could still have conceived of finding a way back into the priesthood. *Then* he could really have tried to be good, *then* it would have made sense for him to ask perfection of himself. Well, did it not make sense now? In an ephemeral moment of humility he went to a retreat house. On his return he started to write his Memoir. And he made jokes about the retreat to Millie.

At the same time, with a self-tormenting casuistry, he kept alive the pain of his other total loss. If only he had not been married he could have been so content to be Millie's fool. Perhaps after all he was not so unlike his father. How much he enjoyed making her laugh! He would be her ass and she should drive him in harness. It was only the nagging thought of Kathleen that spoilt this happiness for him. He started to spend a great deal more time reflecting about himself. The book on the Irish Church began to seem to him a piece of mushy devotional nonsense; or rather, the factual parts now seemed dried up and devoid of interest and the speculative parts seemed pure sentimentality. The whole thing collapsed, went soft; and Barney soon abandoned it and concentrated on the Memoir.

His failures to practise his religion, for which his wife reproached him only by her own increased piety, did not indicate any slackening of the bond which united him to his Church. On the contrary, it seemed to Barney that this bond grew ever closer and more painful. He had so much thought himself into the priesthood and he could not now undo this. He was ordained in his mind and his heart and he had no other profession. He was by vocation a failed priest. Yet it was an almost unlivable vocation. Barney would ask himself: could not even now some miracle of regeneration occur? It seemed as if, all along the way, he had exaggerated his faults, he had despaired too soon: suppose he had turned back then, or then; for what happened later was worse, whereas then it would have been possible to hope. Well, he found himself saying, yet again, was it not still possible to hope? His life was like the Sybil's leaves; there was always, for the same price, less to salvage. And he followed, as it were at a distance, the yearly cycle of the Church, the pilgrimage of Christ from birth to death. Even now He was drawing near to Calvary. He was riding upon an ass into Jerusalem to die.

'And a very great multitude spread their garments in the way: others cut down branches from the trees and strewed them in the way. And the multitudes that went before and that followed cried saying, Hosannah to the Son of David: Blessed is he that cometh in the name of the Lord; Hosannah in the highest. And when He was come into Jerusalem, all the city was moved, saying Who is this?' Who indeed? Barney felt that if he could really believe, even for a moment, in redemption by love he would be instantly, automatically redeemed. He dreamed of being punished and then restored to the flock: when even punishment would fade within that love and be transformed, becoming the spectacle itself of the suffering induced in a pure being by the existence of evil. But for all his cries of *Kyrie eleison* the faith eluded him that would have made him whole. His self-abasement provided a not wholly disagreeable emotional occupation; and not only was there no large change, there was not even the smallest, most momentary change in the pattern of life which he deplored. He was inside, indeed he was, the machine.

Tears started into Barney's eyes. He had been drinking that afternoon with some friendly *bona fides* in the Big Tree in Dorset Street. Just lately he had noticed that he was never entirely sober. Tracts of time were blotted out and he was not always sure where the line came between what he had imagined and what was real, what he had intended and what he had done. He recalled with pain the scene of that morning when Millie had abused him in front of his stepson. Unfortunately, that was no dream. He had been cuffed and sent about his business. He felt a physical pain to think that Pat had witnessed this. Barney loved his stepchildren, though feeling rather in awe of both of them. He knew they could not respect him; but it seemed so very sad that therefore his love for them must be wasted and nullified. He had made one effort to draw closer to Pat by joining up with the Volunteers in the early days, and this had gained him one moment of pure pleasure, when Pat had made the discovery that Barney was a good shot. Barney had been moved too by a vague notion that he was going to strike a blow against social injustice. He had long had fantasies of himself as a slum priest defending the poor against the rich. He now proposed to divert his attention from his own sufferings to the sufferings of humanity. But humanity proved too elusive an object and the Volunteers like everything else turned out not to be the answer.

As Barney mused painfully upon his humiliation of that morning he was walking down the hill from the tram in Kingstown, down past the People's Park, over the mysterious cleft of the railway, towards the sea. Praise be to God it wasn't raining, for it was his day for Frances. Every Tuesday Barney met Frances in the afternoon and they walked down the pier and then had tea at O'Halloran's Bun Shop. Barney looked forward to this time: it was a time of innocence. Barney had a happy relationship with Frances, his only relationship which was not now in some way soured and twisted. Frances was the only person who had always *simply* loved him. He had known her since she was a child and had got to know her well since her move to Sandycove. He was aware that, for Frances too, he had the fascinating role of a sinner. His religion also fascinated her; and for her he could somehow wear all the complicated tragic finery of his story, although of course she knew none of the details. She sensed the wreckage within and felt compassion, although there was also something of the self-conscious stooping of the pure young girl toward the fallen man. Frances knew nothing of his relations with Millie, though she had heard the rumour that 'some woman' had got him slung out of Maynooth. She was very curious about his past and often tried to draw him on to talk about it. Barney had amused himself by hinting at a liaison with a notable prostitute. Keeping it up, he gave Frances to understand that he had once been a great frequenter of Dublin's brothels. This idea, which seemed to Barney to have a sort of symbolic truth, gave a certain thrill both to him and to the girl.

Barney had known from long ago, as everybody had, that Frances was destined to marry his nephew Andrew. He used to feel pleased about this as it represented an inclusion of Frances more closely in the family. But now that the time for the marriage had drawn so very near he had other feelings. He guessed that Andrew intended to take Frances to England. There Barney could not go. He too much needed, not only to see Millie, but also almost superstitiously in the intervals of seeing her to watch her. Now the withdrawal of Frances seemed suddenly to abandon him to the devices of nightmare. Frances had been a source of light. There was also, Barney was surprised to find, an element of pure jealousy in his attitude to this marriage. He was fond of his nephew, but he simply did not want him to have Frances. This was an absurd thought, from which Barney rapidly switched to edifying pictures of dear old Uncle Barnabas, grown curiously ancient and sage-like, dandling little children upon his knee. This sometimes worked. But he was now very unhappy about Frances.

It was a windy day. The wind pursued spherical golden and black cloudlets through a yellowish sky over Kingstown and out towards the soft hazy bands of more slowly shifting sea-cloud which always lay upon the horizon like a distant range of hills. The sea would be rough. Barney could see it ahead of him now, a cold and scaly green with flecks of white. He reached the bottom of the hill and entered the gloomy patch of vegetation known as the Crocks' Garden. This consisted of paths of blackish earth which trailed about between the thick clumps of veronica bushes which clothed the slope down to the sea: a sad place which had seemed a labyrinth of mystery to him when he had been young. Below it the waves roared on to a little muddy beach of green untidy stones and foamed along a broken breakwater which had seemed to the youthful Barney like some piece of Roman antiquity. Beyond, like a strange yellow coastline, stretched the great rocky arm of the pier, on this side of which, hollow and majestic as Egyptian temples to the eyes of the child, rose two stone shelters wherein he had spent many happy hours of his holidays watching the rain falling interminably into the sea.

Barney now took the way past the shelters before climbing up on to the top of the pier where he was to meet Frances. The shelters, whose speckled stony concrete looked like living rock, had been decorated, as usual, by small posters which the Royal Irish Constabulary had not yet had time to remove. *England's Last Ditch. Pretence of the Realm Act. Fight for Catholic Ireland not for Catholic Belgium.* Barney passed by and climbed up to the top where he could pass through the thick wall to the harbour side of the pier. He looked back for a moment as a touch of sun illumined the multicoloured stucco fronts of the marine terraces, and behind them the two tall rival spires of Kingstown, Catholic and Protestant, shifting constantly in their relation to each other except when from the Martello tower at Sandycove they could be seen superimposed.

The pier itself, upon which he now set foot, had always

seemed to Barney an object ancient and numinous, like some old terraced Ziggurat, composed of immense rocks of yellow granite and scarcely raised by human labour: something 'built by the hands of giants for god-like kings of old'. Its two great arms, ending in lighthouse fortresses, enclosed a vast space of gently rolling indigo water and a miscellany of craft riding at anchor. The inner side of the pier was terraced and decorated at intervals by strange stone edifices, wind towers and obelisks and great cubes with doors, which made it seem all the more like some pagan religious monument. Beyond were the waters of Dublin Bay, now a harsh streaky blue, the outskirts of Dublin to the left, a purplish mass in the uncertain light, the dark low line of Clontarf and the rising hump of Howth. Barney noticed uneasily that it appeared to be raining on Howth. But then it was always raining on Howth.

And there was the dear girl herself down below, waving and hurrying on towards him.

'Are you all right, Barney?'

'Oh, all right, struggling along. A bit battered, you know, a bit battered. But struggling along.'

Frances always asked this question and Barney always gave this sort of answer. That anxious 'Are you all right?' of Frances was perhaps the nearest he ever got to a token of the love for which his heart craved.

Frances was wearing a mackintosh cape and motoring hood, and a tartan pleated skirt which swirled about her ankles. She took a firm grip upon the skirt as she walked, gathering several of the pleats carefully between her fingers. They set off along the pier in silence, mounting again to the upper terrace where a gleam of sunshine made the powerful stones a chilly sandy gold. They did not always talk then. The wind often made talking impossible.

'What's that, Frances?'

'I just said there's the mail boat.'

'Why, so it is.'

117

'How very clear and bright its colours are in the sun though it's still so far away. Which one is it?'

'The *Hibernia*.' From long experience Barney could tell the almost identical boats apart. He hardly knew how he did it. He added. 'She's late. There must have been a U-boat alert.'

'How awfully frightened they must be.'

'You mean the passengers—'

'No, the Germans down in the U-boats. It must be terrible.'

It had never occurred to Barney to feel sorry for the Germans down in the U-boats. But of course Frances was right, it must be terrible. His thoughts reverted to himself. With a perverse desire to cause himself pain he said to Frances, 'You'll be off on the mail boat one of these days.'

'What?'

'I said you'll be off on the mail boat one of these days.'

'Why?'

'I mean, young Andrew will take you; I mean, when you're married.'

Frances was silent.

'When will you be married?' said Barney. He had put off asking Frances this question, he did not want to know, it would be horrible to know.

'I'm not sure, Barney, Andrew hasn't actually fixed anything yet, and until—'

'Oh well, he'll fix it soon. He'll have to before he— He's a lucky boy.' Some people have all the luck, Barney thought. Why had he not grown up with a dear lovely girl just holding out her arms and waiting for him?

Frances thrust her arm through Barney's and they forged ahead together against the wind. 'Well, even then you know, I probably wouldn't leave Ireland—'

'Yes, you would. You know Andrew hates Ireland.'

She squeezed his arm in comfort or protest and they went on for a while in silence. When they got as far as one of the 'temples', a square stone hut with a pediment, surmounted by three iron cups which whirled chasing each other with desperate speed, they stopped for a moment to give their whipped glowing faces a rest from the wind, and leaned back against the great wall of the pier. The sun had gone in now and the landward clouds had turned to a bright pewter grey. The spires of Kingstown rose blackened as if dipped into some infusion of darkness, but a mysterious glow lit the terraces of houses and reflected light gleamed in the windows. Beyond, the mountains were almost black save where the sun fell very far away upon a slope of rusty green. Barney began to try to light his pipe.

'Are you still in the Volunteers, Barney?'

'I suppose so. I haven't actually resigned. But I've rather fallen out of things lately.'

Frances was silent for a while, looking towards Kingstown. The spire of the Mariners' Church emerged from its veil of darkness and shone a silvery grey.

She said suddenly, 'I can't think why it doesn't all blow up.'

'What?'

'Oh, I don't know—I mean society, everything. Why do the poor people put up with us? Why do the men go and fight in that stupid ghastly war? Why don't they all say, no, no, no?'

'I agree with you, Frances. It's extraordinary what people will put up with. But they just feel helpless. What can they do? What can any of us do?'

'People shouldn't feel helpless. Something ought to be done. I saw today by Stephen's Green—I was in town this morning —oh, it was so sad—a girl, a mother, she must have been my age, with clothes, well they weren't clothes, just jumbled bits of stuff, and four little children, all of them barefoot, and she was begging, and the little kids were sort of dressed up like little monkeys, and trying to dance, and they were crying all the time—'

'I expect they were hungry.'

'Well, it's scandalous, wicked, and a society which allows it deserves to be blown to bits.'

'But dearest Frances, you must have seen girls like that girl a hundred times. Dublin is full of them.'

'Yes, I know, and that's awful. One gets used to it. I've just been thinking more about it lately. It shouldn't be. And I can't think why they don't attack us, jump on us like wild animals, instead of just humbly holding out their hands for a penny.'

Barney agreed with her that it shouldn't be. But after all what could one do? The begging mother, the starving children, the men in the trenches, the Germans down in the U-boats. It was mad and a tragic world. Now if he had been a priest—

'Barney, do you think there'll be any trouble in Ireland?'

'You mean fighting here?'

'Yes, about Home Rule and so on.'

'No, of course not. Home Rule will come automatically after the war.'

'So there's nothing to fight about, is there?'

'Nothing at all.'

'And any way, Father was saying they have no arms. They *can't* fight.'

'No, they can't.'

'Barney, what will Home Rule do for that woman begging in the street?'

Barney thought for a moment. 'Absolutely nothing.'

'It won't really touch that level of people at all?'

'Well, they'll have the pleasure of being exploited by P. Flanagan instead of J. Smith.'

'Then the thing's not *worth* fighting for anyway.'

'Wait a minute. It's worth having one's national freedom,' said Barney. He felt a bit vague about it. 'Once Ireland's free of England it'll be easier to set the house in order.'

'I don't see why. Some people say there ought to be a rising against the whole thing, against the English and against the Irish employers too. James Connolly says that, doesn't he?'

'Yes, but it's all dreams, Frances. They couldn't do it. And it would be just a very nasty mess if they tried. Those people don't know how to run the country.'

'Do the people who let that woman beg and her children starve know how to run the country?'

'Well, I see what you mean. But law and order are important too. The workers should stick to the Trade Unions, that's how they'll better themselves.'

'But the government and the employers won't allow the Trade Unions.'

'They will, they'll have to. You're getting quite a political woman these days, Frances. We'll see you in uniform next!'

'I ought to be in uniform. But I don't know which one to wear!' She spoke bitterly, striking the palms of her hands against the damp stone behind her. The wind had spread the tartan skirt and flattened it against the wall. She added, 'Oh, I don't know what I'm talking about. How I wish I'd had some proper education. I'm so muddled. Perhaps women really can't understand politics. It can't be right to shed blood for anything. I do think this dreadful war against Germany is so wrong. All those terrible things in the trenches and the shell fire. There must be some way of stopping it. The soldiers should all just throw down their arms.'

'Come, come. You wouldn't like to see Andrew being a conchie!'

'If Andrew became a conchie I'd fall down and worship him.'

As Barney turned in some surprise to look at her she jerked from him impatiently saying, 'Let's go through and look at the rocks.'

This was something they always did. On the inside of the pier were the great terraces and the temples. On the outside, where the open sea beat against it, was a mountainside of immense jagged rocks heaped together. Periodic gaps in the upper wall allowed one to pass through to this side. Barney and Frances went through and stood looking down.

The blows and caresses of the sea had made no impression upon the shape of the rocks or even upon their colour. They remained senselessly jagged and yellow, a random pile of unalterable many-surfaced solids. Here and there a huge stone, balanced between two neighbours, would tilt to and fro at the touch of the waves. In other places the rocks seemed more closely fused as if some semi-intelligent hand had wedged them together. But mostly they lay like things tossed down, one idly resting upon another. And between them were great holes and crevasses, ugly slits and irregular gashes, within which the sea would roar or come suddenly surging upward to boil out over the indifferent granite surfaces. Barney had always felt frightened of these rocks, even when as a boy he had leapt familiarly from one to another. He feared the deep crevasses down which a man might slide into some awful sea cavern. More perhaps he feared the huge weight, the appalling hardness, the senselessness of them. They were like the great weighty stupid world which had rolled off the lap of God. They were the most meaningless things that he knew, as meaningless as death.

He looked at Frances. She seemed to feel as he did, looking down with a puckered alarmed face at the huge waves which were rushing in in quick succession to destroy themselves upon the rocks with a deafening ferocity of foam. It was impossible to speak here. A mist of spray, picked up by the wind, was carried rainily into their faces. Frances shivered and turned back through the opening. Over her shoulder as he came through Barney saw that the mail boat was just entering the harbour.

Back again on the inside of the pier he realized that it was in fact raining. The sky above was hazily grey and thick bunches of ebony cloud were coming up from behind Dublin. The waters of the harbour were black now.

'Come on,' said Frances. 'Oh, it's so *cold*!' She sounded almost tearful. Lifting her skirt well up, she set off at a smart pace along the pier. For a while, not trying to catch up, he followed her. The *Hibernia* had docked. It had turned its lights on dimly and stood out strangely vivid in the darkened scene. The people were coming off it now, hundreds of people streaming off it and streaming away in all directions into rainy Ireland.

Chapter Eight

' "*Charge it again, boys, charge it again,*
Pardonnez moi je vous en prie,
As long as you have any ink in your pen,
With never a penny of money!" '

'Don't sing that song, Cathal.'

'Why not?'

'I don't like it.'

'Why don't you like it?'

'I don't like that sort of song.'

'Why don't you like that sort of song?'

'Do you want your ears boxed?'

'You're in a nice friendly mood today, I don't think. All right, I'll sing another sort of song.

"*Sure 'twas for this Lord Edward died and Wolfe Tone sunk serene,*
Because they could not bear to leave the red above the green." '

'If you sing that song you ought to sing it seriously.'

'Sure I am singing it seriously. How does one sing a song seriously or not seriously? One just sings it. Anyway, you know I love Wolfe Tone and I wouldn't—'

'Your head is full of bad poetry. "Sunk serene" is rotten. And it's not grammar either. Dying isn't "sinking serene". Bad poetry is lies.'

'Well, it's better than no poetry at all and no one has told us about Lord Edward and Wolfe Tone in good poetry yet. I wish I'd been called after him. Wolfe Tone Dumay.'

' "*As I lay on the sod that lay over Wolfe Tone*
And thought how he perished in prison alone—." '

I did that, too,'

'Did what?'

'Lay on the sod. Last time we went out to Bodenstown. When you and the others went off to the meeting, I lay down there and thought about him. Not right on top but near by.'

'You're too young to go lying on people's graves.'

'I'm going to die young, so I'm really older. Like cats and dogs, you have to reckon my age differently.'

'You're a tiresome little brat now and you'll live to be a tiresome old fellow with a grey beard spouting bad verse.'

It was Tuesday evening and the ceremony of Pat's bath was in progress. This ritual had started long ago when the boys shared a cabin in Connemara for part of a summer and Pat had trained his young brother to heat the water in iron pots on the range and then to pour it for him into the big tin bath and to stand by with warm towels while Pat washed off the mud of the bogs and the ferocious coldness of the sea. Although he complained ceaselessly of being 'enslaved', Cathal enjoyed this ritual which had somehow continued in the less primitive surroundings of Blessington Street, a piece of religious drama surviving in a modified form perhaps because it represented for the participants some half-conscious, half-forgotten spiritual need.

So Cathal always attended Pat's bath, his role as acolyte now limited to the handing over of the towels. It was a time, traditionally, of communication between the two brothers, or at least a time when Pat made himself more than usually approachable, so that advice could be covertly asked or misdemeanours defiantly owned to. Sometimes thinking himself rather ridiculous in the role of a steamy oracle, Pat had been inclined to discontinue the custom, but Cathal now claimed his attendance as a right, attaching himself like a small child to 'the way things had always been'.

Now while Pat meditated or splashed gently Cathal sat

opposite to him on the large wooden cover of the lavatory, on top of Pat's clothes. The lavatory, in an arched recess, fitted discreetly inside a long chest of reddish highly polished mahogany, one section of which lifted on a hinge. The wall behind was papered with a design of ivy and blue cabbage roses upon which Cathal's head, inclined always in the same place, had made a blurred brown mark. Lazily relaxed, one leg tucked under, the other crooked at the knee, Cathal displayed the long brown trousers of Irish tweed to which he had lately been promoted. Self-consciously he smoothed them and leaned forward from time to time to smell them appreciatively. He seemed, since the trousers, taller, a very slim boy with a narrow intent face, smooth and straight as a piece of ivory, rather close eyes and longish blackish straight hair. The long-nosed crested head resembled that of a bird, and he had too a bird's capacity for alternating between darting speed and stillness. He sat now perfectly still watching Pat.

At such moments Pat was conscious of resembling his younger brother, though usually they were held to be unlike. Pat's face, which he shaved clean twice a day, was broader and more ruggedly bony, and his eyes were cold blue while Cathal's were brown. Cathal laughed oftener. But his mouth in repose was harder than Pat's. Yet at times when Cathal looked at him Pat saw his brother's face as a mirror, the mask of expression, something poised and fierce, as of a head glimpsed inside a helmet, seeming the image of a grimness which he felt to flow outwards from himself.

Pat turned on the hot tap again. He had noticed lately that he was a little troubled at being seen naked by Cathal. He would not of course have let any other person see him bare. But the brothers had never troubled themselves about this. What had changed? Perhaps it was simply that Cathal was growing up; and Pat perceived this growing up as something very purely, sharply painful, like the touch of a clean knife or a flame. Something here, he scarcely knew what, hurt him and made him wish to withdraw and to hide. Was it this which made him suddenly conscious of his body, which though it was so supple and hard was also white, white as an underground defenceless thing? Or perhaps this whiteness seemed to him now so especially shameful and pathetic since, as he touched his warm limbs in the sticky water, he apprehended himself in an entirely new and urgent way as destructible and mortal. Since the news about Sunday every cell in his body announced itself as precious.

After a pause Cathal said, reverting to a topic which they had in fact been discussing almost continually since the arrival of the afternoon papers, 'So you think it's a forgery?'

'Yes, of course.'

The papers had carried the text of a most alarming document, which had just 'come into somebody's hands', which purported to be a British military plan for a concerted swoop upon the Citizen Army and the Volunteers. All 'nationalists' in arms were to be disarmed and all 'disaffected' premises seized. The places which were to be occupied, including Liberty Hall, the Volunteer headquarters in Dawson Street and a number of other institutions and private houses, were listed in the document, which had many, perhaps too many, marks of authenticity. Dublin was outraged. And the British authorities had at once declared the thing to be forged.

'Well, *they* say so, but of course they would. What makes you think it's not genuine?'

'The bit about the Archbishop's house at Drumcondra. The English wouldn't be so stupid as to interfere with the Archbishop. He's not an extremist, he's well known to be against violence. He's useful to the English. Besides, if they were to touch him Dublin would go mad with rage.'

In fact Pat, who had been startled by the document, had rapidly formed his own theory about its provenance. He attributed it to the Machiavellian pen of the romantic and devious Joseph Plunkett, and when he had taken in its purpose he paid homage to the ingenuity of his comrade. Patriotic indignation spiced with fear, this was just the stimulant which Dublin needed now on the eve of her trial. All the same, it was just possible that the document was genuine, and it was just possible that its publication might lead the authorities to carry out their plan quickly before the threatened persons could take counter-measures.

'But the English *are* stupid,' said Cathal. 'Well, let them try! Then there'll be ructions. General Friend will get a pretty hot reception if he tries to walk into Liberty Hall.'

That was what Pat had for some time feared. If the English had been a little less stupid and a little more callous they would long ago have attempted to disarm their potential foes, and when resisted would have used machine guns. Such a very excusable 'incident' might well be overlooked in the midst of a war where casualties on an astronomic scale were happening elsewhere. A scheme like that could have destroyed the whole movement overnight. Pat wondered if it had been mooted. Fortunately one could rely upon the English, who were certainly not intelligent, to be also less than ruthless. Against a ruthless enemy there would have been no chance at all.

'Do you know what happened at Liberty Hall last Sunday?' said Cathal, pursuing his own line of thought.

'I neither know nor care what happened at Liberty Hall last Sunday.'

'Connolly said anyone who didn't want to fight was to drop out of the ranks. He said it was better for them to go now than later on when they might be needed. He said there'd be no reproaches. No one dropped out.'

'Of course no one dropped out! That theatre business has gone to Connolly's head. He thinks he's the great dramatist of the Irish nation. He's on the stage all the time. It doesn't mean those fellows will actually fight. It's all moonshine anyway.'

'Fight? Of course they'll fight. It's the Volunteers that'll be hiding their heads when the day comes. And the Volunteers are beastly to the Citizen Army. They keep trying to prevent them from having halls and—'

'You shouldn't be surprised. Isn't it the Class Struggle? And I thought I told you to keep away from Liberty Hall.'

'Well, I was there on Sunday and I heard a jolly good lecture on street fighting.'

'Cathal—'

'And I saw those pictures of the civil war in Cuba. One's got to pick up tips. Did you know that you ought to learn to shoot with your left hand? Tom Clarke was telling me—'

'I told you not to be hanging round Tom Clarke's shop either.'

'Think of Tom Clarke being fifteen years in prison. He was in prison longer than my whole life. If I'd been fifteen years in prison I'd hate everybody. But he doesn't seem to hate anyone, not even the English.'

'Sure he's a great man.'

'Then why don't you want me to go and see him?'

'You're too young for this, Cathal. Your turn will come. This isn't for you.'

'So there *is* a plan?' Cathal was rigid with attention. His body, scarcely moving, became taut.

Pat cursed his incautious words. Almost anything he said to Cathal now could be dangerous. 'Of course there's no plan! I just don't want you to be wasting your time romancing with a lot of old Fenians when you ought to be working for your exams.'

'Exams! Connolly says that the failure to take the offensive is the death of all revolutions.'

'How can you take the offensive when you're armed with broken bottles and old shot-guns tied together with twine?'

'If I were Connolly I'd bring the I.C.A. out and that'd force the Volunteers to follow.'

'Well, thank God you're not Connolly so maybe we'll have a bit of peace.'

'Anyway, the Germans will be coming soon.'

'Oh, will they? I see you know all about it!'

'Yes. I don't much like the Germans, but I'm quite prepared to use them.'

'Listen who's talking!'

'Yes, and then we'll carry out Robert Emmett's plan. Take Dublin Castle, while the Germans will be landing in Kerry and arming all the south and the west, and they'll advance, and Roger Casement's Irish Brigade will come—'

'All three of them.'

'And at the same time the Germans will attack all along the front in France, and they'll bombard the English coast and there'll be Zeppelin raids on London—'

'All to set the Irish free.'

'And the U-boats will come streaming up the Irish Sea and cut off the English in Ireland so no more troops can come over and no one will feed the English and they'll have to surrender.'

'The British Navy seems to have been pretty successful so far at keeping the U-boats out of the Irish Sea. The mail boat arrives every day, doesn't it?'

'But there are secret U-boat bases all round Ireland now and wireless transmitters—'

'Besides, even if we did maroon the English troops, which we couldn't, they're still armed to the teeth, aren't they? What about all those field guns?'

'The Irish regiments wouldn't fight against their own people. The Dublin Fusiliers—'

'They'd fight. They'd fight, not "against their own people", but against a little gang of terrorists. And when one of them was killed they'd fight with hatred.'

'Besides, Connolly says a capitalist power will never use artillery against capitalist property.'

'That's the stupidest argument I ever heard. The French used artillery against the Paris workers in eighteen seventy-one. Your great hero ought to read some history.'

'Well, and then the Americans—'

'The Americans! The only sensible thing your hero ever said was that the snakes that St Patrick drove out of Ireland swam the Atlantic and became Irish Americans.'

'It may interest you to know that the Americans are going to make a special treaty with Germany because of the submarines and declare war on England because of the blockade.'

'Why not the other way round? The Americans will never fight the English. It's inconceivable.'

'Well, they don't like the British Empire, do they? A blow in Ireland against the British Empire has a hundred times more political significance than an equal blow struck in Asia or Africa. A child may stick a pin in a giant's heart.'

'Who said that, as if I didn't know.'

'Well, it wasn't. It was someone called Lenin, he's a Russian and I bet you've never heard of him.'

'Well, I have so.'

'The eyes of the world are upon us—'

'That's what the poor Irish always think.'

'Whenever it's the turn of a country, however small, to rise against its tyrants it represents the oppressed peoples of the whole world.'

'I thought William Martin Murphy and the Dublin employers were the tyrants your friends hated, more than the English.'

'Have you heard that Murphy has persuaded all the employers to sack all the able-bodied workers to force them to enlist?'

'If I were your schoolmaster I'd beat a bit of accuracy into you. The employers would do no such thing, it would hit their pockets.'

'Well, there's no call for you to sneer—'

'I'm not sneering.'

'You are so.'

'I am not.'

'The Irish worker is the worst fed and the worst housed in the British Isles, and that's saying something. And it was a Government Commission said that, not James Connolly. Have you been over to Jinny's place ever and seen how she lives? Do you know that they're living six in a room all over Dublin? Do you know how cold they are in winter? Do you know what they have to eat? Do you know what happens to them when they're ill?'

'I know these things, Cathal, don't shout.'

'Well, once we get started we'll shift the whole lot. We'll shift the bloody English and William Martin Murphy all at the same time. And they can put the Home Rule Bill where the monkey put the nuts.'

'Haven't I told you not to be using that bad language.'

'We'll hail the English workers as our brothers. And all over Europe the workers will rise to stop the war. We'll ride on top of the workers' movement like Toomai on the elephant. "Kala Nag, Kala Nag, take me with you—".'

'I'm surprised to hear you quoting that Imperialist writer!'

Cathal was silent for a moment. Then as if deliberately putting his exaltation from him he lifted his other knee and began with wrinkled nostrils to sniff the tweed of his trouser leg. He massaged his ankles and then slowly lowered his feet to the ground, leaning far forward so that his straight heavy sheet of hair fell down over his brow. With face hidden he said, 'So you think it is—impossible—to fight?'

Pat stared at the bowed head. Then he answered slowly. 'Yes, impossible.'

Impossible. That was what all his arguments had proved it to be. But on Sunday they were going to do the impossible.

'Pass me the towel, Cathal.'

The boy jumped up quickly and then laughed. 'Why are you covering yourself up like that, like a girl? Patrick Pearse says the Red Branch heroes went naked into battle. He says shame of nakedness is a modern English thing—'

EIGHT

'Pearse talks almost as much nonsense as your friend at Liberty Hall. Shove over the bath mat, would you.'

For a while Cathal watched Pat drying himself. Then he said, almost under his breath, 'When you go, I am going with you—'

Pat said nothing. His fierce love for his younger brother had expressed itself in a tyranny which had deceived many outsiders. He loved Cathal, and only Cathal, with all the intensity of that place of weakness which he called his heart; and he had always known and knew it now with an especial terror, that Cathal was his vulnerable point, his Achilles heel. Though he were to make himself into a man of iron, here he would always be naked and totally without defence. When Sunday came, what could he do about Cathal?

Chapter Nine

O N Wednesday, at about five o'clock in the morning,
Christopher Bellman, who had been unable to sleep,
arose from his bed. It was today that Millie was to give him her
momentous answer. Since last meeting her he had pursued an
inward dialogue of great length and complexity. He could not
clearly remember doing anything else, though in fact he must
somehow have conversed with Frances, Andrew and Hilda,
and gone about a semblance of his daily work. In fact he had
sat for long hours in his study, staring out of the window and
listening to the uproar of his thoughts which rattled away in
his ears, sounding now like schoolmen and now like fish-
wives.

He was chiefly troubled by two things. First and most
fundamentally he was afraid that Millie might say no. His view
of her as 'cornered' depended upon an assumption about her
rationality which could very well prove false. Of course Millie
did not want to sell Rathblane and the house in Upper Mount
Street and go into cheap lodgings. But was Millie rational
enough to keep this prospect steadily before her face? Might
she not prefer to drift vaguely on, trusting that her luck would
change? This might result, indeed would certainly soon result,
in her ruin, the dissolution of her empire: and at that moment,
or on the brink of it, she might well turn to him again. Yet if
things went that far, and especially if her situation were to
become public, would she in fact turn to him? She might, when
really faced with it, positively prefer the catastrophe and feel
that it was now too late to buy back the continuity and the
splendour of her previous existence. He could negotiate with
an unrealistic, comfort-loving, imperial Millie who simply
wanted the preservation of her advantages provided she was
just rational enough to know what must be done to ensure this.

NINE

But Millie was also capable of enjoying disaster. A desperate, exposed Millie would be an entirely different person, and one who might well find the strength within herself to prefer her freedom. He must see to it that this person did not come into existence.

The other thing that troubled him was the plain thought that he was acting wrongly. Of course, he had had this thought before, but in a different form. He had been ruthless with a certain dash. It seemed to him that after a lifetime of quiet decency this sudden act of selfishness had some elegance about it. For once, and in a wonderful cause, he was going to go straight for what he wanted. Millie was a rich prize, and he would take her in spite of the demon of morality. He had pictured his wrong-doing entirely in terms of himself, in terms of a really rather brave, and certainly rather stylish overthrowing of moral barriers which perhaps his timidity rather than his virtue had previously respected. Now he began to think more closely about Millie.

Of course, if he pressed her too much against her will to marry him she might well resent it in ways which would later make his own life a misery, so there were clear self-interested motives for caution. But Christopher somehow did not fear this. He knew Millie very well and knew the sturdy cheerfulness of her temperament. She would make the best of a bad job. But if it was indeed such a bad job why force it upon her at all? Ought he not simply to rescue her financially, which he could fairly easily do, and expect no reward? The trouble was, he would probably get no reward. He had been exact in saying that moderate faithfulness was all he could expect from a Millie married. Not that he anticipated positive love affairs, though that was possible too, but Millie would never be able to resist a conquest or to contain her roving affections and he could not reasonably, in all the circumstances, ask her, if she became Mrs Bellman, to do so. From a Millie unmarried, however greatly indebted, he knew he could expect very little. Millie would, in a short while, almost literally *forget* what had happened.

Nevertheless, it now appeared before him more precisely, like an alien tablet held up before his face, that his duty was to make the money available and lightly and generously to drop the other idea which would never, except in this graceless context, have occurred to him as in the least feasible or to Millie as in the least interesting. When the argument reached this point the question promptly arose in a new form: was he going to do his duty? He had been prepared to perform the stylish act. Was he equally prepared to perform the ugly act? But here his desire for Millie, the sheer dazzling image of her, like a miraculous icon suddenly laid open before him, struck him dumb with a comforting sense of the inevitable. He simply could not resist her. Then almost at once the whisper of the argument would begin again from the beginning. And now on the morning of Wednesday he was still unresolved, weakly inclined to wait for Millie's words to bring about some new mood in him. With a supreme frailty, of which he was thoroughly conscious, he handed the moral decision over to his future self.

These matters had occupied Christopher for a greater part of the night, in the intervals of storms of nightmare which had departed from memory leaving only a dark stain behind. Unable now to lie still, he got up into the twilight, rather shakily pushing himself out of bed and lowering his feet which curled stiffly and reluctantly on contact with the floor. Sleep still buzzed and swarmed about him. Drooping his head, he noticed how extremely thin his legs were. He sat on the edge of the bed and contemplated his bony knees and ankles and the narrow white shaft in between sparsely scattered with long spidery black hairs. The flesh seemed like a kind of solidified paste, rigidly tubular yet without significant shape or colour. With this came a disagreeable intuition of his whole body as stiff and old and flaky. Unclothed he would be found to be a stick-like puppet, something so crude and primitive that its connection with the human form was merely conjectural. He could ask nothing of Millie. But at that moment it was not even the thought of her that appalled him: it was some old fear of death which had not visited him now for many years.

He got up and mixed himself a little chlorodyne in some water. Then, holding the glass, he went over to the window. The garden was very still, hazily present in a bluish twilight which only just allowed the eyes to see. It seemed to him now an alien scene, something reflected in an old dim looking-glass, a strangely altered mirror garden. Never by day did the trees and plants look so monumentally quiet and abstractedly aware, as in a wide-eyed trance. He shivered and then found that he was listening, perhaps for the sound of the dew dripping from the spikey tips of the palm trees. But the blue air was silent, no sound diffused in it even of the sea, an opaque and sterile air. He was about to turn away to the comfort of his room when he became aware of something unusual in the dim space before him. He saw, or thought he saw, a human figure standing in the garden. He stared, trying in vain to make his eyes see clearly. The bewitchment had shifted, the diffused menace of the blue twilight concentrated in this motionless intruder, quieter and more intent than the waiting trees. Christopher drew in his breath slowly; then suddenly his vision shifted again and he recognized the figure. It was his daughter Frances.

Frances began to move slowly across the lawn. She was wearing a long dressing-gown of a whitish colour which dragged behind her leaving a dark trail in the dew. She came as far as the swing. She was now, underneath the chestnut tree, barely visible. Her pale gown moved behind the leaves and for a moment she seemed to be kneeling on the seat of the swing. Then she emerged and stood looking up at the tree. She touched one of the lower branches and made it sway as if to be sure that something other than herself could move. Her gestures had the dreadful completeness and self-absorption of those who do not think they are observed. Then she swung slowly away and began to drift across the grass, abruptly pausing from time to time to think or listen. She moved heavily, in a way quite unlike her normal gait, as if her entry into the mirror world had weighed her down, powdered her over with some resistant silvery stuff; and indeed her figure seemed now to shimmer slightly, perhaps in the increasing light, like something metallic. Then when she stood still she was very still, fading a little, gathered into the dim morning silence where not even a bird was stirring.

Christopher was extremely troubled. There was something distraught about the quiet figure with its heavy menaced gait. He would have been unwilling now to see her face. She seemed like a person deliberately frightening herself, trying perhaps to still one fear by another. Yet what was so appalling about the garden? It was the girl's own fear which he had seen in the twilit garden, diffused in the blue grains of the dawn light. With a quick horror of being seen by her he moved back from the window. The figure watching from inside could only seem a terrible demon to the figure wandering without. He sat down shuddering upon his bed. How did he so certainly know that she was afraid? And what was it that she was afraid of?

* * * *

'Oh, what fun, you've had the old swing mended!'

'Yes, Andrew mended it.'

The sun was shining brightly and the birds were singing. It had been raining in the earlier part of the morning, but now the sun shone upon the sparkling wet garden which smelt and looked a sort of light salty green.

'Has the dear boy popped the question?'

'Not yet.'

Christopher followed Millie down the garden. He was uneasy at her presence here, uneasy at her insistence on coming to his house, although he knew that Hilda and Frances were safely in Dublin. He would have kept her indoors, but she had, on her arrival, walked straight through the house into the garden.

'Have Andrew and Hilda moved yet?'

'They slept last night at Claresville, just camping out. The furniture from England arrives tomorrow.'

'I must go down and inspect. Do you approve of Hilda's new place?'

'I don't like a sloping garden, but the house is pretty enough. Millie—'

'Your gardener hasn't pruned the roses properly. Look at all those spindly branches.'

'I know. His mind hasn't been on his job lately. Millie—'

'How early the roses are in bud here. But the buds won't open, will they, for nearly another month.'

'More than that. Millie—'

'Isn't it funny the way one *forgets* every year the way things happen in the spring? I never know what order the flowers come in, do you?'

'I envy you all those surprises. Dearest Millie—'

'Is the Castle going to raid all those Sinn Feiners and take their guns away? Did you see that thing in the paper yesterday?'

'No, of course not. That order was obviously a fake. I rang up MacNeill's brother about it and he just laughed. Mr Birrell has gone off to England for Easter as usual. This country's the same on both sides of the fence. All talk and no action.'

'And you think the others won't do anything beyond their usual playing at soldiers?'

'No, they'll sit about waiting for the peace conference. They can't lose by waiting. Now, please—'

'It's so sad. I always thought something wonderful would come out of Ireland. Some great glittering event that would change everything, some great act. But no, it's all toy, it's tiny and provincial after all.'

'There could be no great event, Millie, there aren't the

historical conditions for a great event. A few people might commit a few murders—'

'Well, perhaps it was just something in my own life I was waiting for, some golden thing which never came.'

'Millie, I do wish you'd come inside.'

'No, I like it out here. It's so gorgeously wet. It keeps my ankles cool.'

'Dearest, there was something you were going to tell me today.'

'Oh, the future, the future! I keep on consulting the cards but I draw nothing but the Queen of Spades.'

'You ought to be consulting your heart.'

'My *what?*'

'Millie, please don't torture me.'

'You refer to your suggestion that we should get married?'

'Of course—'

'Well, naturally the answer's yes.'

Christopher stared at Millie, who was now retreating from him across the grass. She was still wearing her grey outdoor coat with its militaristic trimmings in red velvet. Beneath it her silk skirt was visible, patchily darkened by the rain water, and her neat little boots. Christopher watched her plump, slightly swaying figure moving away and now leaning a little over the roses. For a moment it all seemed a picture, as if a golden light had shone upon a stage and made uncertain random things into a beautiful tableau. The relief he felt made him quite dazed with joy. He wanted to kneel down on the wet grass. Instead he stooped and touched it and drew his wet rainy hand across his brow. He followed her.

'Oh, Millie, I'm so glad.'

'Yes, I give in, I surrender. I'm coming out with the white flag. You have all the big guns.'

'Is it as bad as that?'

'Oh, worse—But no, I'm only jesting! Here, I've picked you a lovely green rosebud. Mind the thorns.'

'May there be no thorns in our life together.'

'Nothing sharp with which we can hurt each other. Oh, if you knew how frightened I am of being hurt by you, Christopher.'

'Millie! As if I could ever hurt you. I worship you.'

The unexpectedness of her cry pierced him, causing a little sweet pain which became a warm glow of power. As he spoke he knew still that he ought to be saying something very different to her, he ought to be using all the intelligence he could command to make her, at this last minute, feel utterly free of him. He should be offering her his help and her freedom too. But already, loaded deep with joy and absolutism, the new situation had gained its own historical momentum.

'You think Frances won't mind really?'

'No, no,' said Christopher. 'When she's married, when she's got her man and her own place, she won't be troubled about this.' He recalled the haunted figure that he had seen that morning. But that was a ghost, and this sunny garden and its certainties were the real world.

'I wonder why men always think that about women. Well, I hope you won't falter for Frances. For myself, for what's left of my heart, I've got to think of you as desperate about me.' She gave him a quick look and then turned her back again, going toward the swing.

'But I am desperate about you, Millie.'

'Could you dry the seat for me?'

He dried the seat of the swing with his handkerchief and she sat upon it, digging the heel of her boot into the lawn.

'You know, Christopher, I did love Arthur. A lot of people thought I didn't but I did.'

'I'm sure you did.'

'Really I don't know any way of being fond of people except being in love with them. Arthur was very beautiful when he was young. Well, I suppose in a way he's still young. And I am old.'

'You know you're not old, Millie—'

'Yes I am. I'm doing an old person's thing. I'm giving up waiting. Christopher—'

'Yes?'

'I shall want another motor car. We shall want another motor car.'

' "We"—oh yes—whatever you say, my darling. But we shall have to have a mechanic. I couldn't manage—'

'We won't need a mechanic. We'll use my young men. I shall have a troop of young men, you know, to follow me about. Like young Andrew. He knows all about engines. You won't mind, will you?'

'If you marry me I won't mind anything.'

'I wonder. Will you give me an engagement ring?'

'Of course! But we can't make anything, you know, public for a bit—'

'What an ardent impetuous fellow you are! I suppose I could wear my ring underneath a glove! No, you'd better not buy the ring just yet. You may still change your mind.'

'Millie, I'll get you a ring this afternoon—'

'No, no, of course not! Anyway I want a little breathing space. I want a little time, time for a sort of holiday—'

'You don't mean a last fling do you, my darling?'

'A last fling? Good heavens no. Whoever could I have a last fling with? No, don't swing me, I can swing myself.'

She began to move the swing to and fro. She had opened the front of her coat, revealing a high-necked blouse of innumerable white frills pulled tightly over her bosom. Her legs bent and straightened vigorously with a flash of plump grey-stockinged calf and a hint of petticoat. The rope groaned on the tree and the fragments of bark fluttered down on to the red velvet epaulettes. Millie swung higher. Then something solid and glittering, dislodged from one of her pockets, plopped heavily on to the grass at Christopher's feet. It was a revolver. He picked it up and saw that it was loaded.

Millie let the swing lose speed and in a moment, with a great swirl of skirts, she jumped out of it, her hand seizing Christopher's shoulder. Her other hand gripped the revolver, crushing it against his palm and slipping it from him. As Christopher felt the weight of her body suddenly against him he made as if to embrace her, but she moved quickly from him to the other side of the swing.

Someone appeared at the side of the house and was now going in through the glass doors of the conservatory. It was Barnabas Drumm. He noticed them, hesitated, gave a vague wave and went inside.

Christopher felt suddenly uneasy. 'He must be looking for Hilda. He doesn't know she's moved. He can't have seen or heard anything, can he?'

'No, of course not. He's only just come.'

'I don't trust him. He's full of malice and I believe he spies on you.'

'Nonsense, he's just a dear old sheepdog. Let's go in, shall we? I think it's beginning to rain again.'

They moved out from under the tree into the first drops of the rain. The weak sun still touched the tips of white flowering cherry trees against a leaden sky. Christopher halted. There was, to make his happiness complete, one thing he must say, one hazard more he must run. And surely now it was safe to run it. He meant to say, You know you needn't marry me. I'll do it all, but if you don't want to you needn't marry me.

The words came out differently. 'You know you can always do anything that you want, Millie.'

She looked away from him. The small rain was already laying its drops in her dark hair and upon the shoulders of her coat. 'I won't want to do anything.'

'You may do. You know you can command me. You can do what you please with me.'

'So you think *now*,' she murmured. 'But there are deep roots of selfishness in both of us. And when we struggle you will always win, always.'

Chapter Ten

' AT this period of my life I again became a frequent visitor
at the house in Upper Mount Street, where I knew that a
gay welcome always awaited me. It was, I knew, improper,
doubtless unjust, to prefer the lively affection of the light-
hearted "Millie" to the dour and dumb attachment of my wife.
But the order of the world is unjust and with a natural spon-
taneity like moves to like and life flows towards life. My own
congenital gaiety, so muted in the gloomy atmosphere of my
home "had its fling" at Upper Mount Street, and at times Lady
Kinnard and I would make each other laugh until the tears ran.
The return to Blessington Street was always something of a
penance. The house was usually untidy and often far from
clean; and I was, I confess, offended by the, as it seemed to me
deliberate, tawdriness and ill-kempt appearance not of my
home only but of my wife's person. That most regrettable, that
unexpected but implacable physical distaste which had led me
so unforgivably to fail my wife in the central sanctum of our
marriage, early and silently divined by her, had led the poor
sufferer perversely to accentuate just those features of her
personal appearance which had been the initial occasion of my
abstinence.'

These words, which he had penned early that morning in
the National Library, ran automatically through Barney's
head, giving him but little pleasure since his thoughts were by
now engaged elsewhere as he sat in the Butt Bar in Beresford
Place on the afternoon of Wednesday, April the nineteenth.
Previous to his arrival at the Butt Bar he had been in Little's
Public House in Harcourt Street, and before that in Nagle's
Bar in Earl Street, and before that at Bergin's in Amiens Street.
He had lunched, or it seemed likely that he had lunched, at the
Red Bank Restaurant, but that was a long time ago by this time.

Barney was still in a shocked condition. Seeking Hilda that morning at Finglas he had, coming up the lane at the side of the house, become aware of Millie in the garden. From behind the hedge he had heard the greater part of her conversation with Christopher. Millie flirting with Christopher was one thing; Millie married to Christopher was quite another, and Barney had immediately felt: I cannot endure it. If Millie were married he could not go to her any more. This, which he had never thought, since he had never conceived of her second marriage, was instantly and horribly clear. His presence at Millie's depended on certain assumptions, certain, he had to admit it, perhaps fictions or illusions. He had to feel himself, with her, 'as good as anybody'. He had to feel her somehow potentially his. And Millie was often so gay with him, might he not really be the most necessary man of them all? He could be Millie's spaniel now, but not the tolerated pet of a married Millie, even if he were in fact tolerated.

He was appalled too, almost frightened, by the sudden image of Millie under duress. With an ear attuned by love, or by his own specialized self-interest, he had heard in her bantering voice the hidden whine of despair. Millie was acting under coercion, and there could be only one reason for this coerced decision: she was marrying money. Barney was not so much shocked by this revelation as horrified by it on Millie's behalf. Millie was so essentially a free animal. What awful desperation must lie behind this choice to wear the collar of slavery? Barney could not envisage her as in love with Christopher. That pain at least was spared him. She was not in love; but she would with all the vitality and all the duplicity of her nature play the part of a rapturously happy wife. And she would be utterly lost to him.

At a certain point in these miserable reflections, possibly in Little's Public House, Barney felt an obscure lightening. This sense of relief shortly became explicit as the resolution: it must not be. She would certainly regret her decision: better then if she were prevented from carrying it out. Whatever Millie's financial embarrassments, and Barney had for some time had an inkling of their existence, they were better for her than a forced marriage which her free nature would resent and soon detest. Barney, who after all knew her better than anyone else did, was certain of this. It was for him, doubtless not unrewarded, to rescue Millie from herself. She must be stopped. But how?

To turn from fruitless grinding pain to the envisaging, however vague, of counter-measures, is an invigorating change. Barney had sat up, ordered another whiskey, and focused his eyes sternly upon the Meeting of the Waters which was wanly represented in a diamond of stained glass in the window of the bar. And at once there arose, commanding the new perspective of his thoughts, the figure of Frances. Frances was not yet to be told of her father's intentions. Why? Clearly because Christopher wished the girl to be safely married and packed away before he made his move. Again why? Because he was afraid of his daughter's reactions. Barney, who had by now conveyed himself as far as the Butt Bar, beat his forehead and tried to focus his eyes upon the Snowy Breasted Pearl who was wanly represented in a diamond of stained glass in the window of the bar. The young lady, who would otherwise have been hard to identify, was thus labelled. The letters danced before his eyes, but he had read them on a previous occasion. The matter of Frances was complicated.

Barney had always experienced with Frances a simplicity and gentleness of communication which he had otherwise hoped for in vain from the world of women. Through Frances he had glimpsed that absolute of love, which is the only thing which heals the humiliated spirit. But he was aware too, inside this quiet girl, of a woman both strong and complex. The will of Frances was a powerful machine. If he were to release that machine into the situation he had just discovered, what would happen? That Frances was capable of preventing her father's marriage Barney did not doubt. Though whether she would decide to do so was another thing. The beginning of the argument was that Millie *ought not* to marry Christopher. But granted that, it was still not absolutely clear that it was wise to involve Frances. Frances would be desperately upset; and was it right to upset her just upon the verge of her own marriage? Though of course if Frances did engage in a struggle with her father this might induce her to put off leaving Ireland or even to put off getting married, especially if her struggle were successful. She would feel it necessary to stay with her father and comfort him if she had effectively crossed him.

This introduced a new consideration so interesting to Barney that, scarcely noticing, he put on his hat, heaved himself up and walked with dignity out of the Butt Bar on to the quay. The Butt Bar stood next door to Liberty Hall, the head-quarters of the Transport and General Workers Union, and now of James Connolly's Citizen Army. As Barney crossed the cobbles in the direction of the Loop Line Railway he noticed that a number of people were gathered outside Liberty Hall. There was a familiar figure in the group. He realized that it was Pat, and stopped with a quick instinct of concealment. Pat was dressed in the vivid green uniform of the Volunteers, complete with slouch hat and Sam Browne. He carried a revolver at his belt and a rifle slung at his back. The other men in the group wore the darker green uniform of the Citizen Army. Some sort of argument seemed to be going on. After a moment they all moved inside the building.

The glimpse of Pat sobered Barney and made him realize that he had in fact drunk quite a lot of whiskey. He was glad that Pat had not seen him; and he felt a spasm of that special, unique pain which was caused in him by his stepsons. This pain was compounded of love, shame and an acute sense of injustice. Barney saw his stepchildren as superior, almost perfect, beings, and he loved them with a peculiar, private, incapsulated love. He had never been able to find any language for this love. There was no touch, no look, no gesture, no tone of voice which could give expression to it at all. At the same time he knew, and knew it daily, that he was a cause of scandal to the two boys. They resented what they saw of his attitude to their mother. Even more perhaps they simply resented their stepfather as an object upon the scene, as a debased version of human existence. The contrast between the purity and perfection of his inward love and the meanness and absurdity of his outward performance, between the gravity of his heart and the oafishness of his manner, seemed to Barney something miserably unjust. At the same time he felt ashamed before the two boys with a genuine piercing shame which seemed itself to belong to what was most profound and uncorrupted in him, and which was sometimes almost pleasurable in its intensity.

Barney walked a little way and then leaned against the warm rounded granite of the quay. The sky above him was that particular sort of cold Irish pale blue, looking like thin wet paper down which highly diluted blue paint is almost imperceptably running. A steady wind tilted the masts of ships outside the Customs House and kept the rippling Union Jack squarely on display. Dublin, or perhaps it was the Liffey, smelt of yeast. Barney looked down at the river. Great iron rings hung upon the river walls, joined by loops of rope, shaggy with seaweed, resembling huge coarse Georgian decorations, and below the gluey water passed slowly by, foaming a little like stout, its dark, dirty brown smudged with rusty white lights and thin overlaid blues and shimmers of old tarnished gold. A flight of whitewashed steps was chalkily reflected and now a tower of white gulls descending to investigate some more than usual opacity in the viscous stream. As Barney stared at it and smelt it, and listened to the clatter of the traffic and the quarrelling of the gulls, he thought about the silent unpolluted Shannon at Clonmacnoise and the big open-handed Christ upon His ancient cross, and the empty land there.

He walked on as far as the bridge. Ahead of him the multicoloured quays of the cluttered city meandered away, starkly clear, in the direction of the Four Courts with its green pencilled dome. A construction of clouds, whitish brown like the light upon the Liffey, was rising above Guinness's brewery. Perhaps it was going to rain after all. Barney stroked his moustache, sniffing the whiskey from it. He paused to gaze idly at the array of posters on St George's quay. A large one affirmed, with a modesty which always puzzled him, that Monkey Brand would not wash clothes. Smaller notices announced that *Vaseline Helped the British to Victory*, and *His Skin Turned Black, Zam-buk the Only Cure*. A recruiting poster showed a white-haired woman admonishing her dubious son, *Go, Lad, it's Your Duty*. A photographer's advertisement claimed a willingness to *Enlarge Any Photo of Your Wife, Sweetheart, Child or Dearest Friend to Full Life Size* for only one and sixpence. Did they really mean it? Barney imagined himself in possession of a Full Life Size picture of Millie. He would have to keep it locked in his room. Probably the only safe place would be under the mattress. This led to other disturbing thoughts.

He began to walk up toward the Pillar. Sackville Street was full of the blue uniforms of wounded soldiers, conspicuous in the weak sunshine. A small detachment of lancers, armed with carbines and lances, trotted past in the direction of Phoenix Park, and after them a brake full of police. Barney detached his mind from the interesting possibilities of a life-size replica of Millie, and began to wonder again about Frances and whether her deep dislike of Millie, which he had observed but never fully understood, would lead her, should she be apprised of the situation, to oppose her parent's wishes in the matter of his marriage. As it began to seem to him bleakly probable that Frances would prove all that a magnanimous daughter should be, it occurred to him that there was yet another card which he might play. He might tell Frances about what had happened at Maynooth. He paused at the corner of Rutland Square. The clouds were massing now above the green dome of the Rotunda Hospital, and the clock on Findlater's Church stood at ten minutes to five. Frances had always wanted to know what woman 'had been his downfall', and Barney had often wished to tell her, not in order to discredit Millie, but simply in order to draw Frances closer to him. He had sometimes envisaged telling her everything and making her his confessor and his judge. But a sense of loyalty to Millie had always prevented him from unfolding to Frances the full pattern of his woes, though she herself had often prompted him to do so in O'Halloran's Bun Shop. Frances intuited wickedness in Millie. Should he not, in revealing that this woman was to marry Christopher, also reveal how far that intuition had been correct?

* * * *

Barney let himself in very quietly at the front door of the house in Blessington Street. It was just beginning to rain. He paused in the dark hall to hang his hat upon the stand, and drew out of the drawer a velvet skull cap which he had lately bought at Finnegans, the Gentleman's Outfitter, and which he liked because it kept his bald head warm and gave him a slightly ecclesiastical appearance. He noticed that the hall-stand was thick with dust. He drew a face quickly in the dust, then carefully fitted on his velvet cap and peered at his dim image in the mirror. The cap, in a way which he found satisfactory, made him look much older. He observed how white his eyebrows had become. He was aware of an urgent desire to lie down somewhere and close his eyes. He began to creep quietly up the stairs. He always went up like a mouse so as to avoid any possible interview with his wife.

He passed the stained-glass lavatory window, inhaling the smell and avoiding the stair that creaked. On these occasions he eschewed the ostentation of the lavatory, reserving himself for the discreet quiet of his own chamber-pot. He passed through the glass bead curtain, grasping it with a practised hand to prevent the jangle, and had his foot upon the next flight of stairs when he heard Kathleen's voice calling from the drawing-room. 'Barney, is that you? Could you come in for a minute?'

Barney groaned. He turned back and inserted himself non-committally through the drawing-room door. It now seemed to be raining hard outside, and the room was dark and cold. No fire had been lit in the grate, which was still full of yester-day's ashes. There was the usual stuffy musty smell of dust and old thick feathery textiles.

Kathleen was standing at the far end of the room by the window, plucking at the lace curtain. She must have seen him come in. As she turned her head he saw the big outline of her bun, from which some untidy hairs were sprouting. Her face was a worried pale blur out of which those big light brown eyes glared at him with a luminous intensity. She was wearing her usual old-fashioned brown skirt down to the ground and had drawn a knitted shawl round her for warmth. Not feeling very strong, Barney sat down on an upright chair near the door. The shiny slippery seat, unaccustomed to being sat on, nearly ejected him. He experienced the immediate physical sense of guilt which a confrontation with Kathleen always occasioned. His skin turned black. Zam-buk the only cure.

'Barney, I'm so worried.'

'What about, dear?' Had Kathleen found out something?

'About Pat.'

'Oh, about Pat. I shouldn't worry about Pat.'

'Barney, do you know of anything—anything Pat's going to—do?'

'No, nothing at all. Funny, I saw Pat today by Liberty Hall. He was just going inside.'

'Liberty Hall? But that's not his headquarters. His head-quarters is in Dawson Street.'

'I know. But I expect they were just planning a joint march

or something with the I.C.A. boys. We're great pals with them these days.'

'Yes, I've noticed that. So you don't know anything about it, Barney? I really think you ought to tell me if you do.'

'Honest, Kathleen, I don't know anything. I just don't know what you're worrying about.'

'Oh, well—they wouldn't tell you, anyway.' She came and sat down by the untidy hearth, and crumbled a piece of half-burnt coal with her boot.

Barney was a bit annoyed by this. He got off the reluctant chair and came over to the mantelpiece. 'Of course I'd know if anything was on. I don't understand what you're imagining anyway. What makes you say that about Pat?'

'Oh, I don't know. Nothing definite. He's been two days away from his job without giving any explanation, and Mr Monaghan called in last night to see him. He asked me if Pat was ill and of course I told him he wasn't. It's so discourteous. And when I said Mr Monaghan had been Pat just laughed and said something about not going back at all. He seems to be living in another world.'

'Oh, I shouldn't worry,' said Barney. He was relieved that what troubled Kathleen was not something about himself. He shuffled his feet to produce an atmosphere of departure.

'And now every time he goes out he carries a gun. And he was wearing that uniform again today. And he seems terribly excited and unnatural, and Cathal's excited too.'

'Cathal's always excited.'

'He spends so much *time* out. What's he doing all day? And he simply ignores things I say to him, he doesn't even bother to reply. Barney, couldn't you say something to him?'

'Good heavens, what could I say?'

'Well, ask him if they're thinking of—' Kathleen stopped, and Barney suddenly realized that she was in some state of extreme emotion. She did not weep, but her white face puckered blindly and she covered her mouth with her hand.

'Come, come, Kathleen,' he said, touched and infected by her agitation. 'You know nothing will happen. Nothing ever happens in Ireland.'

'Please speak to him, Barney.'

'I have no authority over Pat.'

'Just to find out. Oh, it's so *wrong*—'

'What is?'

'This hatred, these guns—'

'You don't understand,' said Barney. 'Women don't understand.' Did he understand himself? He was flattered by Kathleen's appeal, but he was also frightened by it. Could her intuition have told her of something which was really the case? But that was impossible.

'You see, it *is* sometimes right to fight—' Barney began. His words sounded blundering and childish in the cold darkened room. Was he only now trying to think about those possibilities which the sheer physical infection of Kathleen's fear had conjured up? He felt sudden fear himself, coldness.

'I'm so frightened about Pat—' Kathleen had turned back to her particular concern. She murmured it as if she knew that there was no help and that she was alone again. Barney saw that she was shivering.

'Don't worry,' he said in a loud voice. 'I've seen these young people getting excited. It comes to nothing.' He felt he would have to get out of the room quickly. He began to move away. 'Shall I light the gas? It's gloomy in here.'

'And that rifle of yours upstairs—' Kathleen went on, suddenly addressing herself to Barney as she saw that he was going to go. 'You oughtn't to have that rifle, it's wrong, it's a wrong thing. You older men should set an example. What can you expect of the young? You should get rid of that rifle. One can't live by violence. The whole world is mad with violence.'

'Oh, well, that's just an old thing—' said Barney. In fact it was a new Lee Enfield in beautiful condition.

'All the guns ought to be dropped into the sea. It's a man's world, a world of hate. Why do you always lock your door now? You're getting as bad as Pat.'

Kathleen had an intuitive gift, a sort of artistic talent, for jumbling together the personal and the impersonal into a sort of inconsequent yet compulsive ensemble. This, Barney often thought, was what made her so good at making people feel guilty. All Kathleen's complaints were threaded together and then somehow attached to her interlocutor. 'Well, you see—' Barney, who now locked his door because the Memoir had reached such monumental proportions that it was impossible to hide it, fumbled for an invention.

Fortunately Kathleen went straight on. 'Must you wear that ridiculous little hat in the house? It makes you look like a Jew.'

'I like looking like a Jew.'

'Have you been to confession?'

'No.'

'Oughtn't you to go?'

'Maybe.'

'Will you go?'

'I don't know.'

'It's nearly Easter.'

'I know it's nearly Easter. I've been thinking about Easter.'

'Won't you go to Father Ryan?'

'I don't like Father Ryan.'

'Confession isn't a personal thing.'

'I know it isn't.'

'Well, go to some other priest. Go to some priest that you don't know somewhere in town.'

'Perhaps I will, perhaps I won't,' said Barney. There was something timeless about his quarrels with Kathleen. It was as if it was always the same quarrel. She reduced him to the status of a petulant child and then goaded him to naughtiness. Helplessly on each occasion he watched himself move from a condition of humiliated stupidity to a condition of spiteful rage.

TEN

'Go to Tenebrae. You always like going to Tenebrae.'

'I will if I choose.'

'We are all sinners. At this holy time of all times we must remember it.'

'I know I'm a sinner.'

'We are in Lent, and that speaks of austerity. Religion is a great simplicity, Barney. Is not that what your life needs, simplicity?'

'It's simple enough already if by simple you mean dull!'

'You know I don't mean that. What troubles you is that you are ashamed,'

'I'm damned if I'm ashamed!' Of course the central trouble of his life was that he was ashamed, but that meant to him something that Kathleen would never never understand, so that he was right to reject her words which had a meaning so far away from the truth. He was not ashamed in her way. He writhed before her, half turning towards the door but unable to escape. She was looking up at him. He could not see her face in the gloom but he somehow felt the naked careworn piety of her expression. It drove him mad.

'Sometimes I think you're just going to pieces, Barney.'

'Well, if I am going to pieces whose fault is that?' If he had not married this women he could have been a good man. If he had not married he would have known how to perfect himself and how to achieve that simplicity which Kathleen was quite right to say was the essence of religion. It was she who prevented him from being simple.

'What's to stop me going to pieces?' said Barney. 'No one looks after me or loves me. And you go round looking like an old hag just to spite me. Why don't you get yourself some proper clothes? You go round looking like an old hag from the tenements. Cathal said the new people down the road thought you were my mother. You're punishing yourself just to punish me. You even use your religion to spite me.'

'That's a wicked thing to say,' said Kathleen quietly.

'Well, you do. You're eating me up. And I'm not looked after. No one does my room upstairs—'

'You lock your door.'

'And the house is a shambles. Look at this room with the fire not even cleared out. And there's dust everywhere. What does Jinny think she's doing? She's a single girl, she hasn't got a place of her own to look after, you'd think she'd have enough time in the day to dust the place a little. You haven't trained her properly. You should be getting after her with a stick.'

'Jinny's away.'

'What's the matter with her?'

'She's pregnant.'

'Oh—' This sudden intrusion of someone else's troubles into the recital of his own left him for the moment confused.

'Didn't you see her crying the other day on the stairs?'

'No.' In fact Barney had noticed Jinny crying on the stairs, but he had been hurrying to see Millie at the time and he had forgotten her tears the moment after. The lie was too base. He put his hand to his cheek and muttered, 'Yes, I did see her crying, but I was in a hurry and I forgot.'

'You're always in a hurry. You're always forgetting. You're only half here.'

'Poor Jinny. What can we do?'

'Very little. But you might go and see her for instance. The doctor's told her to stop work. And you know what that place she lives in is like.'

'Go and see her?' Barney was about to pronounce it impossible. Then he sat down abruptly in the nearest chair. He had been ready in imagination to open his compassionate arms to the whole world. And now he was scarcely able to bring himself to visit a poor servant girl who was in trouble. He said aloud, 'What is the matter with me?'

'You know what's the matter with you. You're so sunk in yourself you hardly know that anybody else exists at all. Why don't you this Easter—'

'Well, and what about you?' said Barney raising his head. He forgot all about Jinny. 'Aren't you sunk in yourself? Do you know that I exist? You don't seem to. All you—'

The door of the drawing-room swung silently open and a figure appeared. It was Cathal, carrying a tray. He circled Barney adroitly and put the tray down on one of the brass-topped tables with a light clatter. 'Why, Mother, how dark it is in here! It's raining cats and dogs outside. Shall I light the gas?'

A match flared at once in his hand, and Cathal was moving along the wall lighting up the gas mantels. Each mantel flickered a pale orange under its silk beaded shade, and then as Cathal turned the tap glowed into a globe of brilliant white. The room lightened and the rainy window darkened as the gas hissed quietly.

'I just wet the tea,' said Cathal, returning to the tray. 'I thought I'd bring some up. Oh, I wish I'd remembered to light the fire, I meant to now poor Jinny's away. There, Mother.' He poured out a cup of tea and handed it to Kathleen.

Kathleen looked up at him, smiling. Her face, pearly-golden in the soft glow of the gas, seemed still a little tearful and puckered, as if it had been lightly plucked at, but her features drooped with a calm, loving weariness, the brow bland and the big eyes bright with affection as she lifted an almost ecstatic gaze upon her son. Cathal, with his gauchely deliberate grace, trampled about her for a moment as if he were weaving some invisible protective cocoon. He pressed his dark hair back behind his ears, giving his mother his intense close-eyed stare. His whole figure was sharp with youth and brilliant with consciousness. Then he turned to Barney.

'Here, for you,' he said. He never called Barney by any name, but he spoke now in a low coaxing voice as if to an ill person. He handed him the tea. 'And look, I've got you your biscuits. Those special biscuits you like. The lemon creams. I got them at Lipton's. I had to queue up.'

Barney looked at the tray. He saw the plate with his special biscuits, the lemon creams, which Cathal had queued up to get at Lipton's.

He felt the tears rising to his eyes. He saw Cathal close to him and saw as if it were a separate thing, a passing bird, Cathal's hand moving in a gesture towards the tray, urging him to eat. He took hold of the boy's hand. Some sort of confused words seemed to be coming up with the tears. 'You are so good to me. You are innocent and pure in heart. Oh, remain so always. Do not ever let evil into your life. Forgive me.' He lifted Cathal's hand to his lips and kissed it.

There was a moment of silence and immobility. Then Cathal stepped back, a little confused and embarrassed. He hesitated, and then put his hand on Barney's shoulder, squeezing it slightly. He turned quickly to his mother. 'Well, I'll go and get the sticks to light the fire—' He was gone from the room.

Barney stood up. His sudden consciousness of Cathal's goodness, his equally sudden and automatic unconsciousness of himself, made him light and bouyant. He felt he had had a revelation.

'So you're drunk,' said Kathleen. 'I hadn't realized it. But I might have known.'

'I'm not drunk!' Was he? Did he always know now whether he was drunk or not? He turned his back to her and the tears spilled out on to his cheeks. It was unjust. He had, for one good moment, spoken to his stepson with the voice of pure love, and all his wife could think of to say was that he was drunk. All right, he was drunk. The tears seemed uncontrollable. They were drunken tears.

He saw through a haze the crucifix upon the wall. He said, 'Where did we lose the way, Kathleen? Can we not find some love for each other?'

His wife was silent.

Barney blundered to the door. He did not want to meet Cathal again. And as he went up the stairs to his room the awful black consciousness of Millie returned to him. He unlocked his door. There was the Lee Enfield rifle leaning in the corner. He sat down at the table and rubbed his tears away. Then he gathered together the scattered pages of his Memoir and began quickly to write.

Chapter Eleven

The misty rosary of morn, my fair,
Marks me your footprints in the holy dew.
Daylight is amethystine where you are
And every floweret of the dawn is you!
Such festal favours feed the sanguine day,
Our plighting day that blushes graciously!
You are its glow, its glimmer and its ray
Which falls from far into the deeps of me.
Now as you trip with little tiny steps,
Your petal hands and water-crystal voice,
Your flower-fragrant, oh-so-sighed-for lips
Make my dull essence tremble and rejoice.
Oh thou my dawn, in thee my noonday glints,
In thee my sun sets with a million tints.

It was early on Thursday morning and Andrew had at last decided that it was time formally to propose to Frances. He was glad that he had waited. He knew now that he had not been idly prevaricating. They had been parted, after all, for a matter of over a year, since Frances' visit to England early in the war, and there was a little strangeness to be got over. He had been upset by his return to Ireland, upset by the fuss and flurry of his mother, upset by his relations. Only now had he, with a certain cool relentlessness, calmed himself and begun to favour Frances with his complete attention.

He had penned the sonnet late last night at Claresville, where he had been camping out with his mother for two nights now, doing the innumerable jobs which had to be finished before the furniture arrived. He looked his effort over with satisfaction. He was pleased with 'amethystine', which provided just that vivid dash of colour which Andrew, a disciple of Gautier, knew that any poem must have. 'Amethystine' emphasized and developed the image of the sparkling dew in which Frances' footsteps, from which of course the epithet 'holy' was transferred, were spread out like a rosary or rosy necklace. 'Little tiny steps' was not perhaps quite realistic as Frances rather tended to stride along, but it was symbolically right, expressing the tripping, gliding motion of the beloved compared to the slow breaking of the dawn. The half-rhymes which he had failed to eliminate troubled him a little, but a friend at Cambridge who published poetry in the *Cornhill Magazine* had told him that half-rhymes were now an allowable device. Andrew himself had once nearly had a poem in the *Cornhill*. The Editor had sent it back with a very friendly note.

The thought that he was shortly going to make himself and Frances so extremely happy made Andrew quite dazed with pride. Suddenly he was omnipotent, the benevolent despot of his little world. He would make everybody happy. He would lay an egg of pure good which would nourish them all. Humility followed pride. He did not deserve this sweet clever girl. A sort of laughing rapture followed the humility, because of course he knew he did deserve her, or rather knew he didn't really feel he didn't! This peculiar private exultation merged into a diffused physical desire. His physical feelings about Frances had always been muddled and fluctuating. He had never really wanted any other girl. Yet he had not always sharply wanted her. Now it was as if his desires were coming into focus and revealing Frances unambiguously as their object. In this self-finding and self-defining Andrew more plainly realized how much he had been afraid of physical love. He had not shared the obvious and obsessive fears which drove his brother officers to places he would shudder to visit. But he had deep deep fears all the same. And with a calmness of resolution it occurred to him that if he could properly conquer those fears all other fears would be conquered too; or if not conquered, at least they would receive an intelligible place. The blind black hole in his consciousness which was the awful prospect of returning to France would be lightened, filled with manageable items. Once married there would be no more nightmare.

Andrew had been extremely upset by his encounter with Pat Dumay. The memory that he had been so undignified and stupid as to taunt his cousin made him hot with shame and on the following day he had been able to think of nothing else. Immediately afterwards he had wished to apologize but had been prevented, perhaps fortunately, by the presence of Cathal. A straight apology stammered out upon the occasion of the fault would only have made things worse. He had, however, very much wanted to see Pat alone, had in fact all through Tuesday pined and fretted simply with this desire. He felt, with an almost physical humiliation, how absurdly much he had counted on achieving with Pat, now that they were both grown-up, some quite remarkable friendship. Pat's magic for him had not faded, and entering the Blessington Street drawing-room on Monday he had felt the pang of a delicious fear.

On Wednesday morning, in order to escape from his mother and to think some decisive thoughts about Frances, he walked over from Dalkey to Killiney and stood on the beach in a hollow of blue conical mountains. Here there came to him a great enlightenment and a great peace. He would never be friends with Pat. Pat belonged to some other race of men. Even if he were to seek Pat out and somehow beg his pardon, even if he were to seek Pat out and somehow defy him, the response would be the same. Pat would be cool, ironical, amused, polite, distant, and finally bored. The realization that there are people we shall never conquer comes to us as a part of the process of growing up. With a clarity of mind which he felt did him credit, and which brought with it a new moral vigour, Andrew faced the fact that Pat was a lost cause. Now was the time to think of Frances and of Frances only.

Standing with his bare feet in the freezing sea he told himself that he had become a realist. He would take Frances away to England, at once if possible. And after the war he would insist on his mother's return to England. After all he was a man and a soldier and must be expected to exert some authority over a female parent. The obvious idea that his mother need not stay over here forever came to him with a revelation of how much, up to now, he had sheerly been afraid of Ireland. It had seemed like a dark pit full of demons. Now it was suddenly clear that he had only to snap his fingers at these chained-up bogeys. Having 'given up' Pat Dumay was perhaps the crucial step. Henceforth he would act like a free person. He saw himself suddenly in the future, a strong *pater familias*, ruling his womenfolk and his children with a benevolent firmness. Even the idea of making Frances pregnant before he returned to the Front was no longer distasteful. Even the idea that he might never survive to see his son was now something at which he could look.

The sand and pebbles in the shallow foam beat on his feet which were almost too cold to feel pain. He stepped back and hobbled to a rock and began to dry his benumbed feet on his socks. A moving shaft of sunlight came across the beach and made the sea sparkle in front of him and gave him a shadow on the sand. His thoughts reverted to the matter of his Aunt Millicent. Millie, as he now rather self-consciously thought of her, had never in fact been very far from his mind since the incident of the lapis lazuli earring. He had wondered again and again whether she had dropped the earring into the pool on purpose. He kept coming to the delightful conclusion that probably she had, and smiled every time he reached it. The situation in which she had put him, of having to make teatime conversation while at the same time keeping the earring under control in some reasonably secure part of his underclothing, had embarrassed him exceedingly at the time and amused him exceedingly afterwards. He felt, about it all, a sense of achievement. He had returned the earring in an envelope next day with a short note which, after numerous re-writings, simply read: *And thank you for my tea!* Really the little drama had excited Andrew quite considerably. He was not sure whether he had been played with as a child or flirted with as an adult, but again successive examinations of the subject brought the more flattering conclusion. His charming aunt had flirted with him. Andrew had never been flirted with in quite this way by an older woman. There came with it, with Millie herself, the faintest whiff of wickedness which he laughed to find so attractive. Women were gay and beautiful and he was young and free. But of course he knew this in any case. And Millie was only his aunt.

He was young and free, but now he was going to bind himself to the dearest girl in the world. He was so happy to find himself eager, to find, when it came to it, no grain of regret. He could give his whole heart. He had rehearsed the scene so often in imagination. Only he had not anticipated the sonnet. That arrived, sent by the gods at just the right moment, like an engagement present. He decided that he would, her clothes permitting, tuck the sonnet into the front of Frances' dress. Then he laughed to think that he was copying Millie. There was also the matter of the ring. On the previous day Hilda, displaying for once some sense of the tempo of others, had produced for him a gold ring set with a ruby and two diamonds which she had got in Dublin with Christopher's help and which she said she was sure would fit Frances. She handed it over to him with no further admonitions. The ring, when Andrew brooded over it later, seemed an almost heart-breakingly beautiful and significant object. Suddenly the romance, the sweetness, the innocence of his union with Frances came before him with an intensity which wrought him to tears.

Now on Thursday morning he was waiting in the garden, waiting near the red swing for Frances to come out of the house. She had been busy with some domestic task when he arrived and had told him to await her outside. Andrew, who had earlier envisaged, indeed planned, the scene quite calmly, now felt dizzy with excitement. He had the sonnet in one pocket of his jacket and the ring wrapped up in his handkerchief in the other pocket. He kept fingering them both and the sonnet was becoming rather crumpled. His heart was hitting his side as if it wanted to fly out of him like a cannon ball and his breath came in short desperate sniffs of the quiet stifling morning air. The day, bright to begin with, had clouded over. He began to fiddle with the swing, and then turned to find Frances quite close to him.

The dear girl was looking so beautiful this morning, her plump round face rosy and smooth, cool and sleek as the surface of an apple. It was one of the days when she revealed her big brow, and her hair was pushed back, still in something of an early morning tangle, behind her ears. She was wearing a long grey dress of coarse cotton, rather like a nurse's overall, caught in at the waist, and over it rather quaintly one of Christopher's tweed jackets, caught up no doubt as she left the house. She had turned up the collar of the jacket round her neck and her hands were thrust into the pockets. She had never looked sweeter.

Seeing something portentous in Andrew's look, Frances was silent waiting for him to speak.

Trembling all over he began. 'My dearest Frances, I have something of very great importance to ask you. I wonder if you can at all guess what it is?' His voice trembled and quavered too.

'No,' said Frances.

'I wish you to do me the honour of becoming my wife.'

There was a silence. Then Frances abruptly turned her back upon him.

Andrew stood quite still, staring at the tousled pile of Frances' dark hair appearing over the top of Christopher's jacket. He felt startled and breathless as if he had inadvertently struck her. He had not realized that his sudden words would arouse so much emotion in her. But of course the gracious imaginary Frances was not thus taken by surprise. He put out a reassuring hand to touch her sleeve. Without turning she moved a step away.

'Frances—'

'Hang on a minute, Andrew.'

The silence continued. Andrew stood staring at her back. His hands in his two pockets twisted the sonnet and fumbled the ring. A light wind was blowing now from the sea, stirring the chestnut tree and the tall leaves of the montbretia, stirring the red swing.

Frances began to turn slowly about. Her hand had not left her pockets. But now she raised one and drew it over her face as if erasing whatever expression had been there before. She coughed, as if a cough would set some helpful tone of ordinariness. Then she said, 'Thank you very much, Andrew.'

Andrew stared at her face. It was the strongest face he had ever seen her wear and the grimmest. Her long mouth curved downwards at the corners with a positive force and her eyes were wrinkled into what seemed two dark narrow rectangles.

'Frances—'

'Oh , my dear—'

'Frances, darling, what is it? Don't be upset.'

'Andrew, it's that I can't say yes. At least, I can't just say yes.'

Andrew opened his fingers and drew them out of his pockets. He wiped his hands together. 'I see—'. He felt completely confused and frightened. He felt as if he were in the presence of Frances for the first time, as if the real Frances had just broken through a screen upon which a picture of her had been painted. It was difficult to put words together. Speech between them had been a kind of silence. Now suddenly it had become something noisy, crackling, arduous. 'What do you mean by "just", that you can't "just" say yes?'

Frances seemed to find it equally difficult to speak. She

stared down at the ground. 'Well, I can't say yes. But I mean it isn't that things are different. It's just—oh dear—'

'But, but—you do love me? You haven't stopped loving me?' He had never known a world without Frances' love.

'Of course I love you.'

'And I love you, dearest Frances, and I want you to be my wife. I expect you're cross with me because I didn't say anything sooner, but you see—'

'It's not that and I'm not cross with you. I'm cross with myself.'

'I don't understand.'

'We've both taken it—so much for granted—too much for granted. And, everyone else assuming it too. It hasn't some-how been quite right—'

'I see. You feel I ought to have courted you properly—that we know each other too well. But I *will* court you—'

'No, no nonsense like that. You see in a way we are like brother and sister.'

'I don't feel we are like brother and sister at this moment,' said Andrew. He had never found Frances more ferociously attractive. She looked up at him quickly. 'And neither do you,' he added.

She gazed at him, her fiercely controlled face relaxing a little. 'Yes. Odd. Well, not odd. But, Andrew, I'm sorry. I've given you a rotten answer.'

'You've given me an incomprehensible answer. But I do understand about—how it's all been taken for granted. As if we weren't private people. I've felt funny about that too. But that can't have spoilt everything. Suppose we were to start again at the beginning as if we'd never met?'

'But we can't—'

'I don't know. For the last five minutes I've been talking to a most exciting stranger.'

'I feel like that too. But it's just that our friendship has had a shock. Oh, dearest Andrew, I do love you—'

'In that case—Frances, is there somebody else?'

'No, of course not,'

'Well, then—is it just that you'd like to wait a bit? We may have known each other since childhood, but we haven't seen a lot of each other lately. Maybe we need time to get used to each other again.'

'There's been so much sort of—quiet pressure—'

'Of course, of course. I know, all these people expecting us to get married next week—it's awful—and I know—for a girl —Oh, Frances, I'm sorry I've been so stupid. What you're really saying to me is yes, only let's wait a longer time before getting married. That's it, isn't it?'

'Well, no it isn't quite. I'm not saying that.'

'Then you're saying no?'

'Not exactly—but I have to be fair—I can't tie you—'

'But I am tied—I love you. You mean you *are* saying no?'

'You're forcing me to say no!'

'No, I'm not. I'm just trying to understand,' he said, miserably.

'I can't tie you,' she repeated, 'so if you force me to say something I've got to say no.'

'I'm not forcing you to say anything. I'm just asking you to marry me. I would have asked you much sooner if I'd thought you'd changed.'

'But I haven't changed.'

'You must have. I just want to know what your feelings are. Do you want me to wait a while and ask you again?'

'Perhaps I do—but this is so unfair, so unfair. I should only say no again. It's that I don't want to hurt you and I want everything to be happy like it was.' She closed her eyes and a great many tears streamed down her cheeks. She took a large white handkerchief smelling of tobacco out of the pocket of Christopher's jacket and blew her nose. It was beginning to rain.

'Well,' said Andrew, 'I'll ask you again later.'

ELEVEN

'I should only say no again,' she said in a frantic tone.

'I'll ask you all the same.'

They stood for a moment silently in the light rain, each looking down at the other's feet. Frances said, 'Please don't say anything about this to anyone just yet, not for a few days. I'll have to break it to my father first—and I'll have somehow to find the right moment.'

'All right. But I can't hold out very long. My mother will be so upset—and I'm not very good at telling lies.'

'Oh, Andrew, forgive me. Oh dear, I must think, I must think. Won't you come in and have some coffee? It's really going to rain hard.'

'No,' said Andrew, 'I won't come in. I suppose I won't be able to come here any more.'

'But of course you must come here—'

'I don't think I'll want to, with everything different.'

They looked at each other suddenly terrified. Even the most dreadful words can be treated as a bad dream through which one reels with a kind of intoxication of horror. But the cold touch of action awakens the spirit to a world where what is dreadful has slowly and minutely to be lived.

For a second Andrew felt it all beyond his strength. He reached out clumsily to Frances as if to seize her arm, perhaps embrace her. But she drew back. They faced each other for a moment. Then she whispered, 'I am sorry, I am so very sorry,' and turned and ran into the house.

Andrew went out of the garden gate, turning up the collar of his greatcoat against the rain. He walked down the road to the sea. The very calm sea was lazily washing the rocks and for miles and miles over its level grey surface the heavy rain was falling.

Chapter Twelve

PAT was giddy with impatience. It was still only Thursday morning. Sunday rose up in front of him like a black cliff. The mountain must open to admit him, how he knew not. He could foresee nothing except that he would be fighting. This time next week he would have been fighting. Perhaps he would be dead. His first startled fear was diffused now into an aching desire for action, and his body was weary of the interim. In the two days since he had been told he had grimly lived the reality of it into himself. To the mystery of Sunday he was dedicated and resigned, become in every cell of his being a taut extension of that violent future. When it came he would enter upon it coldly. It was only the waiting which was an agony and a fever. He could hardly sleep at night but lay telling himself vividly and lucidly how much he needed sleep. His flesh twitched and ached with expectation.

There was much to do each day. He had attended a staff conference at Liberty Hall about the dovetailing of plans between the Citizen Army and the Volunteers, and had been impressed, as always, by the efficiency of Connolly's men. He had visited a quarry at Brittas where some gelignite was hidden which was to be rushed into Dublin on Sunday morning. He had checked over all the ammunition allotted to his own company, which was hidden, often in small quantities, in various places throughout the city, and made arrangements for it to be moved at short notice. He had made a point of seeing individually all the men under his command, and, without revealing anything, satisfying himself that they were equipped and ready.

Pat was one of the most junior officers to have been told of the plan. The great majority of the Volunteers, including some officers, knew nothing except that 'very important manœuvres' were to take place on Sunday and that 'the absence of any Volunteer would be treated as a serious breach of discipline'. Of course, the men had been told, from long ago, that they must be prepared for anything on any occasion when they marched out in arms. But they had marched out in arms so often and returned afterwards to their tea. There was a ferment in Dublin all the same, which it was to be hoped was not attracting the attention of the Castle. Visiting Lawlor's gun shop in Fownes Street, Pat had found it almost emptied of stock. Streams of people had been in to buy bandoliers and water bottles and even sheath knives; and it was said that you could not get hold of a bayonet from one end of Dublin to the other. Perhaps the men were simply 'stocking up', for the 'important manœuvres'. Or perhaps the news was gradually leaking out to the rank and file. If so, this was dangerous. It was still only Thursday.

To most of us at most times past history seems like a brightly lit and faintly clamorous procession, while the present is a dark rumbling corridor off which, in hidden shafts and private rooms, our personal stories are enacted. Elsewhere in that obscure continuum, and out of quite other stuff, history is manufactured. Rarely are we able to be the intelligent specta-tors of an historical event, more rarely still its actors. At such times the darkness lightens and the space contracts until we apprehend the rhythm of our daily actions as the rhythm of a much larger scheme which has included us within its composi-tion. Pat felt for the first time this nearness of history, this almost physical sense of a connection with it, when he learnt that on the previous day at a secret meeting Patrick Pearse had been appointed President of the Irish Republic.

At the same meeting James Connolly had been appointed commandant general of the Dublin district and MacDonagh commandant of the Dublin brigade. Final decisions had also been taken about what points of the city should be occupied. There was argument about where the military headquarters should be. Connolly had favoured the ready-made fortress of the Bank of Ireland. But eventually the choice fell upon the General Post Office in Sackville Street. The fate of Dublin Castle was then debated. Pearse had been for attacking the Castle, but Connolly had opposed this. The 'Castle' in fact consisted of a straggle of buildings which would be hard to defend, and there was also a Red Cross hospital inside it. A full attack on the Castle seemed to present too many problems, and it was resolved instead to isolate it by occupying the City Hall and the offices of the *Evening Mail* opposite the gates.

Pat, who had thought long and soberly about the shortage of arms, had food now for further gloomy reflection as he reviewed the gratuitous folly of his leaders. It was surely essential that Dublin Castle should be attacked and preferably burnt. It was the Bastille of the regime, the symbol of its brutality. The Post Office was an insane choice as head-quarters: a building hemmed in by others and quite unsuitable for a prolonged defence. In any case, the whole scheme of establishing fixed strong points inside the city was ill-considered. Faced with an enemy who possessed and would use artillery, some degree of mobility was essential. Mobile troops could also make more use of the good will of the civilian population. A number of flying columns, able to retire rapidly out of the city if necessary, would do the enemy more damage, and baffle and scare him far more than a number of isolated strongholds, however bravely defended. There were two thousand five hundred British troops in the city itself and more at the Curragh. The joint forces of the I.C.A. and the Volunteers might reach twelve or fifteen hundred at a good turn-out. Mobile forces could seem more numerous than they were. Static forces could be studied and counted. But revolutionary leaders can be just as childish and old-fashioned and romantic as the most reactionary of regular soldiers. There was even a plan to occupy Stephen's Green and dig trenches there, although it was agreed that there were not enough men to take the Shelbourne Hotel; and this particular 'strong point' could be dealt with in a matter of minutes by a Lewis gun on top of the Shelbourne.

Pat reflected coolly on the folly of it all, the shortage of arms, the absence of sensible plans, the lack of elementary medical supplies and medical skill. He thought that he could accept death now, for himself and others, a death for Ireland. But driving his imagination on to savour the worst that was possible he pictured himself, unaided and horribly wounded, unable to stop from moaning and crying out, lying in the back of some wrecked blood-spattered room, while his comrades knelt at the window returning the enemy fire. At that time he would be empty of destiny. History would exist no more. Even Ireland would exist no more. There would be just a half-crushed animal screaming to be allowed to live: screaming perhaps to be allowed to die. He wanted now to be beyond prayer, to ask nothing more for himself as if he had already ceased to be. But he could not help clasping to him, as an amulet, the hope that if he were to die he might die quickly.

Yet in spite of all these reasons for a steady pessimism Pat could not, at the same time, at the back of his blackest arguments, help feeling a most tremendous glow of hope. He had heard Pearse say that the armed rising was to be thought of simply as a sacrifice of blood, after which Ireland would be spiritually reborn. Pearse said that Ireland needed martyrs. Pat agreed that Ireland needed martyrs. But he felt, felt within his own body, as if it came up out of the old tortured soil, the great angry strength of Ireland. At one with this power he felt superhumanly strong; and if there were but a few others like him they would make an irresistible tide. These were feelings rather than thoughts and did not belong to his rational part. Eamonn Ceannt, who had given him the news of the secret council, had said, 'If we can last a month the British will come to terms,' and Pat had replied, 'We won't last a week!' But he had not judged this with his heart. He could not stop imagining that as soon as the first shot was fired the whole of Ireland would rise.

It was only Thursday and between now and Sunday much could happen for good or ill. There were the persistent rumours about German arms, constantly revived from some mysterious source, to which Pat gave little credit. There was, more seriously, the possibility that the Castle might strike first. The document giving details of the planned military 'swoop' was, he was still sure, a clever provocative forgery by some such genius as Joseph Plunkett. But it was just possible that it was not, and it was always possible that with so many men in Dublin in the secret the news of the rising would leak out and the military would act quickly. If that happened, Pat knew that he would resist, he would fight, even if he were alone. To be, at this last moment, tamely disarmed would break his heart forever.

There was also the problem of MacNeill and Hobson, nominal leaders of the Volunteers, indeed in the eyes of the innocent rank and file the true leaders: MacNeill and Hobson, the 'moderates', who viewed the idea of fighting with horror and who were entirely unaware that the organization which they headed had been hollowed out by a secret hierarchy of power which left them at the top, isolated. At some point before Sunday they would be told, or would find out. At some point, somehow, the real leaders had got to sweep the nominal leaders aside. Pat felt uneasily that his masters had not got the answer to this problem: that they were waiting to see and hoping for the best. They would act on the spur of the moment. He also, with a pain that never left his consciousness, knew that there was a personal problem to which he himself had not found the solution and which he too would perhaps have to solve, when it came up, on the spur of the moment.

Pat was about to leave Millie's house in Upper Mount Street. He had detailed men to remove the arms and ammunition from the cellar on Saturday night and take it to a house in

Ballybough Road which was being used as an arsenal. Dublin would be full of mysterious horses and carts on that night. But these risks had to be run, and Pat, who had often performed such operations under the noses of the British, did not regard them very seriously. He had just now, with the help of his sergeant, packed the goods up into manageable bundles, and the man had left unobtrusively by the side door. Millie's servants were, happily, creatures of habit. For Millie herself Pat had invented a good enough story about why the arms had to be moved. In any case she might well be at Rathblane for the weekend.

Pat had been frequently questioned by his superior officers concerning Millie, initially concerning her reliability. He had on one occasion been disgusted to detect an assumption that his relationship with Millie must be of a sentimental kind. He had satisfied others, as he had satisfied himself, concerning her trustworthiness. Millie was a very silly woman; in a word, she was a woman. But she was capable of a strength of discretion which Pat somehow connected with her undoubted physical courage. More lately his superiors had asked him different questions. Millie had been trained as a nurse. She was also a good shot. Should she not simply be enlisted? To this Pat had said curtly no. It was not that he was not prepared to trust Millie all the way or that he thought she would necessarily draw back if asked. She was reckless enough for anything and might well embrace the project simply as an adventure. But he just did not want, at this sacred and holy crisis of his life, to have to bother about Millie at all. When Sunday came Millie and all she stood for would be left behind.

'Pat!'

He stopped in the hallway and cursed. In another minute he would have been clear of the house.

'Pat, come up here. I've got something important to tell you.'

He looked up through the dim cage of the stairs and saw her

somewhere farther up sitting on a step and peering down. He hesitated and decided he had better hear what she had to say. He came slowly up.

When she saw him coming she jumped up, enticingly, like a dog, and ran ahead of him. He noticed with repulsion that she was wearing trousers.

The door of Millie's 'shooting gallery' stood open and it was grey and murky within. A light rain rapped the skylight and ran steadily down the big window at the near end of the room where the small satiny chairs, thickly fringed down to the carpet, stood grouped about Millie's white dressing-table. The mirror was leaden, reflecting nothing, like a dull slab of metal behind the altar-like table. There was a faint unpleasant smell of flowers. In the dim light the scene had the air of a derelict chapel which had been perverted to some other purpose.

Pat came in reluctantly and Millie at once whisked round behind him to close the door. She returned to the dressing-table and stood there posed, as if at attention, her prominent eyes glistening with appetite. In the black tight trousers she looked like a principal boy in an operetta, vivacious, vulgar and about to become extremely noisy.

'Well?' He wondered if she had heard something. If she had, this was going to be awkward.

'Pat, do sit down.'

He looked round for a hard chair. There wasn't one. 'I'll stand, thank you.'

'Have some madeira. I've got some awfully good madeira here and some cake. See, it's all set out.'

'No, thank you. You had something to say?'

'It's so dark in here. It always gets so dark when it rains. I wonder if I should light the gas? One might as well draw the curtains really, it's like the night time.'

'I've only got a minute.'

'Do you like these white daffodils? They're rather unusual, aren't they? They're from Rathblane. I think it's so uncanny when flowers don't have their proper colours. How late the spring is this year. Well, I suppose one says that every year. Do you mind if I have some madeira?'

Pat watched her silently. Her hand shook as she poured out the madeira and the decanter struck the rim of the class with a loud ring.

Millie examined the glass to see if it was cracked. 'How clumsy I am. Pat, do sit down.'

'I can't, I'm in a hurry.'

'Don't be. I do wish you'd come down to Rathblane now and again. You haven't been there since you were a boy, have you. And I've got such a fine grand horse for you to ride, he's called Owen Roe, and you could have him any time.'

'If you've got something to say, say it.'

'Well, it's nothing special really. I just wanted to talk to you. We never seem to meet and talk to each other properly and that seems such a shame.'

'I have very little time for social conversation, you must excuse me.' Pat began to make the movements of departure. He did not think now that Millie knew anything about Sunday.

There was a sudden noisy flurry in the dark room and Millie moved quickly, plunging forward as if she were going to pick something up from the floor. She half fell, half darted forward, grunting like an animal, and blundered past him, butting him with her shoulder. In a moment she was leaning back against the closed door holding something in her hand. He saw her mouth open, moist and almost round as she drew breath, and saw that what she held in her hand was a revolver pointed at him.

For about two seconds Pat speculated. He had once, at the start, put it to himself that Millie might be or might become anything. She was an irresponsible, a person without a centre. She could be a spy in the pay of the Castle. Now suddenly and vividly he saw her as a traitor. In the third second he realized that of course this was only a piece of play-acting, a piece of Millie's usual tomfoolery. He stepped towards her and took the gun out of her hand. She held it lightly, scarcely resisting his fingers. He laid it down on the dressing-table, and as he turned back to her he inhaled the sweet disagreeable odour of the white daffodils.

Millie was still leaning against the door, but her body which had been taut and fierce was now quite limp. She seemed like a figure made of soft wax which might bend or sag slowly to the floor, at any moment. Her face was vague and dazed, her eyes half closed. She said very softly, 'Just for a second you were afraid of me. Oh, oh, oh—'

'You shouldn't play with those things,' said Pat. Of course he had not been afraid of her, but he was angry that she should have seen his mind, and disgusted at the way she had suddenly transformed herself into an animal.

'I was in earnest, you know—for a moment anyway. You were so *rude*. Why can't you be ordinarily polite to me? I've stored all that stuff for you and never questioned you or bothered you. And you know I've told nobody.'

'If I've been rude I apologize.'

'You can't apologize just by saying "I apologize", not in that tone of voice. Of course you've been rude. But it's not that I mind. Sit down.'

Pat sat down.

He felt Millie lean heavily on the back of his chair, and then she had sat down close opposite to him, staring. Her face resembled a Roman mask, huge-eyed and open-mouthed, strained and painful and yet at the same time lewd. The rain seemed to have stopped and there was a little more light and colour in the room. Beyond her head the daffodils were a white blur against the wet silvery window pane. Near to him Millie's features trembled for a moment, quivered all over like something seen through disturbed water. 'You don't like me very much, do you, Pat?'

'I wouldn't say that.'

'And yet in a way too you do like me, I feel it.'

'I don't know you at all—'

'That's just it. But you will get to know me, you will. I wish we could meet sometimes and talk, just talk of anything at all, that's in our minds. It would be good, wouldn't it? I feel we have so much to give each other. I wish you'd come sometimes, here or to Rathblane. Just to talk. I so much want to know you better. I need to.'

'I doubt if we'd have much to say to each other.'

'Please, Pat, please, please, please. I beg you to come and see me.'

'Really—I have no time for visiting—I shall have to go directly.'

'I beg you.'

'I've got to go.' He got up hastily and kicked the soft chair aside, shuffling backwards.

'Pat, I'm so useless, my life is so useless, so empty. You could help me. You could tell me what to do to be of use. I would obey you.'

'There's nothing I can do—'

'I might really have shot you just now. Shot you first and myself after. Do you know how often I think of killing myself? Every day, every hour.'

Pat had got to the door. Fumbling behind him he found the handle, opened the door an inch and closed it again. He had been almost prepared to find it locked.

'I can't help you.'

'How can you be so cruel? You can help me with your little finger, with any look, any word. Don't you understand what I'm telling you? I love you.'

Pat's immediate feeling was simply of an embarrassed shock. Then there was something darker, like intense anger. He said at once, 'That's a foul lie.'

There was a pause in which he heard Millie's indrawn breath, a gasp like a gasp of triumph. She rose and circled behind her chair, keeping her distance from him. He curled with loathing, but his hand upon the door-handle seemed paralysed. The directness of his response to her seemed to have flung out a taut tingling connection between them and they were, as never before, present to each other.

Millie breathed slowly and deeply. Her face, clear in the brightening light from the window, wore an intense expression of happy cunning. She said softly, coaxingly, argumentatively, 'Well, it may be that it is not love. Yet it is fierce enough, deep enough to be love. Will you not test it? I want you.'

'Don't talk like that.'

'And you want me. All right, I know I disgust you. Strike me then.'

'Stop—'

'I know you better than you think. I know the twistings and turnings of your heart. I know you because at the bottom you and I are as like as two pins. You want to humiliate yourself. You want your will to drive you like a screaming animal into some dark place where you will be crushed utterly. You want to test yourself to the point where you can will the death of all that you are and stand aside coolly and watch it die. Come to me then. I will be your slave and your executioner. No other woman can please you. Only I, because I am hard and clever like a man. Only I can understand you and lift to you the face of the beauty that you really desire. Come to me, Pat.'

'Stop—'

'Come soon. Come before the month ends. Think that I shall be at Rathblane, in my bed, waiting for you. Come.'

Pat fumbled desperately with the door. He seemed to be turning the handle the wrong way. Then before he could get it open she had tumbled herself at his feet in a sort of animal onslaught. Her arms entwined him fiercely, pinching and pawing, while she babbled out incoherent supplications. Pat jerked the opening door violently against her and kicked himself free. As he rushed down the stairs and out of the house he felt his trousers damp at the knee from Millie's tears or kisses. He ran away as fast as he could along the shining wet pavements in the direction of Merrion Square.

Chapter Thirteen

ANDREW was riding to Rathblane on a bicycle borrowed from his mother's new gardener. It was Thursday afternoon and he was going to have tea with Millie. On Monday she had asked him and Frances to come to tea. Now he was going there by himself.

Andrew felt that he had received a violent blow which had in reality killed him, although he was still moving blindly about. He felt as he had felt when his father died. Grief had destroyed his ordinary self and now there was nothing but the grief and a body racked with physical pain which somehow accompanied it. Frances had been there so long, so long, an ultimate and invincible source of comfort. He had taken her to be eternal, and this deep sense of the permanence of love had been the essence of all his joys, even those apparently unconnected with her. To lead a life without her he would have to remake himself entirely. But there was no vital being left. She had been the hidden sun of his world. He had thought that world was beautiful just for him, an offering to his youth and his hope, whereas it was only she who had lent it brightness. Her affection and her intelligence had gilded everything. Now all that beauty was withdrawn into her veiled, forbidden figure and the world was ashen. He turned to and fro in despair, seeking a familiar support which should enable him to live through such misery, but the support was Frances.

He tried resolutely to become more rational and to confront his situation. He realized how dreadfully he had undervalued Frances, how stupidly he had taken her for granted. He ought to have behaved like one of Malory's Knights and treated her as a great and difficult trial of his worth. Yet they had known each other so well, with a simplicity which now seemed to him a source of infection.

Surely things *had* been all right, their long love had not been illusion? What had gone wrong? Was it perhaps that Frances had thought him too casual, and was thrusting him away so that he might return again more ardently? But such a policy was inconceivable in her. She was incapable of ruse. There were no mysteries here out of which dramas could be made. She was his oldest friend, and if she wanted him she would take him as he was, without gallantry. The truth was that she was exercising her last inalienable and terrible natural right, the free disposition of the heart. She simply did not want him.

Absolute devotion of one human being to another is comparatively rare, yet such is the dazzling light of egoism in which each of us lives that when devotion fails us in some quarter where we have looked to find it we feel amazement, shocked surprise, that so great a value should not be an object of love. And amid his shame and his misery Andrew felt also quite distinctly this surprise, which he did not then recognize as the germ of a healing selfishness which would in time make his pain diminish. How *could* Frances abandon him? It seemed inconceivable that she should have deliberately ended their long happy companionship and made it impossible for him to come to her any more. Would it not, tomorrow, be as it was? But he knew in his slowly sobering heart that he had not been teased, provoked, played with or simply asked to wait. He had been rejected.

He was already nearing Rathblane, which he had not visited for a number of years, and was surprised to notice that he had found his way there quite unconsciously. Looking at the road now, he found it uncomfortably memorable, loaded with some pungent but undeclared consciousness out of his childhood. Some vanished self had made that landscape live. And it accosted him now like an old friend who fails to realize that one has changed utterly.

Rathblane was about fifteen miles south of Dublin, situated in a fold of the Dublin mountains not far from the river

Dodder. Without reflection Andrew had taken the road through Stillorgan and turned inland at Cabinteely. It was a windy day. Little round clouds like smoke rings hung high over the sea, but inland the sky was crowded with bulbous folds of grey and golden stuff which formed a huge and alarmingly three-dimensional world, gathering, rearing and toppling with slow speed only just above the tops of the mountains. The peak of Kippure, now coming into view, was a dark slatey blue against a diminishing strip of fading yellow sky, as if the peak had already absorbed the dark ray of the coming night. But the little won fields of the nearer mountain sides, pressing upward almost vertically against the thick rusty surge of the heather, were an almost silvery light green, and the gorse hillocks, round which the black-faced sheep stood in circles, glowed a rich yellow in the afternoon sun with a light which seemed to come from within their dense humps of golden flowers.

Andrew had dismounted now and was walking on the rough road up the ridge which separated him from Rathblane. The crumbling domain wall on his right, overgrown with brambles and valerian, seemed like a natural excrescence. A little rain had welcomed him into the wilder country, but now it was dry again. Near by the left side of the road they had been cutting turf, and the thick dark undersoil of the bog, the consistency of sticky fudge, glistened in the momentary sun. Weary with pushing his bike over the stones, Andrew wondered why he had bothered to come at all. There was little point in it now and he could easily have sent an excuse. Well, it was something to do. And it was a pretext for escaping from Claresville where the arrival of the furniture had sent his mother into a state of unbearable excitement, setting up all sorts of painfully domestic trains of thought. Hilda had even uttered the word 'nursery'. His imposed silence was a torture to him, and to be taken to be happy when he was in fact the most wretched man in the world. He mounted the bicycle again and jolted down the hill, through the entrance gates between the battered stone griffins, into a sudden windless hush.

Rathblane was a Georgian house of moderate size, grey and rather tall, with an irregular front, bowed and buttress-like at one end, and smooth and balustraded at the other. Some further extension of the house had been intended but never built. It stood in a large square of trees which separated it entirely from the open country. An eighteenth-century print showed the house in a vista, but nineteenth-century Kinnards had zealously planted innumerable varieties of trees, many of them rare ones, so that boughs of gingko and catalpa and liquidambar, grown into a dense matrix, now concealed the house in a web of closely woven quietness so intense, after the windy expanse of the mountain road, as to make the unsuspecting visitor gasp. Seen only at the last moment within its thick green architecture, Rathblane had that formidable sinister stillness of the Irish country house, a stillness which is perhaps something to do with the Irish air, or is more simply due to the continued absence of the owners or to the premonition that, on coming close to the handsome façade, one will suddenly see the open sky through the upper windows.

Andrew turned the last corner of the drive and saw the big grey buttresses still deep in trees. The bumpy drive led on beside a stone wall toward the stables, but the front door of the house had to be approached across a small unmown lawn where a semicircular stone staircase with white painted railings descended directly into the rough rye grass. Andrew propped his bicycle against the wall and walked across to the steps. He pushed open the heavy door and came into the hall which always smelt of stale bread. There seemed to be no one about, so he wandered through into the big bow-windowed drawing-room.

'Why, Andrew!'

It was immediately and painfully apparent that he was not expected. Millie had forgotten all about inviting him, had forgotten all about his existence. Andrew stared at her miserably.

'Andrew, how lovely that you've come. Tea will be in directly. I was just expecting you to arrive. Where's Frances?'

'She couldn't manage it after all. She sends apologies.'

'What a shame. Excuse me for a second while I hurry on the tea.'

Andrew went and leaned his head against the window which looked out at the back of the house. Here there was a narrow pavement of irregular stones, much overgrown with long fluffy yellow moss, in the crannies of which numerous little blue flowers were growing. Beyond that was a small paddock in which a chestnut horse idled, and beyond that the circle of the trees again, each motionless leaf distinct in the sombre vivid light. The sun was clouded and there was an expectation of rain.

'I see you're admiring my scillas. Aren't they little darlings? The bluest things in the world. I wish I had eyes that colour! However did you get here?' Millie was wearing a big swirling gown of some scaley mauvish material which looked as if it were wet, a black sash and a large black silk collar which looked arbitrary enough to be part of the clothing of a nun. Above it, her plump pretty face was smiling almost too vigorously and for a second it occurred to Andrew that she might have been crying.

In answer to her question Andrew, feeling very unhappy and now sulky as well, said, 'Bike'.

'Bike? Over all these hills? You're a hero. Oh, thank you, Maudie, just put the trolley here, would you, and could you put some more turf on the fire? Indian or China, Andrew?'

'Indian.'

'You should have hired a horse, you'd have been here in half the time, and there's a lovely way you can ride by Glencree.'

'I don't like horses.'

'You, *what?*' This information for some reason amused Millie very much. It seemed to cheer her up. 'The little pet! And you a cavalry officer! I hope you've kept it a secret. But of course I don't believe you. Now I want nothing so much as to see you on board. You shall come down here often, and we'll have a gallop together. I've got such a fine grand horse for you to ride, he's called Owen Roe, and you could have him any time.'

'I'm afraid I shall be leaving for Longford almost at once, Aunt Millicent.'

'Aunt Millicent, indeed! It was today, wasn't it, that you were to start calling me Millie. What a pity dear Frances isn't here, you could have begun the new regime together. Eh, Andrew? Now you must say "yes, Millie".'

'Yes, Millie.'

'That's better. Well, well, Longford is it? I suppose King and Country are after you. What's your regiment, I always forget.'

'King Edward's Horse.'

'And a fine lot of fellows they are too. How the uniform suits you, especially those boots. I'm sure you'll distinguish yourself. Have some of Maudie's lemon cake. Dear God, I think it's going to rain again, what a country. Listen, can you hear the nuthatches singing? Quee, quee, quee. They always sing like that just before it rains, or maybe it's just that the air is clearer then and one hears them. They're building in the old wall, I'll show you the nest. You'll stay for dinner and the night of course?'

'No, sorry, I've got to get back, Aunt Millicent.'

'Well, I won't keep you from your Frances. But I shall have to punish you every time you call me "Aunt Millicent"! You're getting a bit big to slap. How old are you now, dear boy?'

'Twenty-one.'

'You lucky child. I wish I were. You look quite the young

man, I must say, and I adore your moustache. I shall come and sit beside you.'

Millie drove the tea trolley away with her feet and bounced heavily on to the sofa beside Andrew.

Andrew edged himself away from her. He fumbled in his pocket for his handkerchief to wipe the lemon cake off his fingers. As he drew out the handkerchief something else came out too and fell on to the rug at his feet. It was the ruby and diamond ring.

Millie saw the ring and promptly picked it up. At once she slipped it on to her finger and held it up to admire it, flashing it to and fro. 'What an awfully pretty ring! And it just fits me. But of course, it must be Frances' engagement ring. How romantic! Am I the first person to see it? You shouldn't carry it loose like that in your pocket, silly boy, you'll lose it. Haven't you got a little box for it?'

Andrew said, 'I've got a box—'. Then he stopped. His voice was not under his control and he felt that if he continued to talk he would croak and then burst into tears. He sat in paralysed silence staring at the carpet.

After a pause he felt Millie touching his shoulder. 'Something's happened, something's gone wrong?'

He nodded.

'Very wrong?'

He nodded.

'Oh God. She's refused you.'

'Yes.' He put his hand to his eyes which were suddenly wet with tears. He realized that Millie had left him, getting up abruptly and going to the window.

'Why?' she said. 'Why?'

'Why not?' said Andrew, mopping up the tears with his handkerchief. 'Just because we've always been sort of promised to each other it doesn't mean—in fact perhaps that's the reason. In a way we've been too close. She says we've been like brother and sister.'

'Brother and sister!' Millie laughed shortly. 'You don't think there's any special reason, anything to do with her father perhaps?'

'No. Christopher's always been in favour.'

'She'll come round, surely?'

'No, I'm certain she won't. That's why I'm going away as soon as I can.'

'Your mother must be knocked by this.'

'She doesn't know yet. Frances asked me to tell nobody for a few days until she's had time to break it to Christopher.'

'Ah— Don't worry, I'll be discreet. I *can* be. But I'm being so thoughtless questioning you like this. Why, the child's in tears! Come now, let's have some sherry, shall we? You need a drink. And I rather think I do too!'

In fact, Millie's brisk questions had done Andrew good. The tears had come and gone. He felt a little better. He sipped the sherry and felt warmer and more alive.

Millie came and sat beside him and took hold of his hand. 'You're infernally like my dear brother, your father. Did you love poor Henry?'

'Yes, of course.'

'I'm glad. Not all children love their parents these days. I loved him dearly. Well, well, so it's not to be Frances after all. But don't grieve. You're young and quite confoundedly good-looking. Just keep your head and you can have your pick of the fine girls of England and Ireland. I'll help you choose one.'

Andrew shook his head. He looked wearily at the sulky flames of the turf fire. 'No. There won't be anything else for me. Anyway I'm going to die young.' The thought was curiously cheering.

'That's always a solution, isn't it? Nonsense! I'm already looking forward to teaching your children to ride.'

'I don't think I could marry anybody but Frances. Maybe I'm not the marrying type.'

'Sweet boy, just look in the mirror! I wonder if you're really afraid of it, though. Have you ever had a girl?'

'No, of course not.'

'Now I've shocked you. But really never? Don't you want to terribly? Have some more sherry.'

Andrew settled back in the sofa, drawing his knees up. He found that he was still holding Millie's hand, and released it. Millie wriggled into a more comfortable position with her knee touching his. He was very embarrassed by the turn the conversation had taken, yet the sudden crudeness of it was a distraction, almost a consolation. 'I suppose I am frightened. I'm afraid it would be, well, a failure. Anyway the question doesn't arise any more.'

'It *will* arise, my child. You are a soldier. Damn it, Andrew, you are a man. You are inconceivably young. The next two or three years will be more full of events and changes than you can possibly imagine. Here, give me your hand again. How did it get away?'

'Oh, Millie, I don't know. Sometimes I feel frightened of everything. I'm so frightened of going back to France.'

'Any rational person would be frightened of that.' She pressed his hand, kneading it comfortably between her palms.

'It's good to talk to you.'

'You're a lonely chap really, aren't you? I wish you were staying here, there's a lot I could do for you! I must cheer you up, though. Don't you feel, even now, a little tiny bit pleased to be free, pleased to think that after all the big wide unpredictable world lies in front of you?'

'No, I just feel utterly wretched.'

'Well, it's a bit early. But that feeling will come. God, if I were your age and free, knowing what I know now! *Si la jeunesse savait, si la vieillesse pouvait!*'

'But you aren't in the least *vieille*, Millie, and I'm sure you can *pouvait* anything you like.'

'You're very sweet. Let me kiss you.'

The silky mauve knees edged a little over the khaki knees and Millie put her arm round Andrew's neck. She drew his head down towards her and kissed him on the cheek. Then shifting her arm to his shoulder and sliding more closely up against him she kissed him on the lips.

Andrew accepted her kiss with a kind of surprise. He had been conscious of her as a diffuse, warm, comforting animal presence. Now he became precisely aware of her body, aware of its posture and its closeness, of just where it touched his own and how it might be taken hold of. With a hurried gesture, half impulsive, half grateful, he slid his arm round her back and pressed his face awkwardly against hers. Then he drew away in confusion.

They stared at each other. Millie said softly, 'I didn't expect this.' She lifted his hand and laid it against her cheek. 'There you are—the big wide unpredictable world at its tricks already.'

'I'm sorry—' said Andrew.

'What for? You've done me so much good. I'm a disappointed person like you. And a person in a terrible fix. Never mind. But your coming today, and *this*—it's part of something just happy and innocent. You aren't frightened of me, are you?'

'No.'

'Then come kiss me, sweet and twenty, and kiss me properly this time.'

Andrew took a deep breath and then as Millie's body moved to him promptingly he took her firmly in his arms and thrusting her head back against the cushions of the sofa kissed her. It was difficult to let go. Half horrified and half exhilarated, he pulled himself away and stood up. 'I'm terribly sorry, Aunt Millicent.'

'There you go again, I shall really slap you in a minute. Do sit down. There at the far end, I won't touch you. That's right. Dear Andrew, you've altered the world for me. I was utterly miserable when you came. You remember what I said about the scillas being so blue? Well, they weren't blue, they were grey. They're blue now. You've made them blue.'

Andrew sat down. He felt both alarmed and ashamed, but he could not help also apprehending, in the very glow of his shame, his sheer male power over this handsome older woman.

'And you know, you know, Andrew, we can't leave it at that. It would be a crime.'

'What do you mean?'

'You said you were frightened of it. You said it might somehow be a failure. Well, let me teach you. With me it won't be a failure.'

For a moment Andrew did not understand her. Then he stared at her, silent, appalled.

'I've shocked you again. But let me persuade you. There's nothing wrong in it, no sin, you know. With you and me it would be just innocent and lovely. And it would take away all your fears.'

Andrew looked at her and his eyes were really frightened like those of a scared child. 'No, no, it's not—No—'

'Don't be a coward, Andrew. It's a beautiful, wonderful, God-sent chance. Nobody would know. And after that you would be really free. And you would make me so happy.'

'I couldn't—'

'I want you, Andrew. And you want me. That's something one can't be mistaken about.'

'No, really—Millie, I think I'd better be going.'

'What a cowardy custard you are. But I know I've rather sprung it on you. Well, I've rather sprung it on myself! And you're shocked to the core too. Just think about it. But oh, think quickly, my dear and beautiful boy, think quickly!'

They had both risen and Andrew was struggling into his greatcoat.

'Dear Andrew, you're not angry with me?'

'No—forgive me—' He took her hand and kissed it and laid it against his eyes, bowing before her.

'Well, I'll let you go now. Why, I'm still wearing Frances' ring. I'll give it back to you now. But when you come, when you *really* come, you shall give it to me as a present. No, no, sure I'm only joking. Are you going back on that bicycle? Wouldn't you like to ride back on Owen Roe? You could leave him at the stables in Harcourt Street.'

'No, thanks.'

She had led him to the front door and out into the damp darkening evening. A little light rain was just beginning to fall. The woolly black-faced sheep had come close to the steps, a crowd of quiet presences. The sky was a thin papery yellow and the peak of Kippure, just lifting above the trees, was jet black.

'I love it when the animals come right up to the house. You will come back, won't you, I mean come back anyway, just to talk. Why I'm almost crying, how absurd. There now, dear boy, you move me so—and I envy you. And it's not your freedom or your youth I'm after envying at this moment, it's your innocence.'

Chapter Fourteen

WERE there four candles or eight candles, Barney wondered as he knelt in extreme discomfort on the stone floor. He ought to know from the number of the psalm. The fifteen candles, burning upon the triangular candlestick, were extinguished one by one at the close of each psalm. But Barney had long ago lost his place. All he knew was that he had been there some time and that the floor was not only hard but also rather wet from the rain water which had trickled off the mackintoshes and umbrellas of the people who surrounded him. He had been there some time and before that he had been in a bar. He could not remember coming from the bar to the chapel. He had decided after all to come to Tenebrae, or evidently he had decided since here he was.

The chapel, which belonged to a small Dominican community, was a narrow concrete cave, situated off an obscure courtyard in Upper Gardiner Street. Barney knew none of the community, had found the place by accident, and liked it because of the austerity of its furnishings and because it was anonymous and unfrequented. Even now on the Thursday night the chairs provided for the congregation were only half filled. The chapel was entirely dark now except for the sanctuary light and the flickering candles which dimly and intermittently illuminated the two bowed lines of hooded black and white figures stretching away to the altar whereon rose the blurred shape of the shrouded crucifix. In the body of the chapel people knelt here and there in untidy heaps, hunched and sagging in the attitudes of those who have been kneeling for a long time, their mackintoshes piled up beside them. There was a smell of wet clothing and of wet stone.

Tenebrae factae sunt, dum crucifixissent Jesum Judaei: et circa horam nonam exclamavit Jesus voce magna: Deus meus,

ut quid me dereliquisti? Barney shifted his knees a little on the
floor and then sat back on his heels. In order to be more acutely
uncomfortable he had refused himself a hassock, and now his
knees felt like two cold alien metal plates rather roughly
attached to his legs. His thighs ached, his shoulders ached, and
there was a little creeping chilly pain in the small of his back.
He resisted the temptation to sit sideways on the floor. He
screwed up his eyes to look at the candles again and decided
there were four of them.

The intoning of the brothers continued monotonously,
expressionlessly, wearily. The penitents were huddled upon
the floor, a few of them peering at the words in their books, but
most of them humped in attitudes of stupefied abandonment
induced by spiritual misery or physical discomfort. What does
it all mean, thought Barney. Why had he come here? Wasn't it
the same to him now whether he was here or in the Mountjoy
bar? His emotions were the same, the familiar round of his
intentions and compulsions the same. He could have enacted
all this elsewhere. Even here it was only play-acting, only,
despite the dull voices of the brothers, despite the pain in his
knees, indeed because of these things, a kind of cosiness. He
was no stranger to remorse. Bitterly every day he regretted
what he had done, bitterly he regretted what he was doing in
the moment when he lifted his hand to do it. And the power to
change himself by an iota was simply not included in the
complex that he was. That power, if it existed, resided in some
other world, and since it was not native to him it could not
help him. Then he must cast himself on God's mercy. But
could there be such a thing; was it not, must it not be, a contra-
diction? Could a perfect being be merciful to what was imperfect? If he were to go *there* would he not simply be burnt up
automatically? *Ego autem sum vermis et non homo.*

Barney wondered if he ought to go to confession. Well, of
course he ought. Yet now the great austere impersonal
machinery of the Church which had once so much drawn him

seemed a hollow clattering mumbo-jumbo. Perhaps he had never become entirely used to the sacrament of confession. He could go at random to some unfamiliar priest, interrupting him in his perusal of the *Irish Times*, and kneel down and whisper some vague uncriticized account of what he had been doing and receive a flimsy penance and a preoccupied absolution. But he ought to be interrogated, he ought to be beaten. Punishment had no meaning where there was no personal relation between the punisher and the punished. And only punishment, it seemed to him, could now reintegrate him into the order of love. He would have to be punished by God Himself, nothing less would serve. *Quoniam ego in flagella paratus sum.*

How can guilt be taken away, how can it not drag the guilty one down and down? Did redemption exist, *could* it exist, was it not a strictly senseless idea? Could another save me by his suffering? If someone who is good suffers because I am evil and I see and contemplate that suffering might that not alter me and purify me almost automatically? But such contemplation is impossible precisely because I am evil. Human beings cannot look at affliction with uncorrupted eyes. If the suffering of a good person on my behalf could redeem me Kathleen would be an instrument of my salvation instead of being, as she is, an instrument of my damnation. *O vos omnes qui transitis per viam, attendite et videte.* But though he might look and look he could not really attend and see. The spectacle of Christ crucified changed nothing in his heart.

Why should not the sight of any innocent suffering have power to save? He remembered live fowls he had seen in the market, their legs tied together, thrown into dusty corners. Every hour, every second, the young rabbit squealed in the jaws of the fox, the owl flew silently through the night with the vole hanging limp from its beak. He knew of these things, this terrible knowledge was in him as it was in all human beings. But because of his own darkness it was all turned to darkness too and not to light. The appalling tenderness and guilt he had felt before the helpless creatures in the market made him in the end turn away with a curse. That the innocent suffer: this should startle the spirit into a self-denying purity forever. But instead there is only the callous indifference of a guilt felt to be ineradicable. He was on the side of the bad thief. *Me minavit et adduxit in tenebras et non in lucem.*

Was not even the bad thief saved perhaps in the end? Yet what could save him? It is as oneself that one must be saved, and not as another, if salvation has meaning at all. Barney could see plainly, as if a surgical light had been shone within him, that the machinery of his virtuous intent was simply not attached to the living animal that he really was. Nothing that moved here touched the great powerful thing underneath which went its way regardless. It was the strength of that thing, its fat strength, which made him despair. He had thought of himself as a man haunted at least by goodness, but these hauntings were merely the bog fires of his own psyche. His 'good resolutions' were not even play-acting, they were babbling. He did not know what the word 'good' meant. It was a parrot cry in his mouth. His whole substance was fit only for burning. *Non est sanitas in carne mea a facie irae tuae, non est pax in ossibus meis a facie peccatorum meorum.*

Barney had not yet made up his mind to tell Frances about Christopher's intentions. He wanted to desperately, if only in order to be able to act somehow in a situation which tortured him. He told himself that it was his duty to bring the truth out into the open so that everybody should be able to understand what they were doing. But ought people always to understand what they were doing and would that anyway be the result in this case? How was he, sunk in the muddle of his own life, to distinguish between virtuous truth-telling and wicked trouble-making? Frances would be extremely upset. But what would she do? She might postpone her own marriage and prevent her father's, both things which Barney wanted. Then what would

Millie's vengeance be? Could he hope to survive as Millie's favourite? It was too risky. Yet how tempting it was to tell Frances and see what happened. Had he really anything to lose? These debates, which usually began on a high moral level, ended inconclusively with the yapping and scratching tug-of-war of different forms of self-interest.

Of course there was one way in which Barney could be fairly sure that in telling Frances his motives would be good, and that was if he really resolved to give up Millie. It was odd how often he came back to this idea, odd considering how sunk he was in his devotion to her, sunk and drowned like a fly in treacle. It was meaningless to think of giving her up. Yet, quite abstractly, he would think of it again; and he would think of it because he knew perfectly well that what utterly poisoned his life was the beastliness of his relation to Kathleen. Kathleen was his wife, she was *there*, with the authority of an obligation which was rooted so deep in the nature of things that it continually compelled the attention if not the respect of the corrupted will. Kathleen could not be ignored, got round, shuffled away to suffer quietly in a dusty corner like the poor birds in the market. She could not suffer quietly, however silent she was, because she was a human being to whom he was irrevocably bound and he had to see her suffer, he had to see himself making her suffer.

There was no limit to his offence against her, or the limit came only with the limit of himself. Everything he was, was offence. It was the sense of this which made him despair and curse. She seemed to turn every part of him into the stuff of his own damnation. His Memoir, into which he had put so much of his creative power and which had proved such a consolation, was in the end simply a weapon against Kathleen. There had to be somewhere which was safe from her, some place where he was justified and she was judged. In real life she was all judge, even when she said nothing. In the Memoir everything was reversed and the unfairness of life was done away with and that dreadful power was quenched. There were times when the Memoir seemed to Barney the only clean and clear thing in the world. Yet there were always other times when he knew that it was a sin, perhaps his greatest sin, the final corruption of what might have remained unstained, his intellect, his talents. What he wrote in the Memoir was not quite true, and that 'not quite' was the stuff of a most wicked lie. *Vinea mea electa, ego te plantavi. Quomoda conversa es in amaritudinem ut me crucifigeres et Barabbam dimitteres?*

*　　*　　*　　*

Barney opened his eyes. He was sitting sideways on the floor and leaning against the next chair which he had pulled towards him. His head and arm were resting on the chair. He must have fallen asleep.

The chapel was dark and silent and empty. The office had ended and everyone had gone away leaving him there sleeping. The plain walls of the chapel seemed like a dark tunnel at the far end of which the sanctuary light flickered dimly, seeming to give out no illumination but to be a light completely surrounded by darkness up to the very confine of itself.

Barney looked at the light. The last thing he remembered before sleeping was that piercing reproach, *Vinea mea electa* . . . It seemed to him that it was the most annihilating reproach in the whole world. Yet why was it so? Because it was also, in a way which one could not possibly mistake, the voice of love. Could reproach and love become so nearly identical? Yes, for this is the nature of the magnet by which what is good draws what is partly evil, by which perhaps mysteriously it may even draw what is wholly evil. The light cast from a perfect centre cannot but define what is imperfect in a revelation which is both rebuke and summons.

Barney returned to his knees. He was extremely stiff and cold and his head ached. It must be very late now, perhaps it was already the morning of Good Friday. He stared at the sanctuary light and felt the certain almost bodily presence of perfect Goodness. And with this he felt, as he had not felt it before, an absolute certainty of his own existence. He existed and God, opposite to him, existed too. And if he was not, by that juxtaposition, simply dissolved into nothing it could only be because God was love.

At the same moment it also became perfectly clear to Barney that everything which he had dreamt of vaguely as good in some way which simply did not concern him was not only possible but even easy. He could give up Millie, he could tear up his Memoir, he could confess everything to Kathleen and start a new life with her and learn to love her properly. He could make everything simple and innocent once again, and in that instant he knew too that if he lifted so much as a finger to attempt that simplicity and that innocence he would receive, from the other region which had seemed so far away outside him, the inrush of an entirely new strength. He had thought himself so lost, so astronomically far removed that there was no nearer or further any more and no sense in the idea of a way. But all the time he had been held so close that he could not escape even if he would. *Quoniam sagittae tuae infixae sunt mihi et confirmasti super me manum tuam.*

Chapter Fifteen

'OH, I feel so happy!'

Hilda threw her gloves down on a packing-case in the hall and began with delicate exact movements to pluck the hat-pin out of her large velvet hat. She had just returned from attending the earlier part of the three-hour Good Friday service at the Mariners' Church.

'I'm as hungry as a hunter. I expect you are too, Andrew. I'll bring out the cold luncheon directly. You really should have come to church, it was wonderful. Such inspiring addresses. I suppose one ought to be feeling sad on Good Friday, but I always feel so exalted, even more than on Easter day.'

Andrew looked down at her gloomily through the banisters. He was engaged in tacking down the carpet on the upper landing. 'Yes, Mother. I'm just coming down. Where do you want the gilt mirror put? I've found the hooks for it.'

'Oh, opposite the door, I think, it will enlarge the hall, and we'll put the tropical birds in front of it. It's going to be such a pretty house, isn't it, Andrew? It really makes me terribly happy. Christopher is coming round to see it after luncheon. I saw Frances at church, but she said she couldn't come as she had a Comforts for the Troops meeting. But of course she'll have told you.'

Hilda bustled away into the kitchen, humming loudly. A moment later he heard her voice raised in rather self-conscious shrillness above the purr of the taps. '*When I survey the Wondrous Cross...*'

Claresville was indeed a charming little house, but everything about it filled Andrew with misery. It was situated in the steep labyrinthine part of Dalkey below the Loreto convent and above Bullock Harbour, convenient (as the prospectus said) to St Patrick's (Church of Ireland) and commanding from its upper window a handsome view of Dublin Bay. It was a solid nineteenth-century villa with Gothic windows and a high-peaked lattice porch, 'quaint' features also commended in the prospectus. The smooth stucco was painted a dark dusty pink, except for the raised bands of white which outlined the windows. There was an extensive garden on several levels with two fine eucalyptus trees, an old ragged monkey puzzle, and a rockery made out of large sea shells which delighted Hilda. To the drawbacks of the house, obvious to Andrew, Hilda was blind. It was a long way up the hill to the shops and the tram. The road was dark and lonely at night. The steepness of the slope made the house feel precarious as well as making the garden difficult to work. Andrew was even prepared to accept Kathleen's view, scornfully quoted by Hilda, that Claresville was damp. Exploring earlier to find Hilda's nearest shops, he had entered a bar and for the first time since his arrival in Ireland had had his uniform sneered at. He decided that he hated Dalkey.

The inside of the house was at present in extreme confusion. The removal men had arrived on the morning of the previous day, and after hastily pushing everything in through the front door had gone away, to some religious service they said, promising to come back shortly to complete the installation of the heavy furniture. Hilda had incautiously tipped them and Christopher had laughed and prophesied that they would be seen no more. Meanwhile Hilda's grand piano, dismantled and perched on its side, a very large bookcase and a substantial tallboy were left standing in the hall. Andrew thought that he and Christopher could probably manage the bookcase and the tallboy, but the piano would need three or four men. Hilda's suggestion that Pat Dumay should be asked to come and help was received by Andrew with a silence so profound that even his mother quickly changed the subject.

Andrew was tormented by the fact that Hilda did not yet

know. Her little gaieties, her joy in the house, her coy references to Frances, her even more coy references to 'when we're a bigger family', continually beset him with detailed images of the happiness he had lost. He measured too the shock which Hilda herself was going to receive. He had not thought of it at once, but of course for her everything, Ireland, everything would be utterly ruined by this new situation. He knew that his mother was assuming that when he had to go away Frances would remain, a married, perhaps even a pregnant Frances, to be fussed over by Hilda, and that this represented a very real consolation. And then there was Christopher. Hilda was deeply attached to Christopher and relied upon him completely. 'Christopher will know', or 'Christopher will arrange it', was her answer to any practical difficulty. What would happen to her relationship to the Bellmans when she knew that her darling boy had been rejected? Would she want to stay on in the pretty house with the monkey puzzle and the sea-shell rockery? And if she did not stay on, where should she go?

The dreadful blank pain of deprivation and the frightened, miserable tenderness for Hilda did not however compose quite the whole of Andrew's mind. There was also the thought of Millie. What this thought exactly was, was not entirely clear to him; it was persistent, significant, but veiled. At intervals, like a small spark in his memory, the events at Rathblane kept recurring to him, always with a little impetus of interest. And he recalled too, as if this were something unimportant now but which he must not on any account forget, what Millie had said about freedom and about the big unpredictable world. He had certainly not expected what had happened at Rathblane, and the mere fact that, after Frances' rejection of him, anything at all could still *happen* was in itself a kind of salve. He recalled reading once in some French writer that the interpolation of anything, even if it is only a broken arm, between oneself and the experience of unhappy love, is a consolation.

Andrew had been extremely shocked by Millie's unthinkable proposal. But it was an event, it must be admitted, as momentous as a broken arm and certainly more agreeable.

Now he could hear from the sounds below that Christopher had arrived. Hilda was saying, 'You've caught us just at the start of luncheon. Everything gets late on Good Friday, doesn't it, because of the service. Will you have a bite? Oh, you've eaten already. Well, you'll excuse us, won't you? It looks as if we'll have to eat off sheets of the *Irish Times* so it's not very elegant anyway! Andrew! Christopher's come!'

Andrew went down reluctantly. Christopher and Hilda were standing in the bright bay window of what was to be the drawing-room. Against the deep feathery leafage of the garden the sunny room floated in space, dotted with objects, not yet anchored down by the heavy significance of furniture. The keen sunlight revealed the ghosts of old pictures upon its rose-sprigged walls. Christopher and Hilda turned about with faces radiant with happiness. It was clear that Christopher did not yet know. Andrew had never seen him looking so happy.

Andrew's boots resounded in the unmuffled space. 'Hello.'

'Hello, Andrew. Are you going to conscript me to deal with that piano?'

'I'd rather not think about the piano.' Their voices echoed like distant halloos.

'Those men will come back,' said Hilda. 'They said they would.'

'Precisely. But this is Ireland.' Christopher laughed with the ready pointless laughter of the happy man. 'Hilda shouldn't have tipped them,' he said to Andrew. 'They went straight off to the bar. And Hilda was imagining them on their knees!'

'Well, I thought they were very nice men,' said Hilda complacently, pleased to be teased by Christopher.

Andrew thought miserably how pleasant to him this little family scene would have been if only all were well. He would have been glad to see his mother so happy and so befriended.

'Don't let me keep you from your grub,' said Christopher. 'The godless must not prevent the godly from eating!'

'Andrew, would you mind lifting those boxes off the chairs? Be careful with them. The Royal Worcester dinner service is in that one, at least I *hope* it is. And the flower vases should be in that one. Oh, how I am longing to bring some flowers in from the garden and make it really look like home!'

Andrew moved the boxes, and Hilda seated herself at a green baize card-table, putting down the sheets of newspaper under the plates of cold tongue and salad. 'Come, Andrew. It's our first meal in Claresville. Isn't that exciting?'

Andrew scraped his knife and fork on his plate in a pretence of eating. He wanted to weep. He loved his mother so much.

Christopher, humming and almost skipping about the room, kept up a disjointed chatter. 'You should lay down a pavement really. It's not expensive. That grass is so damp and mossy. And I do think you should cut a vista through those bamboos. You might even get a glimpse of the sea from here. Oh—'

Andrew looked up sharply. In the haze of sunlight he saw Christopher suddenly stiff, looking with surprise and alarm toward the door. In that instant Andrew was sure that Frances had come herself, grim and unsmiling, to accuse him publicly of having failed her. He leapt to his feet. But the figure in the doorway was Kathleen.

Kathleen, her long coat pulled shapelessly about her like a cloak, stared into the room with a face haggard with fear and distress. The features were strained and pulled downward in a grotesque terrified leer.

Hilda, looking up short-sightedly, noticed nothing amiss. She was annoyed at Christopher's visit being spoilt by the arrival of Kathleen. 'Why, what a nice surprise!'

'What is it, Kathleen?' said Christopher.

'I just thought I'd call,' said Kathleen in a voice which was surprisingly calm, only just slightly too monotonous to be natural.

'Would you like to join us? It's just a cold meal I'm afraid.'

'No, thank you.'

'I expect you'd like to look round the house and garden. You haven't really seen it except on that wet afternoon.'

'I'll take Kathleen round,' said Christopher. 'I'll show her the garden while you're finishing luncheon.' He marched Kathleen out again into the hall and out through the back door.

Andrew went to the window. He watched Christopher and Kathleen walking slowly down the little pebbled path in the direction of the rockery. Something awful had happened to Aunt Kathleen, but he didn't care. He hated them all.

*   *   *   *

'What is it, Kathleen?'

Christopher was in that condition of sensitive availability to the troubles of others which is produced by certain kinds of happiness. His world had been made perfect, and by that perfection he was himself increased, filled suddenly to the brim with a new abundance of free affections. He felt, positively, a better man. He longed to help others and almost felt that he could do so miraculously just by touching them.

He had not seen Millie since Wednesday when she had given him her world-changing yes. She had told him, though not at all solemnly, that she was going into an Easter 'retreat' at Rathblane and that she wished to be left alone. She had spoken again, with a laugh, of the 'holiday' which she needed before what she called, even more laughingly, 'the fatal event'. Prayer and fasting and meditation were her programme just now. Spiritually refreshed, she would return to Christopher to celebrate the new era with rivers of champagne.

Christopher understood her wish and even welcomed it. With a slightly grim affection he appreciated her need to steel herself in solitude to carry out a plan which was not entirely to her liking. She would succeed in reorganizing her mind and even her heart to meet this new necessity. Millie was an amazingly efficient organism. Christopher had been in fact a little uneasy in case she should press him, once it was all decided, into some immediate action. He was anxious lest she should hold against him his continued silence on account of Frances. He feared the charge of being insufficiently in love to carry all before him, even the opposition of Frances. Well, perhaps he was insufficiently in love. But in any case it would all be much easier and more agreeable if Frances could first be married off and, amid the preoccupations of a newly married girl, be unable to bend her formidable will against her parent. 'Abandoned' by his daughter, Christopher's act must look more understandable, more forgiveable. A married Frances would be in a less strong position to object, might indeed, Christopher suspected, not be on the scene at all: though he had not mentioned this to Hilda, he anticipated that young Andrew would promptly remove his bride to England. So, since everything pointed to silence and discretion, it was as well that the interval should be imposed by Millie herself and not by him. Thus deprived, he could by gentle complaints forestall her possible protestations about his own pusillanimity. In a more straightforward way, having achieved his end at last he was content to be alone for a little while simply to gloat. Lotus-like he floated, sufficient to himself, upon his own felicity.

'What's happened, Kathleen? You look quite distracted.' He propelled her down the humpy path, between two straggling roses bushy with briars, past the chipped muddy shells of the rockery, to a wooden seat. The damp air smelt of eucalyptus.

'Nothing's happened yet. I'm sorry, Christopher. I looked for you at Finglas, and when I couldn't find you I got upset.'

Kathleen and Christopher had known each other for a very long time without becoming close friends. Each accepted the other as a familiar feature of the landscape and this acceptance had become, with the years, a sort of affection. Though she was quite unlike himself, and though he found her outlook in many ways depressing, Christopher respected Kathleen as a decent independent character. In his view, most people were slaves; but Kathleen was no slave and this was noticeable. His contempt for Barney partly took the form of sympathy for Kathleen; and he liked her too because she appreciated Frances. Kathleen sometimes afflicted him, as she afflicted so many, with feelings of guilt; but since he was more rational than other persons thus stricken he understood the ailment and forgave her for it.

'Well now, tell me all about it.' He was rather touched that she should have sought him out.

'I'm sorry to trouble you with this, but you're the only man who's near and I've got to talk to somebody. I said something to Barney, though I wasn't sure *then*, but Barney can't do anything and anyway he's part of it himself.'

'What on earth are you talking about, Kathleen?'

'They're going to fight.'

'Who are?'

'The Sinn Feiners, the Volunteers.'

'My dear, they're always going to fight, only they never do.'

'But there really is a definite plan. I don't know when it'll be, but soon. They're going to take over Dublin.'

'Oh, nonsense, Kathleen. What in heaven's name makes you think this?'

'I broke into Pat's room. He was so secretive and so excited about something, I had to try to find out. So I broke in and there were some plans. I couldn't really understand them, but they were plans for a military occupation of Dublin. And there was a map of Dublin showing what buildings were to be occupied.

'But, my dear Kathleen, they've been doing this for years. Don't you know that James Connolly 'captures' Dublin Castle practically every weekend? They thoroughly enjoy it! I'm sure every young man in the movement has got a plan for the military occupation of Dublin in his pocket.'

Kathleen stared at the black rain-sifted earth of the rockery. Her face had lost the haggard look of terror and was stern and thoughtful. Christopher saw her old lost handsomeness. 'No,' she said. 'It's serious this time. I'm quite sure. I'm sure because of the way Pat is.'

'Pat's young and excitable. He might be that way for lots of reasons. Perhaps he's in love.'

'He's not in love. He isn't interested in girls.'

Christopher was about to suggest that he might conceivably be interested in boys, but decided that this speculation, which was not new to him, was not suitable for Kathleen's ears. 'Have you said anything to Pat yourself?'

'No. He's almost entirely stopped talking to me about anything. Up to now I've simply prayed.'

'Shall I have a word with him?'

'Oh, if only you would! This was really what I came to ask you. I felt I must do something. You might be able to use logic with him.'

'Logic! How like a woman to think that logic is a kind of stuff you just apply to a situation! Anyway, I don't know what the logic of this one is.'

'But you might be able to persuade him that it's mad.'

'I doubt if anyone could persuade that young fellow of anything. Besides, it's not clear that it is mad.'

'What do you mean?'

'It's arguable that the only way for Ireland to become really independent is to fight. England will delay Home Rule and pare it away until there's practically nothing left. An imperialist power won't really budge without a show of force. And a show of force is one thing one can't be too rational about, it comes when it has to. Anyway, Ireland's honour demands a fight. Only I mustn't say things like that to you.'

'It's wicked and insane what you say. Why should Ireland be really independent? How can she be really independent? Ireland's honour means nothing but the vanity of a few murderous men.'

'Well, you argue like a woman. If you like I'll certainly see Pat and try to find out something. But I do assure you there's nothing in it. I know the MacNeills and I'd have heard if anything was in the air. These plans you saw are just for the usual routine manœuvres.'

Kathleen stood up. She looked down at Christopher with eyes big and dazed with thought. 'I wonder if I ought to tell the Castle.'

'*What?*'

'If the Castle knew now they could circumvent them, they could take their arms away.'

'Kathleen, are you mad? That would certainly be the way to start a fight! Anyway, the Castle wouldn't believe you any more than I do. And it would be such, well, treachery. Do you want to break Pat's heart?'

'I don't want to lose both my sons.'

'Cathal's only in the Fianna! No one's going to give him a gun!'

'He'd follow Pat anywhere and it would be impossible to stop him.'

'No, no, Kathleen, do stop worrying. All this is in your imagination. Now I must take you back to the house or Hilda will be cross. Anyway it's starting to rain. Have I convinced you you're wrong to worry?'

'Well—perhaps—'

'Good. But I will talk to Pat. And I'll use logic with him; oh, I'll use logic!'

Chapter Sixteen

IT was Saturday afternoon. Barney had enveloped his Lee Enfield rifle in a long roll of brown paper and was binding it around with twine. He had at last come to a decision.

When it had seemed to him, at his moment of illumination in the Dominican chapel, that if he were simply to lift a finger he would gain a great access of spiritual strength, he had not foreseen how difficult the lifting of his finger would prove to be. He had returned home in the early hours of Good Friday moving in a spiritual rapture which seemed as intense and as pure as his numinous experience at Clonmacnoise. He was resolved on three things: to stop seeing Millie, to confess everything to Kathleen, and to destroy the Memoir. He had lain down and slept, in anticipation, the sleep of the just.

Later on on Friday, and this morning, it had all appeared less simple. The thought of not seeing Millie any more was not just painful it was absurd. It now seemed morbidly gratuitous, like punishing himself for nothing. He might go and see Millie less often, but the difference between less often and never was the difference between sanity and madness. To drop Millie would be a pointless act of self-mutilation. His little visits to her did no harm. It was all in his mind. Yes, that was it, it was all in his mind. He did no real harm to Kathleen by cheering himself up with Millie; on the contrary, he was a more kindly person at home just because he had this consolation. The idea of making a general confession to Kathleen now also seemed somehow an unnecessary penance. He would upset Kathleen, he would upset himself; and anyway Kathleen probably understood the essence of the matter already. To set it out crudely in words was just to make extra trouble. It would not make things simple and innocent, it would make them nasty, emotional and complicated. He had much better keep quiet and try hard, within the structure of his life as it now again seemed to him that it had to be, to be a better husband to Kathleen. Didn't that make sense? Yet he felt, with all this, disappointed. He knew in some refined pinpoint of his heart that what he had glimpsed in the chapel was true and was far more important than the reasoning which could make such nonsense of it. The trouble was that his quick vision of the truth was not commensurable with any plan of action which suited his capabilities. The acts it enjoined now seemed, not necessary, but isolated, arbitrary and senseless. He had no energy for them. Sure, it's all in my mind, he came back to saying.

The conclusion he had reached about his Memoir, that it was a sin against his wife, had seemed, even late on Friday night, both more clearly right and more practically manageable. He knew, as soon as he started to reflect seriously on the matter at all, that the Memoir provided a continual source of bitterness against Kathleen. He was not really soberly and before God trying to write down what was the truth of their relationship, he was deploying an elaborate private argument against her. He was using his intelligence simply to take her captive in the imagination and belittle her, and correspondingly to enlarge himself. He was the wise, detached, shrewd observer, ironical and invulnerable. This must stop. If he was going to lead, even in a rather modified way, a new life, he must destroy the Memoir and blot out from his mind the picture of Kathleen which it contained.

He took out the manuscript and opened it at random. 'I observed with sorrow the progressive estrangement of my wife from her two sons. On one or two occasions I even felt bound to upbraid the boys separately for an "off-hand" treatment of their mother which amounted almost to rudeness. They heard my admonitions with respect but seemed unable to promise any amelioration. It was clear that their mother afflicted them, as she afflicted so many people, with an uneasiness similar in structure to a sense of guilt. That this was not "true" guilt it took me indeed some years to perceive. A prolonged study of my wife's character led me in the end to conclude that the phenomenon was caused, not by any moral superiority on her part, but by something much more simple, her curious lack of vitality. She was, in the end, one of those who "have not" and from whom therefore, in the harsh words of the Gospel, "shall be taken away even that which they have". There was a negative quality in her, an un-life, in the presence of which ordinary healthy persons, such as myself and my step-sons, quite perceptibly shuddered.'

The trouble was, it was so dashedly well written; and it was the only thing he had ever really created. It seemed a pity just to tear it up, in fact it seemed rather a crime. The Memoir existed now in its own right as a sort of personality, and the violent physical act of destroying it would seem like a murder and surely quite a needless one. He would stop writing it of course. Well, it was almost finished anyway. Perhaps he would just quickly finish it and put it away. And in case anyone ever found it he would write at the bottom in large letters ALL THIS IS NOT QUITE TRUE. Or perhaps one day he might change all the names and turn it into a novel.

He reached this conclusion on Saturday morning, and after reaching it, feeling distinctly more cheerful, he went out to the Reading Room in Lord Edward Street and looked at the newspapers and thought about Frances. If he had decided, which he had not, to give up Millie it would have simplified the decision whether to tell Frances about Christopher since, as he would have lost Millie anyway, he would not have to fear her displeasure nor would he have to worry about the purity of his motives. But given that he was still aiming at the preservation of Millie not only from herself but for himself, if Millie knew that Barney had told Frances that Christopher . . . He decided that he would read the newspapers first and think about all this afterwards.

There were two articles in the newspapers which interested

him. The first one, which was in the *Irish Volunteer*, gave an account of how to ambush your enemy at a crossroads. Suppose you have forty men, armed with five rifles, twenty shotguns, fifteen pikes, and as many revolvers or automatics. Find a reasonably high wall and build up a footing behind it and put sandbags on top with loop-holes between. Know your left-hand shots and where to place them. For yourself, if you use a revolver or pistol with lance or bayonet, practise shooting with your left hand. Keep open your lines of communication and retreat. Throw up a barricade on the road in front, always on the right side of a bend so as not to be visible to an enemy till he comes right up to it. Do not put men behind it. Place the shot-gun men and the pike men behind hedges at the side. When the column comes down the road hold your fire until it is well into range; while it is thrown into confusion by fire let your pike men charge through it and back; then another volley.

It sounded easy. Barney liked reading things like that in the *Volunteer* and feeling that they were meant for men like himself. 'Know your left-hand shots and where to place them.' He would know. 'Practise shooting with your left hand.' Left-hand shooting was child's play to him. Being an expert marksman had always made him feel himself to be an honorary soldier. Yet he had never in fact joined the Territorials nor had he been distinguished either for zeal or performance in the Volunteers, although he was respected as a crack shot by the younger men. Perhaps after all he had not got a soldier's temperament. He read the instructions for the ambush over again. Could he really imagine himself there? 'Hold your fire.... Let your pike men charge ... then another volley.' He had seen men training with pikes though he had never handled one himself. What would it be like to thrust one of those things into a human body? 'Then another volley.' He pictured the men lying in the road, some lying still, some twisting and crying out. Could he be there? He closed the *Volunteer* with a shudder. The Irish spent so much of their time imagining what they would do to the English once they got hold of them. Perhaps these fancies really were, as Kathleen thought them, a poison of the imagination, a corruption of the heart.

He next opened the *Irish Times* and started reading an article, reprinted from the *New York Times*, by Bernard Shaw called 'Irish Nonsense about Ireland'. Shaw was at his usual game of deriding Irish nationalism. 'I invite America to contemplate the spectacle of a few manifesto-writing stalwarts from the decimated population of a tiny green island at the back of Godspeed, claiming its national right to confront the world with its own army, its own fleet, its own tariff, and its own language which not five per cent of its population could speak or read or write even if they wanted to. . . . If Ireland were cut loose from the British fleet and army to-morrow she would have to make a present of herself the day after to the United States, or France, or Germany, or any big Power that would condescend to accept her: England for preference.'

Of course, Shaw was right. Could Ireland stand alone? No, of course she couldn't. No little nation could stand alone in these days. And it was true, as Shaw said later in the article, that Ireland's first natural ally was England. Barney had heard the exalted talk of his stepsons, had heard Pat speak of a transfigured Ireland that would shine in the eyes of the nations, had heard Cathal tell how a magnanimous Ireland would raise a defeated England from the dust. But these were dreams. Ireland would always be the half potty second-rate provincial dump which it had always been, with its stupid clergy and its stupid poor. It was not worth shedding men's blood, sticking them through with pikes or knocking them off with shot-guns at country cross-roads, to try to change what could never really be changed.

And yet was Shaw entirely right? All over Europe men had fought savagely for their freedom in scenes just as petty and hopeless as the Irish scene. Was it a bad thing that they had done this, and not chaffered rationally with their local tyrants for a slightly better bargain? Like almost all the Anglo-Irish, Barney had a strong peppering of Irish patriotism in his blood. He felt what it was like to belong to the persecuted and the broken though he himself had never suffered hunger or blows. The history of Ireland was such a tale of misery and wretchedness, enough to make the angels howl and stamp their golden feet. England had destroyed Ireland slowly and casually, without malice, without mercy, practically without thought, like someone who treads upon an insect, forgets it, then sees it quivering and treads upon it again. Was there under heaven no tribunal where such a wrong could be set right and where the voices of the starved dead could mount into a mighty tempest at last? Were the young men wrong to imagine that an Ireland set free by its own righteous anger would be an unimaginably different place?

What could he do? As his thoughts returned to himself, taking him unawares, he felt a familiar pain which was his timeless assumption that he was a priest and then the quick jolt of the truth. He might, for all the horrors of the cross-roads, endorse the fighting of others. He could not fight himself. His battles were battles of the spirit, his only task his own regeneration. And then as he remembered again the pure yet untranslatable summons of the little light which shone so withdrawn and self-contained in the thickness of the dark, he suddenly realized what the thing was which he could do for Kathleen. He could sacrifice his rifle.

The one clear idea which had remained with Barney from his spiritual half-hour in the Dominican chapel was that he ought to act. He ought to do *something*. He ought to lift his finger. He ought, as he put it to himself, to give God a chance. He should shake himself into performing some movement which might be just violent enough to let loose the avalanche of goodness which he had, in that dazed but indubitable encounter, apprehended as reserved in especial for his own address. But there seemed after all to be no action which he could perform. He had decided that at least he could go and visit poor Jinny at the 'little hell' and bring her a present. But Kathleen had told him that Jinny had gone back to her parents in County Meath. So even that little decent act was taken from him. There was nothing left except lighting a candle in a church and resolving to be more polite to his wife. Was that all that had come of such an overwhelming sense of the presence of the Almighty?

The idea of sacrificing his Lee Enfield suddenly seemed the perfect solution. It was something that would cause him pain. It was something that would please Kathleen and win her approval. She had said that she wanted that rifle out of the house. It was a gesture that would symbolize a return to a purer and simpler life. Guns and uniforms were all very well for young ones like Pat and Cathal who were not dedicated men, but he had much better stay away and purge his imagination utterly of these pictures of violence. He must become a man of peace, asking little, harming no one. And he felt in an almost superstitious way that if he could undertake this positive penance this might indeed be the lifting of the finger, the joining of action to good intent from which a whole sequence of improvement might follow.

But how was he to get rid of the rifle? It seemed improper and insufficiently dramatic to sell it or give it away, he could not destroy it bodily and could scarcely leave it on a tram. Again the answer came to him as if from a divine source: he must take it to Kingstown Pier and cast it down a hole in the rocks! Feeling himself once more a man guided and inspired, he ate a hearty meal of sausages at the Red Bank Restaurant and then returned to Blessington Street and tied up the Lee Enfield into a brown-paper parcel.

*　*　*　*

It was an extremely cold day and there was nobody about on the front at Kingstown. Holding his parcel cradled in front of him like a child, Barney began to walk along the pier. The sharpened wind blew into his face and brought tears. He felt, with his strange burden, like a man dressed for a part, one garbed for a Passion-tide procession who by back streets makes his way toward the Cathedral. Yesterday Christ had been crucified. Today He lay in the tomb. Tomorrow He would rise victorious over death. Barney felt, as never before, that he was a part of that mystery. His instinct had been right. An action, even a mad arbitrary action, was needed to break the spell of his despair and set free the promised grace. Penance, sacrifice, these were symbolic movements whose effects were incommensurable in the world of the spirit. His single act would bring the full circle of his reconciliation. God who had asked for Isaac had also sent the ram.

He had gone about a third of the way along the pier on the upper terrace. There was nobody about. He approached one of the gaps in the wall through which one could pass to the other side. The wind screamed in the aperture. In a drenching of spray Barney went through and shuffled sideways with his back to the wall facing the open sea. The sea was extremely rough. It roared into the mountainous random rocks in a break-neck surge which creamed almost as far as Barney's feet and was withdrawn with an equal ferocity, sucked back through holes and crevasses to howl in chambers far below, vanishing in boiling foam under the high dissolving front of the next wave. In a mist of spray Barney gazed, wondering which was more horrible, the huge savage sea or the piled rocks with their shapeless crannies. He found suddenly that he had to sit down against the wall.

A veil of rain farther out concealed Howth and even Sandy-cove from view. There was nothing ahead of him except that line of great glistening light yellow rocks stretching away on either side on which a sort of diffused sunshine fell, and the rolling backs of the waves, dark grey, almost black, coming steadily towards him out of the wall of rain. Barney sat with

the salt trickling upon his face and stared, stared at a manifestation of something far older and more primitive than the god
who today lay sleeping in the quiet tomb and tomorrow would
rise out of a casket of daffodils and lilies.

He could not think why he was so affected by the sea. After
all he had seen rough seas before. Or perhaps it was something
to do with the rocks. He had always hated and feared those
rocks; and now perhaps catching him in this rarefied, this
spiritual condition they were suddenly able to get at him. He
closed his eyes to blot them out for a moment and to collect
his strength. The din of the sea inside his head, the clatter of
Chaos and Old Night, dulled into a ghastly replica of silence
and he almost feared to fall into a drugged perilous slumber.
He opened his eyes quickly and began to look about for a
suitable hole or crevice down which to drop the Lee Enfield.
There were plenty of huge triangles of blackness between the
rocks into which the broken waves drained and echoed away.
Once thrust in there and released from the hand the rifle would
slip away into some other world. It would not just disappear,
it would cease to be. Barney sat still for a while. Then he began
to wipe the spray slowly off his face with a handkerchief. He
had realized that he could not do it.

He had known that the surrender of the rifle would be painful for him, but he had not foreseen that it would be like a
mutilation. At that moment the Lee Enfield seemed like an
extension of himself. He could not sever it, he could not
thrust it into one of those appalling caves and let it go. He felt
that he might perish himself at the moment of release. The
prospect was like a descent into madness. He pitied the rifle,
he loved it. He could not surrender a part of himself to that
evil howling power. He got up hastily and went through the
gap and began to run back along the pier clasping the rifle
against his chest.

He went on running with occasional gasping pauses until
he got as far as the Crock's Garden. The misty rain had

receded momentarily and the sea was a blackish blue scattered with points of light. There was a luminous pallor at the horizon. Overhead the sky was suddenly clear and a weak yellow sun shone on to the Crock's Garden. Barney had again that sense of dream, of belonging to another dimension from the people about him, of taking part in a ritual. Only before he had felt himself the glad master of his steps. Now, in some mysterious enactment into which he had not been initiated, he was being conveyed along.

There were a few people sitting gloomily in their mackintoshes upon the wet seats of the garden looking at the sea. Barney took one of the labyrinthine paths which wound uphill between the thick round veronica bushes. He felt now that he must get rid of the rifle as quickly as possible. If he kept the thing in his hands much longer some doom would fall upon him. He looked quickly about. There was no one to be seen. He thrust the long brown paper parcel far in under one of the bushes and out of sight. Then he walked quickly on till he came to a seat at the top of the hill and sat down.

He was panting with exertion and excitement. He stared at the Martello tower at Sandycove, caught in a grey luminous shaft of sunny rainy light. After a few minutes he thought he would go again and look at where the rifle was. Perhaps after all he should now simply pick it up and go back to Dublin on the tram. He had performed the movements of an act of penance. It was all symbolic anyhow. It's all in my mind, he said to himself. Could he remember under which bush he had put the gun? He started off down the hill, panting again. But several elderly ladies were now coming up the winding path. He returned to the seat at the top. It was raining now in Sandycove and the Martello tower was almost obscured. He waited three minutes and then began to descend the hill again.

He turned the corner of the path and saw a group of people beside a bush. Some children had already found the rifle and pulled it out on to the path. The paper was being unwrapped. Someone was saying confusedly to someone else that hadn't a policeman better be called. Barney pushed quickly past and went down the hill. He expected at any moment to be called back and accused of something. Then it suddenly began to rain extremely hard. Everyone started to run. Barney ran.

He ran toward the nearest of the big Egyptian temples, the concrete shelter upon the near end of the pier. The rain was spilling down, beating violently upon the heads of the running people. It stretched away in front of him like a series of bright metal curtains. Just as he reached the shelter he heard somebody call his name. An umbrella jerked against his shoulder. Underneath the umbrella he saw the pale face of Kathleen.

Barney slithered into the damp gloom of the shelter. There were a lot of people already there and others arriving in haste. Kathleen followed him in, closing her umbrella. They made their way into a corner.

The sudden appearance of his wife did not surprise Barney very much. In his present weird state of mind it seemed to him natural that Kathleen should materialize since she had been in a sense the spiritual agent of whatever it was that had just been happening to him. She was a performer in the same ritual and perhaps its directing genius. However, he asked her, 'How did you know I was here?' It seemed natural too that she should have been out looking for him.

'I asked you when you were leaving the house where you were going and you said Kingstown Pier.'

'Oh. I'd forgotten.'

'I came to look for Christopher really, but there was no one at Finglas, so I came down here in case you might be here with Frances and she might know where Christopher was.'

'It's not my day for Frances.' So Kathleen had not been looking for him after all. 'Would you like to sit down? It's terribly wet.'

Kathleen spread out a newspaper on the rough concrete seat

at the back of the shelter and they sat down. Behind them out of holes in the wall a little water trickled over the pebbly surface. The dreary damp smell of wet concrete mingled with a human smell of wet tweed. A large number of persons were standing up just in front of them, hemming them in, and steaming slightly in the sudden closeness. Their voices echoed in the hollow space.

Barney suddenly felt that he and Kathleen were very private here at the back of the crowd, sitting together in the dark. He felt a desire to touch her, to pat her knee, but felt too shy to do so. A moment later he decided that he must make his confession. The sacrifice of the rifle had worked. 'Kathleen—'

'Barney, I'm so worried—'

'Listen, Kathleen, I must tell you something. I've got to tell you now and it'll make everything all right again between us. I know it'll upset you, but it's right to tell the truth isn't it and won't you forgive me for it? It's about Millie, well it's about me really, but there are two things and one of them is about Millie, that I've been going to see Millie still. You didn't know that, did you? Well, for ages now I've been going to see her at her house, just to talk like, but it was very wrong and I'm very sorry and I won't go there any more at all. And the other thing is about Saint Brigid, I mean about the early church that I'm supposed to be writing. I haven't been writing it at all but I've been writing another thing a sort of autobiography thing about you and me in a way I shouldn't but I'll stop doing that too and—'

'Saint Brigid?' said Kathleen. Perhaps she could not hear very well in the crowded echoing shelter.

'I say I'm not writing about Saint Brigid but about you and me in a sort of Memoir like I shouldn't have been. But did you hear what I said about Millie?'

'Don't talk so loudly. I can hear you quite well. You mustn't talk like that here.'

'But did you hear?'

'Yes. I knew you went to see Millie.'

'Oh. Well and wasn't it wrong of me to?'

'I still don't understand what it has to do with Saint Brigid.'

'That's *another* thing, I'm doing two wrong things but they're not connected, forget about Saint Brigid, it's just that all the time I've been at the National Library I've been writing that thing about you and me, and—'

'Sure, why shouldn't you?'

Barney had often imagined himself making this confession to Kathleen, but it had been in a scene quite unlike this one. He had pictured himself shaken by emotion, the words rent from his breast. He had pictured Kathleen's stricken face, perhaps her tears, her bitter reproaches, and then the great reconciliation. But this was as random and senseless as the sea roaring through the rocks.

'Barney, I'm so worried—'

The people in front of them suddenly surged forward. There were exclamations, 'It's stopped.' The sun was shining outside. Everyone started to troop out of the shelter.

Barney and Kathleen got up automatically. Kathleen began to pull pieces of damp newspaper off her coat, and Barney pawed at the seat of his trousers which felt very uncomfortable indeed. Automatically they walked out towards the sun.

The sunshine was warm and fragrant after the chill atmosphere of the shelter. The wind had dropped and the sea below them was a thick glassy green. The people dispersed along the promenade whose drenched surface steamed in the sun. Kathleen started to speak again, but before Barney could hear what she was saying they both saw, with a sudden dismayed premonition, someone running towards them. There was a sort of explosion and Cathal arrived, cannoning into Barney and saving himself by grasping him violently round the waist. The boy was in a state of incoherent excitement.

'Pat wants you,' he said to Barney, and had to say it twice because the words got all mixed up.

'Whatever is it, Cathal?' said Kathleen, her hands at her mouth with fright.

'I knew you were coming down here and I told Pat I could find you at once and he says you're to report to him directly so come now.'

'Cathal, *what is it?*'

Cathal turned to his mother. He was almost tearful with emotion. 'We're going to fight them now. We're going to take over Dublin tomorrow.'

He darted away, receding along the wet promenade, dodging the people who were standing about enjoying the sunshine. Kathleen ran after him awkwardly, her half-closed umbrella underneath her arm. Barney ran after Kathleen.

Chapter Seventeen

'PAT, Pat, let me in!'

Pat groaned. He had hoped to avoid seeing his mother. He had intended indeed to be out of the house entirely that day, but it had been necessary to come back to destroy some documents and to remove a copy of his will which he wished to leave with a solicitor. He had also wanted to interview Barney about a particular matter. And now he was caught.

When he had noticed on the previous day that the door of his room had been forced he had immediately thought of the police, but Cathal had then appeared and told him what had happened. Kathleen, after searching his room, had gone away in great agitation saying she was going to see Christopher, and had returned rather more calm later in the afternoon. She had said nothing to either of her sons.

Pat, who had jammed a tilted chair against the door handle so that the door could not be opened from the outside, said, 'All right, Mother, I'll come down in a moment.' Her steps receded.

Pat stamped on the smouldering ash in the grate and thrust the copy of the will into the pocket of his green jacket. The other copy was in the unlocked drawer of his desk. All his papers were neat and in order, the room bared and tidied, already unfamiliar. He looked about him. He would not come back that night. Perhaps he would not come back at all.

The authority of tomorrow had made him by now utterly hard and quiet. He had received his final orders and now knew as much as he would know until the firing of the first shot. To his profound joy he had been appointed to be at the centre of the conflict at headquarters, with Pearse and MacDonagh in the General Post Office. He closed the door and went down to his mother.

'Pat, what is this about tomorrow?'

He looked at his mother coldly down the length of the long narrow drawing-room. It seemed to be raining again outside and he could not see her face very well. 'Do sit down, Mother, and take your coat off. You seem to have got soaked.'

'Pat, what are you going to do? They've planned an armed rising for tomorrow, I *know* it, so don't pretend. What are you going to do?'

Pat decided there was no point in a denial. 'How did you find out?'

'Cathal told me.'

'Damn Cathal.' Pat had of course not told his brother anything of the plan. Cathal must have found it out from someone at Liberty Hall. The Citizen Army men had always encouraged Cathal, treating him as if he were grown up.

'So it is true. And you are going to be in it.'

'I'm going to be where every decent Irishman will be on that day.'

'I would do anything to stop you,' said Kathleen in a low gruff voice, uttering every word with an effort.

'Fortunately there is nothing you can do.'

'I could reveal everything to the Castle.'

'That would not stop us from fighting. It would merely increase our chances of defeat. It's too late. There is nothing whatever that you can do, Mother.'

Kathleen slowly took off her wet coat and let it fall to the floor. 'And if I beg and implore you not to—'

'My dear mother, your disapproval is not likely to weigh with me very much at this stage.'

'Not my disapproval, my misery—'

'Or your misery either. I thought of all these things long ago. Be sensible now. Would you really be pleased to have a son who kept out of danger for the sake of his mother's tears? I'm sorry to cause you pain, but I know where my duty lies.'

SEVENTEEN

'It *can't* be your duty,' she said. 'It *can't* be. What's wrong can't be your duty.'

'It's not wrong to fight to free your country.'

'But you won't be *doing* that. You'll just be killing people pointlessly. You'll have innocent blood on your hands. And you may be killed yourself or maimed for life. That's what it will be. And what for? Think about later on, think when people will look back and see that nothing has been changed. You cannot change Ireland by firing a few shots. Don't you see? Nothing can be *done* in this way at all. All that great action is in your mind only. You'll commit crimes and you'll destroy yourself utterly and break my heart, and for nothing. Can't you see it all from that place in the future and see that it's for nothing?'

'I don't inhabit that place in the future, Mother, and neither do you. This is the moment when Ireland has got to fight and she's come to it over a long road.'

'She! She! Who is Ireland indeed? Are you and your friends Ireland? You use these grand jumped-up words, but they mean nothing at all. They're empty words. You're caught all of you in the tangle of your dreams and it just needs a few sane men to halt you. Have you not the courage to stop this thing?'

'It's too late to argue.'

'And what about Cathal?'

Pat was silent.

'Have you thought about your young brother in this? Have you the right to destroy him too?'

'We'll keep Cathal out of it.'

'And how will you do that? You know he'll go wherever you go. Are we to tie him up or what?'

'No one will let him do anything, he's too young.'

'Who'll trouble about his age? Those fellows of James Connolly's he's always about with will take him with them if you don't.'

'I'll manage about Cathal.'

'Pat, child, please don't go. You must have some influence with these men. Put it off at any rate, think a little longer. You know you haven't got a chance against the English, sure you all know you haven't a chance. MacNeill must know that. He's not a madman. "

'It's not the point whether we have a chance.'

'You're going out there to be killed for nothing, to die for nothing.'

'It won't be for nothing. If I die I shall die for Ireland.'

'There is no such thing as dying for Ireland,' she said.

There was a heavy sound of running feet upon the stairs and along the landing, and as they both turned quickly towards the door it burst open and Christopher Bellman rushed into the room.

* * * *

'Kathleen, would you mind leaving me alone with Pat for a few minutes?'

Kathleen said, 'They are going to fight tomorrow,' She went to the door.

'Tomorrow is it?' Christopher stared at Pat. He waited for Kathleen to be gone and then strode forward and gripped Pat's arms above the elbow. He shook Pat with a violence which was half affection and half anger and then suddenly, closing his eyes and baring his teeth, he dropped his hands and turned away. 'Tomorrow? Oh God, you fools, you fools, you fools. You haven't heard what's happened down in Kerry?'

'What?'

'Your precious German arms. A whole shipload of them. Now they're at the bottom of Queenstown harbour. Oh, you idiots, you dolts—But tomorrow—Pat, you're mad.'

'What's this about German arms?'

'You didn't know? A ship crammed with arms for you from Germany—God knows how they did it—I heard it all from MacNeill—got through the blockade—they were disguised as

228

Norwegian fishermen or something—got as far as Tralee harbour—and there they sat for nearly two days waiting for some of your people to pay some attention to them! God, how can you have been so *stupid*? The Germans do this absolutely marvellous thing for you and you have to muff it. Why, why, why didn't somebody get those arms ashore? But no one seems even to have noticed the wretched Germans! God, what were your people thinking of? And then they felt they had to move and they sailed a bit along the coast and ran smack into a British sloop which took them into Queenstown harbour. Even then the Germans were beautiful, beautiful—the captain got everyone off and blew his ship up under the nose of the Royal Navy! My God, the Germans know how to do things. But they might have known the Irish would mess up their end of it. All that stuff sitting in Tralee bay and no one there to land it! God, what a nation of dunces!'

Pat turned away. He was silent for a moment. 'Well, that's gone.'

'Yes, it's gone all right! And they've got Casement.'

'Casement? But Casement isn't in Ireland.'

'He is now. He's in the R.I.C. barracks at Tralee. The Germans landed him from a submarine and he walked straight into the arms of the police.'

'Oh God,' said Pat. 'Casement.' He sat down heavily in a chair. 'They'll hang him.' He covered his face with his hands.

Christopher was in a state of intense excitement which he hardly himself understood. He had comforted Kathleen, but after she had gone he had suddenly felt quite certain that she was right. MacNeill evidently knew nothing of it, but it now seemed to him obvious that if violence was planned MacNeill *would* know nothing of it. Something was going to happen. The certainty came upon him not as a thought-out conclusion but more like a physical visitation, making him leap to his feet and gasp and tremble; and like a man for whom an ambiguous picture has abruptly shifted he saw only the new shape and could not now recapture the old.

Christopher had always played the cynic in political discussions. But in fact, though this would not have led him to lift a finger himself, he felt a strong romantic sympathy with the whole tradition of rebellion in Ireland and with the Sinn Feiners as the present representatives of that tradition. He loved the history of Ireland as if it were a personal possession; and although he freely mocked the person of the 'tragic woman', there was more than a touch of heated gallantry in his reaction to the whole miserable story. He enjoyed here an indignation which he kept entirely private. Like many scholars who ostentatiously eschew the field of action, he had a strongly developed sense of the heroic. While with the sensibility of an artist he apprehended an epic splendour always latent in the tragedy of Ireland.

Now he felt in the most terrible confusion. His misery, his fury at learning the news about the German arms, made him realize how utterly he identified himself with the rebels. He was desolated too by the plight of Casement, a man whom he greatly admired. His heart was already in revolt. Yet he knew too that whatever happened now could only be another miserable failure. He had lightly agreed to Kathleen's request to 'use logic' with Pat; but now that he saw the boy in front of him, illuminated in Christopher's sensitive vision by the bright light of history, he could not think what to say, nor what to do with the sudden tumult of energy with which the new situation had filled him.

'Yes, they'll hang Casement,' he said to Pat. 'They'll hang you all. If you want to end your young life on an English gallows, you're certainly going the right way about it.'

Pat lifted his head and smiled slightly. 'Don't worry. They won't hang us, they'll shoot us. After all, we are soldiers.'

'They won't treat you as soldiers. They'll treat you as murderers. They'll treat you as rats.'

'They'll soon find out we're soldiers. Where did you hear this about Casement? I suppose it's true?'

'I heard it at MacNeill's. I'm very sorry about Casement. But, oh, that you should have muffed those arms—!'

'I don't understand about the arms ship,' said Pat, 'but our men in Tralee will rescue Casement.'

'You won't have time. You'll all be disarmed by tonight.'

'Then we'll all be fighting by tonight. You'll keep your mouth shut about what my mother said just now?'

'Yes, I will, God forgive me, but I think you're insane.'

'I don't think they will jump on us before tomorrow. We may be stupid, but they're stupider. What is it, Mother?'

Kathleen had opened the door. She went up to her son and struck him fiercely upon the arm. 'Someone has just seen Cathal going away down the road with a rifle—'

Pat put her aside and left the room at a run.

Chapter Eighteen

PAT had put off solving the problem, had put it off because he could see no solution. In a way he simply could not think about Cathal at all, could not treat him as an object of rational reflection, could not put to himself questions of the form would this or that be 'advantageous' to Cathal. His brother had always been as close and as connected to him as his own hand. He had always associated Cathal with his view of his own life as if they looked out through the same eyes; and his long tyranny over him had been a form of self-discipline, and experience of living in two bodies. There would be, at moments, the sudden apprehension of the boy's separateness, making him gasp with surprise as at a felicitous audacity. Then as they returned again into each other Pat would feel, in an easing and enlargement of time, his own childhood not only preserved and continued, but perfected.

Would he not have risked Cathal if they were to climb a mountain together or swim a flooded river together? He had indeed so risked him. But this was simply a way of risking himself, and in those open solitudes their joint strength and their youth had seemed invincible. Pat had always so closely associated Cathal in his mind with all his decisions, they had seemed to exist together in perfect unity at a level only a little below that at which they constantly bickered. Pat had indeed been aware of this unity simply as a sense of including his brother. So it was that even in this thing he had seemed to bring Cathal along with him, to bring him absolutely to the threshold over which he was now so determined not to take him.

Pat had of course asked himself if it were not really best after all to keep Cathal with him, to have him, in whatever ensued, positively beside him and under his eye. Then at least he could

be sure the boy would do nothing insane: which if left un-
controlled he would be certain to do. But Pat knew at once
how unrealistic this idea was. He could not help seeing the
coming events in a heroic light; but he also knew, though not
with his heart, that when these events arrived they would be
incoherent and terrible. He would simply not be able to keep
an eye on Cathal or to protect him. And to be less than single-
minded would be a gross failure of duty.

Pat was well aware that he himself, at Cathal's age, would
have reacted in exactly the same way, and he asked himself
whether, in trying to keep him out of the conflict, he were not
somehow tampering with the boy's honour. But he could not
sufficiently make sense of this idea or see Cathal as having, in
this respect, separate rights. If the boy had been a little older,
even two years older, even perhaps one year older, the sacrifice
would have had to be consented to, it would have had to be
accepted as part of the ordinary world. Where he was together
with his brother was still the sacred land of childhood.

It was not exactly that he wanted Cathal to survive him,
that he wanted to keep that most precious piece of himself out
of danger; nor did he care at all about his mother's need for
sons. He had a deeper, more physical, sensation of being, where
Cathal was, entirely exposed and naked, and his instinct was
to hide and cherish this unprotected part. He wanted to stand
entirely in front of Cathal, to shield him completely, to press
him back behind him into a place of safety. He was ready to
expose himself to the English bullets, he had thought about
them often enough, and it was as if he were already physically
hardened, a veteran of the imagination. But the idea that any
harm might come to his brother made him writhe and shrink.
It made an utter coward of him.

When Pat emerged into Blessington Street there was no
sign of Cathal anywhere and Pat began to run down the hill
into a light misty rain which was materializing softly out of the
warm air. It occurred to him that Cathal might have gone to

confession at Saint Joseph's Church in Berkeley Road. It was a time when confessions were heard there. And that day all over Dublin, as intimations of the morrow spread wider through all ranks of the movement, men in green uniforms were to be seen queuing up outside the confessionals. Pat himself had been to confess that morning; and it was possible that Cathal, apeing here his brother, or whichever of Connolly's men was his latest mentor, had had the same idea.

Pat shouldered his way through the door into the stale incense-laden darkness of the church and peered about him. The East window glimmered faintly, bleakly, above the Lenten simplicity of the high altar, and between vegetable pillars the many lights of adoration flickered, blue before the Queen of Heaven, red for Saint Joseph, and yellow for the Little Flower. A few old women, black murmuring bundles, crouched or trotted here and there, but the body of the church was full of men, and there was a deep buzz of men's voices, only just quiet enough for reverence. Looking about him, Pat saw everywhere the uniforms of the I.C.A. and the Volunteers. The interior of the church seemed like a busy encampment. The chairs, which had been moved out of their neat rows, stood higgledy-piggledy, piled with knapsacks, with rifles leaning up against them; and the men waited in long patient lines beside the confessionals, or knelt among the chairs or out in the open aisles. The gathering seemed impromptu, unorganized, yet strangely solemn. The men bowed their heads low, or when they lifted them threw them back in a free way and their faces were clear and relaxed and seemed to shine in the darkness. The men smiled at each other as they passed, took hands in silence, or spoke briefly, holding each other's shoulders. There was a sense of happiness in the church, a sense of all sins forgiven.

Pat pushed his way forward, brushing against people that he knew. As he passed the confessionals he scanned the army boots of various types whose soles were displayed while their

owners murmured quietly to the priest. But in fact the queues
were so long that Cathal would not have had time to get to
the front. He passed through into the side chapel where
innumerable candles, dazzling not illuminating, mingled with
the dark without dispelling it, and God's Blessed Mother,
muffled from head to foot in purple cloth, leaned over him as
he scanned the kneeling figures. Eyes which did not see him
were lifted in the darkness and rosaries clicked, bumped on
wooden chairs or trailed upon the floor as hands fell to sides in
unconscious gestures of self-surrender. Cathal was not there.

Pat pushed his way back again through the murmuring
shifting crowd, reached the door, and jostled out again,
shading his eyes, into the very pale clear light of the late
afternoon. The rain had just stopped and there was a diffused
sunny atmosphere, thick and low, over Dublin, which made
the pavements shine cruelly and outlined every brick in the
façades of the houses. Pat started to run down the hill toward
Rutland Square. Now he must go to Liberty Hall.

Thick and huge, gross with imperial confidence, the Pillar
rose above Sackville Street, and from its summit Nelson gazed
thoughtfully over the head of the Liberator to the Liffey and
the masts of the ships and the open sea. The street was full of
people, the usual Saturday crowds, ambling the pavements
with deliberate slowness and trailing in slow mobs to and from
the trams. Under the low ceiling of sunny light the voices of
women and children were mainly heard, producing a continuous animated clacking. As Pat forced himself along, the
surge of cheerful faces resisted him, clear detailed little human
surfaces, glowing in the brightening air, thrust close up against
him and jerked past. Frantic now with need and fear, Pat
struggled on through the herd of happy people. He hated
them all. Tomorrow this cackling would be put to silence and
he would be separated from the like of these by a line of
English soldiers. As he came to the middle of the street he
looked quickly across at the Post Office.

Near to the Liffey the crowds were less dense and Pat turned to the left along the quay. The sun was coming out properly now, patterning the pavements with reflections and shadows, and there was a sky of the faintest feeblest blue above the glistening wet dome of the Customs House. As Pat approached Beresford Place he saw the gaping doorway of the Butt Bar and heard the sound within of drunken men singing the Soldier's Song. Groups of men in Citizen Army uniform were standing about in the roadway. On the façade of Liberty Hall the dripping banner still proclaimed *We serve neither King nor Kaiser but Ireland.*

Then Pat saw Cathal, standing on the pavement opposite, underneath the shadow of the Loop Line railway, talking to one of Connolly's men. He was holding the rifle awkwardly, like an acolyte holding a very large candle, and conversed with the man with a solemn air, nodding his head in an exaggerated way. As Pat drew near the Citizen Army man turned away, leaving Cathal, and made for the main entrance of Liberty Hall. Cathal stood still for a moment looking down at the rifle, hesitating whether to rest the butt of it upon the wet pavement. Pat recognized the gun as his own crack Italian rifle which Cathal had evidently purloined from his room. Pat crossed the road at a run and almost cannoned into his brother. He took the rifle lightly out of his hand and struck Cathal hard across the side of the face. Then he took Cathal's wrist in a firm grip and began to pull him back in the direction of the quay. Cathal resisted him and began to sob.

As Pat forced him along, ignoring the sobs, a large group of uniformed men were seen approaching Liberty Hall at the double. They thrust Pat and Cathal back against the wall as they passed, and Pat saw the figure of James Connolly in the midst of them. As the bright light fell upon Connolly Pat felt a sudden shock of apprehension. Connolly's face expressed an appalled shocked grief.

Following the group of men with Connolly came three

Volunteer officers, all known to Pat and senior to himself. As he pressed forward now, still automatically dragging Cathal with him by the wrist, one of these, a man called Owen Magillivray, saw Pat and at once beckoned to him. Magillivray's face expressed the same misery and shock. Pat and Cathal followed the Volunteer officers in through the door of Liberty Hall and on into a dark office where a number of men were talking in low agitated voices. Magillivray, shouldering the others aside, half pushed Pat into a corner of the room. He said nothing to him, but thrust a folded piece of paper into his hand. Pat fumbled it open and read. *Owing to the very critical position, all orders given to Irish Volunteers for tomorrow, Easter Sunday, are hereby rescinded and no parades, marches or other movements of Irish Volunteers will take place. Each individual Volunteer will obey the order strictly in every particular.* The signatures were those of MacNeill, MacDonagh and de Valera. The rising had been cancelled.

Chapter Nineteen

PAT DUMAY propped his bicycle against the wall and looked up at the darkened house. The moon, shining through a brown haze, was a large vague blur of light, seeming to move rapidly through the disturbed night sky. In this faint illumination Rathblane looked thicker, squatter, more like a fortress than a country house. Its shadow, an indeterminate hump or blot of darkness hanging from the walls, contained half of the expanse of rough grass, while on the other half, just fading into visibility, the sheep, grouped near the steps, were motionless, fuzzy, seemingly spherical. The windows of the house, very lightly smirched by the moon, bore upon their blackness little streaks and drips of light, as if some liquid silver had been thrown upon them and almost all washed away. Although it was not yet midnight the house and the countryside were deep, not exactly in sleep, but in trance. There was a profound silence in which the wall, the trees, the great black and grey block of the house, seemed submerged, more completely full and present than by daylight, as if the night and the stillness had filled them to the brim and weighted them with a quieter, denser element. The plantation beyond, faintly animate, seemed to breathe without moving, not exactly visible, but perceived in some further solidifying of murky air. Pat fingered the key in his pocket like a man fingering a weapon.

What had happened in the last two days in Dublin Pat had by now largely discovered. On Thursday a rumour had reached Bulmer Hobson that an armed rising was planned for Easter Sunday. He went at once to MacNeill, who was still of course the nominal head of the Volunteers, and in the early hours of Good Friday morning he and MacNeill visited Pearse, who admitted to them that the rumour was true. MacNeill said,

'I will do everything I can to stop it, except ringing up Dublin Castle.' There was a violent and inconclusive dispute after which MacNeill went home. A little later Pearse went with MacDermott and MacDonagh to MacNeill's house to argue with him again. MacNeill refused to see Pearse and Mac-Donagh, but allowed MacDermott to come in. MacDermott told MacNeill that the rising was now unavoidable and that the real command of the Volunteers was no longer in Mac-Neill's hands. He also told him of the German arms which were about to be landed in Kerry, and pointed out that after the arrival of the arms the British were certain to attempt to disarm the Volunteers, and this would mean a fight anyway. So it was better to strike first. MacNeill gave in and agreed to sanction the rising.

On Saturday morning came the news of the catastrophe to the German arms ship. MacNeill began to waver. He was visited by the O'Rahilly and other officers who were opposed to the rising. At last he went to Saint Enda's to see Pearse and there was bitter argument. After that MacNeill went home and wrote out countermanding orders which were dispatched with couriers to the Volunteer organization throughout the country. He prepared a statement, cancelling all 'manœuvres', which was to be published in the *Sunday Independent* next day, and cycled personally to the office to deliver it. Finally he ordered MacDonagh, as commandant of the Dublin Brigade, to inform all his men officially of the cancellation. MacDonagh, who judged that by now the plan was irrevocably spoilt, agreed, and sent out a Brigade Order over his own signature and that of his adjutant de Valera. It was the end of the enterprise.

'If we don't fight now, all we have left to hope and pray for is that an earthquake will come and swallow Ireland up, and our shame.' These words of James Connolly expressed what Pat felt, what they all felt, in those amazed and disappointed hours. Pat went back to Blessington Street. He sent Cathal on ahead to tell his mother. He could not have endured her happy relieved face. He climbed to his room and shut the door and fell face downwards on his bed.

It seemed that life was over. He had only, ever, had but one purpose and now that had been quite suddenly twisted away from him. It was snatched, gone, quickly, meanly, quietly, and without remedy. Pat knew that what was lost here could not be retrieved. If they did not act at once they could not act at all. The impetus would be spent, the movement discredited, the moment missed. There was to have been martyred blood, but now everything would collapse into absurdity and those who had called them shirkers and dreamers would have been proved right. The English would disarm them. Pat, who had felt that he would surrender his weapons with his life, now felt that it no longer mattered whether he kept his gun or not. Everything had been betrayed.

He cursed the leaders, he cursed Pearse. He grieved un-utterably for Casement. MacNeill ought to have been arrested days ago. Why could the Irish get nothing right? Such dunces deserved their slavery. But it was no use cursing and grieving. There was the rest of the day to be got through, there was the rest of his life to be got through, without a plan or purpose. He sat up and stared about him. He felt as if he had been pushed through a very small aperture into a completely other world. He felt giddy and unable to focus his eyes upon the little room which had become an entirely different place. He had nodded for a moment and awakened in prison. The rush of time in his ears had ceased and there was empty space and idleness and silence. Leaning his head forward in his hands Pat felt that he could hardly bear to go on being conscious. He wanted death.

How and when the idea of Millie came into his mind he was not sure. Somewhere in the flashing centre of his unfocused gaze her image had come to be, like a deity seen by a saint in an ellipse of light. The wretchedness of his body demanded violence, the whip, the brand. Thought, even consciousness, must be choked in feeling, drowned in pain. He recalled how

Millie had offered herself, and the disgust he had felt for her, and yet also, as it seemed to him now, how in a totally horrible way she had attracted him. She was a slut, not exactly a woman, but a kind of degraded boy. He pictured her as dirty, sallow, dishevelled, stinking. She had said that she would be waiting for him in her bed, and he pictured her bed. Could he force himself to that?

He sat very quiet now. If this was despair it was a deeper pit than any he had ever dreamed of. And then it seemed to him almost like a duty to go there, to perform this, as it appeared quite final, act of will. There would be an action and an ending after all, not this well lighted idleness but a swift rush into the dark. This would be the last triumph of his will over his fastidious mind, and over the foul animal of his body, for although he now desired Millie he knew that it was only by pure volition that he could so degrade himself. He went downstairs and found his bicycle.

Now that he had reached Rathblane, desire and cool intent had fused into a single thrust. He wanted Millie as an enemy, a victim, a quarry. What she had asked for she would get. He moved forward through the wet grass toward the steps, bringing out the key. It was fortunate that he had provided himself with a key to Rathblane. He did not want to be seen by the servants, not because of any discretion, he was far beyond discretion, but because he did not wish the momentum of his action to be checked. He edged the big key into the lock and the door gave quietly in front of him.

Pat was fairly familiar with the interior of Rathblane but he did not know which was Millie's bedroom. He did not want any apparitions of screaming housemaids. He guessed that it would be safe to try the big bow-windowed room above the drawing-room. He began very cautiously to mount the stairs which creaked at every step. It was extremely dark and the darkness seemed to be getting inside his eyes and mouth. For a moment he felt stifled as if the black air were foul with soot.

He paused on the landing trying hard to see and made out the window with difficulty. The moon must be obscured now, and there was a soft hissing sound of rain. Something white glimmered near by, and reaching out his hand Pat touched the cold smooth globe of an oil lamp. He struck a match and lit the lamp, still breathing hard, and turned it up slowly. Furniture, flowers, pictures and the half-curtained window with its rainy whisper, came into shadowy being about him.

He had no qualms about waking Millie suddenly. She was not the kind of woman who would scream. In fact, he was so dazed with his own purposes that he hardly conceived that he would surprise her. He moved across the landing carrying the lamp and very quietly opened a door. He leaned through, holding the light above him, and saw a small empty room, perhaps a dressing-room, with the low embers of a fire in the grate. There was a smell of turf and a slight smell of whiskey. Some clothes lay untidily upon a sofa beside the fire. At the far side of the room there was another door.

Pat closed the first door carefully behind him and crossed the room. He was gasping for breath as his hand touched the handle of the second door. As the door moved and the dark aperture widened before him he lifted the lamp high and tried to murmur Millie's name. At once, in the sudden wavering light, he discovered a bed. And a second later he saw that there were two people in it. Millie was not alone.

* * * *

Pat closed the door abruptly and stepped back. He put the lamp down on a table. He covered his eyes and shook his head to and fro. He felt shocked, ashamed and stupid, and intensely hurt, though whether this was pain for damage he had received or damage he had done he was not sure. Stupidity had come upon him like a physical condition, like an ass's head. He could have taken hold of Millie without a thought for her mind or her heart. But now he was suddenly related to her differently,

242

shocked into some more childish puritanism. He thought, I have been made an utter fool of. He had not conceived of a rival, that a rival could exist. When Millie had said that she would be waiting for him he had believed her quite simply, quite naïvely. He had imagined her like a helpless quarry, like a victim tied to a post. Now in an instant he had been robbed of his active role, reduced to a gaping spectator, a shameful watcher. He had expected, he had wanted, violence and pain, not muddle.

He wondered if he should not just go away straight out of the house, and he pictured himself going, but his body stood there stiff and paralysed. Then as he still stood, almost at attention, and uncovered his eyes, the door of the bedroom opened and Millie came out, wearing a white frilled dressing-gown.

The appearance of Millie, the movement of the door, made Pat suddenly aware of his rival as an individual. Who was in there with her? But he could not feel angry. He felt humiliated and utterly, primitively, shocked. That another should do *that* was simply something horrible.

Millie, not looking at him, moved to the lamp and turned it up. The white scalloped frills of the silky gown dragged slowly upon the carpet. She leaned over the fire, thrust a long spill into the embers, and lit another lamp. Then she faced him.

Millie looked unfamiliar. Her hair, which he had never seen undone, fell in thin dark sheets about the shoulders of her gown and down on to her breast, making her look like a young girl, vulnerable, caught. Her plump face wore an expression of rueful, quizzical sadness. With the conscious dignity of a youthful princess facing her executioner, she seemed perfectly calm.

'What a pity, what a very great pity. If I had known you might come I would have been more than ready. I despaired of you too soon.' She spoke in a detached way, as if to herself, as if knowing the words could not have much significance for him.

243

Pat stared at her and then looked down at the floor. One bare foot, half emerged beneath the frilly hem, seemed to clutch the carpet like a clenching hand. He had no way of dealing with her now, he felt like a child. He was almost ready to say that he was sorry.

'How did you get in, Pat?'

'I had a key of the place,' he said in a hoarse low voice.

'Ah well. I know this can never be mended or forgiven or even explained. But I think I regret it more than anything that has ever happened to me. I did not conceive that you might come. If you had given me the least hint I would have been eternally patient. I most bitterly regret not having been alone when you came, and I shall regret it forever.' Millie spoke softly, but very slowly and clearly.

'Sure I—' Pat started. He could not face her. He could not feel angry. He felt the hurt confused ashamed resentment of a child who, without understanding, has spoilt some grown-up plan. He half turned as if to go.

'I don't want to act stupidly now,' said Millie, speaking more quickly. 'I know we can't talk now. But your having come, it's so important. If there was any satisfaction I could give you I would undergo anything. I suppose it's hopeless, but I can't help saying—'

'Who's that in there?' said Pat. Even this question, which should have been brutal, was broken, hang-dog. He stared at the closed bedroom door.

Millie hesitated. Then she said, 'Well, I'll give you this, and remember that I gave it to you.' She walked over to the door and opened it wide: 'Come out, Andrew.'

Andrew Chase-White, clad in shirt and breeches, emerged from the bedroom and leaned against the jamb of the door. He was very pale and shuddering slightly. He too appeared entirely different. He stared Pat full in the face with a look of dazed bleak misery.

Millie said 'I'm sorry, Andrew. I'm sorry, Pat. There's

nothing more I can say.' Then she added, 'All the same, it's quite an achievement, isn't it,' and gave a short laugh.

The two young men gazed at each other. Then Pat turned abruptly and left the room. He half fell down the stairs in the dark and found the front door and the moist night air. The rain had stopped and the moon shone clearly through a jagged gap in the clouds. The figure of a man materialized close in front of him upon the steps. Pat thrust the man violently aside and heard him fall with an exclamation into the long grass. Without looking back, Pat reached his bicycle where it stood against the wall. He now saw, revealed by the brighter moon, two other bicycles near it. He swung his left hand hard against the wall, and swung it again and then a third time, until the moonlight showed a dark stain upon the stone.

Chapter Twenty

CHRISTOPHER BELLMAN had suddenly decided that he absolutely must see Millie. After her wonderful 'yes' to him, he had felt happy and at peace and quite content not to see her for a while. He had felt her to be delightfully stored up and safe, a prize reserved and labelled, a perfume sealed, and he had returned to his work and felt more serene, he thought, than ever in his life. This serenity had been disturbed by two things. First, he had been extremely excited and upset by the news of the projected rebellion, which had been followed so soon by the news of its cancellation. This sudden glimpse of another Ireland, so close and yet so hidden, filled him with a distress which seemed like guilt. For a second he had felt the warm quick movement of Irish history risen out of books alive, alive-o. He was stirred, magnetized, then disappointed, relieved. The second thing was that Frances, later that afternoon, had told him that she was not going to marry Andrew. Then it became essential to see Millie.

He set off on his bicycle and would have arrived at Rathblane earlier in the evening, only just as he was beginning to get into the mountains he had a puncture. He left the bicycle and walked on, imagining that the distance was shorter than it was. Then it became dark and he missed his way. When, very tired and drenched with rain he at last reached Millie's front door he was extremely startled at being jumped upon by a man suddenly issuing from the doorway. As he picked himself up it seemed that the man, who had now faded into the moonlight, was Pat Dumay. He went in through the open door.

The hall was very dark and as soon as he came in it seemed to him that someone who was standing in the darkness moved away, with a soundless displacement of air, into one of the rooms. Almost at once a moving light was seen up above and

Millie appeared, wearing a white gown. She began to glide quickly down the stairs carrying the lamp, her gown flowing out behind her, her loose hair lifted. When she was halfway down the lamp light showed her Christopher and she stopped abruptly.

'Millie, what on earth's happening? Somebody rushed out at me. I thought it was—'

'Hello Christopher', said Millie. 'Good evening.' She put the lamp down on the stairs and sat down beside it. Then she began to laugh helplessly. She rocked quietly to and fro moaning with laughter.

'I'm sorry I've come so late,' said Christopher. 'I'd have got here much earlier only I got a puncture and had to walk the last bit. But, Millie, what—'

Millie stopped laughing. 'Please, Christopher, would you go into the drawing-room and wait there? I'll put on some clothes and join you in a few minutes.' She went back up the stairs taking the lamp with her and leaving Christopher in darkness.

Christopher fumbled his way to the drawing-room door and fell through it, knocking his head on the big Chinese screen whose position just inside the door he had forgotten. There was no fire and the room smelt of damp textile and turf ash. He stood still until he could discern the squares of the windows and shuffled towards them. There was a sound of scuffling overhead and he thought he heard voices.

Christopher was feeling very confused. During his long walk along the dark mountain road he had been all the time anxious simply to arrive. He disliked walking. The mountains were frightening at night, there were sounds, presences. He had hurried on, looking forward to finding Millie up, a blazing fire, a welcoming glass of whiskey. But the uphill walk had taken such a long time. And now here he was, hustled away, left in the dark and the cold, not looked after in the least. And who was that person who had rushed out of the door and knocked him down? He realized that his arm was hurting from the fall and his head was aching from the encounter with the Chinese screen. Was it Pat Dumay? What was he doing bursting out of the house as if the devil was after him? And who was the mysterious moving figure in the hallway? And what was all that curious scuffling going on in the room above? Christopher felt very puzzled and very ill-used. He pawed several tables looking for matches but only succeeded in over-turning something which fell on to the floor with a crash. It sounded as if it was broken. He began to feel his way back to the door.

Before he could reach it Millie came in with the lamp. She was wearing her plainest grey walking-dress with a red woollen shawl over her head. She put the lamp down, carefully pulled the curtains, and then lit another lamp.

'Please sit down, Christopher.'

'I'm so sorry, I've broken that vase. I was looking for the matches.'

'It doesn't matter. It's only Ming or something. For God's sake, Christopher, sit down.'

'My dear Millie, I'm only too anxious to sit down once you've given me time to take off this extremely damp mack-intosh. And I think you might give me some whiskey. I've had a very long walk.'

'Oh yes, of course, whiskey, there's some in the cupboard. Wait a moment. Here you are.'

'Millie, is something funny going on here? Was that Pat Dumay? And is there somebody else in the house? I thought I saw someone in the hall as I came in.'

'No, there's no one here but me. The maids all sleep in the annexe.'

'What was Pat doing here and why did he push me like that? I nearly broke my arm. I'm sorry I came so late, but as I told you I had a puncture and—'

'I should think he pushed you like that because you were in

248

his way when he wanted to go out of the door. I'm sorry about your arm and I'm sorry about your bicycle and I'm sorry—'

'But what did he *want*?'

'What did he want? He wanted me.' Millie laughed. She kicked a piece of the broken vase across the floor and turned to stare at Christopher.

He now took in her elated, excited face, flushed with an onset of laughter or tears. Her hair was plaited in a single plait which she had drawn forward over her shoulder and was convulsively clutching and tugging together with the folds of the red shawl.

'What on earth do you mean?'

'He came here to seduce me.'

'Millie! Surely you hadn't given him any reason to think—'

'No, of course I hadn't given him any reason to think. I sent him away with a flea in his ear.'

'But he can hardly just have taken it into his head—'

'Why shouldn't he just have taken it into his head? Or do you think I'm not attractive enough?'

'Of course I think you're attractive enough—'

'Then there's nothing more to explain, is there?'

'Millie, I'm very surprised indeed.'

'Well, I can't help that. Nothing happened. I just sent him off. That's why he was in such a hurry. You do believe me, don't you?'

'Of course I believe you. But as I say—'

'Why did *you* take it into your head to come, Christopher?'

'I had to see you. So many things have been happening. I'm sorry to arrive so late, but as I told you—'

'Yes, yes, your bike. Tell me some of the things that have been happening.'

'Well—Frances has decided not to marry Andrew.'

'Ah—' Millie let go of the red shawl which fell in a heap behind her. She moved forward and began quickly picking up the fragments of the Chinese vase. 'It's so cold in here, we could do with a fire, couldn't we.' She put the fragments of the vase on the table. She advanced on the fireplace and bent to put a match to the paper and sticks. 'Hand over a couple of those little logs, would you?'

'Millie, did you hear what I said?'

'Of course I did, but what am I supposed to say about it? I'm sorry.'

'It won't make any difference to us, of course. That's what I wanted to come and tell you. I'll manage about Frances.'

'Have you told Frances about us?'

'No.'

'That's just as well, perhaps.'

'Why—?'

'Christopher, I think I can't marry you after all.'

'Millie, what on earth are you talking about?'

'I just can't. I'd be no use to you.'

'Is this because of Frances?'

'No, it's nothing to do with Frances. I just can't do it, it would be wrong. Please forgive me. I should never have let the idea exist at all.'

'Millie, I can't let you say this—' He got awkwardly and stiffly to his feet, stretching out his arms towards her. Millie continued to stare down at the crackling sticks, whose light flickered on her face, showing a serene exhausted smile.

'Millie, my darling—' Christopher took her hand, lifting it from her side. It was heavy and limp. Her hand was familiar to him, and as he touched her his fingers became aware of something unusual. He looked down and saw that she was wearing a ring adorned with diamonds and rubies. He recognized the ring.

When Millie saw Christopher's expression and saw what he was looking at, she withdrew her hand with an exclamation and moved away from him.

'Millie, why are you wearing Andrew's ring?'

She pulled it quickly off and laid it on the table. 'Because Andrew has been wearing my ring.'

'I don't understand.'

'Well, why should you, with such an awful lot going on. I've just seduced your would-be son-in-law. I didn't mean to tell you. I just forgot about the ring. I never seem to be able to do wrong with impunity. What an unlucky girl I am!'

'Millie, do you actually mean that you—'

'Yes. I was in bed with Andrew when Pat turned up. I'd invited Pat to be my lover, only I didn't think he would oblige, so I made do with Andrew instead. It was all most unfortunate and I'm a very disappointed woman.'

'Millie, are you seriously saying that you and Andrew—'

'Yes! I've said it as clearly as I can. Do you want me to say it again?'

'How can you talk in that tone.'

'Well, a woman caught in my situation has got to adopt some tone, and it's not easy to combine devastating frankness with calm dignity. What tone do you suggest?'

'I just can't believe you.'

'Have a good try. The fact is I'm in love with Pat, I'm desperately in love with Pat and I have been for ages, only of course it's hopeless, and it would have been hopeless even if Andrew hadn't been here tonight. And our thing would have been hopeless even if you hadn't found out about Andrew. I really think you'd better go, Christopher. Oh, hang it, you can't, you haven't got a bike.'

'In love with Pat. I see.'

'Yes, the real thing. I'd let him walk on me. If only I'd just wanted the best and stayed true to it, it would have come to me. It *did* come to me, and I muffed it.'

'But you said it would have been hopeless anyway. And you have a rather quaint idea of the best. One night in bed with Pat Dumay. You know he'd have hated you in the morning.'

'Yes, you understand Pat. But you don't quite understand me. I'm an odder fish than you imagine, Christopher. Perhaps one night would have been enough, perhaps it would have been everything, and perhaps such hatred would be purer than the purest love. But it's all lost now. I've been unfaithful to my own code . You muddled me, the money business muddled me. And now he despises me and I expect you do too. I think I'll have some whiskey.'

'So you took Andrew. And that was why Frances refused him. I see it all now. It was because of you. I knew you were pretty irresponsible, but I didn't think you were utterly wicked.'

'Oh God, you don't think *that*?' Millie jarred the whiskey bottle back on to the table. 'I'm not that bad. I didn't do anything with Andrew, it didn't enter my head, until after he'd told me Frances had turned him down. Honest, Christopher. You can't really believe I'm capable of—'

'I'm afraid, Millie, that I think you capable of anything.'

They stared at each other in silence. Then Millie took the bottle again and unsteadily poured some whiskey into her glass. She murmured, 'It's funny. At this moment I think I'm almost in love with you. I told you I was a bit odd.'

'There was obviously some guilty secret between you last Monday when you had the boy to tea with Hilda. I thought he was behaving very strangely. But I didn't dream—'

'Oh, that. That was just a silly joke I played on him, it's not even worth explaining.'

'Frances could have had no other reason for refusing Andrew. It was all fixed up.'

'It wasn't all fixed up. And she could have had any reason for refusing him. He's not very clever. He's not even all that good-looking.'

'You say this just after you've dragged him into bed with you.'

'All right, I'm vulgar as well as wicked. But it's true.'

'Where is he now, by the way?'

'Half-way back to Dublin, I hope. He was supposed to slip out just after I came down again. What a pity, you might have borrowed his bike.' Millie started to laugh again, but stopped abruptly. 'You *can't* believe it, Christopher, you just can't believe that I would have seduced Andrew while he was engaged to Frances. I couldn't possibly have done anything so cruel; I'm not cruel, I'm just silly. And anyway I wanted Andrew to marry Frances just as you did because of us.'

'But you said just now you were in love with Pat and you knew our thing was no good anyway.'

'Yes—I do seem in rather a muddle, don't I. But I swear I didn't—'

'You might have done this deliberately to break up Frances' engagement so as to have an excuse for dropping me. I regard you as an utterly mad and destructive person and I always have.'

'Then you shouldn't have envisaged marrying me.'

'I entirely agree I shouldn't.'

They stood now facing each other across the table. What on earth is happening, Christopher asked himself, why are we shouting like this, am I dreaming? His weariness, his wet clothes, the strong dose of whiskey, made him feel dazed and light-headed. The figure of Millie stood out before him with a ghastly sharpness, an object detached from a flat background. He swayed, then went and sat down heavily.

'Anyway, it's not going to happen now,' said Millie in a dull voice. She began to push the ring about the surface of the table with her finger. 'I know it all serves me right. If you behave rottenly you can't complain when other people don't realize just *how* rottenly you're prepared to behave. But, Christopher, you must believe what I said. Andrew came and told me that Frances had turned him down, and then, just to cheer him up you know, I suggested—'

'How long had it been going on?'

'It had been going on for about two hours when Pat arrived, and—'

'I don't mean that! How long before today?'

'Not at all before today.'

'Why did you say our thing would have been no good even if I hadn't found out?'

'Because of Pat. Well, no, not because of Pat. Pat wasn't really anything to do with that. I thought of these things in separate parts of my mind. It was no good anyway, it was a bad kind of idea. We don't love each other enough, Christopher.'

'I suppose it's true,' he said slowly, 'we don't.'

It was raining again. The wind blew the light rain against the windows in intermittent sighing gusts that were like a soft ripple of waves.

'Well, there it is. God, I feel wretched. Damn, we've let the fire go out.'

Christopher got up and found his mackintosh. 'I must go now.'

'You can't go in all this rain. And I haven't got a bike to lend you.'

'Don't worry, I'll walk.'

'Don't be idiotic, Christopher, you know perfectly well you've got to stay here. There's a room ready. You'd die of exposure walking all the way down the mountain.'

Christopher threw down his coat. He was ready to weep. 'All right, all right.'

'And here, you'd better take the ring to give back to Andrew. I don't suppose I'll ever see *him* again. Everybody hates me now.'

'I don't want the ring—Oh, all right, I'll take it.'

'Well, no, maybe you'd better not. It would hurt him so terribly to know you knew—'

'I don't care how hurt he is.'

'You must forgive Andrew. He was very miserable and he's so young.'

'Oh, hang Andrew.'

'You know, you should have given me a ring, Christopher, it might have protected me. Ah, well. I'll show you to your room. The bed's not aired, but I'll get you a hot-water bottle.'

'Don't bother, I just want to be left alone now.'

They went out, Millie carrying the lamp, and mounted the stairs slowly together like an old couple.

'This is your room. Are you sure you wouldn't—'

'No, thanks.'

'I'll light your candle for you. There. Oh, I forgot, would you like anything to eat?'

'No, thank you, Millie.'

'Christopher, you do believe me, don't you, that I didn't—'

'Yes, yes, yes, I believe you.'

'Christopher, I'm awfully sorry about everything.'

'It doesn't matter.'

'Well, it does, but anyway. May I kiss you?'

'Oh, go away, Millie.'

'Good night, my dear, sleep well.'

'Good night.'

Chapter Twenty-one

'THE movement of renewal with which I had hoped to associate my wife failed largely because of a complete lack of response on her part. I appreciated later that it was of course foolish of me to expect from her any understanding of the symbolic nature of my action and its sheer difficulty, or even any conceptual grasp of what I had to tell her. A being devoid of theory, living almost entirely at the level of intuition, she condemned me for what I was, but when I positively desired, even needed, her judgment upon what I had done, she withheld it, and seemed incapable of censuring, even of perceiving, anything as definite as an act. Absolution requires a definition of sin. My wife was unable to give me absolution.'

Barney inhaled the fragrance of this paragraph and returned refreshed to consider the pad of paper on which, earlier that day, he had several times begun to compose a letter. It was Sunday afternoon.

Dear Frances,

I feel it is my duty to pass on to you a piece of information which has lately come into my possession. I know for a positive fact that your fiancé has been having a love affair with Lady Kinnard. I am sorry to be a bringer of bad news, but I feel it is my duty . . .

He thrust the sheet aside and picked up a second version.

My dear Frances,

It is sad to be a bringer of bad news to one one loves—and I think you do, you must, know the sincerity of my attachment to you. But there are moments when it is one's tragic duty to shatter a peace of mind which rests upon a misconception.

He studied this for some time, altered 'sincerity of my attachment' to 'warmth of my affection', and then put the paper down again.

Was it really his tragic duty to shatter a peace of mind which rested upon a misconception? Barney was in a state of excited distress with which his experience that morning at the Easter Mass had mingled to produce a turmoil of emotions, now dark, now singularly light and glittering. The crowded church, the high exultation of the choir, the unveiled images, the heaped-up flowers: these impressions, as of emergence into a place of dazzling brightness, contrasted strangely and yet significantly with the sinister, dangerous, thief-like adventures of the night.

Barney had yielded to the temptation to go to Rathblane knowing quite well that he was doing something idiotic and improper. He was increasingly aware of all his activities as a mode of warfare against his wife, and the very fact that it was not altogether for Millie that he wanted to go made the action seem at first even more a wrong one. If Kathleen had only co-operated with him and entered into the drama of his change of heart she could, he felt, really have changed him. He would have given up seeing Millie. But in order to be able to do what he so pure-heartedly intended he needed a motive which only Kathleen could give him. Her inability to see the mechanics, as it were, of his good intentions he read as a condemnation of him far deeper than any he had ever before experienced. He felt suddenly that Kathleen regarded him as hopeless. All right, he would behave accordingly.

This was what he thought at first. But as he cycled toward Rathblane in the evening and breathed the mountain air and saw the quick fugitive sun on distant green fields and watched a rainbow grow slowly from the lower slopes of Kippure he experienced a youthful sensation of pleasure at being a man going toward a woman he loved. He no longer felt that this was part of his fight with Kathleen or had anything to do with Kathleen at all. In thus obeying his heart he was doing something essentially innocent. He needed to see Millie and there was a redeeming simplicity in satisfying the need. Perhaps his whole moral scheme had become too complicated? If he could only get out of the old familiar web of guilt and justification and back to the things he just wanted to do and the doing of them, then he might become innocent and harmless as he had once been. As the sun went down behind Kippure and the fields glowed a luminous dusty gold before becoming dark it began to seem to Barney that his wants and his needs were very simple and without corruption.

He had obeyed the impulse to go where Millie was without having any special plan about what he would do when he arrived. He hoped of course to find Millie alone, to come to her as at their happiest times and be received by that especial laughter which she reserved for him, to be called to her joyously like an animal. The thought that this could still happen made him smile happily as he pushed his bicycle up the steeper parts of the road. If, however, he was unlucky and Millie had company he would have to decide whether to let her know that he had come or whether to remain concealed. At various times in the past Barney had observed Millie without revealing his presence. These experiences, invariably painful, yet gave him a guilty thrill and a pleasure even more obscure and profound. It was something that took him straight back to certain pleasures of childhood. And more reflectively he could treat this pleasure-pain as a gift which he gave to Millie, as a form of homage.

The thought that someone else might be there brought back again to his mind the melancholy prospect of her marriage to Christopher. Since what now seemed to him his mystical experience on Thursday Barney had set aside the whole problem of Christopher and had ceased to feel the temptation to tell Frances her father's intentions. Now the problem and the temptation had reappeared, and constituted in fact an extra motive for going at once to see Millie. Unable in certain moods to believe in his misfortune, Barney felt that perhaps after all it was unlikely that Millie would really marry Christopher. Nothing was fixed, the future was still uncertain. And although he did not really think that he could positively ask Millie what she intended to do, he needed to see her as a sort of reassurance. He felt that when he actually saw her he would be quite sure that everything between him and her was going to be all right and indeed better than ever.

On arriving at Rathblane in the darkness Barney had noticed a bicycle which he knew not to be Christopher's leaning against the wall. On penetrating into the house by methods well known to him he had heard voices. With the thrilled curiosity which caused him such painful pleasure he had crept closer. He had then learnt first the identity, and then the errand, of Millie's visitor. This discovery caused him at first simply an intense moral shock. Millie and Andrew were both quite suddenly revealed to him as wicked, and wicked with a blackness which faded his own moral frailty to the palest grey. After the first shock he felt amazed indignant jealousy, sheer fright at being the possessor of so potent a secret, and finally a childish misery that his Millie, who had played such harmless, pretty games with him, should elect to play *this* game with another. These reflections were interrupted by the arrival of Pat. Barney, who had been standing in the dark on the landing, heard someone enter below and hid himself quickly in one of the rooms opposite. Later he heard Pat's voice in the dressing-room.

Barney, who had been feeling scared before, was now terrified. He was in a state of total confusion concerning the nature and consequences of his discovery, and he had just made a colossal moral judgment which he was still entirely unable to assimilate. With Pat's arrival Barney became suddenly sensitive to another aspect of the matter, his own guilt as an eavesdropper, a guilt vastly potentiated by the magnitude of what he had overheard. If they were to find him there listening to them in the dark there could be no forgiveness then. Pat, moreover, was the last person in the world before whom Barney could have endured to feel that particular shame.

He did not speculate about Pat's visit or attempt to over-hear any more. He tiptoed down the stairs and stood at the back of the hall wondering if it was safe to leave the house. As he was still hesitating Pat came running down the stairs and out of the front door. A moment later the door reopened and Pat, as it seemed to Barney, came back into the house again. Barney waited no longer but slid away into the kitchen quarters and out into the paved yard, where he waited a while until the moon was again obscured and then went to rejoin his bicycle.

The next morning the pattern of his feelings had shifted. His indignation against Andrew was more extreme, while his indignation against Millie was tempered by a kind of pity which made him feel for the first time superior to her. He felt also a kind of triumphant relief at having found out so much and escaped with impunity. His jealousy had diminished, merging into a tender sense of responsibility for Millie, and a sober recognition that he now held a very powerful weapon against her. His previous temptation, to reveal Christopher's intentions to Frances, now seemed a feeble pointless affair. It was, it remained, unclear what could be the result of this revelation. But now Barney had at his disposal an infallible method of achieving both his objects, the separation of Millie from Christopher and the separation of Frances from Andrew. Would he employ this method?

Perhaps it was better not to meddle. Since *that* had happened and would presumably be happening again it was unlikely that the two marriages that he feared would come off anyway. The apple cart was sure to be upset without his intervention. If by any chance, however, Frances or Millie did marry, not only would Barney never be able to forgive himself for not having spoken sooner, he knew that he would be irresistibly impelled to make the revelation later on when it was too late to do anything but damage. So was it not, considering all the facts including his own weakness, his plain duty to write to Frances?

Barney went to the Easter Mass like a sleep walker. He had decided on the previous day to go and now went automatically. Then quite suddenly, as if someone had come into the room and lightly touched him as he sat absent-mindedly, he was reminded of where he was and what occasion was being honoured. He recalled his good resolutions of three days ago when he had decided to simplify his life and make peace with Kathleen. Had that been mere meaningless emotion or had it been truly the pressure of another world upon his darkness? He remembered how he had felt sunk in himself beyond the possibility of change. Then when this freedom had suddenly been breathed upon him he had jerked up, he had certainly moved; but he had moved still in the old way, projecting his stale self in a new direction; and as soon as there was any check to his fantasy he had despaired at once. He had wanted a formal punishment. But perhaps his penance was simply informality. The terrible thought occurred to him that possibly he ought simply to act rightly and expect no one even to notice it.

The mass impressed him with the notion of an event, a change. Attending to it, he began to feel an obscure distress, a pang as at the loss of something. He never really liked the ending of Lent. He was never quite ready to finish with mourning when the great peal of joy rang out. Suddenly now it occurred to him why.

> *Dic nobis, Maria,*
> *Quid vidisti in via?*
> *Sepulcrum Christi viventis*
> *Et gloriam vidi resurgentis.*

Mary Magdalene might indeed have glimpsed Him in the garden somewhere, but for the rest of us there remained only the empty tomb. 'He is not here.' The Christ who travels towards Jerusalem and suffers there can be made into a familiar. The risen Christ is something suddenly unknown. This metamorphosis had always in the past represented for Barney simply a disappointment, like the ending of a play. He had never thought of it as a starting point. He thought of it so now for the first time; and, with this shift of view, it became clear to him, with a sudden authoritative clarity, that it was the risen Christ and not the suffering Christ who must be his saviour: the absent Christ hidden in God and not that all too recognizable victim. He was too horribly, too intimately connected with his own degraded image of the Christ of Good Friday. Easter must purge that imagery now. The scourged tormented flesh appealed to something in him that was too grossly human since he had not the gift of compassion. These sufferings ended for him in self-pity and further on and shamefully in pleasure. This could not alter him a jot though he contemplated it forever. What was required of him was something which lay quite outside the deeply worked pattern of suffering, the plain possibility of change without drama and even without punishment. Perhaps after all that was the message of Easter. Absence not pain would be the rite of his salvation.

As Barney walked home from mass he also recalled to his mind events of yesterday which his visit to Rathblane had made him totally forget. For a short time, a period perhaps of two hours, he had believed that the Volunteers were about to start an armed rising. Even though he had so incomprehensibly, and it now seemed to him stupidly, surrendered his rifle, a sacrifice not to God but to his own vanity, he was nevertheless an Irish Volunteer. He was a careless, lax, muddle-headed one, but still he was a Volunteer, and he had pledged himself to fight for Ireland should the moment ever come. Then by a connection of thought which led him back through what seemed to him the best moments of his life, he recalled Clonmacnoise, and the little roofless chapel and the abandoned stones and the great empty sweep of the Shannon. *Numen inerat.* And the presence there had been not only God but Ireland. Tears sprang into his eyes.

Barney had joined the Volunteers partly but not entirely to please Pat. He had joined too because he loved Ireland and pitied that history of suffering and because he knew that it might in the end be necessary to fight for rights which had been too long withheld. Barney had a strong sense of history but very little sense of politics, and he acted here by intuition. He had expected everything from Ireland, from her darkness and her beauty, he had run to her as to a mother and a place of shriving. And although his life had been a disappointment and a muddle, it did not occur to him to blame Ireland for this. He had abandoned his book on the saints. It was he who was the traitor. That dark perfection remained near him and untouched, and he loved it. He owed Ireland that service. He had thought so when he joined the Volunteers and he had ineluctably thought so again during the dreadful two hours of yesterday. He had been intensely relieved to learn that he had not got to fight after all.

Barney now sat in his room and looked at the letters to Frances which he had begun earlier in the morning before he went to mass. He could still not think quite clearly about the problem, but it seemed to him that the letters were unworthy. Perhaps Frances ought to know, and perhaps Christopher ought to know, what had happened, but this did not yield the result that he ought to tell them. Any meddling of his here would be evil. He could not, just automatically could not, act with a pure interest, and he ought not to cause fear, misery and hatred without one. Andrew, Millie, Frances and Christopher must take their chance and work out the design of their fate without interference from him. It must be as if he had never known, never seen, that which he knew and saw, or as if he must for ever admit that he could not understand it. Inaction, agnosticism were for him the lessons of the empty tomb. And then it had come to him that with Kathleen too it must be the same. He must not expect to understand Kathleen or to be understood by her. He must not expect her to help him to make a tidy drama out of his infidelities or to make him suffer in exactly the way he wanted. He must just do the right thing simply, even surreptitiously, and let what would follow follow mechanically.

Barney, having come through this maze of speculation, now felt himself brought up with a jerk like a horse that has browsed its way to the end of its tether. So he had come to the same conclusion again but by a different route. Now that the working out was different could the act be done? Could he really surrender Millie? He leaned his head forward on the table, closing his eyes, resting, and then realized that he was praying.

*　　*　　*　　*

'Barney, I'm so sorry, I've wakened you up. There was no answer when I knocked so I just came in to leave a note,'

Frances was there.

Barney sat up abruptly.

'Oh, Frances, come in. I must have been asleep for a moment. I'm so glad to see you. I've been so wanting to see you.'

He got up, fussing round about her, murmuring, touching her, and her presence in the room made him intensely happy. He felt as if somehow while he slept a problem had been solved, a burden lifted.

'Here, let me help you off with your wet things. Your umbrella will be all right there in the corner, let it drip, it won't hurt. Would you like some tea? But oh, my dear, what is it?'

Barney, now that Frances had taken off her hood, saw her face and that she must have been crying. She sat down beside the table, flattening the damp streaky hair back against her head.

'I've just come to say goodbye.'

'Goodbye? But are you going away?'

264

'Yes, I'm going to England. I'm going to be a V.A.D. I'm going to the war.' She did not look at him but stared across the little heaped-up table at the lines of faded cottage gardens upon the powdery dry wallpaper. Her mouth drooped.

'But why ever——?'

'Why not? One ought to do one's bit. I may be totally uneducated, but at least I can cut bread and butter.'

'But what about, what about——Andrew?' Barney felt as if his guilty knowledge must all come tumbling out of his mouth attached to the name.

'Oh, that. That's all over. I'm not going to marry Andrew, you know. We've decided not to get married after all.'

Barney circled the room, rebounding from the walls in his excitement. He longed to question Frances, but could not think how to do it. 'Not marry Andrew. All over. Well, fancy. Oh dear. I'm so sorry. What a surprise though. I do hope you're not sad about it. I do wish you weren't going away.'

'I'm sorry to go, Barney, and I'm specially sorry to leave you. I'll miss you. But it'll do me good to get out of Ireland. With the war and so on, Ireland is a bit of a hole. And I have been in such a stupid mood lately. I won't stay more than a minute now. I see you're working. Is it Saint Brigid?'

Frances picked up a sheet of paper from the table.

'Wait, not that!' Too late Barney jumped. She was already reading the letter.

There was a moment's silence as she read it, put it down, then rested her head in her hand with an almost inaudible 'Oh'.

After another moment she said in a tired, spiritless voice, 'How did you know this, Barney?'

Interpreting her tone he said quickly, 'So you know?'

'Yes.'

'How did you find out?'

'First tell me how you did?'

'I was there last night, at Rathblane. I went to see Millie and found——'

'Pat and Andrew. Yes. You didn't see my father. He was there too. There was quite a gathering. Just like comic opera.'

'Christopher—so he knows—'

'Yes, and he told me this morning.'

'And then you broke things off with Andrew.'

'No, no. I'd refused Andrew days ago, I mean we'd decided not to marry. That was nothing to do with Millie. Millie's not a monster. She didn't grab Andrew until after I'd dropped him. And he still thinks no one knows about his little adventure.'

Barney held his head. It was complicated. But was it not now all right, utterly all right? Christopher knew, and Millie was innocent. Well, not quite but almost. So everything would be all right. He would not have to lose Millie after all. But what was he saying?

Frances' voice interrupted him. 'I'm reading the other letter now. I like the bit about your tragic duty. You must have enjoyed writing that. Which one were you going to send?'

Barney suddenly became aware of a different Frances, a Frances with a new vocabulary, a Frances who could talk in a cynical way, who could assess and sentence him. He felt hurt, then appallingly guilty. His instinct had been right. One could not so intrude one's abominable knowledge. He deserved to be hated for what he knew.

'Frances, darling, I was not going to send either of those letters, honest. It would have been utterly wrong and I'd decided not to. I was just going to tear them up.'

'Oh.' She did not believe him.

Barney jerked himself about, jostling the table and spilling the greater part of the Memoir on to the floor. He trampled the pages underfoot. He felt frantic. He was not going to get the credit for anything with anybody. And now she would never forgive him simply for knowing. 'Frances, I *swear* I was not going to send those letters. I know I ought never to have written them—'

'Don't shout, Barney. It doesn't matter, I knew anyway, it

doesn't matter. I really must go now. I've got so much to do.'

'When are you going?'

'Tuesday or Wednesday.'

'So you'll be on the mail boat after all. Frances, you do believe me——?'

'Yes, yes, of course.'

There was a sudden loud bang on the door and they both jumped. The door swung wide open to reveal the large form of Pat Dumay.

'I must be off,' said Frances. She whipped her things together and was gone, fading thinly away under Pat's right arm.

Barney stared at where she had been, and then formed the face of Pat, huge, excited, grinning. 'What is it, Pat?'

'Sit down. I want to ask you two questions.'

Barney sat by the table and Pat closed the door carefully and sat beside him, placing his large hand on Barney's shoulder.

Barney sat open-mouthed staring up at his stepson. He felt he was being apprehended for some fault. But the pressure of the hand was affectionate. Pat seemed to be in a state of anxious rapture. His left hand, which was bandaged, kneaded Barney's shoulder with a rhythmic clutch and caress, while he pressed his other hand flat upon the table as if he were about to vault. He leant over his stepfather.

'Listen now. You know the plan that you heard of yesterday? Well, we are going to carry it out tomorrow.'

'You mean you're going to fight after all, the Volunteers, just like——?'

'Yes. It's for tomorrow. I want to ask you first, do you want to join us, or would you rather be left out? No one will think the worse of you.'

'I'll come with you of course,' said Barney.

There was silence between them for a moment. Then Pat released him and stood up. 'You mean you're willing to fight?'

'Yes.'

Pat stared at him doubtfully. Then he gave a grunt which might have been a sigh or a laugh. 'Good for you.'

'When is it to be tomorrow?'

'Twelve noon at the first stroke of the angelus. I'll give you full instructions.'

'What was the other thing you wanted to ask me?'

'It doesn't arise now. It was something about Cathal. But it would only have come up if you'd said no to the first question. I'm afraid I thought that you would. I apologize.'

'Don't mention it,' said Barney. 'By the way, you'll have to issue me with another rifle.'

When Pat was gone, Barney stood beside his cluttered table and stared at the powdery cottage gardens deep in the old wallpaper. He was extremely frightened. He had too, in a way that was not entirely disagreeable, a sense of being finally cornered. Whatever the state of his soul might be, his old existence was over, a life beyond his own had taken charge of him.

Would he have sent those letters to Frances in the end? Would he really have managed to give up Millie? He would get no credit. He was justly judged. Or rather it did not much matter now how he was judged. That was not so very important after all.

He reached out for the two letters and took them and tore them into long strips. Then he picked up the crumpled sheets of the Memoir from the floor and began systematically to tear each sheet into small pieces.

Chapter Twenty-two

PAT DUMAY began to mount the dark stairs to the attic. A lamp placed on the floor at the top cast thick shadows down beneath each stair and illuminated the figure of a man in Volunteer uniform who had just come to attention. Pat swayed with fatigue. He had been unceasingly active since the news had reached him on Sunday afternoon that the rebellion was to take place after all. Now it was already after midnight, it was already Easter Monday morning.

On Sunday morning MacNeill's countermanding order had appeared in the *Sunday Independent*. At the same time, Pearse, Connolly, MacDonagh and all the chief militants came together for a meeting at Liberty Hall. At this meeting it was decided that in spite of MacNeill they must act. The rising was fixed again for twelve noon on Monday. Couriers were sent out to all parts of Ireland with the new order.

They all knew, and Pat knew perfectly well, that MacNeill's action had damaged the project perhaps irrevocably. The men, who had been keyed up, had relaxed. Some of them had gone away. A few had even destroyed their uniforms in disgust. There was an atmosphere of *détente* and disappointment and irresponsibility. Monday was the day of the Fairyhouse races, the Irish Grand National. Even if the messengers could, in time, reach every part of the organization, would the order be obeyed? Faint-hearts would find an excuse in the obvious confusion of the leadership. The first plan had administered a fright. Those who had learnt with relief of its cancellation would be in no mood to start again. They would say that they knew not whom to believe and they would go off to the races.

On Sunday Pearse and Connolly could have been sure of their numbers. On Monday it was anybody's guess how many men would turn up. This meant that a lot of quite new arrangements had to be made in a hurry, and crucial projects had to be abandoned: such as the cutting of all telephone contact with England, since there would now not be enough men to occupy the Dublin telephone exchange. An elaborate plan, the product of weeks and months of work, had to be scrapped in favour of a congeries of last-minute improvisations.

However, it was necessary to fight. The English might be slow-witted, but they were capable of reflection upon the events in Kerry; and since so many people in Dublin now knew what had been intended an informer would soon find his way to the Castle. It was surprising that he had not already done so. Then the English would have to act, they would have to disarm the whole movement: and the Irish would have the choice of firing a few disorganized shots or submitting tamely. These were compelling reasons for fighting. But they were haunted by another reason which nobody mentioned. History now required of them that they should shed their blood. They had planned and schemed and hoped for so long, and set going a train of events which now seemed to have a momentum of its own. On the morning of Sunday, April the twenty-third, at Liberty Hall they could, in some quite ordinary sense of could, have decided otherwise. But everyone present felt their decision to be inevitable.

Pat reached the top of the stairs and the uniformed man saluted.

'How is my prisoner?'

'All safe, sir.'

'You may go now.'

The guard unlocked the door and stepped aside and Pat entered the room. The prisoner was Cathal.

Pat had decided to spend the night of Sunday to Monday at Blessington Street. This had been made possible by the timely departure of his mother to the country. Because of anxiety about Pat she had been putting off a visit to an ailing elderly cousin. Now her mind had been entirely set at rest. Pat thought that what had impressed his mother most was reading MacNeill's notice in the *Sunday Independent*. After a Sunday paper had said that all was well Kathleen was entirely reassured. Her joy took form immediately as an extreme concern for her ailing cousin and she left Dublin by train after mass on Sunday.

Late on Sunday afternoon Pat had made the decision to detain Cathal. He knew that this was only a temporary solution, but he did not want a repetition of Saturday's drama. He had of course not told Cathal that the rebellion was going to take place after all, but Cathal might at any moment find this out and decide to hide himself from his brother. Hurrying back from the other end of Dublin, Pat was extremely relieved to find the boy in the house and decoyed him upstairs and locked him in an attic, setting one of his own men there to guard him. He informed Cathal briefly about the renewed plan and told him that he would let him know later what his own part in it might be. Pat said this out of prudence so that Cathal might not be driven into a frenzy and attempt to climb out of the window. Pat was in fact determined that Cathal should have no part at all in the coming events.

But how on earth was he to bring this about? Pat was now more certain than ever that if his brother were exposed to danger he himself would become totally ineffective. He realized, realized it only perhaps now on Sunday with absolute clarity, that Cathal was as important to him as Ireland: was conceivably more important. When he knew this he was appalled. If this were so then anything might happen, anything might be decided. Only then slowly he moved again in automatic performance of his tasks, for he knew that there was something else which would always weigh down the balance on the side of Ireland, and that was his own honour. He could not conceivably in any last or smallest particular fail the cause to which he was engaged. But he could not put it to himself that he must be ready to sacrifice Cathal. If anything happened to Cathal he would become incapable, blind, a mad man. He had got to save Cathal, not only because of Cathal but because of Ireland. But how?

When he had seen this problem, as of course he had seen it, from further back, it had seemed to Pat that he would manage either by arranging for his brother to be out of Ireland at the crucial moment, or else by somehow incarcerating him. Pat had had too short a warning to adopt the former plan: he now saw at the last moment the difficulties of the latter. It was not realistic to imagine that Cathal could simply be imprisoned until the rising was either successful or was crushed. This might take weeks, months. All that could possibly be achieved would be to keep him prisoner until the fighting had started and hope that it would then be physically impossible for him to reach any of the places where the rebels were. If he could prevent Cathal from marching with Connolly's men he would have done all that he could. But even this was difficult since, and Pat did not fully understand this until Sunday night, it was not just a matter of ropes or handcuffs or a locked door. Cathal would have to be guarded.

Cathal would have to be guarded or else he would do himself some serious damage. The problem of imprisoning him was like the problem of restraining, without an adequate cage, a strong and desperate animal. Obviously a locked door was not enough; and it is not so very simple to tie someone up in such a way that he cannot escape and also cannot hurt himself seriously in trying to. If Pat was to march away on Monday morning without the most crippling anxiety he must find somebody to stay with Cathal: but who? It was after all unfortunate that his mother had gone away and could not now be reached. He could not honourably spare one of his own soldiers for this odd entirely personal task. He had thought first of his stepfather. But when Barney had so simply and so unexpectedly elected to fight, Pat, taken aback, had felt unable to deny him what was, after all, every Irishman's right. To keep his stepfather well out of his own way he had arranged for him to join the contingent at Boland's Mill, and Barney had already gone to spend the night with a comrade in the vicinity. Pat telephoned Christopher several times but got no reply. He even thought of Millie, but she was presumably still at Rathblane, which was not on the telephone. He continued with his duties, acting as courier between Dawson Street and Liberty Hall, without solving the problem. Would it be all right just to tie Cathal up and lock the door? He visited the store room at Dawson Street and came away with a pair of handcuffs. The problem obsessed and paralysed him; and now late at night and almost unconscious with tiredness he had still not resolved it.

There was a small lamp burning inside the room. Cathal was huddled on the bed in a rather unnatural position and did not stir when Pat came in. He seemed to have been sitting thus for a long time staring at the door.

Pat was now in full uniform. He had left his rifle and knapsack downstairs but was wearing his bandolier and revolver. The handcuffs were in his pocket. He closed the door and sat down on the floor, leaning against it.

The attic had once been a maid's bedroom in the days when there were maids at the house in Blessington Street, and it still contained an iron bedstead and mattress, a washstand and an upright chair and a coloured picture representing the Sacred Heart. The little lamp, which was on the floor, showed the underside of innumerable cobwebs upon the yellow stained walls. Close pattering rain enclosed the room, the roof, the window, made of rain. Pat looked at the picture and thought, but the heart is not there in the middle of the body, it is on the left. Then he recalled someone saying that in fact it was really in the middle though it was popularly said to be on the left. What would it be like to be shot in the heart? He realized that on sitting down he had almost fallen asleep and that Cathal had said something.

'What did you say, Cathal?'

'I said what are you going to do with me?'

What, what, what? Pat saw from the outline of Cathal's shadow on the wall that the boy was trembling. He could not see his face clearly through the rain and the sleep.

'That mattress must be damp,' said Pat. 'You shouldn't be sitting on it.' He simply must not fall asleep. He got up, half staggering, opened the door, transferred the key to the inside, locked the door and put the key in his pocket. He sagged down again to the floor.

'What are you going to do?'

'I don't know,' said Pat. 'You're a problem. Let's start at the beginning.' He felt that there was some sort of logic here, some sort of consequential procedure which if he could go through it step by step he might keep awake and reach a conclusion with independent authority. 'Logic,' he said aloud.

'What?'

'I said logic. Listen. Let's start at the beginning. I don't want you to take part in this business, you're too young.'

'You can skip that bit,' said Cathal. He began to uncurl his legs which were obviously very stiff. He grimaced and rubbed his ankles and then knelt up on the mattress. 'You're right about the damp.'

'You're too young,' said Pat, 'and you must simply obey me and promise me that you'll stay at home tomorrow and not put yourself in danger. This is a job for professionals. You're not trained and you would only be a hindrance. Someone would have to look after you and you would do harm and not good to the cause. I know this is very hard, but you must be old enough and brave enough to understand it.'

'I'm old enough and brave enough to fight,' said Cathal. 'You may still treat me as a child, but other people don't. And I can use a rifle, one of the I.C.A. fellows taught me. And—'

'I'm not arguing. I'm telling you what you are going to do.'

'You're not my da. You used to beat me when you were

stronger, but I'm just as strong now, and if I decide to go out of that door you can't stop me.'

'You know perfectly well I can stop you with one hand. Cathal, be sensible—'

'I'm not going to obey you and I am going to fight tomorrow. Imagine you were me. Would you stay at home because your elder brother told you you were a little boy?'

Pat was silent. His head swayed. He must keep on talking. What was the next step? Logic. 'In that case,' said Pat, 'you'll have to stay a prisoner.' He touched the handcuffs in his pocket.

'Just you try and cage me.'

It was evident to Pat that Cathal had thought just as hard on this subject as he had. 'I can easily cage you. I'll lock the door.'

'I'll kick the door to bits or get out of the window.'

'I'll tie you up. I've got some handcuffs too.'

'I'll scream the place down and drum on the wall with my feet. There are people in these rooms on either side. The whole street would come and rescue me.'

'I'd have to gag you.'

'I'd swallow my gag and choke or else get a scream out somehow.'

Pat knew that he could not gag Cathal. It is very difficult to gag a desperate person with safety. Pat's head swayed again. He was beginning to feel almost tearful with self-pity. He must sleep tonight and soon. He must make himself ready for tomorrow. Oh God, tomorrow. There must be some way out of this agony. Logic.

'Pat,' said Cathal. His face was indistinct among the cobwebs and the clatter of the rain. 'Understand that it is no use trying to tie me up. I'd be like a wild animal in a trap that would bite its own leg off to get away. I'd get out or kill myself doing it. Imagine yourself—'

'I'll leave someone with you.'

'There's no one you can spare. Everyone who knows will be out tomorrow and you can't trust anyone else. Besides, I'd get away whoever you left with me. It's too late now to keep me out of it. Let me come with you, Pat, I want to be with you, see that you've got to let me be with you.'

Cathal's voice now was strained and childish and Pat realized that Cathal too was in the last stages of exhaustion. Something had got to be decided and he must not go to sleep. If he went to sleep now he would wake to find Cathal gone.

Pat moved, trying to keep himself conscious, and his arm brushed the holster of his revolver. He opened his eyes wide. It was perfectly simple after all. He had only to shoot his brother in the leg.

Pat saw the room very clearly, as if it had only now been lighted up, the cobwebs slightly swaying in the air from the lamp, the blotched sloping walls where the rain tapped, Christ displaying His Sacred Heart. Cathal was crouched on the bed underneath his shadow, moving himself about slightly, stiff and chilled upon the damp mattress. Pat saw his face sharply defined, pinched together about his long nose with tiredness and anxiety. There was a pathetic exhausted defiance about the pouting mouth. Cathal's dark hair kept falling forward as if it were wearily trying to draw his head down.

Does he know what I am thinking, thought Pat as he stared. He fingered the revolver. Then somehow out of the dream he was almost in, out of the Sacred Heart, came the thought that he would kill Cathal. That would be simpler still. That would make him entirely safe. If Cathal were dead he would be beyond harm and tomorrow Pat would be free to die himself. Was that not after all the best thing? He loved Cathal too much to allow him to be hurt by anyone else. Only Pat should hurt him, and that would be no hurt but simply to lay him to sleep. He loved Cathal too much.

Pat grunted and tried to get up and lurched to his knees. He had been thinking something that was insane or else he had been in a dream. He groaned and said, 'Cathal, I've got to sleep, I've got to rest. Have some mercy on me.'

'Promise that you'll let me go tomorrow.'

'I can't, I can't.'

'Promise, and then we can both sleep.'

'I shall be lying here on my face in a minute,' said Pat. He was not sure whether he had said the words aloud. Cathal would soon get the key out of his pocket. The room was indistinct again as if it were full of fumes.

'Promise.'

'I promise,' said Pat. 'All right, I promise.'

It was a lie. But what else could he do? He groaned, leaning against the door, trying to get up. He had to sleep. He would solve the problem tomorrow.

'You do really promise, you do?'

'Yes, yes. Where's the key? Here. Come down from here. You must go to your own room. We've both got to sleep now. Come.'

The stairway opened and the lamp still burning at the top of it. It was dark below like a pit. Pat held on to the banisters. 'Can you carry that lamp, Cathal.'

He pushed open the door of Cathal's room and the light showed it. The lamp jolted down on to the table. Cathal, his head drooping, took off his shoes and his trousers and got into bed. He started to say something but it turned into a drowsy mumble and in a moment he was fast asleep.

Pat looked about the familiar little room: the bookcase with Cathal's books staggering upon the shelves, the pictures of birds pinned to the wall, Cathal's model yacht. It seemed his own childhood that was present here. He had had indeed, with Cathal, a second boyhood, a second innocence. For the first time he grasped what was going to happen tomorrow as a nightmare, as something terrible. He had so often seen his brother lie down to sleep like that on holidays, when they were as tired as they were tonight; and they slept and in the early morning went swimming in the cold sea. Would it never be like that again? Tomorrow he would be killing men. Could the nightmare not pass away and leave them innocent and free in the morning? He leaned over his brother, thrusting back the dark lock of hair from his face, and touching that place upon his temple where the muzzle of a revolver might be pressed. Had Cathal got to die? Had he got to die? They were so young. He suddenly recalled and understood his mother's words: there is no such thing as dying for Ireland.

Chapter Twenty-three

SOON after nine o'clock on Easter Monday morning Second Lieutenant Andrew Chase-White was walking briskly up Blessington Street. He had decided that he must have some sort of explanation with his cousin Pat.

Andrew had decided to go to Rathblane not really because his interest in Millie had increased: that interest steadily diminished, reaching zero when he was actually in bed with her. His best, he thought afterwards his purest, moment with Millie had been when he first kissed her. This event, like a rocket suddenly bursting and slowly descending, had cast a shower of fading light over his subsequent movements. He felt drugged, romantic: but it was despair that made him act. The loss of Frances, as the news of it came to the different, the outlying, regions of his consciousness made his whole being into something restless and diseased. He could not see how, moment to moment, to exist any more. He put off informing his mother of the catastrophe and suffered her questions with churlish writhing. He resolved to return at once to England but recalled that he had to report to Longford at the end of the week. This obligation, which might have seemed a consoling necessity of fate, tormented him too, and he thought: I shall be sent out *there*, I shall be killed, and nothing will have had any meaning. I shall have done nothing, I shall not even have understood. Frances was the whole meaning of my life, and now my life has no meaning and is empty.

The sense was one of emptiness and of strewn pieces and of the sudden disappearance of any picture of himself. A week ago he had occupied himself, packed himself tight with satisfied being, and glimpsed all about him the reflection of a handsome young British officer, the darling of the world, a fine young man with a bride. Now he could scarcely believe that his physical appearance was not utterly altered. He could indeed feel the expression of his face puckering and sagging as if his head were shrinking. He was empty and ragged within: and he felt at moments that his whole body must collapse in obedience to a vacuum.

He went to Millie simply in order to have some action, something, to fill up the void. He felt that Millie might make him into a person again. His altered being must acquire a history. He must have something to remember that was un-Frances. What sort of new person Millie might make of him, and whether she might not like Circe change him into a brute it did not occur to him to wonder. He was in the state of misery which dispenses with all question of right and wrong. He wanted an experience, a transformation. The little glow, not yet faded, from the moment of the kiss, cast a rosy light upon Millie's image, like a cult statue seen by the light of a fire. She was all that was electrical, and magical, and naked. And Andrew did not want to die without having been to bed with a beautiful woman.

Even so, he would have funked it if Millie had not, directly on his arrival, made him very drunk with whiskey. He hardly remembered how he had got into her bedroom. But he remembered the rest. Millie reclining unclothed in the lamplight, her hair undone, her legs relaxed and slightly parted, her hands folded on her shiny plump stomach, Millie propped up by pillows, revealed, offered, seemed to him an utter stranger and filled him with fright. He did not know where to look at her. Her face, at once dazed, complacent and vulnerable, seemed to him unrecognizable and obscene. He undressed miserably, hiding himself, and felt as he took off his trousers that he was become spindly and shrimp-like, a little white thing that might at any moment fall through a crack in the floor.

Of course, it had been no good. He had been almost in tears. He shivered all over as if he were cold, and did indeed feel very cold. Pimply gooseflesh rose leprously along his thighs. He did not know how to touch Millie. His hands would not obey him, but like recalcitrant animals curled up or sought refuge beneath his arms or behind his back. He sagged and lumbered in the bed like a paralytic; and Millie's brisk attempts to arouse his interest filled him with a disgust of himself which approached nausea. At the same time he felt intensely sorry for Millie and ashamed for her, wanting to veil, to conceal her too eager face, working away so close to his. The rest of her body he dared not look at, and to conceal his shrinking he became like stone. He longed to leave her, longed for the decency of clothes, but still he slumped there in the bed, sinking into an insensibility which was almost like sleep.

The arrival of Pat awoke him to a pain of quite a different order. He was like someone lying half conscious in the mud who suddenly receives a bayonet in the ribs. With clumsy haste he got himself dressed, listening to the voices of Pat and Millie in the next room. He had no doubt that Pat had recognized him: and when he pictured what it was that Pat had seen from the doorway he wondered whether he had not better just shoot himself and be done with it. When Millie called him out he could hardly force himself through the door and leaned there helplessly, trying to control a pitiful shuddering in his face. He did not then reflect why Pat had come. He only knew that he had been seen thus, and seen by the person who, it was suddenly clear to him, mattered most in the world.

On Sunday Andrew took his bicycle and set off early for the country. He wanted to avoid his mother who was asking whether he and Frances would not come with her to the Easter service at the Mariners' Church. He intended to cycle to Howth, which had nothing to recommend it except that it was the opposite way from Rathblane. In fact, he got as far as Clontarf and took refuge from the rain in a bar where he sat for several hours. It did then occur to him to wonder why Pat had arrived so late at Millie's house and had come straight up to her bedroom. He had been far too agitated to overhear any of their conversation. But he could not really attend to this problem, nor indeed did he care about it. Millie herself had been blotted out of his mind. All that remained was his shame and Pat as the witness of it. With this there returned to him, flooding and burning his heart, all his childhood love for his cousin. Sitting in the dingy bar in Clontarf he buried his face in his hands.

Andrew thought, at first hopelessly and as of something impossible, of going to see Pat and demanding from him some kind of help, some healing touch. Only Pat could heal this wound of which Andrew now felt himself likely to die. If he could only remove that picture of himself from Pat's consciousness forever: or if that was impossible at least in some way modify or overlay it. But how could he do this? There was no possible explanation of what Pat had seen which would make it less disgusting and less base than it was. Yet if he could only talk to Pat about it, perhaps tell him about Frances, or accuse himself in Pat's presence, this might a little lessen the pain. The idea was impossible: Pat would be cold and scornful or would refuse to talk at all. He would simply not participate in Andrew's scene. The idea was absurd; and yet it was also impossible to report at Longford, to return to France, with this horror unresolved and some alleviation, however small, unattempted. By Sunday night Andrew was beginning to be certain that he would make the attempt. On Monday morning, after a sleepless night, he knew that he could not endure any more hours without seeing Pat.

A light rain was drifting down as Andrew approached the Dumay's house and flashes of bright sunlight were making the wet pavements dazzling. The door of the house was unlocked as usual. Andrew did not knock but pushed the door cautiously open. He did not want to meet Cathal or Aunt Kathleen and hoped that he might be able to slink straight upstairs to Pat's room. Sick with anticipation, he stood for a moment in the hall to listen. He heard voices in the kitchen.

Andrew moved quietly toward the kitchen door, deciding that if Pat were in there he would just go on up to Pat's room and wait. He did not want to meet him in company. He listened.

'And you won't worry any more about letting me fight? I'll be all right surely.'

'Yes, yes,'

'And you'll let me have a gun? Sure I can use a rifle.'

'I don't know.'

'Will we be firing on them directly when it all starts at twelve?'

'I'll do what I'm told and so will you.'

'Why can't we go straight to Dublin Castle and throw them out of there?'

'We haven't enough men.'

'What I like to think of is the surprise there'll be this day! And they all saying we'd never fight!'

'Do shut up, will you, Cathal.'

'And when the shooting starts it'll be a revolution, just like James Connolly said. Sure Ireland will go mad.'

'Did you lock the front door like I told you?'

'Yes, I did. Well, I'll just see. God, we'll fry the English! They'll—' Cathal opened the door and came face to face with Andrew.

Andrew had been listening with curiosity. He was struck by Cathal's excited tone, but he had not taken in the meaning of what was said. He now saw over Cathal's shoulder Pat Dumay in full Volunteer uniform and armed. At the same instant he grasped himself as a British officer in uniform and armed. But still he did not understand.

Cathal jumped back with an exclamation and then turned to Pat. 'He was listening at the door!'

Pat said, or rather drawled, 'Come inside, Andrew, come inside.'

Andrew obeyed him automatically. His own private emotions and expectations in coming to the house were still clouding about his head, and this entirely new crisis left him bewildered.

Pat said, 'Did you hear what we were speaking of just now?'

'Yes, but—'

'I'm afraid you must consider yourself my prisoner. Put your hands up, please.'

Andrew realized that Pat was pointing a revolver at him. He tried to think how he should react, but all he felt was blinding surprise and shock. He did not raise his hands, but moved them a little from his sides in a gesture of helpless enquiry.

'Disarm him, Cathal.'

Cathal quickly took Andrew's revolver from the holster and pushed it across the kitchen table. When he saw his revolver lying on the table Andrew began to understand the conversation he had overheard.

'Can I have that gun?' said Cathal, wide-eyed.

'Shut up. Go and lock that door as you ought to have done before. Move over here, will you, and sit down on that chair.'

Andrew moved and sat down. Cathal returned to the room and stood against the door. Andrew knew that he ought to take some initiative now, to try to get out quickly, while his cousins were both as surprised at his arrival as he had been surprised at his reception. He could see doubt, even bewilderment, in Pat's eyes. He ought to act now before Pat had formed any policy or reached any decision. He glanced about, noting the scullery door, the door into the side passage. He began to get up.

'Sit down, I said.'

Andrew sat down. The habit of obedience to Pat, formed in remotest childhood, was too strong in him. He knew then that it was no good and the moment of possibility had passed. He was indeed a prisoner. He stared at Pat with gradual appalled comprehension.

'You're a fine nuisance turning up now.'

'I wanted to see you,' said Andrew. 'I wanted to tell you—'
But this was meaningless talk. Now he was only a factor in a
situation, a British officer in a damnably awkward fix. He
noticed a rifle leaning against the gas stove, a pair of handcuffs
hung upon the back of a chair. He stared at his revolver, which
was lying on the check lino tabletop where so often as a child
he had sat eating bread and honey. He saw the little shut-in
room and the figure of the armed man. Andrew realized that
he was in action for the first time.

He said, 'Oh God, whatever are we going to do.' But this
was not the right way of speaking either.

'I'm thinking,' said Pat. 'It's unfortunate that you heard
that conversation. I ought to be court-martialled for having
left that door open. You appreciate that I can't just let you
go?'

Andrew was silent. He looked down at his highly polished
boots and his khaki breeches and his empty holster.

'I don't want to have to shoot you,' Pat's voice went on
coolly, 'and it won't be very nice for you if I tie you up and gag
you. Suppose we save ourselves trouble and damage and you
give me your word as an officer and a gentleman that you will
remain quietly in this house until midday and communicate
with nobody.'

Andrew looked up. 'I know perfectly well what my duty is
as an officer and a gentleman, and you know it too.'

Pat suddenly smiled at him. 'Well, well, and how else could
you answer. Cathal, go and fetch that rope from my room, and
any handkerchiefs and scarves you can lay your hands on.'

Cathal paused, fascinated. 'Would you really think of
shooting him, Pat?'

'Go on! And don't be after touching that.' Pat tossed
Andrew's revolver onto the gas stove with a clang.

When Andrew said he knew what his duty was, he at last
understood perfectly, and grasped what was about to occur
not just as the occasion of a conflict between him and his

cousin, but as a general catastrophe. When he left this place he would be going into the firing line not to shoot at Germans but to shoot at Pat and his comrades. He gave a groan of pain. 'Why did this have to happen?'

Pat understood him. 'It's necessary.'

'It's insane. You can't hold out against the British Army. You're forcing us to fight you when we don't want to, and we're the same people, we're brothers, we *can't* fight—' Andrew felt the outrage of it. He wanted to explain that he did not want to fight the Irish, they had done him no harm, there must be some mistake. It could not be that he would have to kill his first man here in Dublin, here where his mother had just moved into a pretty house, where Frances—

'Cousins, not brothers. Thank you, Cathal. Now, Andrew, I'm sorry, but I'm to be out of this place in twenty minutes and I want to leave you behind in a neat bundle. You'll be rescued this afternoon when my mother comes home. Could you just stand up and turn round and put your hands behind your back.'

Andrew stood up facing Pat. Then as he turned about to face the window he said, as he had used to say as a child when about to be beaten, 'Oh *no*, oh *no*—' He felt the cold touch of the handcuffs on his wrists.

The square frame of the window opposite Andrew was suddenly darkened by a figure which rose up from below. The sun was shining now outside and the figure appeared bulky and startling against the dirty sunny brick wall. All three inside the room jumped and exclaimed and Andrew found himself stumbling against Pat. The handcuffs clattered to the floor. Then Andrew recognized through the window, close to his own face, the round eager face of Millie. She tapped urgently on the glass, mouthing something.

'Cathal, go and let her in. You sit down again. Oh, Mother of God!'

As Pat grimaced, Andrew knew again that he ought to act. He did not think that Pat would shoot him if he made a dash for it. Pat was physically the stronger, but should he not at least try to force his way out, lock his cousin in a wrestling hold with all the force he had? But his body was timid, submissive, defeated. He sat down where he had been told to sit.

The next moment Millie was in the room. She was wearing trousers and a thick overcoat.

'Well, what a to-do,' said Millie, 'and Andrew's here too. What is Andrew doing? We three are always meeting.' She picked up the handcuffs and put them on the table.

'What do you want here, Millie?'

'I know all about it and I've come to offer you my services and I'm certainly coming with you and you're not going to stop me.'

Millie's hair was curly and shaggy, bundled against the upturned coat collar. Her whole figure looked stiffly youthful and impromptu, like a schoolgirl acting a man in a play. But she stared at Pat, not provocatively and not defiantly. She was cool and bitter with determination.

Pat was gazing at Millie with a strange look. He put his fingers to his parted lips like one calculating. He said very slowly, 'You can't come with me, but there's something very important indeed which you can do for me. Will you do it?'

Millie looked at him, still with her face hard. 'Pat, I want this thing. It's more than you.'

'Will you hear what it is I want?'

'All right.'

'Cathal, will you go outside a moment, please.'

'Why?' said Cathal.

'Go outside because I tell you. I want to talk to her alone.'

Cathal left the room.

Pat suddenly drew Millie right up against him, jerking her half off her feet. Andrew remembered afterwards how Pat's arm sank deep into the folds of her overcoat, how Millie gasped as her feet slithered upon the kitchen floor, and how Pat, all the time he was talking to her, kept staring over her shoulder at Andrew. He spoke in a quick whisper of which Andrew could catch only a word here and there.

'No, Pat dear, I can't. This thing is made for me. Don't ask me to stay out of it. I can't help you. Just let me come along.'

Pat released, or rather dropped her, and she staggered. 'I can't stop you from getting yourself murdered, but you're not coming along with any of us.'

Millie stared at him, biting her lip. She looked at Andrew. 'I still don't understand about *him*.'

'He knows. He wouldn't give us his parole so he's going to be tied up and left here.'

'Hmmm. I see. Wait a minute, wait a minute. If I solve your little problem for you will you let me come with you today?'

Pat hesitated, 'I don't see how you—'

'But if I can, will you promise?'

'Well, yes—'

'Listen then. '

Millie put her two hands on Pat's shoulders and jolted him back against the frame of the window. She stood on tiptoe, hauling herself up towards his face as she hissed out an inaudible stream of words. Again Andrew saw Pat's eyes fixed upon him, now widening a little as Millie's whisper continued. What a nightmare, thought Andrew. And he thought, how jerky and unreal. Surely nothing connected him to this cardboard catastrophe. Should he not just get up and walk away through the door and leave these grimacing puppets? He moved, or twitched himself, like someone under a spell, trying to find if he is still sentient. But Millie and Pat had stepped apart and Pat now blocked his way.

'All right,' said Pat.

'Shall I take him in there?' Millie pointed to the scullery door. 'There's no way out, is there?'

'No way out.'

'Come in here for a moment, would you, Andrew?'

Andrew followed Millie into the dark scullery and she shut
the door. A little square window gave on to the dirty wall on
which the sun was obliquely shining. There was a small table,
a sink full of unwashed dishes, and a smell of decaying wood
and tea leaves. Andrew thought, I have been taken to the end
of the world, and at the end there is nothing but idiocy. I am in
hell and hell is gibberish. He was standing close against Millie
and saw her face below him looking up, not with the obscene
vulnerability of the last time, but with a cruel intentness, like a
stalking cat's face. This is insanity, he thought, this is dishonour, to be standing in this little room up against this
woman.

Millie pushed him as she had pushed Pat, her two hands
hooked upon his shoulders, her chin poking into his chest, her
hair, which now seemed to issue from her mouth, spread on to
his khaki sleeve. She began to speak in a low voice. As he
looked over her shoulder Andrew saw the sun fading in the
window square. He looked at the pile of dishes. He listened to
Millie and began to take in what she was saying.

'I don't believe you,' said Andrew.

'I have the evidence.'

Andrew thrust her violently away from him. He saw her
evil cat face, the eyes screwed with purpose, the lips wet,
bobbing near him in the scullery which had suddenly become
dark.

'I don't believe you.'

'She would.'

'And I couldn't trust you. '

'You've got to.'

'Don't touch me.'

'If you will do what I want I will have everything destroyed.
Otherwise—'

'Oh, shut up. Let me think.'

'Well, think quickly, Andrew. Believe me, dear boy, it is
true. Look, I will write you a letter to take to Upper Mount

Street. I swear to you I won't cheat. And will you then do what I ask? Otherwise I shall be completely ruthless.'

'What is it that you want me to do?'

'Simply to promise to stay inside this house until twelve and keep your mouth shut.'

Andrew sat down and laid his head on the table. The surface of the table was damp, soft and rotten. He said, gazing along the grain of the wood, 'A promise given under duress is not a promise.'

'You are not under duress. You are perfectly free to refuse and take the consequences. You are perfectly free to promise and to break your promise. But if I find out later that you have, I'll tell everything, evidence or no evidence.'

Andrew lifted his head. 'All right. I'll do as you ask. Write that letter and give it to me at once. And if you cheat here I'll kill you.'

'Ah—' Millie breathed with satisfaction and flung open the scullery door. Pat and Cathal were talking on the other side of the kitchen. Millie went through and Andrew followed her. He sat down in a corner and laid his head awkwardly against the wall, turning his face away from them.

'He will,' said Millie.

The three of them came and stood round Andrew. He did not look up at them, but fixed his eyes upon the gas stove. He saw his revolver there. It had fallen down inside the iron framework of the gas burners and hung there suspended. Andrew felt as if he had had a stroke. His eyes seemed to be askew, his limbs recalcitrant and twisted. He listened dully for his sentence.

Pat said, 'Andrew do you give me your promise, your most honourable promise, that you will stay inside this house and say nothing of what you know until twelve o'clock today?'

'Yes.'

'You have a watch, haven't you. Well, you'll hear the angelus. You do faithfully promise?'

'Yes.'

Pat seemed to hesitate. Andrew looked up at their three faces. Cathal was looking puzzled and frightened. Millie's face was plumped with triumph, her cat eyes slanting. Pat was perspiring. The sweat trickled down past his eyes to his cheeks and his lower lip palpitated. What is it, thought Andrew, what is happening, what are they going to do to me? At that moment it seemed to him that they were intending to kill him.

Cathal said, 'You're not surely—'

'Could you stand up?' said Pat.

Andrew stood up.

'Turn round.'

He turned round and saw again the brick wall, sunny now, its crust of dirt shadowed by the slanting sun.

'I'm sorry to use the handcuffs,' said Pat's voice. 'I have to make sure. Cathal, could you just help me hold his wrist. *There.*'

There was a click. Andrew felt the steel on one wrist. Then there was a wild outcry, an animal howl, and Andrew's wrist was jerked and seared. He staggered, exclaimed and then for a moment everyone stood still. He was handcuffed to Cathal.

'Ingenious, eh?' said Millie.

The moment of stillness passed. Cathal began to shout out something in a loud voice and ran towards the door dragging Andrew with him. Pat caught Cathal in his arms and smothered his shouting mouth against his chest. He called out something to Millie.

'Don't worry,' said Millie. 'I'll gag him. Just hold him tight. I learnt all about that in the South African war. We used to gag troublesome patients. You'd be surprised what goes on in military hospitals. The trouble with gagging is the shape of the human head. Those scarves are no use. I need four yards of surgical bandage. In that drawer? What luck. Get him down on his knees, would you.'

Pat forced Cathal down, and Andrew was pulled down too,

slipping half under the table. The dragging handcuff bit into his wrist and his arm moved jerkily, following the convulsive movements of his fellow-prisoner, shifting so as to ease the pain. He did not look at the struggle which was going on beside him.

'Open his mouth. That's right. Keep your tongue down, boy. Ouch, he bites! There, that's comfy and safe. Don't worry, I know what I'm doing, he won't choke. Now wind the bandage so, plenty of room to breathe, over the bridge of the nose is the important bit. It's all a matter of mechanics. Just as well I was here, isn't it. You couldn't have managed this alone. Now he won't be able to shout for help. Safety pins are best. That's done it.'

Millie and Pat stood up.

Now Millie had placed a sheet of paper against the window and was writing on it. Andrew shifted along the floor as Pat pushed Cathal to the wall and began to bind his free hand. Pat groaned softly and rhythmically as he tied Cathal's hand to the foot of the stove. Over Pat's shoulder Andrew could now see Cathal's thrown-back head. His head, entirely swathed in bandage which thickly covered his mouth, wound over his nose and round his brow, leaving only eyes and nostrils free, looked like an old picture of Lazarus, or some faceless monster glimpsed in a dream. As Andrew watched, tears filled Cathal's eyes and streamed down on to the bandage and darkened it. Andrew turned away, saw Pat's feet in army boots, peered up at Pat's face which was red and quivering. Pat looked down, his mouth opening, the lips drawing back in a snarl of pain: then he turned and leaned his head against the door.

'Here's your letter.' Andrew held it automatically. 'I'm sorry, Andrew. I'm a desperate woman. Hadn't we better go, Pat? You will keep your promise, won't you?'

Pat was on his knees beside Cathal. 'I should have been useless if you had come with me. I had to do this.'

'I must say I don't understand why,' said Millie. 'You are

destroying the child. If the world ends, let it end, is how I feel.'

Pat sat back on his heels. He turned to Andrew, and his face was the face of a weeping man although his eyes were tearless. 'Andrew, I just want you to know that I don't know what it was that Millie told you.'

Andrew nodded slightly.

Pat had turned back to Cathal. He knelt awkwardly and his cheek grazed the bandaging as he bowed his head for a moment on to his brother's shoulder. Then he rose and picked up his rifle and Andrew's revolver.

'Cheer up.' Millie squeezed Andrew's arm. She opened the door and moved out. Andrew saw the boots and the green leg-bands follow her. The front door banged. There was a long silence. Cathal was crying with a soft hissing sound behind the bandage.

Andrew said, 'Do you mind if I lie flat for a while?' He lifted his pinioned hand, edging the wrist round inside the handcuff, and managed to adjust himself supine upon the floor. The sun, rising higher, began to shine into the kitchen. The muffled weeping continued.

Chapter Twenty-four

IT was twenty-five minutes to twelve, Easter Monday morning, on the clock at Findlater's Church, as Christopher and Frances Bellman hurried through Rutland Square and on up the hill towards Blessington Street. The sun shone from a sky of pallid, exhausted blue upon the green domes of Dublin, the majestic dome of the Customs House, the lace-cap dome of the Four Courts, the elegant little dome of the Rotunda Hospital. The two figures moved urgently onward against the slow crowd of holiday-makers who were sauntering down to enjoy the sudden sunshine in the centre of the city.

Christopher had spent the previous day, Sunday, in a condition of frenzy. He had woken early at Rathblane to a state of consciousness which he could scarcely endure. It was not just the sense of having lost Millie, it was the sense of having lost her in such a horrible, muddled, undignified way. He recalled with misery and disgust the pathetic, defensive, frivolous tone which Millie had adopted. This hurt him more than jealousy. He could have born a firm, even a mysterious no from Millie. He could even more easily have born a tragic severance with tears. But this confused matter of having 'found her out' made his own position not only painful but unmanageably absurd. Neither he nor Millie knew how to behave. Christopher hated muddle, hated the plunging to and fro in confusion of half-guilty half-frantic human beings caught up together like carriage horses in an accident.

He decided to leave the house early before anyone was up and in fact set off on foot shortly before seven o'clock. He walked for nearly an hour and began to feel extremely tired and it began to rain. Then there was the sound of a galloping horse behind him and he was overtaken by Millie. A ridiculous conversation followed during which Millie tried to persuade him to mount behind her and return to Rathblane. Christopher turned and walked on, stumbling in the mud out of sheer anger and misery, and Millie followed, leading her horse and expostulating. Finally, as it was now raining very hard indeed, he consented to wait under a tree while she rode to the factor's cottage and got the factor to come down bringing a bicycle. After an exceedingly long time the factor arrived riding his own bicycle and pushing his daughter's. Millie once more galloped up and there was another confused conversation in the factor's hearing, with Millie saying she wanted to talk to Christopher and Christopher saying he must be going. Finally, as he began to wobble down the stony track on the factor's daughter's bicycle he could hear, behind him, Millie addressing friendly remarks to her horse.

Christopher arrived back at Finglas wet, exhausted, shivering, to find an extremely upset and anxious Frances waiting for him. He had forgotten to tell her that he would be away for the night, he had not even reflected on whether he would be away for the night. His daughter's distress and reproaches, and the fact that there was no warm meal waiting for him and that the fires had not been lit, sent Christopher into a paroxysm of self-pity in the course of which he told Frances everything: Millie, Pat, Andrew, the engagement ring, everything. He regretted this immediately after. If he had been calmer and less self-absorbed he would have spared her a revelation which was unnecessary and could not but be intensely painful. But a little later still, when he had had his hot meal, and in the lucid brutality of a renewed concern with self, he decided it had been right to tell her after all: for her sake, because she would now have fewer regrets about Andrew, and for his sake, because the bitterness of Frances would now support him in the loss of Millie. He did not really conceive that Frances might have changed her mind again about Andrew.

Yet her reaction to his news was extreme and she gave herself up to weeping and declared, which he did not take too seriously, that she was forthwith going to England to become a nurse. Christopher thought that it was probably the bit about the ring which hurt most. Frances had not even known about the existence of the ring. How touching to know that Andrew had had it ready for her. How humiliating to know that he had almost directly after her refusal given it, and in such circumstances, to another. It is enough to refuse a man without experiencing also the muddy splash of his too precipitate departure. As Christopher imagined the chagrin of his daughter he had dark thoughts about Andrew and then, returning to his own hurt, even darker ones about Millie. He was still utterly unsure whether or not to believe Millie's assurance that she had not tampered with Andrew until after his refusal by Frances. He began to wonder again whether Frances had not somehow found out something. He went early to bed to lie sleepless with these speculations, hearing the soft sound of weeping in the next room.

On Monday morning Christopher became aware that his daughter was in some quite new frame of mind. She was no longer tearful, but seemed excited, frightened, yet resolute. When he asked her what was now the matter she explained at last that she had seen the gardener that morning and she felt sure that something was going on. Further questioned, she explained that she had found the gardener in Citizen Army uniform searching frantically in the potting shed for something which, when found, looked like a box of ammunition. He had mumbled something about 'manœuvres' and departed at a run, but, Frances said, something about the *way* he ran, and his excitement, and his confusion at being discovered, suggested that something extreme might be going to happen after all. And having got this idea into her head it was evident that Frances could do nothing now but worry about it.

Christopher argued; and ended by being infected by her anxiety. He was a little irritated by this evidence of a continued concern about young Andrew, who might, if Frances' guess was correct, find himself in the firing line sooner than he bargained for. But this piece of drama was at least something new to think about; and the idea that, after all the talk and the anti-climax, something violent *was* perhaps going to occur upset and moved Christopher in a great many ways when, even momentarily, he gave it credence. He let himself become worried too, and readily agreed when Frances herself suggested that they should go over to Blessington Street and see if anything could be found out from Barney. It was at least something to do, and something which was not connected with Millie.

Blessington Street was deserted as usual except for a few scratching dogs and Keogh's laundry van, whose horse had mounted the pavement to eat as much as he could of an elder tree which was growing out of one of the areas. Once out of the crowd, the particular desolate peace of Dublin established itself round about them: the wide pale sky, low down even when it was cloudless, the open dusty cliff-like streets, the endless dark façades, spongy with dirt, absorbing light and sound. A half-clad child emerged slowly from a gaping doorway. Keogh's van moved on a few yards. Surely nothing could happen in this quiet city.

Frances had quickened her pace as they got into Blessington Street, her boots briskly kicking back the skirts of her coat, and Christopher was panting and falling behind when they reached the door of the Dumay's house. Christopher started to say something to her about not alarming Kathleen, but she had already rung the bell. The bell jangled harshly inside the dark hallway and they waited until it had stammered itself into silence. Frances rang again. Then she tried the door which was usually left unfastened. It was locked. Christopher, who did not want to meet Pat and who had been having misgivings about the whole project as they came up the hill, was beginning to suggest that they should go and have some coffee and that Frances might come back again later, when Frances, who had been peering through the letter box, gave a startled exclamation.

'What is it, Frances?'

'I don't know. Something very odd. It looks as if someone's lying on the floor in the kitchen. I can see their foot. You look.'

Christopher stooped and looked through the aperture. He saw and smelt the dark hall and saw beyond it the half open door of the kitchen and a sunny segment of the kitchen floor. Something was lying just inside the doorway which looked like a foot, or at least a boot. The rest of the person, if person it was, was hidden. Christopher felt a thrill of fright. A foot, a leg, extended there upon the kitchen floor while the bell pealed in vain seemed to him at first uncanny. What could it mean? An equally vague but more rational fear followed.

'Let me look again.' Frances straightened up with a frightened face. 'Do you think there can have been—an accident?'

'It might be just someone's boot lying there.'

'No, I'm sure it's someone's foot. I can see part of the leg.'

Something about his daughter's agitation made Christopher push her aside. As he looked more carefully it seemed to him that the immobile object in the kitchen doorway resembled the booted foot of a British cavalry officer.

Christopher shouted through the letter box. 'Hello there! Barney, Kathleen, Pat! Hello, hello!' He pulled the bell again so violently that it gave one yelp and jolted to silence. The stillness of the house absorbed the din.

Frances was now stooping at the slot. She exclaimed, 'It's gone.'

'What?'

'The foot. It's gone.'

Christopher looked again. The boot-like object had disappeared. Had they imagined it? They stared at each other.

'I must get inside,' said Christopher. 'There's a lane at the back. You'd better wait here.'

He ran to the corner of Mountjoy Street and round into the lane, a narrow track of cinders and black earth, smelling of cats and dust-bins, which ran along behind the yards of the houses. The houses looked entirely different at the back, made ugly and formless by every kind of jutting annexe and out-building. The yards, behind earthy, weedy walls, were full of sheds and wash-houses and high lines of tossing linen. As Christopher hesitated, wondering which house belonged to the Dumays, Frances appearing from behind his shoulder said 'This is the one,' and began to push the door of the yard. It was locked.

'Look, *you stay here*,' said Christopher. 'I'll see what's happened, if anything's happened.'

The wall was not high. He dragged an empty dust-bin up against it and mounted. The top of the wall crumbled under his knee and he jumped down on the other side. But before he could advance to the house he saw the shadow of Frances who was trying to pull herself up on to the wall. She got one leg over the top and then almost fell into his arms bringing down a shower of broken brick and earth.

'*Please* stay here, Frances, and don't come till I tell you.'

But her eyes, large and vague with fear, looked past him, and he had to push forward to intercept her. Together they approached the kitchen window.

The sun was shining directly into the kitchen. At the moment of looking in Christopher felt extremely afraid. He had no notion what he expected, except that now, somehow through Frances, he expected something dreadful. The combination of the disappearing foot and the silence of the house had produced an effect both of catastrophe and of eerieness. What he now saw, though it was less catastrophic than his fears, was perhaps ever more eerie. Two people were sitting on the kitchen floor opposite to the window with their backs against the wall. They looked unreal, too big, like outsize dolls. Their faces looked so strange that it took Christopher several seconds to recognize them as Andrew and Cathal, and to be certain that they were both alive. What was unusual was their expression, or rather something which had communicated itself to their entire posture. Andrew, in uniform as usual, had taken off half his jacket and loosened his tie. He sat slack and limp, his feet spread out rather wide apart in front of him. He was caressing his moustache in a curiously absent manner. Cathal, who had a great deal of white stuff which looked like bandage hanging loose around his neck, sat with hunched shoulders half turned away from Andrew, his legs drawn right up and his cheek against the wall. Both heads moved slightly as the two figures appeared in the window and with a shock of horror Christopher saw on both faces a look of utter lassitude and indifference. It was impossible not to think of drugs, insanity. Sitting there vacantly on the floor, the one crouched, the other with outspread feet, they looked like two derelict beings in a madhouse.

Frances was pulling at the kitchen door, and now at the window. 'Help me push this up, I think it's unlatched.' Christopher pawed at the window frame and it moved a little. Frances got her fingers underneath it, and in a moment had thrust her arm through and unbolted the door. They went into the kitchen.

Cathal had leaned his head back against the wall and was wiping his face with a piece of the bandage. He appeared to have been crying. His eyes moved a little, observing the new-comers, but he did not change his posture. Andrew peered up with a frightened hostile look but seemed unable to focus his gaze upon them. The blank expression returned. It was as if some appalling meditation had been momentarily interrupted.

'What's the matter with you, what's happened?' cried Christopher. 'Are you ill?' He stooped over Andrew.

'Look,' said Frances behind him.

He followed her pointing finger and saw that Andrew and Cathal were handcuffed together.

Christopher jumped back as promptly as if he had touched

a metal limb. The comatose propped-up figures, and now the handcuffs, produced an effect of the mechanical, the less than human. Frances, who was looking down with a grimace of fascination, had backed away to the window.

'Andrew, Andrew,' said Christopher, 'how did this happen? Who did it? Are you hurt? Have you been here long?'

After a moment's silence Andrew answered, speaking rather slowly and laboriously. 'I've been here several hours. Well, two or three perhaps. No, I'm not hurt.' Lifting the wrist that was bound to Cathal's he looked at his watch, frowning a little. It was nearly five minutes to twelve. His eyes widened again into the vacant stare and he looked away into the corner of the kitchen. He seemed oblivious of Frances.

'Why are you sitting here on the floor?'

'Well, you see until about five minutes ago Cathal was tied on to the gas stove.'

'*What?* But who tied him? And who put these handcuffs on you?'

'Pat did.'

'Pat?' Frances swept round the table to Cathal's side and shook the boy by the shoulder. 'Cathal, are you all right? Tell us what happened? What's all that bandaging for?'

Cathal shrunk slightly away from her touch, but did not otherwise move or speak.

'Are you both bewitched?'

'It was a gag,' said Andrew, with the same slow stolid enunciation.

'A gag? Cathal gagged? But why? Who did it?'

'Pat. Or rather Millie.'

'*Millie*,' said Christopher. 'Was she here?'

'Yes. She went with them.'

'With *who*?' cried Frances. 'Oh, do talk properly!'

'With Pat. With the Sinn Feiners.'

'But where to?'

'To fight.'

'Oh God, I was right.' Frances clapped her two hands over her mouth.

'Millie gone with the Sinn Feiners, to fight?' said Christopher stupidly. 'But there isn't any fighting.'

'There will be soon,' said Andrew. 'They're going to start at twelve.' He drew his legs up in front of him, twitching his shoulder. He said, 'I'm deucedly stiff.'

'But it's almost twelve now!' Frances started convulsively towards the door, then returned to stare down at Andrew. 'But you—why are you here like this? What happened, what *happened*?'

'I shall never be able to explain that to anybody,' said Andrew, speaking in the same slow way and staring past Christopher at a point on the wall.

'At twelve. It can't be. It's impossible.' Christopher stood there stupefied, his arms hanging down as if he too had become a doll. Millie gone to join the rebels, gone away with Pat with a gun in her hand. 'But why did you just stay here? Why didn't you go and do something, tell somebody, if you knew about it?'

'It was your *duty*, what were you thinking of?' Frances was looking down at Andrew now almost with fury.

'I can't explain,' said Andrew. 'I found out about it quite accidentally. Then I gave Pat my word of honour that I'd tell no one and that I'd stay here in this house until twelve. And he handcuffed Cathal to me because he wanted Cathal kept out of the fight. And he gagged him, or rather Millie did, so that he shouldn't shout for help. And I took the gag off and undid his hand just before you arrived because he was crying so much I thought he might stifle and the time was almost up anyway.' He offered the account in a dull voice as if after all it were something obvious. He shifted awkwardly, tugging Cathal's arm with a petulant movement.

'But why, why, why?' cried Frances. 'Why did you give in? Why did you promise? How could he have frightened you so?

Why didn't you run out and try to stop it all? Why did you just sit here for hours doing nothing? Have you forgotten you're an Army officer?'

Andrew simply shook his head. He looked up at Frances for a moment, and then screwed up his eyes as if he had been dazzled.

Frances stamped her foot. Her hands clawed at the muddied skirts of her coat. She advanced on Andrew as if she would have kicked him. 'Your word of honour! Gave Pat your word of honour! You ought to have shot him as a traitor! You've betrayed your King and country. You've dishonoured your uniform. How could you do it? I can't understand!'

'I don't think Pat understood either,' said Andrew slowly.

'You did it because you were afraid of Pat. You've always been afraid of Pat. Oh, I shall never forgive you—'

As her voice dissolved into an incoherence of tears the clear sound of a bell was heard. It was the angelus ringing at Saint Joseph's church in Berkeley Road.

They all paused for a moment. Then with a jerk Cathal threw himself forward and began to rise. Andrew tried to crouch, but was pulled sharply on to his knees. The handcuffed pair swayed awkwardly together and at last managed to get up on to their feet. Frances began to sob again. The angelus went on slowly ringing. There was a distant noise which sounded like rifle fire.

Chapter Twenty-five

ANDREW and Cathal raced down Blessington Street in the bright sunshine. The sky, cloudless and pale golden with light, dazzled their eyes. Swinging between them and concealing the handcuffs was a mackintosh which Andrew had had the presence of mind to pick up as Cathal dragged him through the hall and out of the house. Their feet clapped and slithered upon the still rainy pavements, and the wet sunny houses gave back an echo, as they rushed along, now jerking apart, now drawn violently together by their bound wrists.

The sun was hot. The two figures were running now in step. But by the time they got as far as Findlater's Church Andrew forced Cathal to slow down. Cathal's breath came in wailing gasps, like quick little screams, and his face, as Andrew glimpsed it, strained and moulded by fear, looked no less grotesque than his Lazarus head of an hour ago. They continued at a quick jolting walk. People eyed them uneasily as they passed; and here and there from side streets men with grimmer faces emerged and began to hurry down toward the centre of the city. One or two people now passed them at a run. An increasing murmur of anxious talk hung like a light canopy above their heads. Dublin, a little startled, a little puzzled, seemed already to be aware that this was no ordinary day in her history.

As they came past the Rotunda toward the upper end of Sackville Street there was a sound of rifle fire ahead of them and then, as in reply, a burst of firing in another part of the city. The murmur of talk fell almost to silence and the moving people, not yet numerous, seemed to draw together with an uneasy, eager purposiveness, already aware of themselves as a crowd compelled onward by the mystery of an historical event. Someone laughed nervously. The rifle fire was heard again.

The police had already formed a cordon across the end of Sackville Street and people were standing four and five deep behind them. Andrew and Cathal pushed their way forward until they could see, over the policemen's shoulders, the wide expanse of the street, empty. That sudden utter emptiness, more perhaps than anything else, showed to the wondering gaze of the onlookers the extraordinary nature of what had happened. The Post Office had a strange look. The glass in all the windows had been broken and the spaces barricaded with piles of furniture. The building already had a huddled, beleaguered appearance, the air weirdly of a fortress. A large placard hung upon the façade read: *Headquarters of the Provisional Government of the Irish Republic.* While up above, in place of the Union Jack, a green flag blew out taut and clear, with the words *Irish Republic* written upon it in white letters. There was something miniature, amateurish, improbable about the scene, as if the line between dream and reality had been crossed in a blundering manner and almost unaware.

As they watched, the crowd almost silent now, a figure emerged on to the Post Office portico and began to speak, reading aloud to the empty street from a piece of paper which fluttered in his hand. While the sound of the voice, too far off to be understood, rang out thinly in the clear sunny air, a man near to Andrew who had some field glasses said, 'That's Patrick Pearse.' Andrew could not hear Pearse's words, but he read them later many times and on many days as they nightly appeared upon posters all over the city. 'Irishmen and Irishwomen. In the name of God and of the dead generations from which she receives her old traditions of nationhood, Ireland, through us, summons her children to her flag and strikes for her freedom. . . .'

The figure had vanished now from the Post Office portico and the deserted street seemed quiet, almost sleepy, in the sun. The crowd began to talk again in low voices. There was a baffled painful excitement which was like guilt.

'Why didn't the English take a pot shot at him while he was out there?'

'Sure, that lot have no guns.'

'He's after declaring the Irish Republic, whatever the hell that is.'

'Isn't it the like of the bloody Sinn Feiners to do this on the day of the races, and it fine for once.'

'The murderin' idjuts, they've killed a horse.'

Andrew, peering between the shifting heads of the police, saw that they had indeed killed a horse. The horse lay in the middle of the street opposite the main door of the Post Office, a huge brown glossy mound. Looking at the dead horse, Andrew felt a piercing fright, an anguish which he scarcely understood. Then looking sideways he saw on the nearby pavement, some mounted and some dismounted, a group of Lancers in colourful uniforms and very evident disarray. Bound for Phoenix Park, the Lancers, who carried no firearms, had passed unsuspectingly down Sackville Street at a minute or two after twelve and had received the first volley from the rebels. Four men had been hit and had already been pulled away into the shops opposite. The horse remained. Andrew looked at the Lancers and looked at the horrified, frightened face of the young officer, a boy of his own age. Andrew's heart expanded and contracted with a violence which almost broke it, as if the blood were trying to burst from his body with shame and despair. He touched himself, touched his cap and jacket to be sure that he was indeed wearing them, touched his shoulder with the single pip. He too was a British officer.

He was then at once aware that people in the crowd were looking at him. The crowd was detached, confused, if anything hostile to the Sinn Feiners. But they stared at Andrew and at his uniform without friendliness. By the violence which had already occurred a breach had been opened, and through that breach inevitably would flow the bitterness of centuries.

Andrew began to struggle back. People were pushing now

alarmingly from behind. He edged through, pulling Cathal after him. He tried to manœuvre his pinioned hand so as to get a grip on the boy's wrist, but managed only to catch hold of his limp fingers. Cathal followed him unresistingly now, his head hanging forward. They picked their way back out of the densest part of the crowd.

Why had he done it? He was a dead man now, he had died there in that little room sitting there beside Cathal with his back against the wall measuring the slow hours and minutes of his dissolution. Frances and Millie, the figures of the women paled to nothing, he scarcely now recalled who it was that had been with him when the angelus began to ring. What was colossal, irrevocable and insupportable was the destruction of his honour. He had been murdered in that little room just as surely as if they had shed his blood. Why had he given in and let them destroy him?

Even as he replied Andrew knew that this was ıot the answer and that he was without defence against the appalling nature of his act. When Millie had whispered to him, driving him with her knee up against the scullery wall, that she had had a certain relationship with her brother, his father, and that there were letters to prove it, he had for a second not believed her. Then when she had gone on murmuring into his ear that unless he surrendered she would have those letters sent to his mother, his mind was overwhelmed with a pity for Hilda which had seemed to bring belief with it and to leave him with no other course but to protect her. Such knowledge could blacken his mother's life back through time to its very roots. He could not risk, by any gambling with Millie, the possibility of so hideous a disclosure. He decided to give in at once.

Now he could doubt it all. The first shock, felt for his mother, brought belief. The second shock, felt for himself, brought disbelief. How could anything so horrible have really happened, anything so, as he now apprehended it, insulting to him? Perhaps there were letters, but they might mean nothing or be construed as harmless. Perhaps Millie would not, or could not, in fact have carried out her threat. Or perhaps, with a grotesque ingenuity, she had invented the whole story to terrify him with. That afternoon, he supposed, he would go to Upper Mount Street and find out. After that he would report to Longford.

But the thought of Longford and of his shame brought him to what lay deeper. He ought, whatever else he had done, to have faced Pat. He ought to have ignored Pat's revolver and to have fought Pat with his bare hands. His cousin would not have killed him. Or if he had, that would have been better, far better, than this other death. He had been near to Pat, nearer perhaps than ever in his life, when Pat had smiled and said, 'How else could you answer.' At that moment there had been a bond between them of dignity and respect. But Andrew had merely spoken of his duty. He ought to have done it. He ought to have fought then and there in the Dumays' kitchen with all the fury of his manhood. This was the encounter for which his whole life had been a training. He loved and he had always loved Pat Dumay. To have fought with Pat then up to any extremity of destruction and disaster would have been the last perfect expression of that love. But precisely because he had always idolized Pat the spring of power was broken inside him. He could not command the splendour of will which would have taken his cousin into a wrestler's embrace. He had dishonoured his uniform and this dishonour could not be forgiven, or blotted out by any degree of heroism ever. And he had done it, in the end, because of Pat and for Pat; and in doing it he had done the one thing which would make Pat despise him eternally.

Andrew found that he was still holding Cathal's hand. He looked at the boy. Cathal's face was oblivious, flushed and running with tears. Andrew felt near to tears himself. He said, 'Come on, Cathal, we must find someone to get these things off us. Do you know where we could go?' He pulled the boy along with him, pulling him away from the ominous dreadful emptiness of Sackville Street.

As they walked together, people were hurrying past them from all sides in ever increasing numbers, their talk filling the sunny air, louder now, more confident, already less amazed.

'Is it mad they all are?'

'They're bringing field guns up into Trinity.'

'They've got the Irish Lights boat up the river to shell them out of that.'

'Please God they've got a priest in there with them.'

'God and His Blessed Mother help them now, the poor bloody fools.'

'Ah, sure isn't this a grand day for Ireland.'

Epilogue

Blessington Street
April 1938

Dearest Frances,

I know I should have written to you ages ago but I've been rushed off my feet what with the work for the settlement and getting the house ready for the new lodgers, it's a lot of small things really but there hasn't been a moment. Jinny's a great blessing of course, and her son has been painting the kitchen and scullery, a useful decent boy and not like the run of those kids at all. I hope the new lodgers will be all right. I got so fond of the other lot, we were quite like a big family here at Blessington Street! But I expect I shall soon get just as fond of the new ones. Did I tell you one had been a major in the British Army, a very nice kind of a man, who's taking the two rooms at the top.

I loved to have the news of your family, how quickly they are growing up, it makes me feel so old to think you've got nearly grown up children now, Frances. Well, God help us we can none of us escape from anno domini and I'm lucky to have my health and strength, not like poor Millie. She's a lot better now of course, but she was never the same since her operation. I think I told you I got her out of that damp place in Eccles Street and now she has a dear little room in Dargle Road, that's off the Drumcondra Road. There's a lot of other old crocks in the house and they all call her 'my lady', and that's still good for a wet of whiskey! I took her out to lunch the other day at Jammet's and a waiter recognized her and said she hadn't changed a bit and that pleased her so much, poor thing, though God knows it isn't true. And she started telling the waiter all about Easter Week at Boland's Mill, and I suppose she was very heroic all that time in the back room tying bandages, but she talks so loud now she's a bit deaf and all the restaurant was listening and passing remarks and I was quite embarrassed. Then after that she was on at me about Barney and how good he was to her and how she misses him yet and in the end we were both of us quite wretched. It's hard to believe it's all of ten years since poor Barney passed away, God rest his soul.

And when are you coming over here? I could make room for the lot of you at Blessington Street, there's that big sofa still in the drawing-room and one of the kids could have the camp bed. It'd be so good to talk about the old days. I've found an album full of old snaps I'd love to show you, including such a nice one of your poor father in that old mackintosh hat of his, you remember the old mackintosh hat. And there's one of Hilda at Claresville, such a pretty house and so sad that she never really lived in it. Now that you've all the children away at school couldn't you be spared to give us a visit, even if you couldn't persuade all the family to come? They say there'll be a heat wave this summer and I know it would please Millie so much if you came, she's always asking after you. And we could go and visit all the old places, Kingstown's just the same, though I still can't get used to calling it Dun Laoghaire, and Sandycove and the baths and all. I was down there the other week and went down past Finglas and looked into the garden. The old red swing's still there. You remember the old swing and how poor Andrew mended it for you and took such trouble with it. Only they've painted the house pink now which I don't like and they've renamed it Hillcrest, which is a silly name as it isn't on the crest of the hill at all. I don't know who the people are who are there now since the Porters left. I think they're English people.

Well, I must stop this scrawl and do the laundry. Give my love to the family. And do come over this summer all of you to the Emerald Isle and 'we'll talk of old times till they put out the light' like it says in the song!

Yours with fondest love,

Kathleen

P.S. I've sent you some spiced beef. Don't undo the cloth, just boil it for two hours.

* * * *

'Who's that great fat letter from?' said Frances' tall son.

'From Aunt Kathleen.'

'Is she complaining as usual?' said Frances' English husband.

'Not specially.'

'I suppose she wants us to go over?'

'She always wants us to go over.'

'Well, you can go. You're not getting me over there again.'

'Oh, I don't really want to go,' said Frances.

She saw her husband folding the newspaper in the careful way in which he always folded it at the end of breakfast to make it into a flat square package which would fit into his briefcase. She saw folding inwards the headline *Franco Threatens Barcelona*. She looked at the face of her tall son and quickly withdrew her eyes. Since her son's best friend had gone to join the International Brigade Frances had lived with fear daily.

'What's the latest in your Irish family?' asked Frances' son.

Her children always spoke of her 'Irish family'. It did not occur to them to regard themselves as half Irish. They did not even regard their mother as Irish. They had visited Ireland four times and expressed no wish to go again.

'Oh, they're very quiet as usual. Aunt Millie's a bit better.'

'Quiet! Quiet as the grave, I'd say,' said Frances' husband.

'Well, after all, Kathleen—'

'Oh, I don't mean Kathleen, I mean the whole island. Do you remember how depressed we got last time? I never saw anything deader.'

'Well, perhaps they enjoy it—'

312

'I hope so, they certainly asked for it. They wanted to be by themselves alone, and they're by themselves alone.'

'I liked that place on the west coast,' said Frances' son.

'No, you didn't. You complained all the time because it was too cold to bathe. And it rained every day. I must say Ireland's an object lesson.'

'Well, I don't mind things being quiet,' said Frances. 'There's too much noise and rush over here. And I like rain.'

'A provincial dump living on German capital. A dairy-farming country that can't even invent its own cheese. And if there's another war they won't fight, any more than they did last time. And that'll really finish them.'

'They did fight last time,' said Frances. 'The Irish regiments were famous.'

'Yes, and where are those regiments now? Oh, a collection of mad-caps enlisted. But most of the Irish were looking after number one. And all that nineteen sixteen nonsense that your family was mixed up in.'

'I don't think it was nonsense,' said Frances' son.

'It was unadulterated nonsense,' said Frances' husband. 'Can you tell me what good it did?'

'I don't know—' said Frances.

'It made no sense at all. Home Rule was coming anyway. Only a lot of disgruntled fanatics wanted to draw attention to themselves. It was pure bloody-minded romanticism, the sort of thing that makes people into fascists nowadays.'

'They weren't like fascists,' said Frances' tall son, 'because they were on the right side.'

'When you're grown up,' said Frances' husband, 'which let me once again remind you that you're not, you'll realize that politics is not a matter of sides, it's a matter of methods. That's why there isn't a pin to choose between those two lots in Spain. If you ask me, it's one gang of barbarians against another gang of barbarians.'

Frances quickly intercepted her son's reply. She was used

313

to this task of oiling the waters, a task that consisted in turning all serious discussion between her husband and children into vague generalities or harmless personal chat. 'Father might have agreed with you. He was always against any kind of extremism. He said the Irish talked nothing but history, but had no historical sense at all.'

'Your father sounds a most sensible man,' said Frances' husband. 'I'm sure we would have seen eye to eye on many subjects. I wish I had known him.'

For some reason Frances had never told her husband of the circumstances of Christopher Bellman's death. Christopher died on April the twenty-seventh, nineteen sixteen. What exactly happened was never very clear. As the days of that interminable week succeeded one another, and the rebels, surrounded, bombarded, shelled, still somehow miraculously held out, Christopher became more and more frenzied. On the Thursday morning he set off on his bicycle for Dublin. That evening someone brought the bicycle back to Finglas, together with the news of Christopher's death. It appeared that he had attempted to make his way into the Post Office through Moore Street. He was killed by a sniper's bullet, no one knew from which side.

'Well, I think those nineteen-sixteen men would have gone to fight in Spain,' said Frances' tall son.

'Yes. But on which side!'

'You know perfectly well on which side I mean.'

'Storms in teacups,' said Frances' husband. 'Who's heard of nineteen sixteen now? *You* wouldn't have heard of it if you hadn't heard your mother going on about it. It'll be the same in twenty years with these Spanish war events you make such a fuss over. Guernica, Irun, Toledo, Teruel. No one will remember.'

'Your father may be right,' said Frances. 'People will only remember Guernica, and that will be because of Picasso.'

'I don't agree,' said Frances' son. He had become almost

alarmingly good at keeping his temper lately. 'These names are part of European history. Like Agincourt.'

'There is no such thing as European history,' said Frances' husband. 'Each country tells a selective story creditable to itself. No Frenchman has heard of Agincourt.'

'No Englishman has heard of Fontenoy, if it comes to that,' said Frances.

'How have you heard of Fontenoy?' said Frances' husband. 'It's new to me that you know any history.'

'Some Irish soldiers were there, fighting for the French. The Wild Geese, you know. There was a long poem about it. How did it go?

> *King Louis drew his rein.*
> *"Not so, my liege," Saxe interposed,*
> *"The Irish troops remain"*—'

'Playing traitors as usual! No, no, I'm only teasing. You mustn't take me so seriously, my dear. Now I must go for my train.'

Frances' husband slid the neat square of newspaper into his briefcase, and after it the white handkerchief, fresh every morning, which he used to clean his glasses. The case clicked shut.

He paused at the door. 'What was the fancy name you used to call Ireland by?'

'Cathleen ni Houlihan.'

'Well, in my view Cathleen ni Houlihan is a great bore. In this century, small nations have got to pack up, and the sooner they realize it the better. You've got to belong to a big show nowadays, and you may as well do it with sense and with a good grace. I'm sure your excellent father would have agreed with me. There.' He kissed Frances. He was a kindly man, though much given to sarcasm.

The front door banged.

Frances and her tall son sat down again at the breakfast

table with the slightly guilty air of a relieved complicity which was part of their morning ritual.

'Well, I think nineteen sixteen was wonderful,' said Frances' tall son.

'So do I really. Though I don't quite see what good it did.'

'It was a reminder that people can't be enslaved forever. Tyrannies end because sooner or later people begin automatically to hit back. That's the only thing which really impresses the tyrant and makes him give way. Freedom belongs to human nature and it can't vanish from the earth. Even though we forget the details of the fight, the fight goes on, and men have to be ready to go down among the details that are forgotten. And whenever it's the turn of a country, however small, to rise against its tyrants, it represents the oppressed peoples of the whole world.'

Frances felt the chill touch again. 'What a speech! You sound just like Cathal Dumay when you say that. He used to say that sort of thing. You're even beginning to look a bit like him.'

'What happened to all those people you knew in those days?' said Frances' tall son. 'Do tell me again. I remember you used to tell us all about them, when we were children. But you haven't talked about them for years now and I've got them all mixed up together in my mind. What happened to Uncle Barney, for instance? He was a real comic. I always remember the touching way he told us he'd have been a vegetarian if it wasn't for his passion for sausages! Something awfully funny happened to him in that nineteen-sixteen business, but I can't recall what it was.'

Frances gave a long sigh. 'It wasn't very funny really. Barney was going to fight with the rebels, but before they reached the place they were going to, he accidentally shot himself in the foot, and he had to be left behind.'

Frances' son laughed. 'That sounds just like Uncle Barney as I knew him! I expect he did it unconsciously on purpose.

You know hardly anything we do is really accidental. I was reading about it in a book the other day. Nearly everything we do is our unconscious mind only we don't know.'

'You might be right that it was somehow on purpose. I couldn't imagine Barney really harming anyone but himself. He was the gentlest of men.'

'What happened to Cathal Dumay, the chap you said I was like?'

'He was killed in nineteen twenty-one, in the Irish civil war.'

'The Irish civil war? I'd forgotten there was an Irish civil war. What was it about?'

'Some of the Irish thought that we, they, shouldn't accept the Treaty, that it didn't give Ireland enough freedom, and they were prepared to fight about it. And the English helped the more moderate Irish, who accepted the Treaty, to put down the extremists.'

'I bet Cathal was with the extremists.'

'Yes, he was with the I.R.A. He was very brave, he led a flying column. He was only nineteen when he died.'

'Was he killed in a battle?'

'No. A Black and Tan officer came up and shot him one night in his bed.'

Frances' son looked thoughtful. 'A civil war—that must be a dreadful thing to have in your own country. Were you in Ireland then?'

'No, I was married. I was over here. You existed. It was a terrible business. Your father says the Irish have managed to hush it up completely, and in a way that's true. It was too painful to think about.'

'Well, no one will be able to hush up the Spanish civil war. We're not going to forget *that*. What about Cathal's brother, what's his name, Pat Dumay?'

'Oh, he was one of the nineteen-sixteen rebels, he was with Pearse and Connolly in the Post Office. He was killed in the fighting, on the Thursday of Easter week, the day before they surrendered. He was killed by a shell.'

'And then there was that other fellow, the English chap—'

'You mean Andrew Chase-White? He wasn't English, he was Irish.'

'I always think of him as English. What happened to him?'

'He was killed at Passchendaele in nineteen seventeen. He got an M.C.'

'I remember now. And his mother died of grief.'

'I don't know whether Aunt Hilda died of grief. She developed cancer very soon after the news of Andrew's death.'

'Heroic lot, weren't they?'

'They were inconceivably brave men,' said Frances, suddenly gripping the table.

'And all those leaders, Patrick Pearse and company?'

'They shot most of them. Pearse, Connolly, MacDonagh, MacDermott, MacBride, Joseph Plunkett—And they hanged Roger Casement.'

'It's rather a miracle De Valera survived. Up Dev! You remember how you used to say that to us when we were children?'

Frances smiled, relaxing her hold. 'Up Dev!'

She did not really think all that much about the old days; and yet now for a moment it seemed to her that these thoughts were always with her, and that she had lived out, in those months, in those weeks, the true and entire history of her heart, and that the rest was a survival. Of course, this was unfair to her children and to the man with whom she had journeyed so far into this workaday middle of her life. They, those others, had a beauty which could not be eclipsed or rivalled. They had been made young and perfect forever, safe from the corruption of time and from those ambiguous second thoughts which dim the brightest face of youth. In the undivided strength of their first loves they had died, and their mothers had wept for them, and had it been for nothing?

Because of their perfection she could not bring herself to say so. They had died for glorious things, for justice, for freedom, for Ireland.

'Yes, I do muddle them up though,' said Frances' tall son. 'I remember you said you were in love with one of them. Which one was that?'

'Me?' said Frances. 'Oh, I was in love with Pat Dumay.'

She got up and went to the window to hide some sudden tears. She looked out at the neat garden and at the houses opposite. Tears flowed more freely now; and she heard drumming in her ears, heard, as she had heard it all through that dreadful week in nineteen sixteen, battering and breaking her heart, the thunder of the English guns.

THE END

Also available in Vintage

Iris Murdoch

THE FLIGHT FROM THE ENCHANTER

With an introduction by
Patricia Duncker

'A spirited fantasia in several keys...brilliant,
witty and original'
Sunday Times

A group of people have elected ambiguous and fascinating
Mischa Fox to be their God. While Mischa is charming his
devotees, his *alter ego*, Calvin Blick, is inspiring fear, and
Rosa Keepe, a high-minded bluestocking under Mischa's
spell (who also loves two Polish brothers), is swept into the
battle between sturdy common sense and dangerous
enchantment.

Elegant, sparkling and unputdownable, this is Iris Murdoch
at her best.

'Miss Murdoch's prose has music even as it has intelligence
and wit'
Cyril Connolly

VINTAGE

Also available in Vintage

Iris Murdoch

THE BELL

With an introduction by A. S. Byatt

'A distinguished novelist of a rare kind'
Kingsley Amis

'Of all the novelists that have made their bow since the war she seems to me to be the most remarkable... behind her books one feels a power of intellect quite exceptional in a novelist'
Sunday Times

A lay community of thoroughly mixed-up people is encamped outside Imber Abbey, home of an enclosed order of nuns. A new bell is being installed and then the old bell, legendary symbol of religion and magic, is rediscovered.

Dora Greenfield, erring wife, returns to her husband. Michael Meade, leader of the community, is confronted by Nick Fawley, with whom he had disastrous homosexual relations, while the wise old Abbess watches and prays and exercises discreet authority. And everyone, or almost everyone, hopes to be saved, whatever that may mean.

'Iris Murdoch really knows how to write, can tell a story, delineate a character, catch an atmosphere with deadly accuracy'
John Betjeman

VINTAGE

Also available in Vintage

Iris Murdoch

AN UNOFFICIAL ROSE

With an introduction by Anthony D. Nuttall

'Of all the novelists that have made their bow since the war she seems to me to be the most remarkable...behind her books one feels a power of intellect quite exceptional in a novelist'
Sunday Times

From the elderly widower, Hugh, to his granddaughter, Miranda, the major characters in *An Unofficial Rose* are all looking for love; and so closely is the web woven that the actions and passions of each are constantly affecting the others.

Hugh meditates returning to his former mistress. His son, Randall, dreams of abandoning his shapeless marriage for a perfect partner. Randall's young daughter, Miranda, is adored by her Australian cousin Penn, but has relentless attachments elsewhere. Randall's wife Ann, the central character, takes upon herself the strains and pains of all the others, while being the victim of her own private dream.

The irony and pathos of this tangled situation has extended Iris Murdoch's powers to the full, but her mastery of it is complete. Impelled by affection, lust, illusion, and dissolution, wanting to be free yet needing to be involved, these characters perform the linked figures of their destiny.

VINTAGE

Also available in Vintage

Iris Murdoch

THE UNICORN

With an introduction by Stephen Medcalf

'Miss Murdoch has taken the stock elements of the Gothic novel and wrung hell out of them…a strange combination of fairy tale and blood-and-thunder'
Books and Bookmen

When Marian Taylor takes a post as governess at Gaze Castle, a remote house upon a beautiful but desolate coast, she finds herself confronted with a number of weird mysteries and involved in a drama she only partly understands.

Some crime or catastrophe in the past still keeps the house, like the castle of the Sleeping Beauty, under a spell, whose magic also touches the neighbouring house of Riders, inhabited by a scholarly recluse.

Marian's employer, Hannah, and her retainers, seem to be acting out some tragic pattern: but it is not clear whether Hannah herself, the central figure, the Unicorn, is innocent victim or violent author, saint or witch…

In a novel that has all the beauty of a fairy story and the melodrama of a Gothic tale, Murdoch explores the fantasies and ambiguities which beset those who are condemned to be passionately abandoned and yet hopelessly imperfect in their search for God.

VINTAGE

Iris Murdoch

A FAIRLY HONOURABLE DEFEAT

With an introduction by Philip Hensher

'A distinguished novelist of a very rare kind'
Kingsley Amis

'Iris Murdoch really knows how to write, can tell a story, delineate a character, catch an atmosphere with deadly accuracy'
John Betjeman

In this dark comedy of errors, Iris Murdoch portrays the mischief wrought by Julius, a cynical intellectual who decides to demonstrate through a Machiavellian experiment how easily loving couples, caring friends, and devoted siblings can betray their loyalties. As puppet master, Julius artfully plays on the human tendency to embrace drama and intrigue and to prefer the distraction of confrontations to the difficult effort of communicating openly and honestly.

'The most important novelist writing in my time'
A. S. Byatt

VINTAGE

Also available in Vintage

Iris Murdoch

THE BLACK PRINCE

With an introduction by
Candia McWilliam

Shortlisted for the Booker Prize

'Iris Murdoch's marvellous, heroic novel...A gloriously
rich tale'
The Times

'Miss Murdoch here displays her dazzling gifts at the full
tide of her powers in a novel which will delight her admirers'
Sunday Times

A story about being in love *The Black Prince* is also a
remarkable intellectual thriller with a superbly involved
plot, and a meditation on the nature of art and love and the
deity who rules over both.

Bradley Pearson, its narrator and hero, is an elderly writer
with a 'block'. Encompassed by predatory friends and
relations – his ex-wife, her delinquent brother and a
younger, deplorably successful writer, Arnold Baffin,
together with Baffin's restless wife and youthful daughter –
Bradley attempts escape. His failure and its aftermath lead
to a violent climax; and to a coda which casts a shifting
perspective on all that has gone before.

VINTAGE

Also available in Vintage

Iris Murdoch

THE SEA, THE SEA

With an introduction by John Burnside

Winner of the Booker Prize

'There is no doubt in my mind that Iris Murdoch is one of the most important novelists now writing in English... The power of her imaginative vision, her intelligence and her awareness and revelation of human truth are quite remarkable'
The Times

The sea: turbulent and leaden; transparent and opaque; magician and mother.

When Charles Arrowby, over sixty, a demi-god of the theatre – director, playwright and actor – retires from his glittering London world in order to, 'abjure magic and become a hermit', it is to the sea that he turns. He hopes at least to escape from 'the women' – but unexpectedly meets one whom he loved long ago. His Buddhist cousin, James, also arrives. He is menaced by a monster from the deep. Charles finds his 'solitude' peopled by the drama of his own fantasies and obsessions.

'A fantastic feat of imagination as well as a marvellous sustained piece of writing'
Vogue

VINTAGE

Also available in Vintage

Iris Murdoch

THE PHILOSOPHER'S PUPIL

With an introduction by
Malcolm Bradbury

'The most daring and original of all her novels'
A. N. Wilson

In the English spa town of Ennistone hot springs bubble up
from deep beneath the earth. In these healing waters the
townspeople seek health and regeneration, righteousness
and ritual cleansing.

To this town steeped in ancient lore and subterranean inspi-
ration the Philosopher returns. He exerts an almost magical
influence over a host of Ennistonians, and especially over
George McCaffrey, the Philosopher's old pupil, a demonic
man desperate for redemption.

'We are back, of course, with great delight, the land of Iris
Murdoch, which is like no other but Prospero's'
Sunday Telegraph

'Never for a moment does one want to stop reading...I don't
think that Iris Murdoch has ever written better prose'
Daily Telegraph

VINTAGE